Mikkel Birkegaard lives in Copenhagen. *The Library of Shadows* is his first novel. It was first published in his native Denmark where it was a national bestseller, and has now gone on to be published in seventeen languages.

www.**rbooks**.co.uk

# The Library of Shadows

MIKKEL BIRKEGAARD

Translated from the Danish by
Tiina Nunnally

**BLACK SWAN**

TRANSWORLD PUBLISHERS
61-63 Uxbridge Road, London W5 5SA
A Random House Group Company
www.rbooks.co.uk

**THE LIBRARY OF SHADOWS**
**A BLACK SWAN BOOK: 9780552775021**

First publication in Great Britain
Black Swan edition published 2009

Copyright © Mikkel Birkegaard 2007
English translation copyright © Tiina Nunnally 2008

Published with the support of the Danish Arts Council's Committee for
Literature

Mikkel Birkegaard has asserted his right under the Copyright, Designs and
Patents Act 1988 to be identified as the author of this work.

Addresses for Random House Group Ltd companies outside the UK
can be found at: www.randomhouse.co.uk
The Random House Group Ltd Reg. No. 954009

The Random House Group Limited supports The Forest Stewardship Council
(FSC), the leading international forest certification organisation. All our titles
that are printed on Greenpeace approved FSC certified paper carry the FSC
logo. Our paper procurement policy can be found at
www.rbooks.co.uk/environment

Typeset in Caslon 540 by Falcon Oast Graphic Art Ltd.
Printed in the UK by CPI Cox & Wyman, Reading, RG1 8EX.

11

**Mixed Sources**
Product group from well-managed
forests and other controlled sources
www.fsc.org  Cert no. TT-COC-2139
© 1996 Forest Stewardship Council
FSC

# The Library
# of Shadows

# 1

Luca Campelli's wish to die surrounded by his beloved books came true late one night in October.

Of course this was one of those wishes that was never formulated either in speech or thought, but people who had seen Luca in his antiquarian bookshop knew it had to be true. The little Italian moved among the stacks of books in Libri di Luca as if he were strolling in his own living room, and without hesitation he could direct his customers to precisely the stack or shelf where the book they were seeking was located. Luca's love for literature became obvious after only a brief conversation with him, and it made no difference whether it was a question of a worn paperback or one of the rare first editions. This sort of knowledge bore witness to a long life with books, and Luca's authority among the shelves made it difficult to imagine him outside the comforting atmosphere of muted devotion that suffused the antiquarian bookshop.

For that reason, this particular night was unique because, aside from the fact that it was to be Luca's last, a whole week had passed since he had set foot in the shop. Eager to see his place of business again, he took a taxi straight from the airport to the bookshop in the Vesterbro district of Copenhagen. During the ride he had a hard time sitting still, and when the cab finally came to a halt, he was in such a hurry to pay and get out that he gave the driver a more than generous tip, simply to avoid the trouble of waiting for change. Appreciatively, the driver lifted Luca's two suitcases out of the boot and then left the elderly man standing there on the pavement.

The shop was cloaked in darkness and looked anything but hospitable, yet Luca smiled at the sight of the familiar facade with the yellow letters 'Libri di Luca' painted on the windowpanes. He lugged his suitcases the few metres from the pavement over to the front door and set them down heavily on the doorstep. The autumn wind took hold of his coat as he unbuttoned it, his coat-tails fluttering uneasily as he reached his hand inside to pull his key ring from his inner pocket.

The sound of the bells over the door welcomed him home, and he hurried to drag his suitcases inside and onto the dark red carpet so he could shut the door behind him. He straightened up and stood still with his eyes closed as he inhaled deeply through his nose, savouring the familiar smell of yellowed paper and old leather. He stood like that for several seconds as the sound of the bells faded away. Only then did he open his eyes and turn on the lamp hanging from the ceiling, even though it really wasn't necessary. After roaming these same premises for more than fifty years, he could orient himself in the dark with no problem. Even so, he flipped all the light switches on the panel behind the door so that the lights above each section of shelves and the lamps in the glass cases on the mezzanine also went on.

He went behind the counter and took off his coat. From the cabinet underneath he took out a bottle and a glass, which he filled with cognac. Glass in hand, Luca went to stand in the middle of the illuminated shop and looked around with a satisfied smile. A gulp of the golden liquid completed the moment. He nodded to himself and took a deep breath.

Carrying his glass of cognac, he slowly walked up and down the aisles, studying the rows of books. Other eyes probably wouldn't have been able to see the changes that had occurred during the past week, but Luca registered even the smallest changes at once. Books that had been sold or moved, new volumes that had been inserted among old ones, and piles of books that had been shifted or combined. On his tour of inspection Luca pushed on the spines so that all the books were properly aligned, and he moved volumes that had been incorrectly placed. Every so often he would carefully set down his glass so that he could pull out a book that he hadn't seen before. With curiosity he would leaf through it, studying the typeface and letting his fingers feel the texture of the paper. Finally he would close his eyes and hold the book up to his nose to breathe in the particular scent of the pages, as if from a vintage wine. After studying the title page and binding one more time he would gently put the book back in place, giving it either a shrug of his shoulders or a smile of acknowledgement. There were more nods than shrugs as he made his way through the shop, so the assistant's transactions, undertaken while the owner was away, seemed to be acceptable.

The assistant's name was Iversen, and he had worked in the shop for so long that it was more a question of a partnership than an employer/employee relationship. Yet even though Iversen loved the shop as much as Luca did, there had never been any overtures to form a real partnership. The antiquarian bookshop had been passed down to Luca from his father Arman, and the intention had always been for it to remain in the hands of the Campelli family.

Very little had changed since Arman left the shop to Luca, but the balcony at the height of a mezzanine was the most noticeable. The balcony was a good metre and a half wide, and it ran along all four walls. It was an addition that the regular customers had quickly dubbed 'the Heavens' since it was there that the rarest and most valuable works were kept, protected and displayed in glass cases.

Before Luca headed up to the balcony, he went back to the counter to pour himself another cognac. After that he walked to the very back of the shop where a winding staircase rose up to the projecting balcony above. The worn steps creaked ominously as he made his way upwards; undaunted he continued his ascent and soon reached the top. There he turned to survey the shop. With a little imagination the bookshelves below him might seem like a labyrinth of well-trimmed shrubs, but he was too much at home there to get lost, and his gaze fell on the two suitcases standing just inside the door.

A frown and a concerned expression suddenly darkened his furrowed face, and his brown eyes seemed to be looking at more distant realms than the floor below. Pensively Luca lifted his glass and sniffed at the cognac before he took a sip and moved his gaze from his suitcases, focusing instead on the shelves on the balcony.

The lights emitted a soft glow inside the glass cases, giving the volumes they protected a romantic, golden sheen. Behind the glass the books were displayed like small objets d'art. Some were open to colourful illustrations and fantastical depictions of the stories contained inside; others were closed to showcase the artistry that had been devoted to the binding or the tanned leather.

Luca walked slowly along the balcony with one hand on the railing and the other wrapped round his cognac glass, which he cautiously twirled in little circles as he let his glance slide over the contents of the display cases. Normally there was little change among the works on the second floor since few people could afford to buy them; those who could usually bought very few volumes, carefully selected for their existing collections.

New books were added almost exclusively through purchases from estates or, less often, from book auctions.

That was why Luca froze when his eyes fell on a particular volume. He frowned and set his glass on the railing before he leaned towards the glass pane to study the book more closely. It was bound in black leather with gold type, and the edges of the pages were also gilded. Luca opened his eyes wide when he got close enough to read the title and the name of the author. The book turned out to be a custom-bound edition of Giacomo Leopardi's *Operette morali*, in superb condition and presumably in Italian, the original language – Luca's native tongue.

Clearly moved, Luca knelt down and opened the glass case. With shaking hands he reached for his shirt pocket and fished out his reading glasses, which he set on his nose. Carefully, as if not wanting to frighten the prize away, he leaned forward and grabbed the book in both hands. Having secured the trophy, he lifted it out of the case and with astonishment turned it this way and that. Deep furrows appeared on his brow, and with a sudden lurch he got to his feet and cast a wary glance all around, as if he sensed that someone was watching him – a hidden observer to this extraordinary find. Finding no one, he turned his attention back to the book in his hands and gingerly opened it.

On the title page he saw that it was a first edition, a circumstance that along with the date of publication, 1827, would justify its placement in the Heavens. The paper was of a sturdy texture, and with obvious delight he let his fingers slide over the surface. After that he raised the book up to his nose and sniffed. It had a slightly spicy scent from something he deduced must be bay laurel.

With a lingering, scrutinizing thoroughness he began turning the pages of the book, stopping at a copperplate etching that showed Death wearing a cowl and carrying a scythe. The illustration was exceedingly well executed, and even though Luca examined it carefully, he could find no flaws in the printing. Copperplate engraving, that rather difficult method of printing, was in widespread use during the nineteenth century, notable for its greater degree of detail and subtlety than even the best woodcuts. On the other hand, the paper had to be printed twice, since the ink settled in the grooves of the copperplate, unlike the text itself, which was typically cast in lead and raised.

Luca turned more pages, admiring with enthusiasm the rest of the copperplate engravings the book contained. At the last page he once again frowned. It was here they normally inserted a price slip the size of a business card with the name of the bookshop, but there was no card. That Iversen would have invested in such a valuable work without consulting Luca seemed odd enough, but that he would have displayed the book for sale without a price seemed counter to the man's otherwise meticulous nature.

Again Luca swept his eyes over the room, as if he expected a welcome committee to leap out suddenly and offer an explanation for the mystery, but very few people knew of his trip or his return home; those who did were fully aware that this would not be an appropriate occasion for a celebration.

He gave a shrug, opened the book to the middle and began to read aloud. All doubt swiftly disappeared from his face, replaced by the joy of reading his native language. Soon he raised his voice and let the words slip freely out over the shop's corridors of books. It had been a long time since he had read Italian, so it took a few pages before the accent came easily and he found the rhythm of the poem. But there was no doubt that he was enjoying himself; his eyes gleamed with happiness and his joyous expression offered a sharp contrast to the melancholy of the text.

It lasted only a moment. Suddenly the look on Luca's face shifted from enthusiasm to surprise, and he staggered back two paces, his body slamming into the glass case behind him. With his eyes still on the book, he continued reading as shards of glass rained over him. The surprise in his wide-open pupils changed to terror, and his knuckles turned white from the convulsive grip he had on the volume he held in his hands. With tottering, almost mechanical movements, his body toppled forward, and when it struck the railing, the jolt caused his cognac glass to tip over the edge and plummet to the floor below. The carpet muffled the sound of glass shattering.

The strength of Luca's voice continued undiminished, but the rhythm had become uneven and spasmodic. Sweat appeared on the old man's brow and his face was pink from exertion. A couple of drops of sweat trickled down his forehead, along his nose and hung from the very tip, before dripping onto the book. The thick paper absorbed the beads of sweat as if they were raindrops on a dry riverbed.

Luca's eyes were open as wide as could be, locked onto the text without blinking even once, not even when sweat ran into them. His pupils relentlessly scanned the lines on the pages, and no matter how hard he tried to turn his head away Luca could not tear his eyes from the words in the book he held in his hands. His whole body started shaking violently and his normally kind face was contorted into a horrible grimace.

In spite of all this, Luca's voice kept projecting into the room, stammering and occasionally interrupted by a pause, then followed by a burst of words. There was no longer any rhythm to what he read; the sentences were chopped up and combined with no regard for grammatical rules, and the stress on individual syllables became more and more random as the speed picked up. Even though the words could still be distinguished as words, the enunciation and syntax were no longer comprehensible. The sentences emitted by Luca's vocal cords were devoid of recognizable content. The tempo increased significantly and the flow of words was interrupted only by panicked inhalations, as his lungs were emptied of oxygen. After each breath, which sounded more and more like a wheeze, the words and sentences would again gush out of Luca's mouth.

His body was now shaking so violently that the railing Luca was pressed up against began vibrating, making the wood audibly groan. Sweat poured out of his body, soaking through his clothing in several places. Drops of sweat had formed dark patches on the carpet all around him.

All of a sudden the stream of words ceased and the shaking stopped. Luca's eyes were still staring down at the book in his hands but the expression of panic was gone. A gentleness came into the Italian's eyes and calm settled over his face. Slowly he leaned his old body over the railing. The book slipped from his sweaty hands and, with pages fluttering, fell to the floor below. The railing groaned ominously under the weight of his body and with a snap a section of the balustrade tore away, spraying splinters of wood all over the shop. For a moment Luca's body stood motionless on the edge of the balcony until it plunged forward, lifeless, hurtling to the floor three metres below. The slack limbs flailed uncontrollably out to the sides, bringing down shelves and books in a cloud of dust.

Luca's body struck the floor with a hard thud in a narrow corridor between bookshelves and was instantly buried under a pile of books, wood and dust.

# 2

Every time Jon Campelli had to make an appearance in court, he would sleep uneasily the night before, if he managed to drift off at all. The same thing happened on this night and finally he gave up and got out of bed, pulling on his dark-blue robe. He sauntered out to his small kitchen where he made himself a pot of coffee in a cafetière. He sipped the coffee and again read through the script for his closing arguments. Even though he'd already gone over the pages several times the previous evening, he carefully went over them once more, testing several versions of the same sentences out loud. And so it was that at four in the morning a clear voice could be heard coming from the penthouse flat on Kompagnistræde, repeating the same passages over and over, as if an actor were rehearsing a role.

After a couple of hours Jon went to get the newspaper from outside the front door. He leafed through it as he ate breakfast, supplied with a fresh pot of coffee. His script remained within his field of vision, and several times he stopped his perusal of the newspaper and instead pulled the script close so he could read through a specific passage again before going back to the daily news and his toast.

None of his colleagues had any idea how much work he put into his closing remarks, but in spite of his relatively young age, he was already known for mastering the discipline to perfection. As a barrister only thirty-three years old, he had acquired a reputation that made him a bit of a celebrity among his colleagues, as well as a challenge to his adversaries and the object of unfounded mistrust among older members of the judiciary.

For that reason his court cases were often well attended. It was highly likely that a large number of spectators would also show up today, even though the outcome seemed predetermined. Jon's client, a second-generation immigrant by the name of Mehmet Azlan, was charged with fencing stolen goods; like the three previous charges against him, this one was also without basis. It was beginning to look like harassment on the part of the police, but Mehmet took it with astonishing calm, satisfied to strike back through legal means, which meant suing for damages for pain and suffering.

Jon drained his coffee cup and went to the bathroom, where he turned on the water in the shower. He dropped his robe on the floor, and while he waited for the water to get hot, he studied his body in the mirror. With his thumb and index finger he gripped the love handles just above his hips, examining them as if they had swollen up during the night. Five years ago he'd had a stomach like a washboard, but almost imperceptibly, and no matter what he did to prevent it, the sculpted figure had gradually been erased as if by a rising tide.

As he stood there in the shower his mobile phone rang, but Jon calmly rinsed the shampoo out of his hair and finished the rest of his morning ritual before he checked to see who had called. It was Mehmet. In the message his client had left, he explained in his customary laid-back tone that he'd sold his wheels and was in need of a lift to the courtroom. The line was busy when Jon called back, so he made do with leaving a message that he was on his way.

Outside it was raining. Jon jogged over to his car, a silver-grey Mercedes SL, and tossed his briefcase onto the passenger seat before he jumped in out of the damp. Through the wet windows the world outside seemed to dissolve; figures wearing colourful rain gear melted into one another until they looked like imaginary creatures in a child's drawing. The windscreen wipers switched on when he started the car and the imaginary creatures vanished along with the water, to be replaced by morose Danes fighting their way through the rain or huddled together under awnings.

Even taking into consideration the weather, the traffic heading for the Nørrebro district was moving very slowly, and Jon kept glancing at his watch. Arriving late for a court appearance was never a good way to start, no matter how sound a case he might have, and Jon took pride in always being on time. Finally he was able to turn off Åboulevard and head down Griffenfeldsgade towards Stengade, which was where Mehmet lived. His building was part of a concrete structure covered with red brick, and each flat had its own garden or balcony. There was a large courtyard in between the buildings, complete with frowzy grassy areas, weather-beaten climbing frames and benches faded from the sun.

Mehmet's ground-floor flat made him the owner of a garden that measured six square metres, surrounded by a woven wooden fence a metre and a half high that was algae-green, though it had probably once been white. Visitors to Mehmet's flat always had to use the door facing the Park, as he liked to call his garden, so Jon cut diagonally across the courtyard and through the creaking garden gate. The Park's grass was littered with empty cardboard boxes, milk containers and wooden pallets, which had all served their purpose and were now just waiting for the caretaker to order Mehmet to remove them. A canopy that ran the width of the flat provided shelter from the rain and also covered a storage area for more boxes, barrels and a pallet of dog biscuits in twenty-kilo sacks.

Jon knocked on the living-room window and didn't have to wait long for Mehmet to appear behind the pane, wearing boxers, a T-shirt and, most important of all, his mobile phone headset. Like a typical Mehmet happening, it said 'Corner Shop' in big type on his T-shirt. He loved to use the most stereotypical prejudices in his small provocations, a sort of hobby of his to carry out pinprick operations against Tabloid Denmark, as he called it. This didn't stem from the bitterness or anger to which some immigrants succumbed, but rather from pure and simple amusement and self-mockery.

The door to the living room opened, and with a smile Mehmet motioned for Jon to come in as he continued talking into his headset. As far as Jon could tell, the language was Turkish. The room he entered served three purposes for Mehmet: living room, office and storage room. Occasionally it also seemed as if the space were used as a sauna. At any rate, it was always very hot, possibly so that Mehmet could walk around in boxers and T-shirts year-round.

Mehmet was a 'contest jockey'. That was the label that he used for himself, and it undeniably gave his work a more romantic tone than it actually deserved. With the universal breakthrough of the Internet, many companies had discovered that a good way to entice visitors to their website was to offer a contest or a lottery that enabled participants to win products, money, trips and much more. Electronic versions of scratch cards and casino games also became effective draws. Since most of these contests were not limited by where the player might be in the world, there was access to countless opportunities, with new ones appearing every second.

Mehmet lived off, in many cases quite literally, taking part in as many contests and games as he could find, regardless of what he might win. He then re-sold the prizes he couldn't use himself, which was why his home looked like a merchant's warehouse with cardboard boxes everywhere, containing cleaning products, breakfast cereals, bags of crisps, toys, sweets, wine, fizzy drinks, coffee, toiletries and a few larger items such as an Atlas freezer, a Zanussi electric cooker, an exercise bicycle, a rowing machine and two 'Smokey Joe' grills. To an outsider it might look like the well-stocked inventory of a receiver of stolen goods, and that was also the reason why he was regularly accused of using his flat for exactly that purpose.

'What's up, boss?' exclaimed Mehmet, reaching out to shake hands with Jon. He was apparently done with his phone conversation, though it was never possible to know for sure since he rarely took off his headset.

Jon shook his hand.

'Well, *I'm* ready,' he said, nodding at Mehmet's half-dressed state. 'What about you?'

'Hey, all I have to do is sit there and look innocent,' said Mehmet, holding up his hands.

'Then you should probably change your T-shirt,' suggested Jon dryly.

Mehmet nodded. 'I'm on it. In the meantime, take a load off, it'll only take me a nanosecond.'

Jon's client left the room, and the barrister looked around for a place to sit down. He moved a box filled with tinned goods from a brown leather sofa and sat down with his briefcase on his lap. At one end of the room stood a large dining table that functioned as Mehmet's desk. On the table three flat-screen computer monitors were lined up as if they were headstones. Behind the table stood a desk chair the size of a dentist's chair, and judging by the multiple levers it offered as many possible settings.

'What about the lawsuit for damages?' called Mehmet from the bedroom.

'We can't very well sue them before we've won,' Jon shouted in reply.

Mehmet appeared in the doorway, transformed by a black suit, white shirt and highly polished shoes. He was in the process of tying a grey tie, struggling with the unaccustomed manoeuvres.

'But it could be a fair amount this time,' Jon went on, pointing at the cut on Mehmet's face.

Mehmet gave up on the tie and tossed it aside. 'Yeah, they're going to have to cough up plenty of euros,' he said as he touched his eyebrow. 'What's the hourly rate of a punch bag?'

Jon shrugged in reply.

At the latest visit the police had shown up with six officers and forced their way into the flat through the front door, not knowing that the hall was filled with cases of tinned tomatoes, Pampers nappies, electric kitchen utensils and wine. Of course they weren't aware that visitors, for that very reason, always entered through the garden door, so they interpreted the mess as an attempt to barricade the entrance and the subsequent arrest was significantly more violent than was necessary. Mehmet ended up with two bruised ribs and a cut over his eyebrow when they flung him to the floor. The situation was not helped when eight of Mehmet's friends from the neighbourhood came storming in and, according to the police, behaved in a threatening manner so that back-up officers had to be called in.

The next day one of the morning newspapers pronounced the raid a 'successful break-up of a Turkish fence syndicate'. Even though the court ruling later in the day would demonstrate something else entirely, none of them expected an apology or even a retraction in the same paper.

Mehmet straightened his shirt collar and threw out his arms. 'Okay?'

'Lovely.' Jon stood up. 'Shall we get going?'

'Stop,' said Mehmet. 'I can't let you leave without making you a special offer, just between friends.' He went over to a stack of boxes and opened the one on top. 'How about a couple of fantastic books?' he asked. 'I'll give you a good price.'

Judging by the covers, they were romance novels of the worst kind, so Jon gave him a wan smile and shook his head.

'Er, no thanks. I don't read much any more.' He tapped his finger against his temple. 'I had an overdose as a child.'

'Hmm,' grumbled Mehmet. 'I've also got a few detective novels, even a couple of legal mysteries, as far as I recall. Those interest you?' He glanced at Jon, but the barrister wasn't about to change his mind.

'What about some Tampax?' asked Mehmet. 'For your woman, I mean.' He burst into loud laughter. 'I won a year's supply of Tampax from some women's magazine. First prize was a trip to Tenerife.' He shrugged. 'You can't win them all, but the best part is that when they come over to deliver the prize this afternoon, they're going to take a picture of the lucky winner for the next issue of the magazine.' He clasped his hands behind his neck and rotated his hips. 'So I'm going to be a model.' He laughed again.

'Well, at least your annual Tampax budget should be quite low. But thanks anyway. I haven't got a girlfriend at the moment.'

'I don't understand it,' exclaimed Mehmet. 'With your Latin-lover looks you shouldn't have any problem in that area.'

Jon shrugged his shoulders. His complexion wasn't as dark as Mehmet's, but it still had a hue unlike that of most Danes, and his hair was jet-black. But since he was only half Italian, he was slightly taller, five foot eleven, and with lighter skin than might be expected; perhaps that was why he had never experienced any sort of racism, especially not from the opposite sex.

Mehmet snapped his fingers and dashed over to the computer monitors, where he grabbed the mouse in one hand and pressed a couple of keys on the keyboard with the other.

'But I could get you a woman, boss. There's this contest put on by a Copenhagen nightclub, and you can win a night with . . . let's see, what was her name?'

'I'm really not that desperate.'

'Just say the word. I've fixed the bot on their website.'

Mehmet was trained as a computer programmer, but like many other second-generation immigrants in Denmark, he hadn't been able to find a job in his field, which was otherwise clamouring for manpower. Even though he was a highly skilled programmer, he had realized that his name played a bigger role than his qualifications, and the best way for him to get ahead was to go into business for himself. Opening a pizzeria was too much of a stereotype even for Mehmet, so he had decided to become a contest jockey, which offered him the necessary freedom as well as the opportunity to make use of his expertise in developing bots. Mehmet's bots were tiny computer programs that could be instructed in filling in the contest forms and applications he found on the Internet. Once he had instructed a bot how to go about things, it would obediently repeat the procedure and pump in the names and addresses from his address file, so increasing his chances of winning. His address file contained his family, friends, acquaintances, neighbours and whoever else he could persuade, including Jon. Consequently, one day Jon received a phone call from an enthusiastic secretary at a big chain toyshop, telling him that he had won a pram with cross-country tyres and a detachable hood.

As payment for agreeing to be included in Mehmet's address file, everyone was offered some of the goods he couldn't sell, or a significant discount on whatever he happened to have on hand.

Mehmet nodded towards the door.

'All right, let's get this over with.'

The two men left Mehmet's flat and jogged through the rain to Jon's car.

'What happened to your Peugeot?' asked Jon as they sat in the Mercedes, on their way to court.

'I finally got rid of it. Unfortunately I had to drop the price to a hundred K, even though it was really worth two hundred.' Mehmet shrugged. 'Not many Danes dare buy a car from a Turk.'

'But that's still an okay hourly wage, isn't it?'

'Sure, it's cool. On the other hand, I had to throw out two pallets of cornflakes that had gone bad. But in the big picture, it all works out.'

'So what do you have to eat?' asked Jon.

'Hey, I've got plenty. Two weeks ago I won fifty frozen dinners, so now I don't have to eat breakfast food at night.'

As expected, the courtroom was packed. Some of Mehmet's friends were present, but there were also many of Jon's colleagues and acquaintances from his law-school days. At this stage of the case, everyone was waiting for the final arguments, which affected the last examinations of witnesses. They were routinely carried out, without a great show of enthusiasm from any of the parties involved. Even the judges seemed to be mentally twiddling their thumbs. The decision was going to be made by a panel of five judges – a method Jon didn't much care for. He was better in front of a whole jury, which wasn't biased by previous cases or Jon's own personality.

The prosecutor, a thin, bald man with a drawling voice, gave quite a sober speech, but by now no one had any doubts about the outcome of the case. There was simply no definitive proof, and any remaining speculations or suspicions about Mehmet's operating as a fence were dubious at best.

It was utterly silent in the courtroom when Jon was asked to begin his summation. Slowly he got up from his chair and stepped in front of the judges. Many of his colleagues improvised their final arguments, but that didn't suit Jon. His presentation was written down word for word on the pages he held in his hand, and it was very seldom that he diverged from his script.

Jon started reading but, for the spectators, it didn't sound as if he were reading aloud from a prepared text, and many didn't even notice that he kept on consulting his notes. The illusion was a combination of various techniques he had developed over time. For instance, the text was divided in such a way that he could make use of natural pauses to turn the pages, and the sections were structured so that he could quickly find his place in the text again after having looked away. He also had methods for looking at the papers discreetly, either with a glance or under the cover of other gestures, like a magician.

The purpose of all this meticulous preparation and constant consulting of the text was that during the speech Jon was able to concentrate on the presentation itself. Even though the content was fixed, he could still change the emphasis, taking his audience into account; he could accentuate certain sections and downplay others, colouring the statements as needed.

The only time he had ever tried to explain his technique to a colleague, he had compared it to the work of an orchestral conductor. Except that in this case he himself was the instrument, and he could turn the effects up or down as needed to fit the situation, precisely the way a conductor can alter the experience of a piece of music. Jon's colleague had looked at him as if he were crazy, and since then Jon hadn't tried to explain or teach anyone his approach, even though it had never yet failed him.

The effect wasn't lost this time either. Before long everyone's attention was directed towards him, and the mood could be read in the satisfied expressions on the faces of Mehmet's friends and in the small nods of acknowledgement from Jon's colleagues. Even with his back turned, Jon could sense their support, as if it were a home game. The judges leaned forward in their chairs, their bored expressions were gone, and their eyes attentively followed Jon's performance. The prosecutor, on the other hand, sank lower and lower in his chair, uncertainly plucking at the papers on the table in front of him. He emanated defeat, and Jon was audacious enough to lend the police officers' report of the case a sarcastic tone that provoked a good deal of amusement in the courtroom.

It was over. Jon read the last sentence of his speech and stood in silence for a moment before he folded up the pages of his text and returned to his place, accompanied by spontaneous applause from the spectators as the judges called for order.

His client slapped him on the shoulder. 'Pure Perry Mason,' whispered Mehmet with a smile. Jon replied with a wink but maintained a neutral expression.

The judges withdrew to deliberate while everyone else in the courtroom dispersed, slowly and reluctantly like a group of school kids after an outing. The prosecutor approached his opponent and shook hands, giving Jon a smile of acknowledgement. As Mehmet joined his friends, who loudly greeted him, Jon gathered his papers into two neat stacks.

'Congratulations, Campelli,' said a hoarse voice behind him. He turned round and stood face to face with Frank Halbech, one of his law firm's three partners.

Like Jon he wore a dark suit, a Valentino as far as Jon could tell, but it was his manicured hands that revealed that this man was not encumbered with work; he had people for that. He'd become a partner in the law firm five years ago at the age of forty-five, and judging by his appearance, he now spent his time at hair salons, tanning spas and fitness centres.

'Open-and-shut case, but good argument,' said Halbech, offering his hand. Jon took it. Halbech leaned forward without releasing Jon's hand. 'He's losing his grip, Steiner,' he whispered, motioning with his head towards the prosecutor.

Jon nodded. 'The case should never have gone to court,' he whispered in reply.

Halbech straightened up, released Jon's hand and took a small step back to give him the once-over. His grey-blue eyes scrutinized Jon, while a little smile formed on his lips.

'What would you say to a real challenge, Campelli? A case that will put hair on your chest?'

'Of course,' said Jon.

Halbech nodded with satisfaction. 'That's what I figured. You seem like a man who dares take up the gauntlet, someone who will come through when it counts.' He formed his fingers into a pistol and aimed them at Jon. 'The Remer case. It's yours.' He broke out in a big smile. 'Drop by my office tomorrow and we'll talk about it.'

Before Jon had time to react, Halbech turned on his heel and strode towards the exit. Astonished, Jon watched his boss go until a short, stout man wearing a light-grey suit stepped in front of him and blocked his view.

'Wow, was that Halbech?' asked the man, alternating his gaze between Jon and the disappearing Halbech. The short man was Jon's colleague, Anders Hellstrøm, whose speciality was traffic cases and who had a penchant for Irish pubs and Guinness.

'None other,' replied Jon distractedly.

'Incredible. I can't remember when I last saw him inside a court-room,' said Hellstrøm, sounding impressed. 'What in the world did he want?'

'I'm not really sure,' said Jon pensively. 'But I've got the Remer case.'

Hellstrøm gawked at him in disbelief.

'Remer?' He gave a low whistle. 'Either he wants to gild you, or else he wants to murder you.'

'Thanks for the support,' said Jon with a crooked smile.

'Wait until the others hear about this.' Hellstrøm rubbed his hands and glanced around. 'But that was a hell of a good closing argument, Jon,' he added before he turned and set off for the far end of the room where some of their colleagues had gathered.

Jon needed some fresh air. He felt as if everyone's eyes were directed at him, even though his performance was over. He made his way towards the exit, accompanied by congratulations and slaps on the back. A moment later he was outside on the courtroom steps. It had stopped raining and gaps in the light-grey clouds revealed patches of blue sky. He stuck his hands in his pockets and took a deep breath.

The Remer case had to do with corporate raiding of the highest order. The main player, Otto Remer, was accused of bankrupting no fewer than a hundred and fifty companies over a period of years. There was no doubt that what he had done was morally problematical, but it was much less certain whether it was outright illegal. The case had already gone on for three years, and it was a widespread joke among the firm's employees that the amount of information and the complexity had reached critical mass, where-upon the case had taken on a consciousness and life of its own.

The case files had their very own archives, just as the ever-changing team of lawyers had been given a special Remer office where they could work undisturbed. It was a 'make or break' case, and so far the lawyers who had given it a shot had all broken. A successful resolution of the case would undoubtedly lead to an offer of a partnership in the firm. That was the rumour among the lawyers, at any rate.

The amount of documents and the complexity of the case were not the only challenges. The man himself, Otto Remer, was also a bit of a trial. Several colleagues had completely given up trying to work with him, since he had no fondness for lawyers nor for supplying documentation of his transactions. He behaved without regard for the gravity of the case and wasn't beyond going off on a ski holiday or a business trip during critical phases of the proceedings.

The air was still damp and chilly after the rain, and Jon shivered in his thin jacket. Two men in shirtsleeves came out of the build-ing to have a smoke. They lit their cigarettes, which they greedily inhaled, while they shifted from one foot to the other to keep warm.

A mobile phone rang and Jon instinctively reached for his inner pocket. It wasn't his phone, but he did notice that he had received three calls from the same number during the course of the morn-ing. Without looking at the display, he pressed the familiar combination of numbers that gave him access to his voicemail.

He listened with growing amazement to the message that had been left for him. It was from a Detective Sergeant Olsen, who in a businesslike tone explained that he was ringing with regard to Jon's father, Luca Campelli. Jon frowned. He was accustomed to receiving calls from the police, but he couldn't fathom what the connection could be with his father.

Before he managed to return the call, a bailiff came out to find him. The judges had finished deliberating.

Before a courtroom that was now only half filled, the judges announced what everyone already knew, that there was no real case against Mehmet and that all charges were dropped. Mehmet's friends who were still present cheered, and Mehmet himself took Jon's hand and shook it vigorously.

'Good job, Lawman,' he said with satisfaction.

Jon smiled back and nodded towards the elated spectators. 'Do you want a lift back, or are you going out to party with your fan club?'

'If you're taking the car out anyway, I'll catch a ride with you,' said his client. 'Some of us have work to do.'

Jon started packing up his papers. Several colleagues and acquaintances came over to congratulate him on the outcome, and Jon good-naturedly had to decline invitations to dinner to celebrate. He didn't feel the euphoria that usually followed a victory. The encounter with the firm's partner had been a little too odd for him to be able to concentrate on celebrating.

Mehmet seemed to sense his mood. In the car he said, 'Hey, we scored!' and gave Jon a playful shove on the shoulder.

'I know. I'm sorry,' said Jon with a smile. 'I guess I'm a little tired.'

Mehmet accepted Jon's explanation and began talking about suing for damages – how much money they should demand for damages to the door of his flat, about compensation for his cut eyebrow and about whether they could demand money for besmirching his reputation in the neighbourhood.

Jon gave curt replies as he drove towards Nørrebro. When they arrived at Mehmet's flat, his mobile rang, and Jon switched on the hands-free to take the call. Detective Sergeant Olsen introduced himself and explained why he was ringing. Jon listened to the man's monotone voice and offered brief replies, mostly to acknowledge that he was still there.

When the conversation was over, he took off the headset and sighed.

'Yet another fan?' asked Mehmet.

Jon shook his head. 'I wouldn't say that. My father is dead.'

# 3

Luca was going to be buried in Copenhagen's Assistens Cemetery, among the great Danish authors, just as he had lived his life among their works.

Jon arrived at the last minute and was met by an obviously nervous Iversen, who was standing on the gravel path outside the chapel, waiting for him. Jon recognized him at once as his father's long-time assistant at Libri di Luca. They had spoken on the phone several days earlier. It was Iversen who had found Luca in the shop that morning, dead of a heart attack; he had also taken care of all the practical arrangements for the funeral. He had always been the one who got things done, and he handled all tasks willingly.

When Jon had visited the bookshop as a child, he could always persuade Iversen to read stories to him when Luca either didn't have time or was out on business. During the past fifteen years Iversen's hair had turned whiter, his cheeks were fuller and the lenses of his glasses were thicker, but the same warm smile still welcomed Jon when, with his briefcase under his arm, he hastily approached the waiting man.

'It was good of you to come, Jon,' said Iversen, giving him a warm handshake.

'Hello, Iversen. It's been a long time,' said Jon.

Iversen nodded. 'Yes, you've certainly shot up, my boy,' he said with a laugh. 'The last time we met, you were no taller than Gyldendal's four-volume encyclopaedia.' He let go of Jon's hand and placed his own hand on the younger man's shoulder, as if to demonstrate how tall he had grown. 'But the service is about to start,' he said, giving Jon an apologetic smile. 'We'll have to talk afterwards.' His eyes assumed a solemn expression. 'It's important that we have a chance to talk.'

'Of course,' said Jon and allowed himself to be ushered into the chapel.

To his surprise the place was almost full. The pews were occupied by people of all ages, from mothers with whimpering infants to wizened old men who looked as if the ceremony could just as well have been for them. As far as Jon knew, Luca's only contact with the rest of the world, aside from the bookshop, was through an Italian friendship society, but the crowd was a diverse gathering of people who didn't look as if they were of Italian origin.

A murmur arose as everyone turned to look at the two men walking up the centre aisle to the two vacant seats in the front row. On the floor before the altar was a white-painted coffin surrounded by wreaths that overflowed into the aisle in a river of colour. The wreath that Jon had asked his secretary to send lay on top of the coffin. On the ribbon it said simply 'Jon'.

After they sat down, Jon leaned towards Iversen. 'Who are all these people?'

Iversen hesitated for a moment before he answered. 'Friends of Libri di Luca,' he whispered.

Jon's eyes opened wide. 'Business must be good,' he said in a low voice, looking around. He estimated there to be about a hundred people in the chapel.

From his childhood he remembered well the regular customers who came to the shop, but it surprised him that there would be so many, and that they would feel obligated to come to the funeral. The customers he remembered best were strange individuals, shabby eccentrics who spent their money on books and catalogues instead of on food and clothes. They could roam about for hours without buying anything, and many times they would come back the next day, or two days later, and once again scour the shelves, as if they were checking to see when the fruit would be ripe and ready for picking.

A priest entered the chapel and seemed to float in his embroidered surplice over to the pulpit on the other side of the coffin. The scattered whispering in the room died away and the ceremony began. The priest swung the censer towards those who were present and the discreet aroma of incense spread through the chapel. After that the priest's calm voice filled the air with words about sanctuaries, breathing spaces, about belonging and giving other people experiences, and about the fundamental values in life such as art and literature.

'Luca was a guarantor for these values,' intoned the priest. 'A man generous with his warmth, knowledge and hospitality.'

Jon stared straight ahead. Behind him he sensed the congregation's sympathetic nods, barely audible sniffling and the tears that no doubt welled up while his own eyes were dry. He recalled another funeral when things had been different; a funeral when he, as a twelve-year-old boy, had to be led out of the church, and a distant aunt had tried to comfort him in the biting winter cold. Back then it had been his mother they were burying, dead at much too young an age, in everyone's opinion; but it wasn't until the following year that he found out why it happened. Not the existential why, but the raw, unvarnished reason: Marianne, Jon's mother and Luca's Danish wife, had committed suicide by throwing herself out of the sixth-floor window. It was unclear whether it was the cold outside the church or his own despair that had chopped up his sobs into a heart-rending stammer back then, but the experience of not being able to breathe had stayed with him, and he hadn't been to a funeral since.

At the priest's invitation, the congregation sang a couple of selected hymns before the floor was given to Iversen. Luca's faithful co-worker and friend picked up a stack of books from under his seat and stood up. He stepped over the wreaths on the floor and made his way to the pulpit. There he held the pile of books a couple of centimetres above the surface and dropped them so they landed with an audible thump. That provoked laughter, and the mood lightened after the exalted tone of the hymns.

Iversen's speech was a cheerful farewell to the man with whom he had spent the last forty years. He peppered his talk with anecdotes from their friendship, and readings from passages of the books he had brought along. Just as when he read stories to Jon as a child, Iversen captured the attention of his audience with a lively reading from *The Divine Comedy*, one of Luca's favourites. Then he continued with excerpts from the great classics, which everyone in the chapel seemed to know by heart. Even though Jon hadn't read these works, he was still moved by Iversen's interpretations and the evocative images blossomed on his internal canvas, precisely as they had when he sat on Iversen's lap in the leather chair in Libri di Luca, listening to stories about cowboys, knights and astronauts. When he closed his eyes, he could almost smell the dust of the antiquarian bookshop and hear the silence, which between the shelves of the shop seemed to resonate like nowhere else.

When Iversen finished his speech, a few people spontaneously applauded until they remembered where they were and fell silent. The priest once again appeared in the pulpit and insisted on singing one last hymn before they said goodbye. Jon followed the text in his hymnal but didn't participate in the song, unlike Iversen, who droned along unembarrassed at his side. For a moment Jon wondered whether he ought to feel guilty about not taking a greater part in the ceremony, but he shook off the thought by directing his gaze at the ceiling. Undoubtedly some of those present were surprised; they might even think he was arrogant, but that was their problem. They didn't know anything. For his part, it was just a matter of getting through the funeral and escaping into the fresh air.

When the hymn was over, Jon was one of the first to stand up.

Outside, those in attendance divided themselves into two groups, and Jon kept close to Iversen, who was the only person he knew. They were quickly joined by several others who praised

Iversen for his speech and offered their condolences to Jon. Apparently everyone knew who he was, but at the same time he sensed a certain astonishment from those he greeted, as if they hadn't expected him to show up.

'You look exactly like him,' a middle-aged man in a wheelchair said bluntly. He introduced himself as William Kortmann, and Jon noticed that the wheelchair he was sitting in was completely black; even the spokes of the wheels were black. 'How strange that he didn't say anything,' Kortmann went on, but abruptly fell silent when he noticed Jon's surprised expression. 'Well, we need to be going,' he said, turning to a dark-clad man who stood alone a couple of metres away. As if by telepathy, the man turned around at once and came walking towards them.

'But of course we'll be seeing each other,' said the man in the wheelchair. 'I'm very much looking forward to working with a Campelli again.'

Before Jon had time to reply, Kortmann's wheelchair turned and he was pushed away from the chapel by his attendant.

'What was that all about?' Jon asked Iversen.

Iversen made a wry face. 'Er, hmm, he's from the . . . Reading Group.'

'But what kind of work did he mean?' Jon insisted.

'Let's take a walk,' said Iversen, drawing Jon away.

They left the gravel path and went into the cemetery. The autumn sun hung low in the sky, sending knife-sharp rays through the tree branches and making wavy patterns on the path in front of them. They walked for a while in silence. It was quiet in the older part of the cemetery, where the shrubs were so thick it was impossible to see through them, even though the leaves had begun to fall.

'Your father loved walking here.'

Jon nodded. 'I know. I once followed him on one of his walks. I must have been about nine; in any case it was before . . .' Jon paused and bent down to pick up an acorn from the ground. He turned it over in his fingers before he went on. 'I pretended I was a secret agent and sneaked after him. I tailed him, imagining he was meeting other spies and passing on information.' Jon cleared his throat and tossed away the acorn. 'Maybe I was a bit disappointed. He didn't do anything except walk among the graves. Occasionally he would stop, and a few times he sat down to read from a book he'd brought along, as if he were reading aloud for the dead.'

'That sounds just like him,' said Iversen with a chuckle. 'Always looking for an audience.'

'I wouldn't know,' said Jon.

They had reached the wall bordering Nørrebrogade, where the ivy grew in abundance, covering the graves along the wall like a green snowfall.

'You realize you're going to inherit the bookshop, don't you?' said Iversen, keeping his eyes on the path in front of them.

Jon stopped and glanced at Iversen, who managed to take a couple more steps before he too came to a halt and turned round.

'There was no will, and as his only relative, you're the sole heir,' said Iversen, fixing his gaze on Jon. There wasn't a trace of bitterness or envy in the old man's eyes; instead, they seemed filled with concern or anxiety.

'I hadn't given it a thought,' said Jon. 'Was that what Kortmann meant when he said we'd be seeing each other again?'

Iversen nodded. 'Something like that, yes.'

Jon looked away. They continued walking.

'I was sure that Luca had left everything to you,' said Jon.

'Maybe your father hoped you would find your way back,' he suggested.

'That *I* would find my way back?' exclaimed Jon. 'As far as I recall, he was the one who didn't want anything to do with me the last time I contacted him.'

'I think . . . no, I'm *certain* he had a good reason for that.'

They had reached the end of the wall and exited the cemetery through the gate to Jagtvej, where they turned right towards Runddelen. The traffic was a welcome contrast to the silence of the cemetery.

'I don't want anything to do with it,' said Jon firmly as they turned down Nørrebrogade and headed back to the chapel. 'There won't be any problems. I have good legal contacts who can take care of this sort of thing. You've always been the right person to take over the place.'

Iversen cleared his throat so he could speak over the traffic noise. 'That's terribly nice of you, Jon. But I can't accept.'

'Of course you can,' said Jon. 'Luca owes it to you, and to me.'

'Perhaps,' Iversen admitted. 'But the bookshop isn't the whole thing. Your father's estate is more than a room full of old books.'

'Debts?'

'No, no, it's nothing like that, I can assure you.'

'Come on, Iversen. Let's not play a guessing game at the man's funeral,' said Jon, unable to hide his annoyance.

Iversen stopped and placed his hand on Jon's shoulder. 'I'm sorry, Jon. But I can't say anything more right now. You see, it's not my decision alone.'

Jon studied the man facing him. The expression in his eyes was both serious and sympathetic behind the sturdy frames of his steel-rimmed spectacles.

'That's okay, Iversen. Whatever the two of you have got your-selves mixed up in, it can wait until a more suitable moment. I suppose it's rather bad form to be discussing an inheritance at a funeral, isn't it?'

Iversen nodded with relief and gave Jon's shoulder an affection-ate pat. 'You're right, of course. I just wanted to make sure that you're aware this isn't the end of the matter. Let's meet at the shop in the next few days so we can settle things.'

They had reached the intersection of Nørrebrogade and Kapelvej, and Iversen made a move to turn back towards the chapel. Jon stopped and pointed to a bar on the other side of the street.

'I'm going to have a drink. Want to join me?' he asked. 'Isn't that part of going to a funeral?'

'No, thanks,' said Iversen. 'We're having a little get-together at the Society. You're welcome to come too, of course.'

Jon shook his head. 'Thanks anyway. See you later, Iversen.'

They shook hands, then Jon crossed the street and went inside the Clean Glass pub.

It was no more than two in the afternoon but the air was thick with smoke and the regular customers had already taken their places. They gave him a brief glance but clearly decided he was of no interest and went back to their beers.

Jon ordered a draught beer and sat down at a heavy wooden table, marred by beer rings and lit by a hanging copper lamp attached somewhere above the clouds of smoke. At a table opposite him sat a scrawny old man with pale skin, a crooked nose and wispy hair. The jacket he was wearing had patches on the sleeves, and the shirt underneath was wrinkled and far from clean. On the table in front of him stood a bottle of stout.

Jon offered the man a curt nod in greeting, but then he pulled out the Remer file from his briefcase so as not to invite further conversation. He sipped his beer as he studied the anonymous ring-binder. It was three days ago that he'd gone to Frank Halbech's office and officially received control of the Remer case. Halbech had to know what a reputation it had, but he ignored that and handed over the case almost as if it were a matter of a bicycle theft or a dispute between neighbours. The actual transfer consisted of Halbech tossing a bunch of keys on the table in front of Jon. The keys were attached to a ring adorned with a Smurf figure – Clever Smurf – and among them were the keys that provided access to the office set aside for the case, along with a number of filing cabinets. Jon would have to review the files on his own. Otherwise Halbech was more interested in which teachers Jon had studied with in law school and whether his father's death was going to affect his work. Jon assured him that Luca's death would have no impact on his work performance.

Jon now opened the file in front of him and scanned the first couple of pages. They comprised his predecessor's attempts to summarize the case, but Jon knew that he wasn't going to get out of ploughing his way through the many thousands of pages of material guarded by Clever Smurf.

Only a few moments after Jon had started working his way through the minutes from court meetings and hearings, the man with the bottle of stout began shifting about and uttering grunts of dissatisfaction. Jon glanced up, and their eyes met. This was clearly not the first stout the man had had; his eyes were bloodshot and bleary.

Jon looked away, took a gulp of his beer and returned to his reading.

'Hey, do you think this is some sort of reading room?'

Surprised, Jon glanced up at the man with the stout. With a jab of his index finger, his neighbour made it clear it was Jon he was talking to.

'I said, do you think this is some sort of reading room?'

'No, of course not,' Jon replied, flustered. 'But surely I'm not bothering anybody as long as I don't read aloud, am I?' Jon gave him a friendly smile.

'That's exactly what you're doing.' The man now jabbed his finger at the table. 'Reading can be very bothersome, even downright dangerous.' He reached for his beer but stopped in mid-motion. 'And not just for those who do the reading, but for everyone in the vicinity . . . passive reading is no joke!'

The man with the stout finally took a gulp of his beer. Unable to work out what reply would satisfy him, Jon did the same.

'Just imagine if everyone around you started recklessly reading,' the man went on after slamming the bottle down on the table. 'All the formulated words and sentences would fly around in the air like snowflakes in a blizzard.' The man held his hands up in front of him and began making a series of circling motions. 'They would get all mixed up with each other, stick together in incomprehensible phrases, then split up and reconnect in completely new words and passages, which would drive you crazy if you tried to find some meaning and sense where no meaning exists.'

'I've never experienced anything like that,' Jon ventured.

'Ha! That's because you're not listening, not properly anyway. But once you've learned to listen, you're lost. Then you have to live with the voices of the books for the rest of your life, whether you want to or not. You have no choice. The most beautiful poems, thrillers or whatever trash you happen to be sitting with, they'll all muscle their way in and poison the air around you.' The man sniggered and drank more of his stout.

Jon pointed at the file in front of him. 'Do you mean to say that this is speaking to you right now?'

The man laughed scornfully. 'Texts without a reader can't speak. A reader is required, but then they certainly do speak. They sing, they whisper, they even scream.' He leaned across the table with a lurch that threatened to topple his bottle of stout. 'Imagine a reading room,' he said, pausing to allow the image to sink in. 'A whole cheering section can come out of a place like that. Bloody awful.' He slumped back in his chair and scowled at Jon with his red eyes.

'But you don't hear any voice in here?' asked Jon.

The man ignored the sarcasm and threw out his hands. 'This is my sanctuary. Not many readers in here, you see.' He picked up the bottle and aimed the top at Jon. 'Until you turned up, of course,' he added and put the bottle to his lips.

'I'm sorry about that,' said Jon.

'Sheesh. You don't understand a thing, do you?' snarled the man and stood up, still holding the bottle. 'Go ahead and read whatever you like.' He swayed a bit before he got his body moving. 'But your father understood.'

Astonished, Jon watched the man as he set his bottle down hard on the bar and staggered out of the door.

# 4

After a fifteen-year absence, Jon decided to visit Libri di Luca the day after the funeral. Over the years he had driven past the place many times and it always looked as if it were open, even late at night. Occasionally he had caught a glimpse of Luca through the windows, busily occupied at the counter or in the process of straightening the books in the window.

The bells over the door were undoubtedly the same as the last time he had been there, and the sound welcomed him back like a distant member of the family. There was no one in the shop and yet he was still met by familiar faces – the long rows of book-shelves, the lamp hanging from the ceiling, the light from the glass cases on the balcony and the old silver-chased cash register on the counter. Jon stopped inside the door and breathed in the air of the place. He couldn't hold back the small, crooked smile that formed on his lips.

Before his mother's death, the bookshop had been his favourite place. When both Luca and Iversen were too busy to read to him, he would go exploring in the shop, acting out the stories among the books from which they originated. And so the staircase became a mountain he had to climb, the shelves were transformed into sky-scrapers in futuristic cities and the balcony became the bridge of a pirate ship.

But what he remembered most clearly were the many hours when Iversen or Luca had read stories to him, sitting in the green leather chair behind the counter with Jon either on their lap or on the floor at their feet. During those hours he became a witness to fantastic tales whose images he could still recreate, even today.

The antiquarian bookshop looked exactly as he remembered it, with the exception of two things: a piece of the railing of the pirate ship had been replaced by a new section of fresh, light-coloured wood; and a bouquet of white tulips stood on the dark counter. Both items seemed out of place in the tranquil atmosphere of the room, as if it were a picture in a quiz that posed the question: what doesn't belong here?

'He'll be back in a moment,' Jon heard behind him.

He gave a start and turned to face the voice. Half-hidden behind the far bookshelf was a red-haired woman wearing a black sweater and a long, burgundy-coloured skirt. Her hand was resting on the edge of the shelf in such a way that it hid her mouth and the tip of her nose. The only parts visible were the red hair and one shining green eye that regarded him coolly.

Jon nodded to her and was about to say something in reply, but then she retreated once more behind the bookshelf. In the front of the shop stood a long table where the newly arrived books were on display. Under the pretence of studying the new volumes, he moved along the table and over to the corridor between the shelves where the woman had disappeared. She had made it halfway down the aisle, and since her back was turned, Jon could see that her red hair was tied in a ponytail and reached to the middle of her back. With light, cat-like steps she made her way down the shelves, running the very tips of her fingers along the spines of the books as if reading Braille or looking for irregularities. She didn't seem to be reading the titles of the books as she passed. A couple of times she stopped and placed her whole palm on the spines, as if she were absorbing the stories through her hand. At the end of the aisle the woman turned the corner, but managed to cast a quick glance in Jon's direction before she once again disappeared from view.

Jon turned his attention back to the books in front of him. It was a collection of fiction and non-fiction, both in hardback and paperback. Some of the books were new, virginal copies without a scratch or a crease, while others had clearly been taken to the beach or on a lengthy backpacking trip.

Until Jon was big enough to read for himself, one of his favourite pastimes had been to look through the newly arrived volumes for bookmarks. It became a collector's mania, just as other people go in for stamps or coins, and the variety was almost as great. There were the official bookmarks, rectangular pieces of cardboard adorned with an image that had – or didn't have – some relation to the book itself. Then there were the more neutral types – blank pieces of paper, pieces of string, elastic bands or banknotes. Other bookmarks indirectly revealed something about the reader's habits or interests. It might be a receipt, a bus pass, a cinema or theatre ticket, a shopping list or newspaper clipping. Finally, there were the personal bookmarks such as business cards, drawings, letters, postcards and photographs. The letter or card might be from a sweetheart, the photo might have a greeting or an explanation written on the back, the drawing might have been a present from a child.

Unless it was a matter of a banknote, which Jon was allowed to keep, all the bookmarks were collected in a wooden box under the counter. When he was a child and couldn't find anything else to do, Jon would pull out the box and place the bookmarks on the floor like playing cards, making up stories about them.

The bells over the door rang and Iversen came in with a red pizza box in his hands. When he caught sight of Jon he broke into a big smile and offered a vociferous greeting as he hurried to close the door behind him.

'It's good to see you,' he said, setting the pizza box on the counter and stretching out his hand.

'Hello, Iversen.' Jon shook his hand. 'I hope I'm not interrupting you?' He nodded towards the pizza. The pronounced aroma of pepperoni and melted cheese momentarily drove out the smell of parchment and leather.

'Not in the least,' exclaimed Iversen. 'But I hope you won't mind if I eat. It's best when it's hot.'

'Not at all. Go right ahead.'

Iversen smiled gratefully. 'Let's go downstairs so we can talk without being disturbed,' he said and grabbed the box.

'Katherina?' called Iversen as they made their way along the corridor towards the winding stairs at the back of the shop.

The red-haired woman popped up at the end of the bookshelf, as if she'd been waiting to be summoned. She was only slightly shorter than Jon, and her body was slender without being lanky. Her red hair framed a narrow, pale face with thin lips pursed into a stern expression. Her green eyes looked at Jon as if he were in the wrong place.

'We're going down to the kitchen,' said Iversen. 'Could you watch the shop in the meantime?' The woman nodded in reply and once again withdrew from sight.

'Your daughter?' asked Jon on the way down the spiral staircase, whose worn steps creaked loudly under the weight of the two men.

'Katherina?' Iversen laughed. 'No, no, she's one of the friends of the bookshop. Lately she's been an invaluable help to the two of us old men. She mostly takes care of practical matters such as cleaning and things like that.' Iversen stopped at the bottom of the stairs. 'She's not exactly the best bookshop clerk,' he added in a low voice.

Jon nodded. 'She seems a bit shy, doesn't she?'

Iversen shrugged. 'That's not really it. She's dyslexic.'

'A dyslexic clerk in a bookshop?' exclaimed Jon in surprise, speaking a little too loudly, which prompted him to lower his voice to a whisper. 'How can she possibly be useful to you?'

'I haven't got a single bad thing to say about Katherina,' replied Iversen solemnly. 'She's smarter than most people. You'll soon find that out.'

They stood at the foot of the stairs in a narrow, whitewashed hallway illuminated by two bare bulbs. On either side of the hall were doorways, one leading to the kitchen, which was where Iversen headed. The room across from it was cloaked in darkness, but Jon knew that Luca used to use it as a workshop where he bound and restored books. At the end of the corridor was a heavy oak door.

The kitchen was small but functional. A stainless-steel sink, a cupboard, two hotplates, a fridge and a table with three folding chairs. On the walls and the cupboard doors hung discarded book jackets interspersed with illustrations, wherever there was space.

Iversen set the pizza on the table, took off his jacket, and hung it on a hook by the door. Jon followed his example.

'I love pizza,' said Iversen as he sat down at the table. 'I know it's supposed to be food for youngsters like yourself, but I can't help it. And it's not even the fault of your father's influence. He hated Danish pizzas.' Iversen laughed. "They have nothing to do with real pizza," he used to say. Too much topping, in his opinion. "Piled up like an open sandwich."'

Jon sat down across from Iversen.

'Would you like some?' muttered Iversen, his mouth already full of food.

Jon shook his head. 'No thanks. On that point I share Luca's opinion.'

Iversen shrugged his shoulders as he continued to chew. 'So tell me a little about what you've been doing while I eat.'

'Hmm,' said Jon. 'Well, I ended up living with a family in Hillerød back then. It was okay, but a little too far from the city, so I moved to a dorm in Copenhagen when I started at the university. In the middle of my studies I took a couple of years off and worked as a legal assistant in Brussels – I was more or less an intern. Back in Denmark I finished my law degree near the top of my class, which led to a position as barrister with the firm of Hanning, Jensen & Halbech, where I still work.'

Jon fell silent, discovering that he actually didn't have anything else to add. Not because there was nothing to tell – he could always talk about his travels, his difficulties at the university, the jockeying for position at the firm or the Remer case. But why involve Iversen now, after so many years of separation, and with Luca's death about to bring their connection to a definite end?

'As you can hear, I haven't had much to do with literature,' he added.

'Maybe not with literature, per se,' admitted Iversen between pieces of pizza. 'But the written word is of great importance in both of our worlds. Each of us in his own way is dependent on *books*.'

Jon nodded. 'More and more is becoming available electronically, but you're right. Everyone in my field has a set of Karnov law books somewhere or other. In some sense it's still more impressive to have a stack of thick reference books than a single CD-ROM.' He threw out his hands. 'So I assume there's still some use for antiquarian bookshops like this?'

Iversen gulped down the last of his pizza. 'I'm positive there is.'

'Which brings us to why I'm here,' said Jon in a businesslike tone. 'There was something you wanted to tell me?'

'Let's go into the library,' said Iversen, pointing to the door. 'There's more . . . atmosphere.'

They got up and walked down the hall. As a child, Jon was never allowed to be downstairs unless accompanied by Luca or Iversen, and he'd never been inside the room behind the oak door, which they were now approaching. The room had always been part of his games about a treasure chamber or a prison cell, but no matter how much he pleaded, he had never been allowed inside. The door had always been kept locked, and after a while he gave up asking. At the door Iversen pulled a key ring from his trouser pocket and selected a black iron key, which he stuck in the lock. The door groaned impressively when he opened it, and Jon noticed that the hairs on the back of his neck quivered.

'This is the Campelli collection,' said Iversen as he vanished into the darkness beyond the door. A moment later the lights went on and Jon stepped inside. The low-ceilinged room was approximately 30 square metres, and the floor was covered with a thick, dark carpet. In the middle of the room stood four comfortable-looking leather chairs around a low table made of dark wood. The walls were covered with bookshelves and glass cabinets filled with books in various bindings. Most of them had leather spines, and the indirect light from the top of the shelves bathed the books and the rest of the room in a soft, golden glow.

Jon whistled softly. 'Impressive.' He let his hand slide over the books on the nearest shelf. 'Not that I know much about it, but I have to admit it's an amazing sight.'

'I can assure you that for those in the know, the sight is no less impressive,' added Iversen. He smiled proudly as he let his gaze roam from shelf to shelf. 'The collection was put together over the centuries by your father and your ancestors. Many of the works have travelled around most of Europe before ending up here.' With great care he pulled out a volume and caressed the darkened leather with his fingertips. 'If only I could hear it speak,' he said to himself. 'A story within a story.'

'Is it valuable?'

'Very,' replied Iversen. 'Maybe not in terms of cash, but it has a high sentimental and bibliographic value.'

'So, is this the big secret?' asked Jon.

'Part of it,' replied Iversen. 'Sit down, Jon.' He pointed to the leather chairs and went over to shut the door. With the door closed it felt as if they were inside a glass bell. No sounds seemed able to penetrate the atmosphere of the library, and Jon had the feeling that no one outside would hear them, no matter how much they yelled or shouted. He sat down in one of the leather chairs and placed his elbows on the armrests with his hands clasped in front of him.

Iversen sat down in a chair across from Jon and cleared his throat before he began.

'First of all, you need to know that what I'm about to say is something that your father would have told you at some point – just as Luca was initiated by his father, Arman. He should have done it long ago, but the climate in your family hasn't been the most conducive to confessions.'

Jon didn't say a word, and the expression on his face didn't change.

'But let's not go into that,' Iversen went on. 'Though I'd like to say that since things are the way they are, I'm proud of the fact that I'm the one who is privileged to tell you what you're now going to hear.'

Iversen's voice quavered a bit, and he took a deep breath before he continued. 'You've experienced personally how unusually good your father was at reading stories aloud, just as his father was. I myself, in all modesty, am rather good at it, but nothing in comparison with Luca.' Iversen paused. 'So what do you think makes someone good at reading aloud, Jon?'

In spite of all the intervening years, Jon still knew Iversen too well to be surprised by the question. He felt himself carried back in time to all the occasions when Iversen, enthroned in the green leather chair behind the counter, had asked Jon about the stories he had heard read aloud. Always penetrating questions about what Jon thought of the stories, the descriptions, the characters.

'Practice, empathy and acting skill, to a certain degree,' he replied without taking his eyes off Iversen's face.

The man across from him nodded. 'The more a person reads, the better he gets at finding the tempo and knowing how to pause at the right moments. As he gains more experience, the language flows more easily from his lips, and he can devote more attention to the two other traits you mentioned: empathy and acting skill. It's no coincidence that actors are often the ones who read stories on the radio.'

Iversen leaned towards Jon. 'But some people have an extra card to play, so to speak.' He paused for dramatic effect.

'Being able to read a text is not an innate skill. The ability to decipher letters of the alphabet is not in our genes. It's unnatural – an artificial skill that we acquire during our first years in school; some people with greater success and talent than others.' He cast a glance at the ceiling and the shop above them, where Katherina was most likely still strolling about among the bookshelves. 'When we read, many different areas of the brain are activated. It's a combination of recognizing symbols and patterns, connecting them to sounds and gathering them into syllables until we're finally able to interpret the meaning of a word. In addition, the word has to be set in relation to the context in which it's found, in order to produce meaning . . .'

Jon caught himself wiggling his foot impatiently and stopped.

'Of course, what I'm telling you is quite banal,' Iversen said in apology. 'But it's something we don't usually think about, and it's merely meant to emphasize what a complicated process reading is, going from the word on the page in front of you to the sound that leaves your lips. Many areas of the brain are involved in the translation from symbol to sound, or to comprehension if you're reading silently to yourself. And it's there, in that interplay, that something amazing can occur.'

Iversen's eyes shone, as if he were on the verge of unveiling some unseen work of art.

'For a very small number of us, that brain activity includes areas of the brain that make us capable of psychically influencing those who listen.'

Jon raised an eyebrow, but apparently that wasn't enough of a response to make Iversen go on.

'What do you mean?' Jon asked. 'That you can make people feel moved by what you read to them? Isn't that just a matter of technique?'

'That will have some effect,' admitted Iversen. 'But this goes beyond that. We're capable of influencing people without them being aware of it, influencing their view of the text, its theme, or something else entirely.'

Jon intently studied the man sitting across from him. Either he was crazy or else this was a joke, yet Iversen wasn't the type to make fun of literature.

'If we want to, we can change people's opinion of the subject matter. To take an extreme example, we could get a Catholic priest to approve of abortion.' Iversen broke into a smile, but there was still no indication that he was not completely serious.

'But how?'

'Well, I'm probably not the best person to explain it, but I can tell you about the general principle and then others can fill in the details.' He cleared his throat before continuing. 'As I understand the matter, it has to do with the fact that when we – and this applies to everyone – receive information, for example through reading to ourselves or listening to readings, or through films, TV, pretty much anything at all, a sort of channel is opened that examines, classifies and distributes the information. It's also here that an emphasis is added by comparing the received data to the presentation and one's previous experiences, attitudes and convictions. In fact, it's this process that determines the extent to which we like the music we hear or agree with the arguments of a speaker.'

'And this . . . emphasis is something you can control?'

'Precisely,' replied Iversen. 'Those of us who practise the art are called *Lectors*, and when we read aloud from a text, we charge it with whatever emphasis we like, thereby influencing the listener's experience of and attitude towards what is being read.'

Jon was starting to feel a little annoyed. He wasn't used to dealing with emotions, sensations and undocumented claims. In his world a case wasn't worth dealing with if there was no reliable testimony or facts or very strong evidence. This seemed like a case of faith, and that didn't appeal to him at all.

'Can you prove any of this?' Jon asked firmly.

'It's not an exact science, and there are many things we don't fully understand. For instance, it turns out that certain types of text are better suited than others. Fiction is more effective than non-fiction, and the quality of the work is also significant. Even more remarkable is the fact that the potential of the text may depend on whether it's read from a monitor, from a cheap photocopy or from a first edition – and the last is far more powerful than the others. It also appears that certain books become *charged* when they're read, so that the next presentation of the text becomes stronger – more effective at communicating the message and emotions it contains. Older and frequently read volumes are therefore more powerful than new, unread copies.' Iversen shifted his gaze from Jon, allowing it to slide over the bookshelves surrounding them.

Jon got up and went over to the nearest shelf. 'Are these books charged?' he asked sceptically, pulling out a volume at random.

'Many of them are. You can actually feel it when you hold the most powerful copies in your hands.'

Jon placed his palm on the book he had taken from the shelf. After a couple of seconds he shook his head, put the book back and repeated the process with another.

'I don't feel anything,' he finally said.

'You would need to possess the ability,' explained Iversen. 'Plus a certain amount of practice.'

Jon put the book back in place and turned to face Iversen. 'So how does someone gain the ability? How does someone become a Lector?'

'It's something a person is born to do. It's not something you can learn, or for that matter even choose. Your father inherited the ability from his father, Arman, who got it from his father, and so on. Therefore it's highly likely you've inherited the ability from Luca.'

He fell silent and then hammered home his point. 'You can be a Lector, Jon.'

Jon stared at Iversen. The smile on the old man's lips was gone and his expression was filled with a solemnity that seemed quite unsuited to the otherwise jovial man. Jon threw out his arms towards the bookshelves surrounding them. 'But I told you I didn't feel a thing.'

'In most people the ability is latent,' said Iversen. 'Some never discover it, others are born with an active talent, while still others can become activated by chance. But most demonstrate some form of talent in that direction, either through their choice of profession or in the way they perform their job.' He gave Jon a searching look. 'What about you, Jon? Have you ever experienced situations where your reading aloud has influenced or spellbound people?'

Even though Jon had the feeling he was affecting people when he presented his closing arguments, he had never noticed anything special about this. No channels or energy or charges of any kind – it was merely a reading technique, nothing more.

'Maybe I'm better at reading aloud than most people,' Jon admitted. 'But that doesn't necessarily mean anything.'

'You're right. A person can have a talent for reading aloud without being a Lector.'

Jon crossed his arms. 'Luca was a Lector?'

Iversen nodded. 'The best.'

'And the friends of Libri di Luca . . . Are they Lectors?'

'Most of them, yes.'

Jon pictured the congregation in the chapel and tried to imagine them as a silent crowd of conspirators instead of the motley group that he had perceived. He shook his head.

'There's one thing that I don't understand,' he said. 'If it's all about being able to read . . . what is a dyslexic doing here?'

'Katherina?' said Iversen with a smile. 'She's a whole different story.'

# 5

Katherina sat down on the top step to the balcony and drew her legs up so that she could rest her chin on her knees. From here she had a view of the whole shop and, more importantly, the front door. Even though it was now a week since Luca's death, she still expected the door to open and the diminutive Italian to step into the bookshop with a contented look on his face, as if he were coming home instead of starting a work-day. For the past couple of years she'd had that feeling too when she pushed open the door and heard the bells welcoming her inside. The sound of those bells put her in a different frame of mind, a state of calm and peace, and she imagined the same had been true for Luca.

But now all that was going to change.

Her gaze fell on the section of railing that had been replaced. The carpenter, who was a friend of Iversen's, had done his best to match the tone of the wood with the old railing, but it was still obvious that repairs had recently been made. It would take a couple of years before the difference was no longer discernible.

Katherina couldn't hear the voices of Iversen and Luca's son from the basement any more, and she surmised they had withdrawn to the library. She'd heard about the son for the first time after Luca's death, and it was news that took her completely by surprise. After ten years in the bookshop and, she thought, a close friendship with both Iversen and Luca, the news had suddenly made her feel like an outsider. Iversen claimed that Luca had had his reasons for keeping the information secret – even Iversen didn't know what all the reasons were – but it had apparently had something to do with his wife's death.

At the funeral Katherina had had a chance to study the son closely. He looked like his father, though he was significantly taller than Luca had been. The facial features were the same, the dark eyes, thick eyebrows and almost black hair, all of which confirmed her assumption that Luca must have been an attractive man in his younger days.

Katherina was not the only one who was surprised to learn that Luca had a son. When Iversen presented the situation to the Bibliophile Society, the news was evidently as much of a shock to many of them as it was to her. The meeting had lasted a long time, and afterwards the only thing Iversen was willing to reveal was that they had decided to include the son. Katherina gathered this went against Iversen's own wishes, but she hadn't delved any more deeply into it.

Downstairs he was most likely in the process of discussing the whole matter. It was no easy task to explain how everything fitted together to an outsider, but Iversen was the best person to do it. She wondered which explanation he would use this time. Probably the one about the channel. A bit too technical for her taste. Katherina had been forced to come up with her own explanation until years later she finally found others who suffered from the same affliction – or gift, depending on how you looked at it, or rather at what moment you happened to ask her.

Iversen had a different perspective on these abilities because he was a transmitter. Katherina was a receiver. Two sides of the same coin, he would probably tell Jon, but for Katherina there was a significant difference that could not be explained by either reversing polarities or flipping coins. As Iversen was in the process of explaining, there were two types of Lectors: transmitters like himself, who could influence those who listened to a reading and were thus able to affect the listeners' perceptions of and attitudes towards the text.

The other type were receivers, like Katherina.

The first time she became aware of this, she was barely conscious. She had been in a car accident and was badly injured, as were her parents. For several days she lay under anaesthesia in a big hospital bed with her small, fragile body broken in pieces and held together with screws and plaster. It was in this state that she experienced someone reading aloud to her. Through the drug-induced fog she heard a clear voice telling a story about an unusually passive man who let his life go by without taking any real part in it or having any opinions about what was happening around him. Even though she was anaesthetized, she was still conscious enough to feel surprised. Partly she wondered who the calm voice belonged to, and partly she was amazed by the strange story, which she didn't understand at all. It wasn't funny or sweet or exciting, but the compelling force of the voice held her attention and led her through the tale.

When she was finally brought out of the anaesthesia, she had other things to think about. Her parents were in very bad shape and unable to visit her. She also had her own injuries, which only slowly began to heal under the thick layers of bandages – a subject that was off-limits for the relatives who visited her with teary eyes and quavering voices.

As she regained consciousness, she started hearing voices. Not the same voice that had read to her, but various voices that seemed almost to merge together, voices that tormented her during the day and kept her awake at night. Sometimes the voices were accompanied by glimpses of images, impressions that forced themselves on her, demanding her attention, only to vanish as suddenly as they had appeared. One day she asked the nurse if she could hear the rest of the story. She was longing for the sound of the calm voice that had kept her company when she was under anaesthesia. The nurse stared at her in surprise. No one had read anything to her. It was true that she had shared the room with an elderly man while she was unconscious, but he couldn't have been the one who read to her. He'd had his vocal cords removed because he had cancer of the throat.

Her family were very indulgent. They knew that being separated from her parents was naturally very hard on the girl, and the voices she claimed were tormenting her must be a delayed reaction to the trauma. Her mother's condition improved, and she was able to visit Katherina, but her father was still on a respirator, and it wasn't certain whether he would survive. Everyone treated Katherina with the greatest care and understanding, but as time passed and she was discharged from the hospital along with her mother, those around her began to think that her mind must have suffered permanent damage after all.

Physically she had escaped with scars on her legs and arms, as well as one in the centre of her chin, which gave it a tiny, masculine cleft in the otherwise so girlish face. The scar on her chin was a constant reminder of the accident to her, and she was often seen rubbing the spot with her index finger, with a remote look in her eyes.

Her distracted air only added to the family's concern and she was sent to a child psychologist, who had nothing to offer except to give her pills – a solution that seemed to keep the voices at bay but had the same effect on all other input.

For that reason she paid very little attention when her father was discharged, permanently confined to a wheelchair and so bitter at life that he spent most of his days behind the closed door of his office with no desire to speak to anyone.

She started roaming around, fleeing from her father's bursts of rage behind the closed door, and from the voices. There were places where they left her in peace. The woods and grassland of Amager Fælled was one of these, and she seized every opportunity to bicycle out to that area where she could sit for hours, enjoying the silence. School was the worst place of all, and she soon began to skip classes and go out to the park instead.

Of course it was only a matter of time before her family became aware of her truancy. She then realized that her condition was not just affecting herself but was also hurting everyone around her. It was at that point that she decided to reconcile herself to the voices. Outwardly she would pretend they didn't exist, that she had been miraculously cured, but for her own part, she would start to listen. She wanted to find out what they wanted, clarify why she was the one they sought out, and whether she really was meant to be their victim. Up until then she had refused to listen to what they said, but now she had begun to suspect that they weren't speaking to her directly – it seemed more as if they were coming from a radio tuned to several different stations at once. Could it be that the voices were actually radio signals she was picking up?

Because she was dyslexic, more severely than most, the world of the alphabet was already foreign to her, and the connection between the incomprehensible symbols on the page and the voices she heard in her head when others read them evaded her for a long time. But one day on the bus she worked it out. She was sitting there staring out of the window and listening to a clear female voice telling a story about a girl with red plaits, freckles and such strength that she could lift a horse. It was an entertaining story, and at a particularly funny scene, Katherina couldn't help laughing – she laughed out loud, to the amazement of all her fellow passengers, except for one. In the very back of the bus, a boy was holding a book in his hands and laughing just as heartily as she was. Even from her seat in the bus Katherina could clearly recognize the girl with the plaits on the cover of the book. It was Pippi Longstocking.

The bells over the door in Libri di Luca rang, pulling Katherina out of her reverie. A man in his thirties, wearing horn-rimmed glasses, a corduroy jacket and carrying a worn leather bag over his shoulder, stood in the doorway. It was clear that he hadn't been to the shop before because he reacted the way most newcomers did: he looked around the room in surprise, paying special attention to the balcony, as if he'd never seen a bookshop on two levels before. Katherina had probably behaved in the same way when she first discovered Libri di Luca ten years earlier, but she was always a little annoyed by the bewilderment of new customers. Yes, it was an antiquarian bookshop. Yes, there was a balcony with rare books in glass cases. Yes, it was a fantastic place, so why don't you just see about buying a few books and then get lost? If it were up to her, Libri di Luca would be closed to customers.

The man in the horn-rimmed glasses caught sight of Katherina at the top of the stairs and immediately lowered his eyes, turning to close the door behind him. Afterwards he headed for the table where the newly arrived books were displayed.

Katherina stood up and slowly went down the steps.

The intruder was scanning the book covers.

'Swann'sWayJoysAndDaysJamesJoyceAbsalomAbsalomWilliam FaulknerBuddenbrooksTheGothicRenaissanceExLibrisJorgeLuis BorgesTheExpelledFiccionesTheDumasClubFranzKafkaItalo Calvino . . .'

The names of authors and titles on the books babbled chaotically in her head like the sound of a reel-to-reel tape recorder whirring at high speed. She clenched her teeth and continued over to the green leather chair behind the counter. The customer raised his eyes for a moment to nod at her in greeting, and the flow of voices stopped. Katherina nodded back and sat down in the chair.

'FootprintsInHeavenTheArtOfCryingGustaveFlaubertCharles DickensTheCastleTheWoodenHorseCarlSchmittBennQHolm PoeticsAndCriticismFrankFønsASeriousConversationJeffMatthews LastSundayInOctober,' chirped the voices, and she leaned back and closed her eyes. Katherina couldn't completely shut out the voices, but she had learned to turn down the volume, mostly thanks to Luca and Iversen.

Ten years earlier she had been walking past Libri di Luca when a voice stopped her. It was late afternoon and raining, so she didn't feel like bicycling out to Amager Fælled. Instead she was wandering around the Vesterbro district, heading for areas of silence – any place at all, if only she could have some peace for a moment. After discovering the connection between the voices and readers, she had tried to avoid places where it was worst, and on this day she had ended up on the street where Libri di Luca stood.

The voice that stopped her was one she immediately recognized. It was identical to the voice from the hospital, which had kept her company while she was unconscious. She looked around, but no one was near. As she approached the bookshop, the voice became clearer, and when she was close enough to look in the windows, she saw a group of about fifty people sitting on folding chairs in the front of the shop. At the counter stood a short, compact man in his fifties with salt-and-pepper hair and a Mediterranean fervour on his face. He was reading from a book he held in his rough hands, and doing so with such energy that his entire body was taking part in the reading.

Katherina cautiously opened the door, and even though the chiming of the bells drew attention to her, the reader didn't interrupt the story, merely sent a friendly glance in her direction. She sat down at the very back of the room and closed her eyes. Although the man behind the counter was an excellent reader, it wasn't *his* voice that she had come inside to hear. She shut it out by placing her hands over her ears and concentrating on the other voice, the one that she recognized from the hospital. That was how she sat there at the back of the room with her elbows propped on her knees, oblivious to all sights and sounds. Inside she was filled with the voice and the images the story evoked, scenes from the city where it was set, the miserable flats, the birds above the rooftops, the dust and filth of the streets. Even though it wasn't a happy story, she felt comforted, and if she hadn't been sitting there looking down at the floor, people would have been able to see the tears on her face.

Suddenly the whole thing was over. The reading came to an end, and everyone around her applauded. She removed her hands from her ears in time to hear that the story was called *The Stranger*. A discussion of the text ensued, but Katherina stayed where she was, with her eyes closed and her face turned towards the floor. People started to get up and wander about, and as they began studying the books on the shelves, the titles and author names and excerpts of the texts flowed towards Katherina. Voices and images forced themselves upon her in an ever-growing torrent, and she had to summon all her forces to stand up and stagger towards the door. The intensity seemed to increase when she got up, as if she were leaning into a strong wind, and it got harder and harder to focus on the exit. After only a few steps, she collapsed on the floor.

When she came to, the bookshop was empty except for the man who had been reading. With concern he asked her how she felt, and then introduced himself as Luca. He was sitting next to her on a folding chair. She was propped up in a soft leather chair behind the counter. The voices had disappeared along with the audience members, but she was so exhausted she couldn't get up.

Luca told her to relax and take all the time she needed. In a soothing voice he continued to chat about everyday things: the bookshop, the readings they had in the evenings, various books, even the weather, until he suddenly asked her how long she'd been hearing voices.

The question took her aback, and she forgot her vow never to mention it to anyone; she told him everything. Luca turned out to know an astonishing amount about her condition, asking her how strong the voices were, whether she was able to shut them out, when she had heard them for the first time and whether she knew anyone else with the same experiences. She answered as best she could, and for the first time she sensed that someone understood her, that she was being taken seriously. In his relaxed manner, which she would grow so fond of in the coming years, Luca explained that she was not the only one – at least half of the people who had been at the reading possessed the same abilities.

Katherina had never regarded it as an ability. For her it was the voices that sought her out, forcing her to pay attention; she was not the one who tuned into them. But that was also possible, Luca explained: she could tune into the channel that opened whenever people read, whether aloud or silently to themselves.

In a matter of fifteen minutes he taught her a technique that enabled her to turn down the volume of the voices so they no longer bothered her. Even though the technique would require practice, the effect was so extraordinary on her first attempt that

Katherina burst into tears from sheer relief. Luca comforted her and invited her to drop by as often as she liked to improve her technique. Of course she could try muting the voices without his supervision, but he implored her never to try to amplify them or alter them in any other way until she'd had more practice. Katherina would later find out why.

The customer in Libri di Luca wasn't focusing. Among the small glimpses of images conjured up from the excerpts he was reading were pictures that had no relevance to the books. That was a residual effect of her powers. In addition to being able to hear the text that was being read, Katherina could often see the images it evoked in the reader. And if he or she happened to be thinking about all sorts of other things at the same time, they would pop up like brief sequences inserted into a film. That was a side effect that had required training, but over the years Luca had helped her with this as well, and she was now able to sense what an unfocused reader, such as the man with the horn-rimmed glasses, had on his mind.

Apparently he was supposed to meet a girl later in the day because pictures of the girl kept appearing along with an image of where they were supposed to meet (at the Town Hall Square), where they were going to have dinner (Mühlhausen), plus his strongly erotic hopes for the rest of the evening. Katherina felt her cheeks flush.

It was by no means everyone that Katherina could read in this manner. Iversen claimed that it had to do with the individual's imagination, how clear the images were that came from the text and the person's subconscious; but it was also a matter of the reading style. People who skimmed the words produced a swift series of pictures which in the most extreme cases became a stylized cartoon that would flicker before her eyes. Other readers took their time – so much time that the images were razor-sharp and so saturated with information that she could go exploring in them, zooming down to the smallest details, as if in a spy photo from a satellite.

'I'll take these,' said a cautious voice, and Katherina opened her eyes. The man with the horn-rimmed glasses stood at the counter holding out two books towards her. He gave an apologetic shrug of his shoulders.

'Eighty kroner,' said Katherina without looking at the paperbacks he had selected. They had already revealed themselves as *The Big Sleep* and *Moon Palace*, which cost 30 and 50 kroner respectively. She stood up and found a bag under the counter while the customer rummaged through his pockets for the money. He paid and left the shop with a black plastic bag printed with the name 'Libri di Luca' in gold letters.

In some cases Katherina's Lector powers compensated for her dyslexia, and in many situations she was able to completely hide her handicap. For a while that was how she'd appeared to show 'noticeable improvement' in her reading classes in primary school. But when the teacher or other pupils weren't following along in the text, she would be cut off from the meaning of the letters. That had produced a setback at exam time.

Luca thought there was a connection between her dyslexia and her abilities as a Lector. During their practice sessions he quickly discovered that she had powerful talents, and in his opinion this was because of dyslexia, not in spite of it. So he tried to get her to regard her abilities as a gift and not a punishment, which was how she had previously thought of them. Even though he himself was a Lector, he was not a receiver and thus could not fully understand everything that Katherina had to endure.

She thought it must be even worse for her mentor's son, who was now being initiated into the secrets of the Lectors in the room beneath her. The scepticism she had felt when Luca explained things to her had soon disappeared, because she had already felt it in her own body. Here was an explanation, incredible though it might be, and yet it was an explanation she could accept. But she couldn't even imagine how it would all sound to someone who was a complete outsider. How would he react?

At that moment Katherina heard the stairs creak, and a few seconds later Iversen came into view. He was sweating and his face was a bit red, the way it always was whenever he got excited or upset by a discussion.

'He wants proof,' he said, out of breath. 'Could you give a demonstration?'

# 6

Which one should he choose?

Jon walked along the shelves in the basement, looking for a book to use in the demonstration. He could choose any volume he liked, Iversen had said, like a magician challenging a spectator to pull a card at random from the deck. As Jon understood it, the plan was for him to read an excerpt from the book while Katherina tried to influence his perception of the text to such a degree that he would have no doubts that such a thing was possible.

As Iversen had explained, Katherina was a receiver, which meant that she was able to hear and to a certain extent see what other people were reading. What seemed even more unbelievable was that she was capable of accentuating the reader's experience of the text at will. In this way her abilities resembled those he himself possessed, according to Iversen, but whereas he should present a text in order to charge it, Katherina was able to affect the reader directly, even if that person was reading silently to himself.

Iversen had seemed very convincing, but when he had hinted at outright mind-reading as a consequence of Katherina's talents, Jon had demanded proof. The fact that the old man had immediately agreed to his request planted a seed of concern in Jon's mind. If there really was something to these abilities, he wasn't sure he cared to have other people rummaging about in his brain as he read.

The way Katherina entered the library hadn't made the situation any better. She emanated neither the flamboyant style of a magician nor the secretiveness of a mystic – it seemed more as if she were a bit embarrassed to be there, and she hardly gave him a glance as she sat down in one of the leather chairs with her hands in her lap. Even so, Jon felt that he was being observed, not only by the two other people present but by the walls of books, which seemed to be studying him with bated breath.

'Can I get one from the shop?' asked Jon, pointing towards the ceiling.

'Of course,' replied Iversen. 'Take your time.'

Jon left the room and went upstairs to the bookshop. Iversen had locked the door and turned off the lights so that only the glow from the street lamps outside lit up the room. Jon let his eyes adjust to the dimness and then walked up and down the aisles at random. Every once in a while he stopped to pull out a book, which he studied but then quickly rejected, putting it back in its place. Finally he realized that it didn't make any difference what book he chose, because how was he to know what was a suitable text for this sort of test? He closed his eyes and let his fingers run along the spines of the books in front of him until he stopped at random on a volume, which he pulled from the shelf. With his trophy in hand, he returned to the reading room in the basement.

'*Fahrenheit 451*,' said Iversen, nodding in acknowledgement. 'Bradbury. A brilliant choice, Jon.'

'Science fiction, right?'

'Yes, but the genre is of no importance. Are you ready?'

'As ready as I'll ever be.'

'What about you, Katherina?' Iversen asked, turning to look at the redhead who was sitting motionless in the leather chair. She raised her eyes and inspected Jon. Meditatively she rubbed her index finger over her chin before she again placed her hands in her lap and nodded.

'All right,' said Iversen, clapping his hands together. 'You'd better sit down, Jon.'

'And I'm just supposed to read to myself?'

'Correct,' replied Iversen, gesturing towards a chair. 'Go ahead and begin, and don't worry. She'll take good care of you.'

Jon sat down on the chair across from Katherina. She nodded, as if giving the signal to start, and instinctively Jon nodded in return and then turned his eyes to the book.

It had once been an ordinary paperback edition, but the owner had laminated the front cover and reinforced the spine and back with cardboard and leather. The edges of the paper were yellowed and slightly frayed from wear, so the book bulged a bit as it lay on his knees.

Before he opened the book, Jon cast one last glance at Katherina sitting opposite him. She was sitting erect with her hands in her lap and her eyes closed.

Then Jon began to read.

At first he proceeded very slowly. He read cautiously, on the alert to see whether he noticed anything unusual. That was how he read a couple of pages, without really taking in what it said, but all of a sudden it felt as if the text seized hold of him, and he read more freely and fluidly as the story sank unhindered into his consciousness.

The main character in the book, Montag, was apparently a fireman, but a fireman who started fires instead of putting them out. His job was to burn books, which were regarded as dangerous in his society. One day on his way home from work he runs into a girl who tags along with him as he walks. The description of the girl was incredibly vivid and Jon could picture her in his mind, lithe, smiling, flirty and spontaneous. His heart started beating faster, and his mouth went dry. This girl was amazing. He couldn't wait to read more about her, he had to find out where she came from and what role she played in the story. She appeared so clearly to him he could almost feel her at his side, walking along with fluttering red hair, her steps light as a feather, on the way to Montag's house, and he was already starting to miss her, to fear the emptiness when she would leave him there on the doorstep to his home.

The description was so convincing that Jon wanted to glance to the side to get a closer look at the girl, but his eyes no longer obeyed him. They refused to leave the page and carried on wandering through the text towards the leave-taking with the girl. In despair, Jon tried to stop reading or at least to slow the pace, but the story moved inexorably forward before his eyes. He noticed that sweat had begun to appear on his forehead and his pulse was elevated.

In the story Montag and the girl reached the fireman's house, where they stood and conversed on the doorstep, calmly, lingering, as if they were stretching out the time, for the sake of delighting or tormenting Jon. He felt an incredible warmth for this girl, as if he had always known her and loved her. Finally Montag said goodbye to the girl, and Jon suppressed a fierce desire to call out to her, to entice her back into the text, which now seemed banal and impoverished. He noticed that his eyes were moist, but at the same time he realized that once again he was able to control them, and he immediately took the opportunity to stop reading.

As he glanced up, Katherina at the same time slowly opened her eyes, but she avoided looking directly at him. He noticed that her eyes were red-rimmed. Jon shifted his gaze to Iversen, who stared back expectantly.

'Well?'

Jon glanced down at the book. It looked like any other book, a stack of pages with letters and words, without a hint of the life and wealth of colours he had just experienced. He closed the book and turned it in his hands, examining it.

'How did you two do that?' he asked at last.

Iversen broke out in a laugh. 'Isn't it amazing? I'm just as impressed every time.'

Jon nodded absentmindedly. 'And you could hear me reading?' he asked, turning his gaze on Katherina.

She blushed and nodded almost imperceptibly.

'Except,' said Iversen, raising his index finger, 'it wasn't your voice she heard. Or her own either, or even the author's, for that matter. That's the most incredible thing about it. Apparently every book has its own unique voice.' He stared with obvious envy at the red-haired woman. 'It's like communicating with the book itself – with its soul.'

'The fantasy of all bibliophiles.'

'Er, well, yes,' said Iversen, smiling with embarrassment. 'I suppose I was rather overcome by the mood. Sometimes I forget that there are significant costs associated with being a receiver. Costs you and I can't even imagine.'

Jon happened to think about the man drinking stout he'd met in the Clean Glass pub after Luca's funeral. At the time he'd written him off as a wino, a drunk spouting nonsense about readers and texts that sang and shouted. Yet the man's words were now adding credence to Iversen's explanation.

'Okay,' said Jon, setting the book on the table. 'Let's say I believe your explanation that Lectors exist and that you can manipulate my thoughts and feelings through a book.' He threw out his hands. 'So what do you expect from me?'

'Who says we want anything to do with you?' said a voice from the door.

All three of them turned towards the new arrival. In the doorway stood a thin young man about twenty years old, wearing a tight T-shirt and a pair of baggy, army-green trousers. He had a narrow face with a goatee, but otherwise he was bald and as pale as flour. His burning dark eyes were fixed on Jon.

'Hi, Pau,' said Iversen. 'Come in and say hello to our guest.'

The young man came into the room and took up position behind Katherina's chair with his hands on his hips. 'Guest?'

'It's okay,' said Iversen soothingly. 'This is Jon. Luca's son.'

'I know that. I saw him at the funeral,' replied Pau. 'The guy wants to sell Libri di Luca. You said as much yourself, Svend.'

Iversen cast an embarrassed glance at Jon, who seemed unaffected by the scene.

'I said there was a risk of that. We don't know for sure, Pau,' said Iversen. 'That's why we're here.'

'So what's going to happen?'

'We were just about to explain everything to Jon when you arrived,' replied Iversen.

'How much?'

'Everything.'

Pau stared first at Iversen and then at Jon. His jaw muscles tightened and his eyes narrowed.

'Could I talk to you for a moment, Svend?' asked Pau, motioning with his head towards the door. 'You too, Kat.'

Jon noticed that Katherina briefly rolled her eyes before she cast an enquiring glance at Iversen. The old man nodded.

'As you wish, Pau. Go upstairs, and I'll be there in a minute.'

The young man marched out of the door, and Katherina slowly followed.

'You'll have to bear with him,' said Iversen when the other two had left the room. 'We literally picked Pau up off the street, where he was making a living by using his powers as a Lector. Luca found him on Strøget reading poems to passers-by, and very successfully too. A lot of people stopped to listen, and most of them tossed coins into the cigar box he had at his feet. Luca recognized him for what he was. Experienced transmitters can sense when other transmitters charge a text, and Pau made no effort to hide what he was doing.' Iversen leaned forward in his chair. 'As you may have guessed, Jon, we have plenty of reasons for concealing our abilities. We can't risk having a young fellow like Pau compromising us, just because he doesn't understand what he's dealing with.' He paused. 'Luca took him under his wing, and for the past six months Pau has been part of the bookshop. We've developed quite a fondness for the lad, and vice versa, even though he may not admit it. And, as you can see, he has a real passion for the place.'

'And he thinks that I'm going to take it away from him?' asked Jon.

'A great deal has already been taken away from him,' said Iversen. 'Often enough that I suppose he has come to expect it.'

Jon nodded pensively.

'Well, I'd better . . .' Iversen pointed towards the door, then got up and left the room. Jon could hear his footsteps move along the hallway and up the creaking stairs. Then everything was quiet.

Left alone, he stood up and studied the books lining the shelves.

There weren't many titles he recognized, and besides, the truly old volumes were in Latin or Greek, which he couldn't read. Of course there were also numerous works in Italian, and even though Jon hadn't used his Italian in years, he was able to read some of the words.

In many cases the titles on the spines were artfully executed, in Gothic script or with little illustrations, and at times he struggled to decipher what it said. A few books had no spine at all; rather, they were a collection of yellowed pages held together with cords made of leather or bast. Others had metal fittings on the spine and on the corners of the cover; still others had covers made of veneer on which the title and ornamentation had been burned into the wood.

After a while the letters began flickering before Jon's eyes, and he sat down in one of the soft leather chairs to survey the room. It wasn't hard to imagine that it had taken generations to compile this collection – a task that had started in Italy and had accompanied the Campelli family through Europe to Denmark. For a moment he pictured the scene in his mind: a little family pushing a cart loaded down with books and a great secret. Jon leaned his head back and covered his face with both hands.

He'd been very stressed lately. The Remer case was taking all his waking hours, and the number of files he was lugging back and forth between his flat and the firm was getting greater and greater. His home had become an extension of his office, and he had no time to sit on his roof terrace or prepare proper meals in his brand-new kitchen. Most often he picked up food from one of the nearby fast-food restaurants or else he ate pre-packaged meals that he cooked in the microwave.

Jon moved his hands to the sides of his face, pressing his index and middle fingers against his temples, massaging his skull in circular motions. He inhaled slowly, taking in deep breaths, noticing how his pulse slowed and his body felt heavy.

Luca's death couldn't have happened at a worse time.

He removed his hands from his face and lowered his arms to the armrests of the chair. With his eyes still closed, he continued to breathe calmly. His chest rose and fell in time with his breath, and he could hear the air leaving his lungs and then being drawn in once again.

But there was something else.

When he listened closely, he could hear a faint, rushing sound. A quiet whispering, almost inaudible, seemed to have seeped into the room, and very slowly the sound grew in strength, as if it were coming closer or simply getting louder. Jon concentrated hard but couldn't make out what was being said or whether they were male or female voices, because there was definitely more than one. Like a low murmur from an entire crowd. The sound seemed so faint and weak that he had to hold his breath to pinpoint where it was coming from, but as soon as he sensed that the sound was coming from a particular direction, it would move. His heart began pounding harder and he gasped for air, only to hold his breath once again to listen.

In an attempt to increase his concentration, he clenched his fists and closed his eyes even tighter.

All of a sudden pictures exploded before his eyes, abstract forms and colours mixed with landscapes and scenes of fighting armies of knights, pirates and American Indians. Underwater pictures of sea monsters, divers and submarines were succeeded by desolate moonscapes and deserts, followed in turn by ice-covered plains, rolling ships' decks – all of it flickering past at breakneck speed, like a turbo-charged slide show. Rain-soaked streets paved with cobblestones were replaced by sun-baked arenas with sweating gladiators, followed in turn by buildings from which huge flames stretched up towards a brilliantly yellow full moon. The full moon then became the eye of an enormous dragon, whose trembling eyelid closed and became a school of tiny fish, which was at once swallowed by a killer whale, which was promptly harpooned by a weather-beaten sailor wearing yellow overalls.

All these impressions, along with hundreds of others that moved too fast to take in, bombarded Jon in the space of time it took for him to open his eyes wide. He jumped up, gasping for air. Unsteady on his feet, he tottered forward until he came in contact with the back of a chair. A violent nausea surged up inside him, and he was hyperventilating, his fingers tingling. Overwhelmed by dizziness, he sank to his knees and leaned forward until he was down on all fours with his eyes focused on the carpet.

After a couple of minutes of gasping for breath and even trying not to blink, Jon slowly straightened up. His face was covered with sweat; he wiped it off with the back of his hand before he cautiously got to his feet. His legs trembled slightly beneath him as he took the first steps towards the nearest bookshelf. From there he worked his way over to the door, the whole time keeping a firm grip on the shelves. The hall from the door to the stairs seemed much longer than before, and it seemed he was walking for an eternity before he reached the bottom step. He practically hauled himself up the spiral staircase, hand over hand along the banister, the steps responding with an ominous creaking under his weight.

When he reached the room above he could hear voices coming from the front of the shop. Unable to make out what they were saying, he headed in that direction, keeping one hand resting on the bookshelves. At the end of the aisle he hesitantly stepped out into the room, no longer having anything solid to hold on to, and as he did, the voices fell silent. Pau was sitting in the armchair behind the counter with his arms crossed. Katherina was sitting on top of the counter dangling her legs and Iversen was standing in front of the cash register with his back turned.

Iversen turned to face Jon and said something to him. His concerned voice followed Jon as he went over to the door and yanked it open with a violent tug.

Outside he greedily breathed in the cold evening air, but he didn't stop until he reached a street light that he could hold on to. The cold metal felt particularly reassuring.

'Jon, can you hear me?'

Iversen's voice finally reached Jon, who nodded slowly, as if in a trance.

'Are you okay?'

'Dizzy,' Jon managed to stammer.

'Come back inside,' Iversen said earnestly. 'You can sit down.'

Jon shook his head violently.

'Thanks,' Jon groaned.

'How about some water?' said Katherina, handing him a cup.

Reluctantly Jon removed one hand from the street light and reached for the cup, emptying it in one gulp.

'Thanks.'

'I'll get some more,' said Katherina, taking the cup from him and disappearing.

Iversen placed his hand on Jon's shoulder. 'What happened in there, Jon?' he asked with concern.

Jon took in a couple of deep breaths. The water and the fresh air had done their job and he was already feeling better.

'Stress,' he replied, looking at the ground. 'It's just stress.'

Iversen studied him. 'As if that makes it any better,' he said, annoyed. 'Come back inside where you can rest.'

'No,' exclaimed Jon. 'I mean, no thanks, Iversen.' He raised his head and looked into the old man's eyes. They were shining with both worry and suspicion. 'The only thing I need right now is to go home and get some sleep.'

Katherina returned with more water, and he drank half of it under the scrutiny of the two others. With a nod of thanks he handed the cup back.

'I think I left my jacket inside,' said Jon, patting his pockets.

'You're not thinking of driving in this condition, are you?' asked Iversen.

'It's okay. I'm already feeling a lot better,' replied Jon, mustering a smile. 'But if one of you wouldn't mind fetching my jacket?'

Katherina left them and a moment later returned with his jacket.

'We still have a lot to talk about,' said Iversen as Jon got into his car.

Jon nodded. 'I'll be back in a couple of days. You've given me something to think about, that's for sure.'

'Take care of yourself, Jon.'

He started the car and waved goodbye as he drove off. The dizziness was gone, but he was overcome with an exhaustion he'd never felt before. He was used to long work-days, but this fatigue seemed to have settled in all the cells of his body.

He had tossed his jacket onto the passenger seat, but out of the corner of his eye he noticed a bulge in one of the pockets. At the first red light, he pulled out what was inside the pocket.

It was a book. *Fahrenheit 451* by Ray Bradbury.

# 7

Katherina fixed her eyes on the car, watching it disappear. Iversen, who was standing next to her, did the same with a worried expression on his face. She rarely saw him look like that, but lately, on several occasions, his otherwise amiable face had been marred by deep furrows on his brow.

When they could no longer see Jon's Mercedes, they went back inside the bookshop, where Pau was waiting. He hadn't moved from his spot in the armchair, sitting there with his arms ostentatiously crossed.

'What got into that guy?' he asked as soon as Iversen had closed the door behind him.

'After everything we've told him today, it's not so strange that he would feel a little dizzy,' replied Iversen.

'Why couldn't he just stay away from here?'

'You're forgetting, Pau, that we're the ones who are the intruders here,' said Iversen, throwing out his arms. 'This shop we're in, the books all around us, even the chair you're sitting on, they all belong to him.'

'But that's a mistake,' Pau insisted. 'Luca would never betray us like that. There must be some way to get the will annulled, changed or whatever it is they do.'

'I don't think there's much chance of that happening,' said

Iversen benignly. 'For one thing, there's no will to invalidate, and besides, I rejected Jon's offer to let him take over the bookshop.'

'You did what?' exclaimed Pau, jumping up from his chair. 'Are you out of your mind?'

Even Katherina gave Iversen an astonished look.

'I think that deep inside, it was what Luca wanted,' Iversen replied, without raising his voice. 'What father doesn't wish to have his life's work carried on within the family? Would Luca want the Campelli collection to fall into the hands of outsiders? I don't think so.' He paused for a moment before he added with a sigh, 'Besides, we need him.'

'If only he doesn't think we've poisoned him,' said Katherina quietly.

The other two looked at her.

Iversen nodded in agreement. 'It would be disastrous to alienate him now.'

'What if he does take over? And what if he decides to sell the whole shitload?' Pau asked.

Iversen smiled uneasily.

'He really has no choice in what will happen. The Council has already approved a reading.'

No one said a word. Pau slowly sat back down in the chair without shifting his glance from Iversen. Katherina stared in disbelief at the elderly man, but Iversen's gaze didn't waver.

A reading was a drastic measure, and she'd never heard of the Council pre-approving one. It was strictly forbidden for anyone to use his Lector powers in any way except to enhance reading experiences. That was the Society's code. Any violation of this rule was a very serious matter and would result in grave consequences for anyone who did so, although Katherina had never heard what those consequences might be. The survival of the Society depended on its members keeping its existence secret, and any misuse of powers would invariably attract attention.

But in very rare circumstances it might be necessary to use their powers for purposes other than enriching a text. This was especially true in situations when the Society, or its powers, were directly threatened with disclosure, and on these occasions the Council would approve a reading for the parties involved, who would then be made to reconsider. The process for authorizing a reading was a lengthy one. Precise plans had to be made for how things would proceed, who would be present, what the result would be and what pretext would be planted. The latter was important, because if the subject did not give a plausible explanation for why he had suddenly changed his mind regarding a particular matter, the whole thing could fail.

After the approval, the Lectors who were to carry out the reading would arrange for an opportunity to read to, or to be in the vicinity of, those individuals who were to be influenced. As a rule, this wasn't a problem. The targets were often public figures such as politicians, government officials or journalists, who all moved about without a large security force.

For the reading, a suitable text was chosen that would touch on areas associated with the sensitive topic. During the reading important passages were charged in such a way that the subject either lost all interest in the topic or rejected it completely. This required skilled and strong Lectors, but it had never failed to produce the desired result, which had secured the anonymity of the Society.

Katherina didn't know how many readings had been approved, but in the ten years she'd had contact with Luca, she knew of only one. She herself was directly involved in it, 'but only to provide reinforcement', as Luca had assured her.

The target was a local politician in Copenhagen who had seen a chance of recouping funds by cutting back on money for reading classes in the schools. His intention was to investigate thoroughly every reading class in every one of the city's schools.

One of the Society's most important tasks was to promote the reading experience and, in particular, improve reading abilities among children who had difficulties. Many of the Society's members acted as travelling reading teachers, offering scheduled tutoring at various schools for children who were in need of help. In addition to sparking in the children a real joy of reading, they often ran into kids who were spontaneously activated Lectors, and thus the lessons were a means of discovering those few who had the special abilities, and an opportunity to monitor and guide them as discreetly as possible. The fear of losing this access to potential Lectors was enough for the Council to approve a reading for the politician.

The reading was carried out on a scorching summer day at the city hall. Beforehand the Society had circulated a petition to collect signatures objecting to the shutdown of the classes. The parents of those children who took advantage of the reading classes showed up willingly at the politician's office, where the signatures were to be presented and a declaration would be read.

In addition to Katherina and Luca, three other members of the Society were part of the delegation, along with a few parents who were totally unaware of the real purpose of the visit. Luca had squeezed into a suit, which did not appeal to him in the least in that summer heat. Sweat ran down his forehead and his face had taken on a distinct red colour. Katherina was wearing a loose black dress, and she was most likely the one suffering the least among the small delegation. In spite of the heat, a young blonde secretary made them wait forty-five minutes in the reception area. In her white summer dress, she didn't seem to be bothered by the temperature.

Finally they were allowed to enter the politician's office, where the group was received by a middle-aged man with steel-grey hair wearing an equally grey suit that fit snugly around his lean body. From under a pair of bushy eyebrows that stuck up like little horns, his stern eyes stared at them. They shook hands with him as they entered, one by one, and Katherina had to lower her glance when it was her turn. The handshake he gave her was crushing, and her hand still hurt several minutes later.

The spokesman for the reading delegation briefly explained why they were there and then handed the signatures and declaration to the grey-haired man, who had taken his place behind a big, completely bare desk. With his elbows propped on the armrests of his desk chair, he regarded them through half-closed eyes. He pressed his long, gnarled fingers together to form a tent.

The declaration was delivered in written form, but it was also supposed to be read aloud. That was Luca's task. Huffing a bit he stepped forward and began his presentation. As expected, the politician immediately picked up his copy, either to follow along in the text or to conceal his lack of interest.

The first part of the declaration was a mishmash of introductory nonsense about the background of the reading classes – a sort of warm-up they could use to home in on their subject's ability and willingness to focus on what was being read.

Katherina sensed how Luca was only slightly accentuating the text, like a painter who starts his work with delicate strokes of the brush that barely touch the canvas. The text had been meticulously prepared in advance, and Luca's presentation was flawless, but it was the minor accents that elevated the experience so that it didn't just feel like a reading but more like a performance.

To enjoy it, the listener had to pay at least a modicum of attention to the words, an honour that the politician had no intention of granting.

Katherina shut her eyes and noticed how he was leafing through the declaration, stopping at random places and reading short excerpts without really comprehending what they said. A wealth of other thoughts dominated the images that the text and Luca were evoking, ranging from other meetings to family members, from rounds of golf to visits to Tivoli, to a dinner party that presumably was going to be held that very evening.

She took a deep breath and let herself drift along with the stream of images issuing from the subject's consciousness. Every time he read a word from the text, she reinforced it just a bit, stimulating his attention by holding onto it just a bit longer than the politician himself had intended. Soon the text began to occupy more of his thoughts, and he started to read longer, more cohesive excerpts, which Katherina did her best to strengthen and maintain.

For a receiver this was rather a trivial exercise. Katherina had countless times sat in trains and buses and used her talents merely to help a nearby reader focus on the text instead of everything else. Many commuters read on their way to and from work, but their concentration would often waver as they read, and Katherina frequently noticed how they would stop reading, only to turn back a few pages to read the section again. For her it was clear what had happened. She could follow along as images from the text were blocked out by all sorts of other thoughts, drowning in worries about a job, a love affair or grocery shopping. Sometimes she would intervene. If she found a good story, she would help the reader keep his focus on the text, a few times so effectively that the person in question would miss his station or bus stop. Other times, if it was a dull text or Katherina just wanted to keep the voices at bay, she would sabotage the reading until the reader became so unfocused that he or she would give up.

The politician, helped out by Luca and Katherina, suddenly became very interested in the text and started turning forward to the place that Luca had reached in his reading of the declaration. Katherina ensured that he maintained his focus – a very easy task since Luca used his accentuation efforts to do the same. She opened her eyes and saw how their subject was now sitting up straight in his chair and studying the documents he held in his hands with visible interest. Now and then he nodded to himself, almost on cue from Luca, who was turning up the emphasis on important sections of the text.

The effect of a transmitter on the listeners was not directional, and if anyone else had been in the room who previously doubted the justification for the reading classes, they too would have been convinced by the time Luca read the last word of the declaration. Katherina smiled when the politician looked up. He clearly had no idea how to react, as if he were embarrassed to say anything at all after Luca's presentation, but finally he managed to stammer a few clumsy, polite platitudes and his reassurances that he would look into the matter again.

The effect was not lost. A few days later the politician declared that the reading classes were fully warranted.

But it was one thing to influence a career politician who had no idea about Lectors or readings; it was quite another matter when the targeted subject had a suspicion about what was being done to him.

*

'Isn't it too late to read for Jon now?' asked Katherina after Iversen's statement had sunk in. 'He'll notice right away.'

'Yeah, why didn't we give him a reading right from the start?' Pau punched his fist into his open palm. 'Bam! No warning. Then we could have made him do anything we liked.'

'This is still Luca's son we're talking about,' replied Iversen. 'He's a good boy. Jon deserves our respect and should at least be given a choice. Besides, he would have found out about it anyway if he became activated. And how would it look then?'

'But what if he doesn't want to participate? What if he chooses ... wrong? What then? Are you going to force him?' asked Katherina.

'Perhaps,' replied Iversen. 'It's been done before. Not recently, but there have been examples when a reading was carried out against the listener's will. In the old days it was used to constrict members in our own ranks who opposed the Society. Not something we're proud of, and it looked like a real torture scene, using straps and gags.' He sighed. 'We just have to hope that it won't go that far.'

'That might be really cool,' exclaimed Pau, who then hastened to add, 'I don't mean with Luca's son, but with someone else, not a volunteer. Reading for ordinary people is too easy; they're like cattle that just need a little shove. But to try it on someone who offers real resistance ...'

'You're too much, Pau,' Katherina told him.

'Hey, maybe you'd like to volunteer? I could find something to read to you, maybe even something romantic?'

'I'm sure you could, but shouldn't you be doing the exercises that Iversen gave you first?'

Pau's crooked smile vanished and he muttered something unintelligible.

'All right then,' Iversen interjected. 'What do you say we close up for the evening?'

For once the other two were in agreement and quickly disappeared out of the door while Iversen made one last round before he too left Libri di Luca.

*

Katherina pumped hard on the pedals of her bike as she rode away from the antiquarian bookshop. With a shake of her head she reproached herself. She ought to know better than to let herself be provoked by Pau, but just like siblings, they both knew which buttons to push to rile the other, and a defensive response quickly turned to attack after the first words were uttered.

Her mountain bike carried her from the Vesterbro district towards Nørrebro. Nimbly she rushed along in the late evening traffic, meticulously timing her speed to the changing of the traffic lights and taking the corners largely without slowing down.

Maybe the sibling comparison was more apt than she wanted to admit. In a sense she had been an only child in the shop with Luca and Iversen until Pau turned up like an unwanted little brother. It hadn't been easy for her to cede territory, and deep inside she felt a bit guilty about not giving him a warmer welcome.

In the area around Elmegade she rode the wrong way along a one-way street, keeping close to the parked cars or moving onto the pavement when a vehicle appeared, heading in the opposite direction. Several times she cast a glance over her shoulder, but she couldn't see anyone following her. At Sankt Hans Torv she cut across the square in front of the cafés and tuned off Blegdamsvej down Nørre Allé.

No doubt their squabbles also had something to do with age. Pau was seven years younger than she was, but mentally he was even younger, in her opinion. Everything centred around him and his needs. His training came before everything else. She shook her head again. Maybe she was just jealous.

Katherina swerved onto the pavement and stopped a couple of metres further along, in front of a grey building with white window frames. There were lights on in only two of the flats; in one the curtains were drawn, but through the other windows she could catch a glimpse of a white plaster ceiling from which hung a big chandelier with real candles.

The fact was that a lot had changed since Pau had started coming to Libri di Luca. The balance had shifted. Now *he* was the baby of the family while she, not without some pride, had become some-one they could count on, and someone who could take care of herself. But the balance would shift again with Jon's return – the question was: to which side?

After parking her bike in the entryway, she checked once again that she wasn't being observed before she pushed open the front door and disappeared into the stairwell. Without switching on the light she headed up the stairs, taking them two at a time. On the fifth floor she stopped outside a panelled door painted grey. The brass plate was clearly legible in spite of the dark, and even though she was unable to read it, she knew what it said: Centre for Dyslexia Studies (By Appointment Only).

Katherina pressed the bell twice, the first time longer than the second, and waited. In a moment she heard footsteps behind the door, and then the sound of a bolt being slid back. The door opened slightly and a strip of light shot out into the hall, capturing her in its glare. The light seemed especially bright since her eyes had grown accustomed to the dark in the stairwell and she blinked, holding her hand up to her face.

'Come in,' said a woman's voice, and the door opened wide.

Katherina stepped into a long, beige-coloured hallway with rows of brass hooks lining the walls. They were almost all taken by jackets and other outdoor garments, but she found an empty hook for her coat.

The woman who had let her in closed the door and turned to face her. She was in her mid-forties and a bit stout around the waist, which she tried to hide under a black dress. Her face was dominated by a pair of sturdy glasses and framed by light-brown hair which seemed a little artificial in the sharp glare coming from a row of halogen spotlights.

'Well?'

Katherina caught the other woman's glance and nodded. 'He's going to be good – better than his father.'

# 8

Jon woke a few seconds before the clock radio switched on.

At first he wasn't sure where he was. The bedroom's bare white walls and ceiling merged into one, looking like a dome of snow as he lay on his back inside an igloo. It was cold too. The duvet had slid off onto the floor during the night, and the crumpled sheet bore witness to a night of uneasy slumber. He remembered he'd had trouble calming down. For a long time he had lain in bed pondering what had happened in the antiquarian bookshop. Right now Iversen's explanation, the demonstration and the visions that had overwhelmed him when he was alone in the library all seemed unreal and far away. At one point he'd got up to find the book, *Fahrenheit 451*, which was in his jacket pocket. Tangible proof that it had all happened, but it was just an ordinary book that didn't presume to be anything else.

It was a long time since he'd read stories in bed. As a child he had loved it, an experience surpassed only by having Luca read a goodnight story to him – preferably *Pinocchio*, and preferably in Italian. This copy of *Fahrenheit 451* was a Danish translation, and when he read through the first chapter again, he discovered that the text was significantly more choppy and jolting than was his impression during the demonstration. The colour of the girl's hair wasn't mentioned at all; it wasn't red, as he had so vividly pictured it.

Jon turned his head towards the nightstand where he had placed the book. It was still there, bulging a bit because of the worn pages. The time on the clock radio next to the book shifted at that moment to 7:00, and the voice of a tired DJ seeped out of the speaker, reciting the latest news. Unrest in Israel, absurd political arguments in the debate about immigrants, a post office robbery. Not until the monotone voice began summarizing the results of a study about children's reading abilities did Jon raise himself up on his elbows to listen. Danish children were apparently worse readers than children in neighbouring countries – a development that the Minister of Education found worrisome and unacceptable. Jon sank down onto his back and closed his eyes with a sigh. Next week they would come out with another study proving just the opposite.

The DJ was replaced by another, a cheerful morning-type who started spewing inanities that roused Jon to get out of bed. He turned on the coffee-maker and went through his morning routine: showering, shaving, drinking coffee, ironing a shirt, knotting his tie, and more coffee. The habitual tasks calmed him, and on his way out it was the day ahead of him that preoccupied his thoughts rather than what had happened the night before.

It was only when he was sitting in his car, rolling along with the morning traffic slowly flowing through the city, that he noticed how many people around him were reading. Passengers on the buses were reading books, people sitting on benches were immersed in the morning paper, schoolchildren on the pavement were reading through their lessons as they moved cautiously along like tightrope walkers, placing one foot in front of the other. Signs in the shop windows were read by passers-by, bus adverts were glimpsed by drivers, flyers were scanned and tossed aside by mothers with prams. It seemed to him that everywhere words and sentences had invaded the facades, windows, signs and buses for the purpose of enticing him to decipher their messages, a decoding process he could no longer be sure he controlled.

Jon drove the rest of the way to the office with his eyes fixed straight ahead on the road in front of him.

He had barely opened the glass doors to the reception area before Jenny, the secretary, came running towards him with a newspaper in her hand. She was a blonde and what might be called a cheerful, plump young woman.

'Listen to this,' she said merrily, waving the newspaper.

Jenny arrived at the office significantly earlier than he did, and they had worked out a routine: she found articles in the daily papers that were either relevant to their work or were simply funny. Then she would present what she'd found to him, often reading them aloud over a first cup of coffee. Frequently he didn't even need to bother looking through the papers himself.

Jon glanced at the newspaper and then at Jenny. He saw how her eyes, full of anticipation, looked down at the paper as her lips began forming the first sentence.

'I'll read it later.' Jon abruptly cut her off and continued on towards his office.

'Okay,' murmured Jenny, clearly disappointed, letting her arms fall to her sides.

Jon stopped and turned around. 'Sorry, but I didn't sleep well last night. Give me half an hour.'

Jenny nodded and slowly folded up the paper.

'Nice tie,' she said and retreated to her desk.

Jon waved his hand in thanks as he continued through the open-plan room towards the Remer office. At the door he fished out the keys with the Smurf figure and let himself in. Safe inside, he leaned his back against the closed door.

He took a couple of deep breaths before an annoyed grimace appeared on his face. It wouldn't do him any good to go about in a constant state of paranoia. It was impossible to do his job without reading, and it wasn't realistic to think he could move around freely without anyone else reading in his presence. He shook his head. If Lectors had ever used him before, he hadn't noticed it, and considering his present position, they couldn't very well have put obstacles in his way – on the contrary.

There was a knock on the door, and he hastily took a few steps forward before it opened.

Jenny stuck her head inside. 'Halbech wants to talk to you,' she said in a businesslike tone. 'In his office in ten minutes.'

Jon nodded. 'Okay. Thanks, Jenny.'

She closed the door without making a sound.

'Of all days,' he muttered to himself.

He'd been expecting this conversation. A week had passed since the Remer case had been transferred to him, and he knew that at some point he would have to present his plan as to how the defence should be carried out. Even though one week was an inhumanly short amount of time to familiarize himself with the extensive case files, he really hadn't expected to be given much more time before he was tested.

Jon opened his briefcase and took out a thin dossier containing five or six typed pages, which he hurriedly skimmed. The pages held his proposal for a strategy regarding the Remer case in accordance with all the rules. But he knew that Halbech wanted creative solutions which, without being directly illegal, would simplify the defence. The short cut in this instance was to win a two-month postponement, which would mean that two of the initial charges in the case would fall outside the statute of limitations. Not a particularly brilliant solution, but it would spare them from the most vulnerable sections in the defence, which was the status of the first companies that Remer had purchased. On the other hand, they would have to find a reason for having the case postponed, or even better, persuade the prosecutor himself to request a postponement. But that meant they needed to toss new information onto the table.

Jon put the documents back in the dossier and left his office with the plan under his arm.

'Campelli,' said Halbech from his chair as Jon entered his office. 'Have a seat.' He pointed towards one of the Chesterfield armchairs that stood in front of his desk.

Jon nodded and sat down with the dossier in his lap.

'Things going well?' asked Halbech routinely.

'Fine, thanks.'

'And what about all that business with your father? Has everything been resolved?'

'More or less. There are still a couple of loose ends to tie up.'

Halbech nodded. 'So tie them up, Campelli.' He smiled. 'There's nothing more distracting than loose ends. "One touch" – that's my motto. Finish a task immediately instead of postponing it. Having to deal with the same issue over and over is a waste of time, and it affects the rest of your work.'

'Right,' Jon remarked.

'What about Remer?'

'Things are in full swing,' replied Jon, patting the dossier. 'I've got—'

'He'll be here at nine o'clock.' Halbech gave Jon a searching look. 'He wants to talk to you.'

'Okay,' said Jon, astonished, automatically casting a glance at his watch. It was 8:45.

'Yes, well, undoubtedly he wants to have a look at his new barrister. Grill him a bit,' said Halbech with a glint in his eye.

Jon shrugged. 'It's his money.'

'Precisely,' said Halbech, leaning towards Jon. 'But try to make the most of the meeting. It's not often we have access to him, and if I know the man, he's on his way to a skiing holiday or something of that sort.'

He stood up and began putting on his jacket, which hung from the back of his chair.

'I can't stay, unfortunately. But it's not me he wants to see, anyway.'

Jon got up. 'I'll ask Jenny to take notes,' he said.

'Take them yourself, Campelli,' Halbech commanded. 'Remer doesn't care for having too many extraneous people at his meetings. And after all, it's . . .'

'His money,' Jon chimed in.

They walked through the door together and continued out to the receptionist's area.

'One touch,' Halbech repeated, giving Jon a parting slap on the back before he made his way out of the front door.

Jon asked Jenny to arrange for a meeting room and refreshments before he locked himself in the Remer office to collect the things he would need.

The rumours about Remer were both plentiful and harrowing, but Jon assumed that most of them were probably urban myths intended to scare law students. Remer didn't care for lawyers, that much was certain, and the fact that he often disagreed with how the case should be handled was a recurrent theme of the stories, but from there it was a big step to throwing himself into a fistfight. One of the stories circulating the corridors described how Remer, in a heated moment, had grabbed his barrister by the tie to give him a good shaking. Afterwards he cut off the tie, right below the knot. A real horror story, not so much because of the physical assault but because of the vandalizing of the expensive tie.

The pile of essential folders and documents grew, and Jon had to use a trolley to transport all of them to the meeting room. As Halbech had emphasized, it was important to make use of his time with Remer, so he didn't want to be missing anything. He had a long list of questions for the main player in the case. There were creative appendices, dates and sequences of events that didn't match up, as well as depositions that later turned out to have been either illegal or improbably lucky. It was a hairline distinction.

There was a knock on the open door and Jenny appeared with coffee and mineral water, which she set down on the table without saying a word. A moment later she returned, this time accompanied by Remer.

The man was about fifty, his grey hair in a crew-cut, which made him look like a stern colonel. If it weren't for his lively, genial eyes, the stories about him might have stemmed from his appearance alone, but his eyes softened the harsh face, and a broad smile with strikingly white teeth also had its effect.

'Remer,' he said, holding out his hand towards Jon.

'Jon Campelli,' said Jon, grasping his hand.

Remer had a firm grip, and he kept his eyes fixed on Jon as they shook hands. 'Campelli?' he said. 'Is that Italian?'

'Correct,' replied Jon. 'My father was Italian. Please have a seat.'

'I prefer to stand,' said Remer casually. 'Lovely place, Italy. I've just come from there. Or rather from Sicily, to be more precise.'

'Would you care for something to drink?' asked Jon, gesturing towards the refreshments on the meeting table.

'No, thanks,' replied Remer. 'I can't stay long.'

'Then we'd better get down to business . . .' suggested Jon amiably as he sat down at the table.

'Campelli,' Remer repeated to himself, glancing up at the ceiling. 'I've heard that name recently.'

Jon cleared his throat and leafed through the documents in front of him. 'I have a number of questions, especially regarding the purchase of Vestjysk Piping in '92—'

'Books!' exclaimed Remer, snapping his fingers. 'It was the man with the books. Luca was his name.' He turned to look at Jon. 'Is Luca someone in your family?'

'Yes, Luca was my father,' replied Jon. 'He died a week ago.'

Remer opened his eyes wide. 'I'm sorry to hear that,' he said, sounding sincere. 'What a sad coincidence. He owned a bookshop, didn't he?'

Jon nodded. 'Libri di Luca in Vesterbro.'

'I've never been there myself,' Remer admitted as he walked around the room. 'It was one of my business associates who happened to mention your father's name.'

Jon studied Remer as he moved along the walls, peering at the paintings. He wore a black jacket, a white shirt without a tie and a pair of dark jeans. His attire sent a rather confusing signal for a business meeting, but that was clearly not the reason he was here. Whether he had a genuine interest in Jon's familial relationships or was just testing him, only Remer himself knew for sure.

'He owns a couple of bookshops, my business associate,' he went on. 'Hugely successful, as I understand it. Something of a book empire, with Internet shops, book clubs and catalogues.' He gave a short laugh. 'Considering the fact that books have frequently been declared dead, there's surprisingly good money to be made.'

He stopped his roaming and rested his hands on the back of the chair across from Jon. Then he leaned forward.

'Well, Jon. What do you have in mind?'

For an instant his expression changed, his eyes shifting from sparkling and friendly to scrutinizing. Jon instinctively reached up to straighten his tie.

'I'd like to start with—' he began, but Remer once again interrupted him.

'May I ask you a personal question, Jon?' He didn't wait for an answer but pulled himself upright and crossed his arms before he went on. 'What's going to happen to the shop?'

'Er, the bookshop?' asked Jon in surprise. 'I haven't decided yet.'

'But it's yours? Luca left the business to you?'

'As the sole family member, yes.'

'Allow me to make a suggestion.' Remer unfolded his arms. 'I can put you in contact with my friend, the bookseller. I'm positive he'd give you a good price for Libri di Luca.' He broke out in a big smile. 'Unless you're planning to set yourself up as a bookmonger, that is?'

Jon smiled. 'No, that's not exactly what I had in mind. But as I said, I haven't yet decided.'

'A word of advice, Jon,' Remer admonished him. 'Stick to what you're good at. I'm good at making deals. You're good at helping get someone like me out of difficulties. But we'll never be book-dealers, neither of us.' He laughed. 'Make some good money by selling the shop, and let my friend take Libri di Luca into the twenty-first century. That would have pleased your father, don't you think?'

'I'm not so sure about that.' Even though he had no idea whether Luca might have made use of computers and the Internet over the past years, Jon found it most unlikely. The very image of a PC in Libri di Luca seemed absurd. It would be like sending a jet back to the Middle Ages.

'Well, surely he was a businessman too,' Remer insisted. 'He would have loved the idea of a shared warehouse for a whole chain of anti-quarian bookshops, of an enormous selection of works and search possibilities so that customers would never look in vain but could order their valuable books directly from their home computers.'

'I thought the charm of an antiquarian bookshop was that you spend a whole lot of time poking about and finding surprises.'

'Oh, sure, by all means. There also has to be opportunity to do that. The shop wouldn't be closed, of course. Just think of it as an expansion.'

Jon held up his hands defensively. 'I promise I'll think about it, when the time comes. But right now I'm going to wait and see.'

'Fair enough. But give me a ring when you've made a decision.' He took a business card out of his inside pocket and tossed it onto the table.

'I'll do that. So, shall we get started?'

Remer glanced at his watch. 'I'm going to have to leave now, Jon. It was a pleasure meeting you.' He reached across the table towards Jon who, greatly astonished, stood up and shook hands.

'I'll see myself out,' said Remer over his shoulder, already on his way out of the meeting room.

Jon sank down on his chair and stared at the door in bewilderment. He felt as if he'd just been visited by a tornado. Remer had done his job and then vanished again like a whirlwind. The question was, what job had he done? Did he merely want to have a look at the 'new guy', and then found himself tempted by a potential deal with the bookshop, or was that his real purpose all along? Jon picked up the card his client had left and studied it. There was nothing more than Remer's name and a couple of phone numbers. No logo, company name or even his first name. Anyone with a computer and a printer could have made something comparable in two minutes.

He stood up and started packing up his things.

'How did it go?' asked Jenny, appearing in the doorway.

'I don't really know,' Jon replied honestly. 'But at least my tie is still intact.'

Jenny laughed and turned to leave.

'By the way, Jenny.' The secretary turned to face him. 'Have you ever seen Remer before?'

She thought for a moment before she shook her head. 'No. I think they usually have their meetings in town.'

'Okay, thanks,' said Jon as he began pushing the trolley with the folders out of the room and towards his office.

It had occurred to him that he had never seen Remer either. After locking himself into the Remer office, he went straight over to the filing cabinet which held newspaper clippings. That was where all the media mentions were kept, and he quickly leafed through the folders. A moment later he found what he was looking for. Only a few of the articles were accompanied by photos, but there was one taken outside the court with Remer in profile on his way up the steps.

It was him, no doubt about it. There was no mistaking that distinctive haircut and the resolute expression. The tornado *was* Remer – for Jon that decided the matter. As the files indicated, Remer was a particularly zealous businessman with his fingers deep in everything that smelled of money. It didn't matter what type of business, so why not an antiquarian bookshop, when he just happened to come across it during a meeting with his lawyer?

For the second time that day Jon shook his head at his own paranoia, and it wasn't even ten o'clock.

# 9

Katherina was about to leave when she happened to glance through the windows of Libri di Luca. There was Luca's son. He was standing at the counter, talking to Iversen, who was repeatedly shaking his head. Because of the darkness, they wouldn't be able to see her, and she could easily disappear without them noticing. Her hand rested on the door handle, and she couldn't decide whether to go in or turn round.

Acting as a receiver could be quite an intimate experience. In addition to the images conjured up by the text, she could pick up small glimpses of the reader's personality as well, fragments that revealed the person's character traits and frame of mind. Ever since the demonstration she'd felt uncomfortable about being in Jon's presence. She had a feeling she knew something she shouldn't, something even he didn't know. During their little show she was both surprised and startled by what she sensed in Jon, but she had no idea what to do about her discovery. Many people didn't like finding out exactly how much her abilities allowed her to comprehend.

She took a deep breath and pushed open the door. The two men turned to face her.

'Hi, Katherina,' Iversen said. Jon merely gave her a brief nod.

Katherina returned their greetings and closed the door behind her.

'Maybe you know him, Katherina,' exclaimed Iversen, pointing at a photocopy lying on the counter. 'His name is Remer. Does that ring a bell?'

She went over to the counter and studied the picture of a man in his forties, making his way up a stairway. Katherina shook her head.

'No, I've never seen him before. Who is he?'

'A client,' replied Jon. 'But he seems to know quite a lot about Libri di Luca, and about Luca.'

'He wants to buy the place,' added Iversen.

She looked in alarm at Iversen, who instantly raised his hands in a reassuring gesture.

'Don't worry, the shop hasn't been sold. Not yet, at any rate.'

'The prospective buyer is actually one of Remer's friends, not him,' explained Jon. 'Apparently he already has a whole chain of stores, as well as an Internet shop. Does that sound familiar?'

Iversen grumbled affirmatively. 'There are a couple of major players in the market, including a few who have previously made your father an offer to take over Libri di Luca, but he always turned them down. Under no circumstances did he want to leave the shop to that sort.'

'What's your position?' asked Jon.

'In my opinion Libri di Luca doesn't belong anywhere near a computer. How can you evaluate the quality of a book without holding it in your own hands?' He shook his head. 'Most of our customers come here for the sake of the atmosphere. We can't leave them in the lurch.'

Katherina agreed with Iversen on that point. Libri di Luca was a free zone, and she, if anyone, knew the pleasure of wandering among the walls of books, holding a fine-quality volume in her hands. Even though she had great difficulty reading the words herself, she loved to touch the paper they were printed on, and the binding that protected them. Since the contents were inaccessible to her, she had to make do with the medium that held the words, feeling neither bitterness nor sorrow, but rather a fascination with the materials and the craftsmanship.

'So, what do you think?' asked Jon. 'What's this man's interest in the shop?'

Iversen and Katherina exchanged looks. She could see that he was burning to tell Jon what he knew, yet at the same time he feared there were limits to what should be revealed to an outsider. In fact, Jon already knew far too much, more than enough to be a security risk for the Society.

'Well, I think his interest primarily stems from the shop's good reputation,' replied Iversen. 'Your father was much liked and respected in these circles.'

'Could it have anything to do with the collection downstairs?'

Iversen shook his head. 'Very few people know about that. I think it just has to do with someone wanting to exploit the void your father's death has left, in one way or another.'

Jon fixed his gaze first on Iversen, then Katherina. He took a deep breath. 'As I'm sure you know, I'm a lawyer,' he said slowly. 'An important part of my job is the ability to see through people who are lying or holding back information, and I think there's something you're not telling me.'

Iversen was about to object, but Jon raised his hand to cut him off.

'I realize that you've initiated me into a situation that is otherwise kept secret. If one chooses to believe you, that is – which I suppose I'll have to do. But I sense there's more. You keep pointing out how important it is for me to understand, but how can I do that if you won't tell me everything?'

Iversen stared at Jon, who was standing in front of him with both hands on the counter. Katherina saw resignation slip into Iversen's eyes, and he turned away to look out of the window. She surmised that behind his mild expression he was thinking like mad about how he could give Luca's son a satisfactory answer without revealing too much.

His expression suddenly changed from resignation to astonishment, and then his eyes widened in fear. Iversen opened his mouth but his shout was drowned out by the sound of breaking glass.

Katherina flinched and then turned towards the sound. The

windowpane to the right of the door shattered and shards of glass flew into the shop like small projectiles.

'Get down!' shouted Jon, throwing himself to the floor. Iversen sat as if paralysed in the leather chair with his eyes fixed on the broken window.

Katherina ducked behind the counter, just in time to avoid the splinters from the other windowpane as it shattered too. She shut her eyes tight, waiting for the sound of glass raining down on her to stop.

Slowly she opened her eyes. There was glass everywhere, but even worse were the little columns of smoke issuing from some of the pieces of glass that had landed on the carpet.

'Fire!' she yelled and leaped to her feet.

Little tongues of fire had taken hold of the carpet in several places, and the display in the left-hand window was in flames. Jon was still lying on the floor, while Iversen was leaning over one of the armrests, away from the window. Quickly Katherina stepped behind the counter and opened the cabinet where the fire extinguisher was kept. In the meantime, Jon got to his feet and looked around in disbelief.

'Here,' she said, handing him the fire extinguisher. 'I'll get the other one.'

Jon grabbed the canister, which was no bigger than a thermos, and ran over to the display window, where the flames were biggest. In the meantime Katherina dashed through the shop and downstairs to the kitchen. There she tore the second fire extinguisher loose from its holder, a heavy model at least a metre high, and rushed back up to the shop with it.

'I'm empty,' shouted Jon when she came over to him. The extinguisher was on the floor and he was stamping out the flames on the carpet as he simultaneously tried to pull off his jacket. The fire in the display window was almost out, but Katherina could see an orange glow outside the window frame, so she tore open the door to attack the flames from outside.

As the door flew open she was met by a wave of intense heat. The whole outer surface of the door was on fire. The flames gladly accepted the invitation to come inside and began licking their way up the top of the door frame and towards the underside of the balcony.

Katherina aimed the fire extinguisher at the door and pressed the handle down as far as it would go. A hoarse hiss drowned out the sound of the crackling fire, and white foam spewed out over the wooden door. With an angry sizzle the flames gave way to the foam and the fire on the door was put out before it could gain a foothold inside. The stench of smoke and burnt paint made Katherina cover her mouth and nose with her left arm as she stepped through the smouldering doorway, dragging the fire extinguisher behind her.

Outside the flames were still licking up the wooden facade beneath the windows, and Katherina immediately began emptying the contents of the extinguisher over the blazing areas. The heat made it impossible to stand close for very long, so several times she had to stop and retreat before she could once again attack the flames. Her arms were shaking from the exertion of holding the heavy canister and her fingers were cramping from their convulsive grip on the handle. At the same time the smoke brought tears to her eyes so that everything appeared distorted and blurry. But she continued her assault on the burning patches, and soon she had put out the right side of the facade.

The left was not blazing as strongly, but by the time she'd put out half of the flames, the foam in the container was gone. Desperately she pumped the handle a few times, then she flung the empty extinguisher on the pavement, where it landed with a metallic clunk.

Angry and in despair, she tore off her jacket and started beating it on the remaining flames. With every blow the fire seemed to taunt her by yielding and then flaring up even more violently than before. She whipped her jacket against the shopfront, but each time she put out one flame, two more tongues of fire would appear in its place.

She felt a hand on her shoulder.

'Step back,' said a voice, and the hand pulled her away from the flames. A figure moved in front of her, and she heard the welcome sound of yet another fire extinguisher.

Katherina dropped her jacket on the ground and rubbed her eyes. Behind her a crowd of people had appeared, standing there and watching the scene as if it were a bonfire. The man in front of her gasped from the heat as he fought the last of the flames, but slowly they gave way, and soon the whole facade was a smouldering shell of charred wood. Behind the smoke she saw Jon's silhouette as he beat the floor with his jacket, cursing loudly. She ran inside the shop just as he stamped out the last of the flames. His white shirt had come untucked and was covered with big black patches of soot and sweat.

'Are you okay?' he asked, without taking his eyes off the carpet as he looked for more sparks.

'I'm okay,' she said, looking around for Iversen.

She found him behind the counter, lying on the floor in a foetal position, shivering with cold. Big burns covered his back, and in several places blood had soaked through his shirt and heavy sweater. Katherina knelt down next to him and placed her hand on his arm. Iversen gave a start at her touch, and then moaned loudly.

'It's me. Katherina,' she said soothingly.

Iversen turned his head towards her. Little pieces of glass were buried in one side of his face and blood covered the rest. Fortunately his glasses were still intact and had protected his eyes, which now gave her a pleading look.

'I think I need a doctor,' he said, trying to smile.

As if on cue, they heard sirens outside.

'An ambulance is on its way,' said Jon, who was suddenly leaning over them. 'I'll show the medics in,' he added and left the shop.

Iversen closed his eyes. 'The books,' he said. 'Are they . . .'

'They weren't damaged,' said Katherina. 'The ones in the display window burned up, but the rest are okay.'

The old man smiled, even though the effort seemed to cause him pain. 'You have to take him to Kortmann,' he whispered.

'Me?' She stared at him intently. Maybe he'd hurt his head. 'Are you sure they'd let me in?'

'They'll have to,' replied Iversen, opening his eyes for a moment. 'Take Pau with you – they can't turn him away.'

'Shouldn't we wait until you're up and about again?' asked Katherina.

'No,' said Iversen firmly. 'It can't happen soon enough. Just look at this mess.'

'All right.'

The medics arrived, accompanied by Jon, and one of them put a hand on Katherina's shoulder to pull her away so they could get to Iversen. After giving him a superficial examination, they cautiously lifted the elderly man onto a stretcher and carried him out to the ambulance. Katherina and Jon followed.

'I'll go with him to the hospital,' Katherina told Jon. 'Will you wait here?'

He nodded. 'Of course.'

Katherina got into the ambulance, the doors were slammed shut, and the vehicle took off. Iversen opened his eyes in time to see the smouldering shopfront receding behind them.

Two hours later Katherina was back in front of Libri di Luca. The windows were covered with sheets of plywood, and the facade and pavement were wet from being hosed down by the fire department.

At the hospital Iversen had been examined immediately; aside from a number of burns and deep cuts from the glass, his injuries weren't serious. Nevertheless he had been admitted for observation, and considering the state of shock he was in, that was undoubtedly for the best. During the long waiting period, she hadn't been able to get a single coherent sentence out of him.

Katherina was in a hurry to leave the hospital; it brought back too many memories of the accident she had been in as a child. She took a taxi from the hospital back to the sorry-looking bookshop, which resembled a building marked for demolition that had been closed up and gutted.

The smell of smoke was still strong outside, and the wall felt warm to her touch. When she opened the front door, the smell was even worse. The fire department had removed a four-metre stretch of carpet from the entrance, exposing the dark floorboards underneath. The display tables had been shoved together, and the books had been removed from them and hastily stacked in the aisles between the shelves.

Jon was standing at the counter, pouring the contents of a bottle into a bucket. His face was streaked with soot, and he had put on his jacket, even though it was covered with little black holes where the flames had licked at the fabric. He looked like a cartoon character who had been in a shootout. She was glad he had been in the shop during the attack, and even more grateful that he was here now.

'Vinegar,' he explained, nodding towards the bucket. 'For the smell.' He emptied the bottle and set the bucket on the floor in the middle of the shop. The vinegar stung Katherina's nostrils. She moved away from the bucket and dropped into the armchair behind the counter.

'How is he?' asked Jon with concern.

'He's in shock,' said Katherina. 'But otherwise it's not so bad. It could have been much worse. But they're going to keep him in for a couple of days. At least.'

Jon shook his head.

'Who would do such a thing?' he asked rhetorically. 'The police suggested it might be some sort of racist attack against the shop, but that seems a bit far-fetched.'

'The police?' exclaimed Katherina in alarm.

'Yes, they arrived at the same time as the fire department.'

Jon told her how the firemen had hosed down the hot spots, boarded up the windows and removed the carpet. In the meantime he had been questioned by the police. They hadn't seemed especially surprised; instead, they asked their questions in a routine manner, but at no time were they interested in what might have been going on in the shop, and he assured Katherina that he wouldn't have told them anything if they had asked. Outside the police had found remnants of the Molotov cocktails that had been used. It was apparently this evidence that had made them conclude it was a small group behind the attack, probably motivated by racism.

'Of course the police would like to talk to you too, but I didn't know your address or phone number, so you'll have to contact them yourself,' he said.

Katherina nodded slowly as she stared straight ahead.

'So what do you think?' asked Jon. 'Who was it?'

She opened her mouth to answer but was interrupted by a loud pounding on the boards covering the window of the door. They both turned towards the sound. The door handle was pressed down, and the door swung open.

Pau came in with a wild look in his eyes. 'What the hell happened here?' he burst out.

It took some persuading before he calmed down enough for Jon and Katherina to tell him. As they talked Pau paced back and forth on the exposed floorboards, as if he wanted to make up for the years of wear and tear that the floor had escaped by being underneath the carpet. His face grew more and more red with fury as their report progressed, but he didn't interrupt them, and he probably wouldn't have been able to speak anyway because his teeth were pressed together so hard.

'Those shitheads,' he exclaimed, his voice shaking, when they finished. His eyes full of hate, he shifted his gaze to Katherina and then to Jon.

'Who?' asked Jon at once.

The question seemed to take Pau by surprise. His eyes wavered, and he looked back at Katherina.

'Yes, who exactly do you mean?' asked Katherina.

'Er, well, that's obvious,' he said, in annoyance. 'You of all people should know.'

Silence descended on the shop. Katherina kept her eyes stubbornly fixed on Pau's face. She knew very well what he was referring to, but she also knew that he was mistaken. In any case, this was not the proper time or place to start a quarrel. Considering the state he was in, it would do no good to argue with him.

'Don't you think it's about time you gave me an explanation?'

Katherina and Pau broke off their staring contest and shifted their attention to Jon. He was leaning on the counter, pressing the palms of his hands into the surface.

'Frankly, I think I've been extremely patient. I've had Molotov cocktails thrown at me, people have lied to me and mysterious things have been going on in this shop, to say the least – this shop that actually belongs to me. So don't you think it's reasonable that I should know what's going on?'

Pau was the one who broke the silence. 'Will you, or should I?' he asked, turning to Katherina.

'Kortmann,' she replied tersely. 'Iversen said we should take him to see Kortmann.'

'We? Do you think he'll let you in?'

Katherina shrugged. 'We'll see.'

'I believe I met this man at the funeral.' said Jon.

'An older man in a wheelchair?' asked Katherina.

Jon nodded.

'Kortmann is the head of the Bibliophile Society,' she went on. 'He has all the answers, and he'll decide what should be done.'

Katherina had a hard time hiding the sarcasm in her last remark, but Pau didn't seem to notice and clapped his hands in satisfaction.

'When are we going to see him?'

'Now,' replied Katherina.

# 10

Jon had driven past Kortmann's house in Hellerup many times without knowing whose it was. The house stood out from the rest because it was enormous and had a big rusty tower reaching up along one wall to the very top of the building. The tower looked like a factory smokestack that had fallen into disrepair. Its presence on a well-maintained four-storey redbrick house in the suburb of Hellerup was so extraordinary that Jon immediately recognized the place.

A wall three metres high surrounded the property, and solid wrought-iron gates prevented unauthorized visitors from entering.

Katherina sat in the passenger seat of Jon's car; Pau sat in the back. Neither of them had said a word except when it was necessary to give directions. Jon stopped the car a few metres from the gate. There was an intercom on the driver's side. Jon rolled down his window, stretched out his arm and pressed the button marked with a bell.

'What should I say?' he asked as they waited for a response.

'Just say who we are,' replied Katherina. 'He'll know it's important.'

Jon glanced at his watch. It was one a.m., but there were still lights on in some of the windows on the fourth floor.

'Yes?' said a dry-sounding voice from the intercom.

Jon leaned towards the speaker.

'It's Jon, Jon Campelli.' He paused for a moment, but there was no reaction. 'I'm sorry for coming here so late, but it's important, and we're here to speak to Kortmann.'

There was still no reaction from the intercom except for a faint rushing sound, and Jon gave Katherina a questioning look. She shrugged. Jon turned back to the speaker. 'Iversen is in hospital,' he ventured. 'Libri di Luca was—'

'Come in,' said the voice. 'You need to go up through the tower.'

The gate in front of them began to open, slowly and soundlessly, as if access to the house were being deliberately delayed. Jon drove the car in as soon as there was enough space to pass through and continued along a short asphalt drive up to the house. There was room for four or five cars in front of the building, but at the moment the space was deserted.

A row of columns dominated the facade of the house, and a wide, illuminated stone stairway led up to a dark wooden door with black hinges and a grille over a little window near the top.

All three of them got out.

'It must be over there,' said Pau, pointing along a flagstone path leading to the side of the house. He started walking that way, with Jon and Katherina following him.

'Have you been here before?' Jon asked.

'No,' replied Katherina.

'Me neither,' said Pau, hastening to add, 'But I don't think many of the others have either.'

The path ended at the huge rusty tower which turned out to contain a wide door lit by a single lamp above the frame. The tower and building were connected at the ground floor and the top storey by enclosed catwalks with the same rusty appearance.

'The receiver has to stay there,' they suddenly heard.

Pau pointed to where the sound was coming from, a speaker in the door frame. They looked at each other. Jon frowned, uncomprehending, and was about to object, but Katherina put her hand on his shoulder and nodded.

'It's okay,' she said. 'I was expecting that. I'll just stay in the car.'

'Are you sure?' asked Jon.

'Positive,' she replied. 'The two of you should go on up.'

Pau had already opened the door. 'Are you coming?'

Katherina turned round and headed back to the car as Jon joined Pau in the tower. Inside they found themselves in a lift with just enough space for the two of them. On their left a door led to the house, and Jon was just about to grab the handle when the lift started to move. They rose upwards, slowly and almost imperceptibly, as if they were being carried on a rising tide. The lift was not hoisted up on wires but by means of giant gears that raised the platform up at an even tempo. The whirring mechanism made Jon feel as if he were locked inside a huge grandfather clock.

Pau impatiently tapped his foot against the metal floor and peered up at the ceiling eight metres above them.

After what seemed to Jon an eternity, they reached the top, and Pau pushed open the door to the catwalk leading into the house. At the end of the passage a door opened to reveal Kortmann in his wheelchair. It almost seemed as if he'd been expecting them because he was fully dressed in a dark suit, a pair of shiny black shoes visible below the hems of his perfectly pressed trousers. The wheelchair was specially built out of brass and significantly higher than normal, which made it easier to have eye contact with the occupant. Yet at the same time it made him look like a boy in a high chair.

With a restrained nod, Kortmann bid them welcome.

'Come closer,' he added in a neutral tone that could be taken as both invitation and command. He moved his chair back a bit so they could get past and then directed them down a corridor with subdued lighting and paintings in gold frames on the walls. At the end of the hall they entered a large room with bookshelves from floor to ceiling. In the middle of the room stood a low, round table surrounded by six armchairs, and above it hung a large prism chandelier.

'Have a seat,' he said, gesturing towards the armchairs.

They did as he asked while they both looked around, impressed. Pau gave a low whistle.

'Quite a place you've got here,' he said. 'It must have cost a fortune.'

Kortmann ignored him. Grabbing a handle on the side of his wheelchair, he lowered the height of his seat.

'What happened?' he asked, looking straight at Jon.

Jon told him about the attack on the bookshop and about Iversen's condition. During the entire account Kortmann kept his eyes fixed on Jon and not once, even when Pau interrupted with a snide remark, did his gaze waver. It was not a suspicious gaze, but a look filled with gravity, concern and attentiveness. When Jon was finished, Kortmann sat in his wheelchair without saying a word, his hands clasped in front of him.

'Did you see who did it?' he asked at last.

Jon shook his head. 'No.'

'But the receiver was there too?'

'Katherina? Yes, she was there the whole time. In fact, she put out most of the fire.'

Kortmann turned towards Pau. 'And what about you?'

'I didn't get there until later,' replied Pau. 'I do have a life besides books, after all.'

Kortmann looked down at his hands. 'It was only yesterday that I talked to Iversen,' he began. 'We talked about you, Jon. You can be an extremely crucial person for the Society, and considering the latest events, it's more important than ever that we make use of you.' He raised his head to look at Jon. His dark eyes gazed at him sorrowfully.

'Recently quite a few disturbing things have happened in our circles. Libri di Luca isn't the only antiquarian bookshop that has been subjected to an attack. Last month a bookshop in Valby burned down, and several of our contacts in the city's libraries have been harassed or fired without warning. And then, of course, there's the regrettable matter of your father's death.'

Jon gave a start and stared enquiringly at the man in the wheelchair.

'What does Luca's death have to do with the fire?'

'Your father's death was only the beginning.'

'Stop just a minute,' said Jon, holding up both hands. 'Luca died of heart failure.'

'Correct,' Kortmann agreed. 'But there was nothing wrong with his heart.'

Jon studied the man sitting across from him. The eyes behind the glasses didn't waver, and his face emanated both seriousness and patience.

'What exactly are you trying to tell me, Kortmann?'

'That your father, in all likelihood, was murdered.'

Jon felt his body grow heavy, and he had a sensation of sinking into the armchair, as if the air had been let out of the leather upholstery. He couldn't meet Kortmann's eye but let his gaze wander aimlessly while the words seeped into his consciousness.

After a pause Kortmann went on. 'I understood from Iversen that you've witnessed the abilities of a receiver during a demonstration at Libri di Luca. Is that right?'

Jon nodded absentmindedly.

'Perhaps you noticed that you didn't have total control over your own body. You were unable to steer the reading or your eyes or your breathing, and maybe you even sensed a change in your heartbeat. Just imagine those small effects increased by a factor of ten or a hundred. Your father didn't have a chance.'

Jon tried to recall what had happened in the basement during his reading of *Fahrenheit 451*. He remembered strong images and a definite impact on the story, but did he have control over his own body or was it being steered by Katherina?

'Naturally we can't prove anything,' said Kortmann with regret in his voice. 'It doesn't leave any traces of drugs or injuries or any sort of marks. The symptoms are an over-exerted heart, subsequently followed by heart failure.'

The feeling of helplessness Jon had experienced during the demonstration returned, and he remembered how his heart had noticeably beat faster. He recalled the heat he had felt on his hands, and the sweat that had appeared on his forehead. He'd been a passenger in his own body, unable to stop it, even if it had walked off a cliff. Jon could easily imagine how this power could be used for other things than conjuring up good reading experiences. But what sort of person would use this control over someone else to such an extent that it ended in death?

'Katherina is a receiver,' said Jon. 'Is that why she isn't allowed up here?'

'Indeed. No receiver has access to these rooms any more.'

'Any more?'

'Forgive me, I keep forgetting that you know nothing about the Bibliophile Society and its history, even though you're Luca's son.'

'Please, just tell me,' Jon insisted.

Kortmann nodded and cleared his throat before he went on.

'Until twenty years ago, the Bibliophile Society was a group that welcomed both transmitters and receivers. That was largely thanks to your father and grandfather – they held the two factions together as long as they could. But twenty years ago a series of events occurred, quite similar to what we're seeing today. Lectors were fired from their public positions for no reason, or they were subjected to harassment of one sort or another. This escalated to break-ins, fires and even murder, and there were clear signs that powers were being used offensively. The receivers accused us of being behind it, while we were convinced that they were causing these events. The powers that receivers possess are less obvious than ours, and we thought we had proof that receivers were involved in most of the attacks we suffered. Everything pointed in their direction. Even in cases where receivers were the target, we could explain them as deliberate smokescreens or revolts within their own ranks. But they denied everything. The accusations ended up splitting the Society in two. The mood was hateful, and at that time your father was out of the picture because of your mother's death. He'd always been an ambassador for both sides and without his diplomacy the Society became, as I said, divided up into transmitters and receivers.' Kortmann pressed the palms of his hands together. 'That's why receivers are not welcome here today.'

'What happened?' asked Jon. 'Did the attacks stop?'

'Instantly,' replied Kortmann. 'After the split, there were no further problems.'

'Until now,' Pau added.

Kortmann nodded.

Jon thought back to his father's funeral. Iversen had said that both transmitters and receivers were present – many of them, in fact. He hadn't sensed any discord or mistrust, but back then he'd had no idea what sort of people they were, or what their connection to Luca had been.

'Why Luca?'

'Your father always had one foot in each camp, and not everybody was happy about that. Some people, both transmitters and receivers, think that it's best to stick with one's own kind. In their eyes he might be regarded as a traitor.'

'And in yours?'

Kortmann hesitated for a moment, but if he felt accused, he didn't show it.

'Luca was my close friend. In addition, he was a talented leader and the very embodiment of goodness, but we didn't always agree. I lobbied for the division between transmitters and receivers back then, and that gave me the position as leader of the Society when your father stepped down. I would have much preferred that he stayed on, but your mother's death took a terrible toll on him, and he had no contact with the Society for several years afterwards. When he finally returned, the split had long since become a reality.'

'So he didn't become the leader again?'

'No, in accordance with his own wishes, Luca became an ordinary member of the Society,' replied Kortmann, and he hastened to add, 'But we always asked him for advice when it came to important decisions. He was, after all, one of the founders, and his word still carried great weight.'

'Was that what made him so dangerous that he had to die?'

'I have a hard time imagining that, but as for what he was doing with the receivers, I can't say.'

'They must have had some reason for killing him,' said Pau. 'You said it yourself, Kortmann. The murderer is a receiver.'

'They deny any involvement,' replied Kortmann. 'In spite of the split, we occasionally communicate with the receivers. It used to be done through Luca. Now we're trying to set up a more official means of communication. Right after Luca's death their leader rang me up and assured me that they had nothing to do with the murder.'

'The whole thing stinks to high heaven,' exclaimed Pau. 'I bet they're the ones behind all of it. So who's going to be the next one to be assassinated? You? Me? We should do something before it's too late.'

'Before you start launching an attack,' said Jon calmly, 'shouldn't you rule out that Luca's death was actually from natural causes?'

'We've certainly had doubts,' admitted Kortmann. 'Until tonight. The attack on Libri di Luca has absolutely convinced me that someone wants to destroy us. But your scepticism pleases me, Jon. You'll need it for the task that we're about to give you.'

'Task?' said Jon uncertainly. Images of himself tossing Molotov cocktails at shop windows popped into his mind. Strangely enough, the situation seemed less repellent than he might have expected, as if the circumstances surrounding Luca's death had stirred up something inside him.

'What sort of task did you have in mind?'

'The receivers deny all knowledge of this, but they've agreed to an investigation. Just as we have no idea whether there might be a traitor among us, they're in the same situation. For that reason, both parties are interested in an impartial investigation, carried out by an outsider – an individual who isn't influenced by the milieu, so to speak. You're that person, Jon.'

Jon stared in astonishment at the man in the wheelchair.

'How am I supposed to . . .' he began without finishing the sentence.

'You're the perfect choice, Jon. The goodwill felt towards your father will help you with both groups. You're still not involved enough in the Society to take sides, and as a barrister you must be used to a certain degree of detective work.'

'But when it comes to Luca's death, you might say that I am anything but impartial,' Jon countered.

'I should think it gives you even more motivation to find the murderer, the *real* murderer.'

It was hard for Jon to find an argument against this. His immediate reaction was that he didn't want anything to do with the matter. He should sell the bookshop as quickly as possible, then forget all about Lectors and get on with his own life. He already had plenty of tasks on his desk. Finally a clear career opportunity had presented itself in the form of the Remer case, but on the other hand it took all his time except when he was sleeping. His inbox was full.

And yet he had a feeling that this was his last chance to find some real answers. Maybe the investigation of Luca's death would provide him with the explanation he'd been lacking for so many years: why his father hadn't wanted anything to do with him after his mother's death. As he sat there surrounded by books in the inner sanctum of the Bibliophile Society, bombarded by conspiracy theories, it occurred to him that it was all connected – Luca's death, his own life, and everything that had happened to him over the past twenty years – they were all pieces in a puzzle which until now he'd been too young to put together. 'For ages thirty-three and older,' it might say on the box.

'I'd have no idea even where to start,' Jon objected after no one said a word for a while.

'First you have to meet the rest of the Bibliophile Society members,' said Kortmann. 'Both the transmitters and the receivers. Perhaps the receiver you brought along can be of use. Apparently she enjoyed Luca's trust, so use her if you can. It's possible that she can arrange something with the receivers. After that you can work out a strategy, assuming that they accept you.'

'He'll probably need a bodyguard, don't you think?' suggested Pau, pointing both thumbs at himself. 'Like me, for instance?'

'As I said before,' explained Kortmann with poorly concealed annoyance in his voice, 'it's important for both sides to have faith in the person or persons who undertake this investigation. They have to be as impartial as possible, and we can't exactly accuse you of that.'

'Okay, okay,' said Pau, disappointed. 'Just trying to help.'

'Besides, there's another obvious qualification that Jon possesses, unlike yourself. Jon is not an active Lector.'

Pau shrugged.

'There's no doubt that you have potential,' said Kortmann, turning to Jon. 'But at the moment your powers are dormant. It would be an advantage to keep them that way until the investigation is completed. The people you're going to deal with need to be certain that you're not manipulating them. The disadvantage, however, is obvious – you won't be able to sense when someone is trying to manipulate you.'

'That makes me feel a lot better,' said Jon, unconvincingly.

'It's not that bad. Your advantage is that you know who you're dealing with. If you stick to a few very simple rules, you shouldn't have any problems.'

'And they are?'

'Don't read anything in the presence of a receiver, and avoid any reading given by a transmitter.'

Jon nodded. 'But I'd still feel more confident if I had someone with me. Call it a bodyguard or a guide. As a stranger in this environment, I could use some guidance on how I should act.'

'I understand,' said Kortmann. 'But the receivers would never accept Pau as an investigator.'

'It wasn't Pau I was thinking of,' said Jon quickly. 'I'd like to take Katherina along.'

Pau sniggered while Kortmann calmly clasped his hands and leaned his chin on them. After giving Jon a long, inquisitive look, he laughed. 'You're truly Luca's son. That's exactly the sort of thing he would have done. All right, have it your way. As long as you realize that there are certain places she can't go, and that some people won't be happy with the arrangement, you're welcome to take her along.' His expression turned serious again. 'So, what do you say?'

Jon shifted his gaze to Pau, who stared back with an offended expression. Kortmann sat with his hands clasped in front of him, regarding Jon expectantly. Again a sense of powerlessness slipped into Jon's mind. It was clear what he had to do, even if he didn't want to. He felt he'd been stripped of the right to choose. But what surprised him was that he *did* want to do it. The opportunity to find out what had happened in the past countered all sensible arguments about career and unfounded conspiracy theories. Something told him that there had to be a connection between the present events and what had happened twenty years earlier.

Jon sat up straight and threw out his hands.

'Okay, when do we start?'

# 11

Even though it was dark, Katherina could see that something was different about the two men as they came walking towards her. Jon came first, taking resolute strides, while Pau scuffed along behind him. They'd been gone for an hour. An hour in which Katherina had roamed around the courtyard in front of the house in the autumn chill. The cold hadn't bothered her, but Kortmann's arrogant dismissal had, and she'd been kept warm by her anger and frustration at not knowing what he was going to say, or what version of the story he would choose.

'Well, what did he say?' asked Katherina when they reached the car. Jon didn't say anything, just got in behind the wheel without looking at her. She shifted her gaze to Pau, who scowled back.

'Congratulations,' he muttered. 'You get to be the tour guide for our friend here.' He opened the car door and threw himself onto the back seat, where he crossed his arms and closed his eyes.

Katherina got into the passenger seat. 'What's that all about?'

Jon took a deep breath. With his hands on the steering wheel and his eyes staring at the darkness beyond the windscreen, he replied, 'I've been asked to undertake an investigation into the circumstances surrounding my father's ... death. Kortmann thinks that Luca was murdered.' He paused for a second before turning to face her. 'I'm going to need your help, Katherina.'

She lowered her gaze and nodded. 'Of course.'

Her worries were suddenly gone and she had to make an effort not to show her relief. After an hour of misgivings and uncertainty, she could now relax. Because didn't this mean that she was still welcome at Libri di Luca? And that there was still hope of a reconciliation between the transmitters and receivers? She hardly dared believe it.

'You don't look surprised,' said Jon. 'Did you realize he'd been killed?'

'There are plenty of indications,' replied Katherina evasively. She could understand it if Jon was feeling left out. 'We can't be a hundred per cent positive, but Iversen is absolutely sure of it.'

'It sounds like everyone except me knew about this.' Jon started the car. 'There also seems to be agreement that a receiver was behind it,' he went on as the car rolled towards the gate which, as if by a secret signal, had begun to open. 'Everybody has warned me against you receivers. Your powers seem to make people nervous, and if that's really how Luca was murdered, then their fears are certainly justified. So the question is whether I can trust you.'

Katherina sensed that Jon was looking at her as they waited for the gate in front of them to open all the way so that they could leave Kortmann's property. If she'd known what to say in order to reassure Jon, she would have said it, but the only thing she could think of was that she felt safe with him.

From the back seat Pau began snoring loudly. Katherina didn't say a word.

'I think I can,' Jon concluded. 'Since the man whose death we're going to investigate trusted you. I suppose that's the best recommendation.'

'What about the others?' asked Katherina. 'Not many people trust a receiver these days.'

'They're going to have to accept it, if I have anything to say about the matter. I'm going to need someone the receivers know and trust. Someone who can decipher the signals coming from both sides. And as I understand it, you've had contact with both receivers and transmitters by virtue of your connection with my father and Libri di Luca.'

Katherina nodded. Suddenly it seemed to her that the time she'd spent with Luca, as well as his efforts to reunite the two factions, had actually prepared her for investigating his murder. As if the whole thing had been planned from the start, and she could now step into the role. She hoped she had the strength for it.

'I wish Iversen were here,' she said quietly.

'We're going to need him,' Jon acknowledged, then paused for a moment. 'He's the one who knew Luca best, after all.'

The undertone of this last remark made Katherina give him a sidelong glance. For the first time she seemed to detect a touch of regret in Jon's voice. His eyes were fixed on the road ahead, but they seemed to be looking further. When his face was lit up by the headlamps of oncoming cars, she could see the muscles of his jaw moving slightly, and if she listened closely the sound of his teeth grinding was audible. There was anger and sorrow in his expression, and she wished she could make these feelings vanish. Maybe he noticed she was looking at him because he turned his face towards her. She immediately looked away.

'There's a lot I need to catch up on with regard to my father,' he said. 'It's been years since I last had any contact with him, and things didn't go very well on that occasion, to put it mildly.'

It was strange to be sitting there talking about Luca with his own son. In many situations Luca had been like a father to Katherina, and in that sense Jon was like a brother, but they had both known him for only part of their lives. Jon for the first part of his, and Katherina for a later part of hers. Together they might be able to form a more complete picture of the man to whom they both, each in different ways, owed their life.

'What happened the last time you saw Luca?' she asked cautiously.

'He rejected me,' said Jon. 'I had just turned eighteen at the time and was no doubt surly and irritating, but we didn't talk long enough for him even to find that out.' He cleared his throat before he went on. 'First I called the bookshop. I'd never understood why he had sent me away when I was in my early teens. Now that I was all grown up, in my opinion, I thought I had a right to an explanation. So I rang him up, with my heart pounding, my hands sweaty, the whole business. At first there was a long silence on the other end of the line, and for a moment I thought we'd been cut off. But then he said there must be some mistake because he didn't have a son. Then he slammed down the receiver.'

Pau grunted drowsily from the back seat, but a more regular snoring soon started up again.

'It had taken me months to muster enough courage to make that phone call,' Jon continued. 'So when I heard the dial tone on the other end, I went berserk. I took the next bus to Vesterbro and crashed open the door to the shop. Iversen was there that day. He was standing behind the counter, helping a customer, but when he saw me, his whole face lit up with a big smile and he gave me a friendly greeting. That made me calm down a bit, and when the customer left the shop, Iversen patted me on the shoulder and said that he'd go and get my father. Then he disappeared downstairs. It took a long time for Luca to appear. He came walking slowly towards me with a kind, inquisitive look in his eyes. For a second I thought that everything was going to be all right again, but then his expression changed and he asked me what I was doing there. I had no reason to be there, he said, and I should never come back.'

Katherina shifted position uneasily. This description of the man whom she had considered her foster father for so long was light-years from her own experience. It sounded like two totally different people.

'I can't understand that at all,' she said, shaking her head.

'Me neither. It made me stubborn and I wanted to know why. After all, he couldn't deny that he was my father, since Marianne was my mother. I suppose I said a number of stupid things and hurled a lot of accusations at him, but he remained utterly calm and just let me vent my rage before he played his trump card.'

They had reached the bookshop. Jon parked the car at the kerb and turned off the engine. He sat there with his eyes fixed on the shop.

'What did he do?' asked Katherina.

Jon grimaced.

'He said he couldn't stand the sight of me. I reminded him too much of my mother. Every time he looked at me, he was reminded of how she died, and that he hadn't been able to prevent it.'

Katherina had heard about Marianne's suicide from Iversen, but Luca himself had never said a word about it.

'Whew,' she exclaimed. 'What can you say to that?'

'As an eighteen-year-old, nothing,' said Jon, taking a deep breath. 'I shut up and walked out of the shop – and out of his life.'

They sat there for a moment, listening to Pau's snoring. As if on cue, it became erratic and he woke up, uttering a grunt, followed by a loud yawn.

'So, are we there yet?' he asked, stretching as best he could in the cramped space.

'We're back,' Jon confirmed.

Pau leaned forward between the seats and looked first at Jon, then at Katherina.

'So aren't we going to get out?'

Katherina opened the door and climbed out, followed by Pau.

'I'll drop by tomorrow,' said Jon before they said goodbye and slammed the doors shut.

Pau shivered in the cold, while Katherina watched Jon's car drive away.

'Are we going the same way?' asked Pau, heading for his bicycle.

'No, I'm staying here tonight.'

'Is that a good idea?' he asked. 'They might come back.'

'Exactly,' she replied.

Pau shook his head.

'Go ahead and play the hero, if you want. But I've really got to get some sleep,' he said, sounding apologetic. 'Will you be okay on your own?'

Katherina nodded in reply.

When she woke the next morning, it was dark all around her, and it took several minutes for her to figure out where she was. The boards over the windows of Libri di Luca kept out the morning light. The folding camp bed under her creaked at the slightest move, but that hadn't stopped her from sleeping. She recalled wrestling with the bed the night before, but she didn't remember taking off her shoes or climbing in.

The sound of traffic outside penetrated the darkness, and she lay listening to it for a while before she untangled herself from the blanket and sat up. After putting on her shoes and woollen sweater, she went over to switch on the light in the ceiling lamp.

The shop was a sorry sight. The missing piece of carpet was like an open wound, and the barricaded windows and bed made the room look like an improvised hiding place for antiquities during a bombing raid rather than a bookshop.

She unlocked the door and went outside. Not a cloud in the sky, but the shop was still in the shadows of the other buildings, so it was bitterly cold. For the first time since spring she could see her own breath, and for a moment she jumped about on the pavement in front of the shop to stay warm. It was past eleven, and Libri di Luca should have opened two hours ago, but the pitiful state of the facade had no doubt kept any potential customers far away.

Katherina left the door ajar and began cleaning up inside. The books that were normally displayed on tables just inside the entrance had been tossed on the floor further back in the shop, so she started by setting up a table where she could put them. Unable to sort them by author or title, she indiscriminately piled them into stacks.

She spent the rest of the day cleaning and waiting for customers, with a lunch break at a nearby pizzeria. Only two braved the barricades to have a look inside, but it was clear to see that the devastation bothered them, and they left the shop without buying anything.

Jon turned up late in the day. He had dark circles under his eyes and it didn't look as if he had shaved. His clothes, on the other hand, were impeccable, up until he took off his tie and opened the top button of his blue shirt.

'Hard day?' asked Katherina after they exchanged greetings and Jon plopped down in the leather chair, heaving a big sigh.

'I suppose you could call it that,' he said and closed his eyes. 'What about here? Any problems?'

Katherina gave him a summary of her day, which took less than a minute.

'All right,' said Jon, opening his eyes. 'We have to see about having the windows replaced. I'll try to get hold of a glass company tomorrow.'

'Have you heard from Kortmann?' asked Katherina.

'He rang just as I was leaving. There's a meeting in . . .' He glanced at his watch. 'Half an hour.'

'Here?'

'No, some place in Østerbro. A library,' replied Jon, adding with a smile: 'Where else?'

The library was on Dag Hammarskjölds Allé across from the American Embassy. Big picture windows faced the street, and passers-by could freely look in at the rows of shelves holding books and boxes of comics. Even from outside they could see that there were still quite a few people in the library, despite the fact that the official business hours would end in ten minutes.

Katherina followed Jon inside through a five-metre-long foyer to the actual front doors. It had been a long time since she was last inside a library. Her powers made it a taxing experience. Even though she was good at blocking out all the input, she could still sense a roaring background noise that refused to go away. The books gave her no joy. The bindings were often merely glued, and the quality of the covers was standardized and impersonal.

Right inside the doors was a counter where a lone female librarian was helping the last borrowers. She was about fifty with long blonde hair and a pair of round glasses that were too big for her narrow, pale face. Katherina thought she looked familiar, and when their eyes met, the librarian broke out in a smile and gave her a brief nod. They continued on past the counter to the stacks.

To the right of the counter was the periodicals department, a glass enclosure where newspapers and magazines were displayed along the walls. In the middle of the glass enclosure were chairs and tables where readers could leaf through the daily papers or selected periodicals.

'Kortmann,' whispered Jon, staring at a man who was sitting at one of the tables with his back turned to them. Upon closer inspection, Katherina discovered that the man was sitting in a wheelchair.

'What now?' she whispered back.

'I think it starts after the library closes,' said Jon in a low voice. 'Let's split up.'

Katherina nodded and began moving slowly past the room with the periodicals and towards the children's section. Jon headed in the opposite direction. It had grown dark outside, and the reflection from the fluorescent lights on the ceiling made the big picture windows look like surfaces of opaque black glass. Katherina had a feeling that someone was watching her from outside in the dark as she strolled past the boxes of comic books. She passed the time by leafing through a few of the comics while out of the corner of her eye she observed the other library patrons. In the fiction section a man in his forties stood with his nose in a thick book – *The Name of the Rose*, judging by the small snippets she was receiving. Katherina cautiously focused her powers on him and had a clear sense that he was also just killing time. When she turned her head to study him, he immediately looked up and she thought she caught a spark of recognition in his eyes. He quickly lowered his gaze, put the book back and continued along the shelves.

In this way Katherina reconnoitred the library and found several more people strolling about among the books with a purpose other than borrowing reading material. In addition to the man in his forties, there was a couple in their thirties immersed in a discreet conversation at the end of one of the corridors in the stacks, a teenage girl in the comic book area and an Asian-looking man wandering around in the non-fiction section. All of them were directing their attention at something other than what they were reading, and they kept sending searching glances at everyone else.

At closing time the librarian walked around to announce the last call for checking out books. None of the individuals Katherina had noticed responded, but the last library patrons who had actually come to borrow books headed for the check-out counter. Slowly Katherina made her way back to the periodicals room, and she noted that the other remaining people did the same.

Jon was already inside the glass enclosure. He was moving along the far wall, apparently very interested in magazines about fishing. Katherina suppressed the temptation to find out what he was really thinking about.

The librarian had let the last borrower out and locked the front door.

'Now we can get started,' she declared loudly and turned off the lights in the rooms facing the street.

The rest of the participants gradually emerged from the rows of stacks and the reading areas. They nodded to each other with small smiles of acknowledgement and headed for the glass enclosure. One by one they sat down at the tables in the middle, and conversations quickly started up about all sorts of things. The librarian was the last to arrive, but just as she was about to close the door, they heard a loud banging at the front entrance.

'Just a minute,' she said and disappeared again. The conversations stopped and everyone listened to the librarian's footsteps and the rattling of the door. There was a brief exchange of words before they heard the door close again and footsteps approaching.

'Whew, I just made it, didn't I?' said Pau, gasping for breath as he came into the room, his face red.

The librarian carefully shut the door behind her and the last two arrivals sat down. Everyone turned their attention to the man in the wheelchair.

'Welcome,' said Kortmann. The others murmured a greeting in return. 'I'm glad that so many could participate at such short notice. It can be risky to meet in times like these, but recent events have unfortunately made it necessary.' Solemn expressions marked the faces of those around the table.

'Last night Libri di Luca was attacked. Molotov cocktails were thrown at the bookshop, which has suffered significant damage. Iversen is in hospital due to burns and shock. We have Jon to thank that the shop didn't burn to the ground.'

Everyone expressed their approval with subdued whispers and nods towards Jon. Katherina clenched her teeth hard and fixed her eyes on the tabletop in front of her. She had never expected a hero's reception from Kortmann, but he could have at least mentioned that she'd taken part in putting out the fire. Surely the very fact that he was willing to be in the same room with her must mean that he trusted her, so why was he downplaying her role? Maybe he was unaware of how it had all happened. Kortmann had only heard the story from Jon and Pau, and it was impossible to say what version they had told him. She looked over at Jon, who didn't bat an eye.

'As you've presumably heard, Jon is Luca's son,' Kortmann went on. 'It's only recently that we've learned about him, or perhaps I should say that it wasn't until he turned up that we remembered that Luca even had a son. For that reason, it's only now that he has been made aware of the Society's existence, and he is not yet an active Lector.'

Everybody in the room looked at Jon as Kortmann spoke, but his expression didn't change, even when the discussion touched on his relations with his father.

'I'm personally very happy he has returned, especially now when we have need for reinforcements to defend ourselves, and I'd like to ask all of you to give him your unconditional support regarding the task he has agreed to resolve.'

'What task is that?' asked the man that Katherina had seen in the fiction section.

'I'll come back to that in a moment,' replied Kortmann. 'First I think you should all introduce yourselves and explain what sort of work you do, both within the Society and outside of it. We all know Pau, so we can skip over him.' Kortmann turned to his left and nodded at the librarian. She immediately sat up straighter and cleared her throat. Her glasses with the big frames now hung round her neck and a pair of blue eyes stared intently at Jon.

'Well, my name is Birthe,' she began, suppressing a giggle. 'As you've seen, I'm the librarian here. Usually I work at the check-out counter or in the children's section. I love being surrounded by children, and I'm so happy whenever I'm allowed to read to the kids – to sense how they become totally absorbed by the story, letting themselves just—'

Kortmann cleared his throat.

'Er, yes,' said Birthe apologetically and giggled again. 'We can always talk about that later. In the Bibliophile Society I'm the historian, which means that I try to map out the history of the Lectors and their expansion through the ages. I worked very closely with your father, such a lovely man. So full of life and humour.' She giggled with delight. 'Always friendly and helpful and—'

'Thank you, Birthe,' said Kortmann. 'Henning?'

The man from the fiction section leaned forward with his elbows on the table. The light from the fluorescent lamps revealed that his greying hair was very thin on top of his head, and little beads of sweat were visible on his scalp. His eyes kept blinking erratically like defective windscreen wipers, making him appear un-necessarily nervous.

'My name is Henning Petersen. I'm forty-two years old, and I work in a bookshop on Kultorvet.' His dark eyes flickered from Jon to Katherina. 'I'm single, as we say nowadays, and I'm fond of cooking and going to the theatre – in addition to books, of course.' He smiled self-consciously. 'I've been active for over thirty years, and I'm the Bibliophile Society's treasurer.'

He leaned back in his chair and nodded to the next person in line, a woman of about thirty who was holding hands with a man of the same age. Both were a bit stout. They radiated great joy, maybe because they were together.

'My name is Sonja,' she began in a bright, somewhat piercing voice. 'And this is my husband Thor.' She lifted his hand in triumph. 'I met him through the Society almost three years ago. We're both teachers. Thor works at a school in Roskilde, while I'm at Sortedam School right over there.' She gestured with her hand past Katherina. 'We don't have any specific tasks within the

Society, but we always show up at the reading sessions, when it's necessary.' She turned to look at her husband. 'Your turn, Thor.'

Thor cleared his throat behind his big, full beard.

'I don't think I have anything to add – after that,' he said and gave a brief chuckle, while his wife chimed in with a shrill squeal.

The next person in line was a teenage girl who blushed bright red and looked down at her hands.

'My name is Line,' she said in a low voice. 'I only became a member a month ago, so . . .' She shifted her gaze to the next person, the man with the Asian features whom Katherina had seen in the non-fiction section. Narrow, rectangular glasses framed his dark eyes, which were turned towards Katherina. His Asian features made it hard to guess how old he was, but she thought he had to be in his mid-twenties.

'The name is Lee,' he said with no trace of an accent. 'I'll spare you my first name, since most people can't pronounce it correctly anyway. For my day job I work in the IT field as a software engineer, if that means anything to you. I try as much as possible to help the Society on that front, but it's not as if we're expanding via the Internet or using IT in that way,' he remarked, with regret in his voice. 'So I don't do much other than collecting data. Well, I guess that's all,' he concluded and nodded at Katherina.

She cleared her throat and was about to introduce herself when Kortmann cut her off.

'Thank you for the introductions. Unfortunately, not everyone was able to be here today. You all know Iversen, but we have three additional members in the Copenhagen area who were unable to make it. But they've all been told that Jon and Katherina will be paying them a visit in the near future as part of the investigation.'

'Could we now hear what this is all about, Kortmann?' asked Henning Petersen, clearly annoyed.

'Yes, you can,' said Kortmann, looking at Katherina for the first time that evening before he continued. 'The receivers feel that *we* are the source of what's been happening lately, that in the *best* case scenario we may have a traitor among us.'

# 12

From his seat next to Kortmann, Jon had an excellent view of the reactions of everyone present. Lee's expression didn't change and he kept his eyes fixed on Kortmann, as if he were waiting to hear more. The teenage girl, Line, looked as if she didn't know how to react, and her flitting eyes sought help from the faces of the others. But there wasn't much help to be found there. The married couple stared at each other in shock, for the first time without smiles or romantic sentiment, while the librarian looked down at her hands, which were shaking slightly. Only Pau looked unconcerned. The whole situation actually seemed to amuse him.

'What do you mean, "In the *best* case scenario, we may have a traitor among us"?' Henning Petersen wanted to know. He spoke the words slowly and with his eyes narrowed, as if it were taking all his concentration, but not for a moment did he take his gaze off Kortmann.

Katherina abruptly leaned forward.

'That it's not the receivers who are behind these events,' she replied before Kortmann had time to respond. 'And if it's not the receivers, then it must be you, the transmitters, but since you deny any knowledge of it, you're either lying or there are one or more traitors among you.' Katherina paused to take a breath. Jon watched her from the corner of his eye. She kept her green eyes stubbornly fixed on Henning; her expression was neutral but her breathing revealed how upset she was, and her chin with the little scar was trembling faintly. 'Of the two possibilities, we regard the latter as a more likely scenario than the former.'

Henning stared at her. His eyes blinked involuntarily, as if they couldn't believe what they saw.

'Ah, now I remember you,' he exclaimed. 'You're Katherina, right? The receiver?' He didn't give her time to reply before he went on: 'And one of the best, from what I've heard.'

Jon noticed that Katherina's cheeks turned a bit pink. She nodded and sent a defiant look towards Kortmann before she again spoke.

'That's right. My name is Katherina. I'm a receiver and have been for fifteen years now. Ten of those years I've spent with Luca Campelli and Svend Iversen, and they deserve all the credit if my powers happen to be better than most.'

'Okay, no offence,' said Henning, raising his hand. 'It wasn't meant to be an accusation.'

'No one should have any doubts as to Katherina's loyalty,' Jon interrupted. 'I saw how she fought the flames last night, and she's really the one you should thank for the fact that the bookshop didn't burn to the ground, not me.' Katherina leaned back with her arms crossed as everyone now turned their attention to Jon. 'Kortmann has asked me to undertake an investigation of recent events, including my father's death, and there's no one else I'd rather have helping me than Katherina. Right now she's the only one I trust.'

Looks were exchanged around the table, but most nodded their approval to both Jon and Katherina.

Kortmann cleared his throat.

'As Jon said, he's going to carry out an investigation among us, but also among the receivers. The purpose is to find out who's behind the attacks we've experienced lately – whether we like what he finds out or not.'

'But...' Birthe began hesitantly. 'Could anyone besides a receiver be responsible for Luca's death? No transmitter would be capable of provoking heart failure like that.'

'I wouldn't say that,' replied Henning calmly. 'A transmitter's powers could very well cause an elevation in the pulse and other physiological reactions in a listener. But no one has yet exhibited powers that are strong enough to kill someone outright in that way. Besides, it would be relatively easy to protect yourself against such an attack.' He shrugged his shoulders. 'All you'd have to do is cover your ears.'

'Forgive my ignorance,' said Jon, 'but is that all? Covering your ears?'

Henning nodded. 'A transmitter's powers depend on having the text heard by a listener. It's the text combined with the emotions that it evokes that open the channel and make the person in question susceptible to the Lector. So the best defence is to cover your ears, or simply walk away.'

'Does that mean we can rule out that it was a transmitter who murdered my father?'

'Well, it's very unlikely that it was done by using a transmitter's powers – unless Luca was tied down, but there was no sign of that, was there?'

Kortmann shook his head. 'It would have left marks.'

'Okay,' said Jon after no one else spoke for a couple of seconds. 'Luca's death indicates that it was the work of a receiver, but it could still be the result of natural heart failure, or possibly poisoning. None of the other attacks points exclusively to a receiver, so I don't want to rule anything out yet.' He scanned the faces of the people sitting around the table. Most of them had a more or less resigned look; only Line displayed something other than dismay. Her eyes shone with fear.

'Maybe we should discuss what the motive might be,' suggested Jon.

After another few seconds of silence Henning cleared his throat. He shut his eyes tight for a moment before he spoke.

'That's what doesn't make any sense,' he said, clasping his hands on the table in front of him. 'No Lector, either a transmitter or a receiver, has anything to gain from all this. It's simply too risky. The connection between these events may not be obvious to so-called normal people, but if the attacks continue, we're going to be exposed, and none of us wants that.'

'Why not?' asked Jon. 'Why all the secrecy? Couldn't your powers be of use to everyone if they became known?'

'Let me answer that by asking you a question,' said Henning. 'How do you feel about the fact that there are people like us who can influence your decisions and opinions without you having any control over it?'

'Well, everything's rather new to me,' Jon began. 'I haven't really thought through all the consequences, but I have to admit that it does make me uneasy.'

Lee broke in by leaning forward and jabbing his index finger at the table.

'That's exactly the reason,' he said earnestly. 'That's the normal reaction. Maybe in the beginning people would be fascinated. We'd become exhibits in a freak show – wearing brilliantly coloured robes, we'd "mind-read" what the people in the audience were reading, or we'd make people do silly things by reading to them, like in one of those phoney hypnotist shows. But after a while people would start to worry; they'd be afraid of being manipulated, and maybe they'd even refuse to read anything unless they were sure they were alone, or at least among friends.'

Jon saw how Henning and the married couple exchanged glances, and Thor smiled indulgently. But Lee didn't notice, or at least refused to be deterred and went on with his explanation.

'Anyone with powers would become an outcast, as if he were a leper, because people would be constantly on guard around him. The growing paranoia would end up forcing the Lectors to be registered, maybe even wear a special symbol so that people on the street could recognize them and take precautionary measures. Before long, society might come to the conclusion that the easiest and safest thing would be to lock us up, put us somewhere far away from other people, and maybe even prevent us from having any access to books and texts.' Lee stopped his tirade for a moment to allow Jon to catch up.

'Soon new Lectors would try to hide their powers,' Lee went on with a shrug. 'Just like we do now, actually, and regular manhunts would be carried out to find those who weren't registered or those who had managed to escape from the prisons. A great deal of energy would be expended to detect the existence of powers, even in infants, and "bloodhounds", either electronic or in the form of trained traitors, would track us down like hunted animals. Underground movements would be created by those of us who had managed to get away, and before long the groups would be forced to defend themselves using violent means. Wars would break out—'

'All right, thank you,' said Kortmann. 'I think we get the point, Lee.'

Lee blushed. 'I guess I got a bit carried away,' he said apologetically. 'But it was just to illustrate that none of us has anything to gain by becoming known. Neither transmitters nor receivers.' He leaned back in his chair.

'Even though Lee's version may seem a trifle exaggerated, he's right,' said Kortmann. 'We're different, and as such we can expect to be treated differently, and not in an especially good way, if what we're capable of doing ever gets out.'

'Hasn't anyone ever given you away?' asked Jon. 'It seems to me very unlikely that something like this could be kept secret for what – a hundred years?'

'Oh, much longer than that,' exclaimed Birthe. 'We're talking about centuries. Our best guess is that the first Lectors were in charge of the libraries of antiquity long before the birth of Christ. Back then it was considered prestigious to be a librarian,' she added with a touch of bitterness in her voice. 'They were regarded as statesmen and scholars. People who had influence on the development of society, whose opinions carried weight, and who were consulted regarding all sorts of issues. As you probably realize, that would be a prime position for a Lector who knows how to make use of his powers.'

'But there are no instances when you've ever been exposed?'

Birthe shook her head. 'There is very little concrete evidence that points in our direction. During certain periods some suspicion was directed at scholars who could read and write, but that was probably rooted in envy and ignorance rather than any justifiable fear. If we look at more recent times, no one has ever even hinted at the existence of our powers.'

'Could that be the motive? Exposing the Society?' Jon suggested.

'A hell of a complicated way to go about it,' said Henning. 'I mean, why not just expose us outright? The chances are slim that anyone would ever figure out the connection between the actions that have been carried out up to this point. If the intention is to expose the Lectors, only a complete revelation would do it.'

Lee nodded eagerly. 'I agree with that. An exposé could only come from someone who's part of the group, and only by demonstrating the powers. So if that's the motive, we would have already read about it in the newspapers, seen it on the talk shows and gone to the premiere of the movie.'

'So what are you saying?' asked Jon.

Lee looked at Katherina for a moment. 'I think,' he began, casting a glance at Henning before he continued. '*We* think that there's something bigger going on. *Someone* is up to something big, and this is just a preliminary manoeuvre meant to wear us out, confuse us or divert our attention – maybe all three. The question you should be asking now is who this *someone* might be, and for me it's obvious.' Again he looked at Katherina. 'Everything points to the receivers.' He waved his hands towards her, making the gesture seem both dismissive and apologetic. 'I'm not saying that you're involved. It could very well be that you've been kept out of it because of your relationship to Luca.'

'So what's our big plan?' asked Katherina. 'World domination, I suppose?'

Lee studied Katherina for a moment with a hint of satisfaction but then shifted his gaze to Jon.

'I have no idea what they're after, but at least I'm searching for the answer.'

'You're searching?'

Lee nodded. 'Every chance I get. The clues are out there, on the

Internet, it's just a question of finding them and figuring out the connections. So far it hasn't produced any result, but it will. It's a little like the wreckage of a ship – something always pops up, even though the beach may have been empty the day before.'

'How long has this been going on?' asked Kortmann in surprise.

Lee shrugged. 'A couple of weeks, I suppose. I didn't think it was necessary to ask permission.'

'No, no, not at all. It would just be nice to know.'

'I didn't realize you wanted to start up this ... investigation,' Lee added. 'And it didn't look like anyone else was thinking of doing anything. So since the Society didn't have any more pressing work for me to do, I permitted myself to show a little initiative.'

Kortmann nodded appreciatively. 'Good work, Lee. I suggest that you continue your searches.'

'That's certainly what I intend to do,' said Lee, his words barely audible.

'And keep us updated,' Kortmann emphasized, pointing to himself and to Jon.

'What about the rest of us?' asked Henning sharply.

'You'll be informed, of course, provided there's some definitive result. The most important thing is that we don't panic or start a lynch mob without having any proof to go on.'

'It sounds more like you don't trust us,' said Henning.

'So we're still under suspicion?' Pau interjected.

Kortmann gestured dismissively. 'As you've all said yourselves, there's no firm proof. All possibilities remain open, even the *worst* of them.' He glanced briefly at Katherina. 'The possibility that one of us is a traitor.' A murmur of discontented voices arose, so Kortmann had to raise his own voice to be heard. 'But I don't believe that. Even so, we're being forced to take every precaution. This isn't a matter of one person maligning someone else or swiping money from the till. People have been hurt – even murdered. Keep that in mind.'

Everyone stopped talking, and for several seconds it was completely silent in the room. Many avoided Jon's eyes when he looked in their direction.

'I think that we should end the meeting here,' said Kortmann calmly. 'The point was for everyone to introduce themselves and for all of us to understand the importance of this investigation. I hope that's been accomplished. Jon will have access to your names and addresses so he can contact you directly if necessary. That's up to him. As I said, I expect all of you to help as best you can.' He clapped his hands together. 'Thanks for coming.'

Everyone stood up amid the scraping of chairs and parting words offered right and left. When Jon said goodbye to Kortmann, the man took a brown envelope out of the side pocket of his wheelchair and handed it to him.

'Keep me posted,' said Kortmann, giving Jon a wink.

Jon nodded in agreement and headed outside with Katherina. Kortmann remained behind with Birthe.

In front of the entrance Pau, Lee and Henning were having a muted conversation, but as soon as Katherina and Jon came out, they broke up and went their separate ways. Pau came sauntering over to them.

'Would you like a lift?' asked Jon.

'No, thanks,' replied Pau. 'I'm on my bike. Besides, I wouldn't want to get in the way of the Dynamic Duo.' He laughed.

'New friends?' asked Katherina, nodding in the direction that Lee had headed.

Pau shrugged. 'I've always thought that Lee was cool. He's going to show me some of his Internet tricks some day.' Pau watched Lee go. 'I suppose he was a little miffed at what Kortmann said. The last time anyone talked to him like that, it was his old man. The Bibliophile Society has turned into a pensioners' club with reading aloud, bingo and all that crap. We've got to recruit some new blood soon – I agree with Lee about that.' He shifted his glance to Jon. 'What do you think, Jon?'

'Hard to say, since I'm not even a member.'

'There shouldn't be any problem about becoming a member since you're Luca's son. But maybe Kortmann won't let you in. Have you thought about why he won't activate you?'

'Not particularly.'

'The others think he's afraid you'll want to take his place.'

'I haven't exactly got the feeling that he's trying to get rid of me – on the contrary,' replied Jon in a neutral tone.

'Yeah, okay,' said Pau, sounding resigned. 'I've got to go. See you!'

They said goodbye and watched Pau cycle away into the darkness, riding an ancient men's bicycle with no lights.

'What do you think?' asked Jon.

'He's just a kid,' said Katherina.

'I meant about the meeting.'

She laughed but quickly turned serious. 'They're scared.'

For the first time in what seemed like ages Jon allowed himself to sleep eight hours straight. Even so, he could tell that he was still suffering from a lack of sleep, but he was alert enough to go through his morning routine without skipping the shaving.

In light of all the recent upheaval in his life, his usual activities and rituals had taken on a new purpose. It was as if he were putting on a different identity – lawyer by day, investigator of secret conspiracies by night. When the two worlds collided, he could see the absurdity, respectively, of going to work when he ought to be investigating his father's death, or of playing amateur detective when he was facing the breakthrough case of his career.

On that particular day three such collisions took place.

The first one happened when he rang a glass company to order new windows for the bookshop. He'd chosen the one that was located closest to Libri di Luca, and it turned out that the glazier had known Luca. Jon introduced himself as the new owner with such ease that afterwards he had stared at the phone for a long time and had to resist the temptation to look at himself in the mirror.

The second collision came in the form of a phone call after lunch.

'Campelli? Remer here,' he heard on the other end of the line, despite the bad connection.

'I'm glad you rang,' replied Jon. 'I assume you received my letter?' After Remer's last visit, Jon had compiled the questions that hadn't been resolved when they met and sent them off to Remer.

'Letter?' repeated Remer. 'No, I didn't receive anything, but I'm in Holland at the moment, so I may be a little difficult to reach. Send an email instead – I usually get those.'

'I did that too,' remarked Jon.

'Oh. Well, that's not the reason I rang you up,' Remer said quickly. 'Do you remember that bookseller I told you about? I met him here in Amsterdam at a reception. Smart guy. He told me what happened at the shop. A very sad story. How serious is the damage?'

'It's not so bad,' replied Jon. 'The wooden facade and the windows have to be replaced, and a bunch of minor things need repair inside, but otherwise not much happened.'

'That's good to hear, Campelli. I can't have my lawyer getting his fingers burned.' Remer laughed loudly on the line while Jon wondered whether the real reason for the call was so that Remer could deliver that punchline.

'It's nice of you to think of me, Mr Remer, but I'd rather have you answer some of the questions I sent you.'

'Oh sure, I'll take a look at them,' said Remer. 'I just wanted to say that he's still interested in buying the place – the bookseller, I mean. He's even willing to overlook any fire damage.'

'As I said—'

'Don't tell me you're still considering becoming a bookseller yourself, Campelli?' Remer interrupted him. 'It does look as if it's more exciting than we both thought, but of course you know where your real talent lies. As I said before, just sell the place and get out of that business. It's much too unpredictable for laymen like us; recent events have proven that clearly enough.'

'Mr Remer,' Jon cut him off. 'I *have* made a decision. Libri di Luca is not for sale. And if you don't mind, I'd like to get back to my job of keeping you out of prison.' He hung up before Remer could reply.

But it wasn't easy to concentrate after that call. He managed to write yet another email and a letter, but Jon's thoughts were more on the conversation than on his work. As he replayed Remer's words in his mind, he sometimes came to the conclusion that Remer had been trying to coerce him into selling for business reasons, but at other times he thought the man had made an outright threat.

The third collision took place during these speculations.

Katherina rang him from the bookshop. On the phone her voice sounded both fragile and gentle, but there was also a note of uncertainty, which Jon noticed at once.

'There's a claims assessor here in the shop,' she told him.

'Yes?' said Jon, as his brain made connections between fire damage, insurance policies and compensation.

'Is this something you requested?'

'No,' replied Jon. 'I think they just show up automatically, don't they?'

There was a pause on the other end of the line.

'The thing is,' whispered Katherina, 'he wants access to the basement.'

# 13

From the moment the claims assessor stepped through the door of Libri di Luca, the atmosphere changed. Katherina felt instantly ill at ease as his enquiring gaze swept over the boarded-up windows, the exposed floor and from there up to the bookshelves and balcony. There was no love for books in his eyes, just a cynical appraisal of what he saw, calculated in square metres and percentages.

Up until then it had been a good day. There wasn't a cloud in the sky, and even though it was cold, Katherina had enjoyed the bike ride from the Nordvest district into town. In the shop she started cleaning up. The bucket of vinegar had done its job, and the last whiff of smoke disappeared after a thorough airing. To add a little ambience to the room, she had brought up a five-branched candelabra from the basement and lit the candles. Somewhere deep inside she felt herself gloating at the idea of lighting small flames in a place where they had so recently fought much larger ones.

Not even the four or five customers who had appeared over the course of the day had bothered her – on the contrary, she had discreetly steered their attention to a couple of excellent purchases.

The only thing the man told her was his name, Mogens Verner, and the fact that he was a claims assessor who 'was going to look things over'. Under his light trenchcoat he wore a dark-blue suit, and under one arm he carried a notebook and a pocket calculator. At no time did he ask for permission to take a look around, nor did he ask Katherina any questions. In silence he surveyed the ground floor, paying special attention to the display windows and the floor. He quickly scanned the bookshelves without focusing on any individual titles. It was only when he climbed the stairs to the balcony that Katherina sensed that something was very wrong.

She didn't honestly know why he needed to go up there. Even from down below it was clear that the only damage the fire had done was on the underside of the balcony, and not on the mezzanine itself. In addition, he started lingering over the books, long enough to read the titles and the authors' names. Some of them he even wrote down in his notebook.

Although Katherina remained below, she could easily follow his survey of the contents of the glass cases above. She also noticed that he was very focused and only a few disruptive images interfered with his thought process. But there was one that showed up a number of times, though not long enough for her to make out the details. It was a picture of two men sitting across from him in a café. One was tall with red hair and deep-set dark eyes. The other had grey, close-cropped hair and seemed jovial and forthcoming. Both were wearing suits. Katherina was convinced she had seen the grey-haired man somewhere before.

As the claims assessor started down the stairs, Katherina made sure she was standing at the foot so that they would meet. He nodded to her and then made for the stairs down to the basement.

'Excuse me, but where are you going?' she asked sternly.

'I have to evaluate the entire property,' he said. 'That includes the basement.'

'Nothing was damaged down there,' said Katherina. 'The fire department didn't use any water indoors, so there can't be any water or fire damage.'

'Nevertheless,' said the man with a sigh, 'it's my job to inspect all the rooms.'

'I'm afraid I can't permit that,' said Katherina. 'Not without the owner being present.'

'The owner?' The claims assessor expressed surprise. 'He's the one who requested the appraisal.'

After the phone conversation with Jon, Katherina persuaded the claims assessor to come back in half an hour. He wasn't pleased. With rising irritation he tried to explain that he had other appointments that day, and that the case couldn't be resolved without his final evaluation. His mood hadn't improved when he returned thirty-five minutes later and Jon still hadn't turnedup.

'What should we do now?' he was asking just as Jon opened the door to the shop and came in, out of breath.

Katherina smiled with relief and motioned towards Jon as he came over to them.

'Mogens Verner,' said the claims assessor, holding out his hand.

Jon shook hands with him.

'Jon Campelli. I'm the owner of Libri di Luca.'

'You're the owner?' replied the claims assessor in astonishment, letting go of his hand as if he'd had an electric shock.

'Yes, is there something wrong?'

'I think there's been a misunderstanding,' said Mogens Verner, smiling uncertainly. 'You really must forgive me.'

'What do you mean?' asked Jon. He pointed at the windows. 'The fire damage isn't a misunderstanding.'

'That's not it,' explained the claims assessor, who was now bright red in the face. 'Although I generally work as a claims assessor, in this case I wasn't hired to evaluate the fire damage. My assignment is to evaluate the shop and its contents for the purposes of selling the property.'

'Selling?' Katherina burst out, giving Jon an alarmed look.

He shook his head. 'That's not something I requested.' He turned to look at the stranger. 'Who hired you?'

'The buyer and . . . well, I thought he was the owner,' replied the claims assessor, clearly embarrassed about the situation. 'I'm afraid I can't reveal their names.'

'Don't you think it's rather strange that one of them would purport to be the owner?'

Mogens Verner nodded. 'Yes, and again I apologize. I'm going to straighten this whole thing out as fast as possible.' He put out his hand again. 'I'm sorry for wasting your time.'

Jon shook hands with the man, and Katherina did the same before he vanished out of the door as quickly as he had arrived.

'What do you think that was all about?' asked Katherina.

'I have an idea,' replied Jon. 'Do you remember the article I had with me on the night the shop caught fire? The man in the photo is one of my clients who's been asking questions about Libri di Luca, wanting to know whether I plan to sell it or not. He was quite insistent.'

Katherina nodded and quickly went behind the counter to rummage through the drawer. In all the commotion when the shop was attacked, the article had ended up on the floor, but she remembered tossing a bunch of loose papers into the drawer when she was cleaning up. Triumphantly she pulled out the article and studied the picture.

It was definitely the same man she had glimpsed in the thoughts of the claims assessor.

'The strange thing is,' Jon went on, 'that I was actually talking to him, to Remer, a few hours before you rang. I even made it clear to him that I didn't want to sell.'

'Some people won't take no for an answer,' said Katherina and told him about the image she had picked up of the two men in the café.

'The other man could be Remer's bookseller friend,' said Jon. 'You didn't recognize him?'

Katherina shook her head. There had been something disturbing about the red-haired man. Images she received in this way were often strongly coloured by the individual's perception of the situation in question, and something had made the claims assessor nervous at that meeting in the café. In reality the man was probably not nearly so tall and his eyes weren't as deep-set or dark, but Mogens Verner had felt uneasy, maybe even threatened by the man, which made him appear as he did in Verner's memory.

'Do you think there's any connection with Luca?' she asked.

'No,' replied Jon hastily. 'Except that they're trying to snap up the bookshop at a propitious moment. I know Remer's type – always on the lookout for a good deal.' He paused, as if he were also trying to convince himself, before he went on. 'Besides, he's not part of the bookselling trade, so how would he know anything about what's really going on?'

'I have no clue about the business side of things,' said Katherina. 'But at least I can say that I've never seen either of them in Lector circles.' She raised her index finger. 'By the way, there's a meeting for receivers tonight. They've agreed to allow you to attend if you have time.'

'Hmm, I was actually supposed to work on the Remer case, but I'm not feeling very motivated at the moment, after that stunt he pulled today. Maybe I should get hold of him right now and tell him what he can do with his appraisal.' He got out his mobile phone and started pressing numbers.

'Is he an important client?' asked Katherina.

'Very important,' said Jon with a nod. He raised his eyes, stared straight ahead and his courage seemed to flag as she looked at him. Finally he gave her an embarrassed smile. 'Well, okay, maybe I should wait a while.'

When his mobile suddenly rang as he was holding it, they both flinched and Jon almost dropped it.

'Jon Campelli,' he said into the phone after fumbling it up to his ear. 'Kortmann,' he said, looking at Katherina. 'Yes, she's here.' He listened some more, shaking his head a couple of times. 'When?' He glanced at his watch. 'We can be there in fifteen minutes. Fine. Goodbye.'

Katherina expectantly studied Jon's face as he folded his mobile closed and stuck it in his inside pocket.

'Do you remember Lee? The IT guy from the meeting yesterday?'

Katherina nodded.

'He's dead,' said Jon. 'Suicide.'

'When?' asked Katherina, shocked.

'Last night,' replied Jon. 'He was found early this morning.'

'But suicide?' The man she had seen in the reading room of Østerbro Library hadn't seemed like a candidate for suicide. On the contrary, he radiated an overbearing arrogance which, even though it was annoying, didn't seem outright self-destructive.

Jon shrugged. 'Kortmann isn't convinced either. He wants to meet us at the flat where it happened. I think it's best if we both go over there now.'

Katherina closed up the bookshop and they drove over to the Sydhavn district in Jon's car. Darkness was in the process of taking over the day, and by the time they reached the place, the sky was coloured from deep blue to red.

Lee's flat was in a complex with a view of a commuter-train station and several other grey blocks of flats. Katherina shivered as they climbed out of the car, both from the cold and from the surrounding atmosphere. The car park in front of the building was half-filled, but one car stood out. Among the Polos, Fiats and a long row of Japanese vehicles was a big black Mercedes. In the dark it looked empty, but as they approached a light went on above the back seat. In the glow of the light they could see the outline of someone in the driver's seat and another figure in the back.

When they reached the Mercedes, they recognized Kortmann as the person sitting in the back. He motioned them closer and gestured towards the back door. The inside of the black Mercedes had been customized. Half the back seat had been removed and the floor had been lowered so that Kortmann could easily roll his wheelchair right into the car. The front passenger seat had been turned round so that anyone sitting there would be riding backwards. Jon sat down on this seat while Katherina got in next to Kortmann.

As if on command, the driver got out as soon as Katherina closed the door. Kortmann made sure the driver was far enough away before he started talking.

'Lee was found this morning by one of his colleagues. They both worked in Allerød, north of Copenhagen, and commuted together in Lee's car every morning. The colleague usually met Lee at his flat because he had a tendency to oversleep. He would often stay up all night, working. That's why his colleague even had his own key, and that was how he happened to find Lee, not asleep but dead.' Kortmann took a deep breath. 'The police found several empty ampoules of insulin on the nightstand. Lee was apparently diabetic. In addition, they found a letter which, according to the colleague, had Lee's signature on it.'

'So it was suicide?' asked Jon.

'All indications are that he took an overdose of insulin,' said Kortmann. 'The police are convinced and have closed the case.'

'But you don't agree?'

Kortmann glanced at Katherina for a moment. For once there was no trace of suspicion in his eyes; it seemed that he was trying to gauge her reaction to what he was telling them.

'I'd like to be sure,' he said. 'Right now this type of coincidence seems highly suspicious, and we shouldn't rule out any possibilities. Partly so as not to overlook anything, but also so we don't panic. Both things could destroy us.'

'But if the police couldn't find anything—' Jon began.

'The police found what they were looking for. They were looking for a suicide and that's what they found. He fitted the profile: young loner-type with no girlfriend or family or social network. Even his colleague confirmed that Lee sometimes seemed paranoid.'

'Then what is it we're looking for?' asked Jon.

'Two things,' replied Kortmann. 'First, any sign that it wasn't suicide after all. Second, we need to know what Lee found on the Internet, if he actually did find something.'

'Are we going to break into a dead man's flat, or do you have a key?' asked Katherina without concealing her sarcasm.

'I actually do have a key, now that you mention it,' Kortmann calmly replied as he pulled an envelope out of his inside pocket. 'Don't ask where I got it.' He handed the envelope to Jon. 'I'll ring while you're up there.'

Jon and Katherina got out of the car, passing the driver on their way to the stairwell. He nodded to them gratefully, rubbing his hands up and down his shirtsleeves as he jogged back to the car.

The flat was on the fourth floor, with the entrance from a hall-way with access to nine other flats. As they walked past the cell-like doors, they could hear TVs blaring, children shouting or crying, and petty quarrels brewing. The only thing that Katherina could sense being read were the Danish subtitles to American movies or sitcoms, and as always with those sorts of texts, the images they evoked were vague and diffuse.

At Lee's flat Jon shook the key out of the envelope and unlocked the door. They waited to turn on the light until the door was shut. A rice-paper ceiling lamp revealed a small entryway with a cramped kitchen to one side and a toilet on the other. Straight ahead was the flat's only real room, a space that was a good thirty square metres with windows running along one whole wall.

Even though they could still hear a television from one of the neighbouring flats, Katherina felt as if they'd stepped into a vacuum. It was less than twenty-four hours ago that Lee had died here, but the flat seemed abandoned and devoid of personality.

Jon turned on the rest of the lights, and they silently walked through the flat, careful not to disturb anything or make any un-necessary noise. The kitchen bore all the signs of a bachelor. Dirty dishes and fast-food containers covered most of the table, and large sections of the floor were littered with empty bottles in bulging plastic bags. The toilet hadn't been cleaned in months, and Katherina stayed only long enough to find out that the small medicine cabinet behind the mirror contained nothing more than shaving gear, a toothbrush and other toiletries.

The main room was obviously where Lee had spent all his time. Two walls were covered with shelves filled with books. Against the third wall stood a chest of drawers, a nightstand and a bed – or rather, a bedstead, since the mattress had been removed. In front of the windows was a wide table on which stood two black computer monitors and a printer. The window ledge was overflowing with books and big stacks of printouts that threatened to topple over if anyone got too close.

For a moment Katherina stood in the doorway and looked at the empty bedstead before she stepped inside the room. She wasn't sure they were welcome here, not even if Lee had been alive, and an invisible barrier seemed to have stopped her in the doorway. It was the bookcases that finally made her cross the threshold and approach the rows of books. In contrast to the disarray that marked the rest of the flat, the books had been meticulously arranged, and they were all in very nice condition.

'What sort of books does he read?' she asked Jon, who was crouched down next to the computer table. He pressed a button under the table and the monitors came to life. Then he stood up and joined her in front of the bookcase. She followed along as he scanned the titles.

'A lot of science fiction and fantasy,' he said after looking over the shelves. 'But also some classics.' He pulled out a leather-bound volume and handed it to her. 'Joyce.' Katherina turned it over in her hands, opening it in several places at random. In the back of the book she found a small business card from Libri di Luca.

A couple of paces further along, Jon pointed to eight or nine other volumes.

'Kierkegaard, of all things.' He went on to scan the stacks of books on the window ledge and those piled up on the nightstand.

'I suppose we could say he had a wide range of interests,' said Katherina, setting *Ulysses* back on the shelf.

Jon nodded and went back to the computer, which in the meantime had finished booting up. He sat down and put his hand on the mouse. Katherina went to stand behind him and watched as he experimented with clicking on various buttons and menus.

'What are you doing?' she asked after a couple of minutes.

'To be perfectly honest, I don't know,' Jon admitted with a laugh. 'Computers aren't really my thing.'

Katherina giggled. There was something endearing about him as he sat there, fumbling with the unfamiliar equipment, well aware that he was out of his element. He was no longer the super-barrister but a human being with his own limitations, and he admitted as much.

At that moment his mobile phone rang. He took it out and studied the display.

'It's Kortmann,' he said, handing it to her. 'Could you talk to him while I keep working on this?'

Katherina took the mobile. 'Yes?'

'Are you inside?' she heard Kortmann ask.

'Yes, we are,' Katherina told him. 'Jon's inspecting the computer right now.'

'Did you notice anything else?'

'In the flat? No, not really.'

'What books was he reading?'

'Lots of different things,' Katherina replied. 'There are a couple of volumes of Kafka on the nightstand – that must have been the last thing he was reading.'

'Kafka?' repeated Kortmann. A few seconds of silence followed. 'Keep working on the computer. I'm going to have to leave now.'

'Okay,' said Katherina, but by then Kortmann had already rung off.

'Arghh,' exclaimed Jon in frustration. 'I can't get anything out of this.'

'Can we take the computer with us?' asked Katherina. 'Maybe someone else could help us with it.'

Jon broke out in a big smile. 'Of course. Why didn't I think of that?'

He got out his mobile again and punched in a phone number.

'It's Jon ... yes, I'm fine ... uh-huh, the case is coming along ...' He nodded impatiently as the other person finished talking.

'Listen here, Mehmet, I need to ask you a favour.'

# 14

It turned out not to be necessary to move the computer. Over the phone Mehmet guided Jon through various menus and programs, allowing him to locate the computer's IP address and switch off the security routines so that Mehmet would have access to the PC from outside. After less than five minutes Jon was able to lean back in his chair and watch as the computer was taken over. On the monitor in front of him windows were opened and closed at the command of the cursor, which dashed between programs like a bee in a field of clover.

'Okay, I'm in,' said Mehmet. 'What exactly are we looking for?'

'First of all, what were the last sites he visited on the Internet?' replied Jon. 'But otherwise just whatever he was working on, in general.'

'No problem,' said Mehmet. 'How much time do I have?'

'As much as you need. The owner isn't coming back any time soon.'

'In the slammer?'

'No, he's dead.'

Mehmet didn't say anything for a couple of seconds, and the activity on the monitor abruptly stopped.

'Was he a client of yours?' he asked. The cursor started up its dance across the screen again.

'No,' replied Jon, pausing before he went on. 'This has nothing to do with my job. That's why I also need to ask you not to talk about whatever you find.'

Again a moment of silence from Mehmet.

'I hope you know what you're doing, Lawman.'

'Take it easy. You know me.'

Jon glanced at Katherina, who had found a place to sit on the window ledge, far away from the bed, which she was staring at with a remote look in her green eyes. Her face was pale, and she had wrapped her arms around her body, as if trying to stay warm. She suddenly seemed very fragile.

'Listen, Mehmet, can you also shut down the computer by remote control?' asked Jon.

Mehmet muttered a reply, which Jon interpreted as affirmative. In the background he could hear keys tapping at impressive speed, and on the screen in front of him lines of illegible commands were appearing, followed by an equal number of incomprehensible replies.

'Then shut it off when you're done. We can't stay here any longer,' said Jon, standing up. 'I'll contact you later to hear what you've found out.'

'Okay, but drop by instead of ringing. For security's sake.'

'It's a deal. See you later, Mehmet.'

'Later.'

Jon hung up and stuck the mobile in his inside pocket. 'Are you okay?'

'Sure, I'm fine. Or rather . . . it's just so strange to think that it happened right here and such a short time ago.'

Jon nodded and cast a glance at the bedstead. It was hard for him to see how they were supposed to find anything the police might have overlooked. There was nothing on the nightstand but a pile of books, and there was no sign of a struggle. He had the feeling that the main reason Kortmann had let them inside was to find out what was on the computer, and not to discover Lee's fate.

'Come on, let's go.'

*

THE LIBRARY OF SHADOWS

Following Katherina's directions, Jon drove them to Sankt Hans Torv, where he found a parking place on one of the side streets. There was still over an hour before the meeting for receivers would start, and since neither of them had eaten, they went to an Italian restaurant on the square.

The colour in Katherina's face began to return, aided by Jon's attempts to take her mind off the flat in the Sydhavn district. He tried to talk about other things: his work, Italian food, trips abroad. They'd been given a table at the back of the restaurant where they could talk undisturbed, though for most of the meal they confined themselves to generalities. But it got more and more difficult to avoid mentioning Luca, or the bookshop, or the Society, and the awkward pauses in the conversation grew longer and longer.

Jon's thoughts were on the upcoming meeting. Luca had been a transmitter, and even though he was apparently the best of friends with everybody, his allegiance still must have been stronger to his own kind. For that reason, Jon had a feeling that he was about to enter enemy territory.

'What should I expect?' he asked, finally breaking the ice.

Katherina glanced around before she answered.

'In any case, a greater unity than among the transmitters.' She looked down at her hands. 'It can be very hard to be a receiver, especially in the beginning when you don't really know what's going on, so those of us who have been through it have a tight bond. We need each other, because no one else has any idea what it's like. Your father had some idea, and he respected us because of what we have to endure, but most other people think that the powers are just something we can switch off and on at will.'

'I'd go crazy,' said Jon.

'Many people do,' replied Katherina. 'Even more are branded as lunatics when they claim to hear voices.'

Jon nodded. He told her about his experience at the Clean Glass pub and the man who was drinking stout.

Katherina smiled.

'We know him well,' she said. 'Ole sometimes shows up at our meetings, but not very often any more. He's found his own way of keeping the voices at bay: alcohol. So we shouldn't expect to see him today.'

'Alcohol removes the voices?'

'For some people it mutes them, for others it makes the voices distorted and incomprehensible, which is even worse. We all have our own methods for keeping the voices at a tolerable level. The most skilful among us can mute them using special techniques, but those who aren't as lucky turn to other solutions. Some recite nonsense phrases or make certain repetitive motions to divert their focus, others go to extremes and resort to pain, by pinching or even cutting themselves.' She sighed. 'But the best method is to meet in a group.'

'Therapy?'

'In a way,' Katherina agreed reluctantly. 'It's always helpful to meet others in the same situation – to know you're not alone.' She looked Jon in the eye. 'As you can tell, our goal is to stay together as a group and help each other, *not* to take over the world or even harass a couple of booksellers. We simply don't have the energy for that.'

Jon nodded. He could see in her green eyes that what she was saying was more than just words.

She looked down as she rubbed her chin with her fingertips. 'Isn't it about time to go?'

From Sankt Hans Torv Katherina led the way along Nørre Allé. Across from the church they entered a doorway and went up the stairs of an older building. She rang the bell on a door with a big brass sign.

'Centre for Dyslexia Studies,' Jon read. 'Does dyslexia always go hand in hand with the powers of a receiver?'

'It's not a prerequisite,' she replied in a low voice. 'But more than a third of us are dyslexic, so it can't be just a coincidence.'

Behind the door they heard someone approach and undo the locks. A plump woman wearing a black dress opened the door. Her round face lit up with a smile when she saw them.

'Come in, come in,' she welcomed them, stepping aside. 'The others are already here.'

Katherina and Jon stepped into the hallway where rows of overcoats bore witness to the presence of more than twenty people.

'I'm Clara,' said the woman, shaking Jon's hand vigorously. 'I'm the head of the centre here.'

'Jon Campelli,' said Jon.

'You don't have to tell me that,' she said with a laugh. 'It's incredible how much you look like him – Luca, I mean. Besides, I saw you at the funeral.'

After they took off their jackets, Clara hustled them down the long corridor towards a white panelled door that stood open at the end of the hall. A buzz of voices streamed towards them from the room beyond. The sound stopped the moment Jon, who was first, stepped inside. Around an oval conference table sat at least ten people, with the same number or a few more seated along the walls.

'Hello,' said Jon, raising his hand in greeting. Everyone nodded and murmured in return.

'Sit down here at the end,' suggested Clara, pointing to two empty chairs at the table.

Jon and Katherina sat down, carefully observed by the others. Clara took her place at the opposite end of the table.

'As I mentioned,' she began, 'we have the pleasure of meeting with Luca's son, Jon, and our own Katherina, of course.' She smiled. 'Let me start by offering my condolences on Luca's death. He was a close friend to all of us, and we considered him one of the group. We miss him very much.' Scattered nods and murmurs of agreement were heard from all sides.

Jon nodded his thanks. He noted that the women were in the majority, making up about two-thirds of the group, but it was hard for him to see all their faces. The people seated around the table were lit from above by a long, oval lamp, but the light didn't reach all the way out to the walls, where the rest of the members sat. Some of them he glimpsed only as shadows or partial shapes, with the top half hidden in darkness.

'That's why we will do everything we can, of course, to help find out what happened,' Clara went on. 'We've followed the latest events with concern. We have nothing to gain from anything that has occurred, least of all from the loss of your father.'

'What function did he serve in your group?' asked Jon.

'First and foremost, he acted as an ambassador,' replied Clara. 'Up until the very end he was trying to reunite the Bibliophile Society, and without his efforts, the relationship between trans-mitters and receivers would be even worse than it is.'

'It's hard to imagine the relationship could be any worse,' said Jon.

'Things have escalated lately,' Clara admitted. 'But before these events started, we were actually very close to a reconciliation. It's not easy to forget twenty years of hostilities and mistakes – that requires a great deal of diplomacy and a willingness to compromise. You might say that Luca had already spent years laying the ground-work by holding evening readings at Libri di Luca, which was regarded by both sides as a neutral zone with a permanent cease-fire. But for the Society's part, the cooperation hadn't yet begun.'

'What would it mean?' asked Jon. 'Why is it so important to be united when your powers are so different?'

'Even though you haven't been activated yourself, you still must have some idea of how effective an instrument the respective powers that transmitters and receivers possess can be. But it's only when these powers are combined that their true force emerges. If a transmitter is supported by a receiver, the result is much more focused and the effect on the listeners is so strong that few can resist.'

'So it's a matter of power?'

Muted protests came from all sides, but Clara raised her voice.

'Power over the story, you might say. We would never dream of misusing our talents. The goal is to present the story as faithfully as possible and convey the message of the text as effectively as we can.'

'And yet these attacks have been occurring,' said Jon.

'That's correct,' Clara admitted with a nod. 'But there's no evidence that any receivers are behind them. We realize that Luca's death bears the mark of being provoked by a receiver, but it's also possible that he died of natural causes, or that his heart attack was prompted by something else.'

'Like what, for example?'

'Poison, or possibly shock,' Clara suggested, though she didn't sound very convinced.

'But if we assume that a receiver *was* behind it,' said Jon calmly, 'and all indications point in that direction, could it happen without you knowing something about it?'

Everyone sitting around the table turned to look at Clara. For a moment she glanced up at the ceiling and then shrugged her shoulders.

'I can't rule it out,' she said. 'But I find it very unlikely. We're a very tightly knit group and an act of betrayal is unthinkable. Besides, we've all enjoyed Luca's company, not just because of his personality and wisdom, but also in a purely practical sense, by training with him. Without his cooperation as a transmitter, our powers as receivers would not have reached the high level they have. Katherina here is a good example. If Luca hadn't taken her under his wing and trained with her almost every day, she wouldn't be one of the most skilled Lectors that we have today.'

Katherina nodded in agreement.

'Could it be a receiver outside the group?' Jon suggested. 'Someone you don't know?'

'In theory it could be a "freelance",' Clara said after pausing to think for a moment. 'But as a rule freelances aren't especially well trained, so they're not strong enough to kill someone. You have to remember that they often have no idea what their powers are, never mind what they might be used for. Sooner or later they end up with us, provided they don't get institutionalized, or worse.'

'Could it happen by accident? If you say they don't know their own abilities, could a freelance kill someone by accident?'

'That's very unlikely,' Clara said hastily. Her gaze shifted for a moment from Jon to Katherina before she continued. 'It requires a gradual build-up in effect, which in turn presupposes a great deal of training and self-control.'

'And nobody has ever left your group after having achieved the requisite powers? Someone who might have reason to seek revenge?'

'No,' Clara replied firmly.

Jon looked at the people who were visible in the light from the lamp. Some of them were whispering to each other, some were waiting expectantly with their arms crossed, as if challenging him to come up with a new and better scenario.

'So if the motive isn't revenge or power,' Jon summed up, 'then what is it?'

There was complete silence in the room. Some of those seated around the table exchanged glances, but most directed their attention at Clara.

'I didn't exactly dismiss either revenge or power,' Clara began, for the first time with a harsh undertone to her voice. 'I simply said it would be exceedingly doubtful that any of *us* would be driven by such a motive. In our opinion, this has to do with someone wanting to prevent the Society from reuniting. Someone who has something to lose, either in the form of power or prestige. The timing isn't coincidental. Only now, after twenty years of separation, did the attacks start up again because the prospect of reconciliation seems possible.' She took a deep breath. 'I wouldn't be surprised if the person or persons behind them also started the attacks twenty years ago. Someone who gained a certain status back then, and now is afraid of losing it.'

Jon fixed his eyes on Clara's. The woman who had earlier appeared so jovial didn't smile, just stared across the table at him without wavering. Those sitting around them studied first her, then Jon, as if they were betting on who would blink first.

'You mean Kortmann? That's a serious accusation,' Jon said at last.

'It's a serious situation. We're being threatened, and our very lives may be at stake.'

'So far it's the transmitters who have suffered the biggest losses,' Jon pointed out. 'Lee died last night. The police say it was suicide, but Kortmann thinks otherwise.'

Clara nodded, as if she already knew about it, but many of the members began whispering and casting looks of astonishment at others in the room.

'I'm sure he does,' she said. 'Even though we didn't know Lee very well, we're sorry about what happened, but that doesn't change our suspicions. Lee wasn't old enough to have taken part in the events back then, and that alone could present a risk for those involved. Maybe he got in the way.'

'Maybe he just took his own life,' Jon insisted. 'The police found a suicide note with his signature.'

'The question isn't really whether he committed suicide or not,' said Clara. 'Though it's very likely that he did. Kortmann is not the only one who has connections to the police.' She smiled. 'The real question is, what drove him to do it?'

'He didn't seem like the type who would allow himself to be pressured into something so drastic,' Jon emphasized.

'All the more reason to be sceptical,' said Clara and then she abruptly fell silent, even though her lips had been about to shape her next words.

Jon sensed there was something he had overlooked. Clara stared at him with an expectant, almost inquisitive expression, as if she'd given him the first part of a sentence that he needed to complete himself.

'You're forgetting that the man you're accusing was the one who initiated this meeting.'

'Not at all,' replied Clara, smiling wryly. 'What would suit him better than to get someone who doesn't belong to the Society to carry out the investigation, someone who isn't aware of his powers, someone he thinks he can influence?'

Jon was about to object when Clara stopped him by raising her hand slightly.

'But I think he's miscalculated, Jon. It may well turn out that he made exactly the right decision, but for all the wrong reasons. Your demand to have Katherina participate in the investigation has convinced us that you're the right person for the job.' She smiled, this time in a friendly and accommodating way, as if exonerating him.

'Thanks for your trust,' said Jon. 'But I've never been accused of being a puppet before. I think you're mistaken about Kortmann. It seems to me that he wants to get to the bottom of this, and that he'd like to see the Bibliophile Society reunited.'

'I hope you're right,' said Clara.

'It's possible that he did campaign for a split back then,' Jon went on. 'But I sense that today he regrets it, or at least he has come to doubt it was the right solution.' He shrugged. 'Maybe he has just become more mellow over the years.'

'Which brings us back to the starting point,' said Clara. 'What's happening now is damaging to all of us, so how can we help you, Jon? What are you going to do?'

No one said a word, and Jon felt as if a blinding spotlight had been directed at him, ready to show his slightest movement. He noticed that his palms grew warm, and he suppressed an urge to shift position in his chair.

'*We* are going to start by studying the individual incidents,' Katherina broke in. 'It's important to find out for sure whether what's been happening was planned or just coincidence. If there's a connection, we have to ask: who might gain by doing this? And in that case, what would they get out of it?'

Jon nodded, sending her a grateful smile.

'I agree completely,' he said and then paused. 'I'm convinced that there's a connection between the events of today and what happened twenty years ago. That fact alone – a gap of twenty years – limits who might be involved.'

After the meeting Jon drove Katherina to her flat in the Nordvest district. They said very little during the drive. Jon was going over the meeting in his mind, but he had a hard time coming to any conclusion. In reality he ought to have been insulted to be called Kortmann's lapdog, yet he felt they did support him, even though he had come to Kortmann's defence. He sensed that the receivers expected even more from him than the transmitters did. They had hopes for what he might do – at the same time they had secrets they wouldn't voluntarily disclose, which he was going to have to dig up on his own.

'This is it,' said Katherina, pointing to a dull yellow building with green aluminium balconies. The exhaust from the traffic had turned the yellow brick almost grey in patches. Holes in the asphalt and the broken pavement bore witness to years of poor maintenance.

Katherina opened the car door but hesitated before getting out.

'I'm going to visit Iversen tomorrow,' she said. 'Would you like to come along?'

Jon nodded, prompting a warm smile to appear on her face.

'See you,' she said, putting her hand on top of his and giving it a squeeze. 'You did good today.'

She got out and closed the door behind her.

# 15

If time hadn't been on Katherina's side that day, they would have arrived too late to save Iversen.

It wasn't often that Katherina felt that time was particularly kind to her. She had often pondered what her life would have been like if circumstances had delayed her enough that certain events never took place or had turned out differently. If she'd been a little faster getting dressed on that morning when she went out with her parents in the car, or if she had insisted on changing clothes one more time, the accident never would have happened. The truck would have passed them by, either before or after that hill where her father was overtaking the tractor in front of them, and it would have left them uninjured and unaware of the family's alternative fate.

On those occasions when chance and timing coincided to her advantage, she didn't always recognize it as such. Yet she had given a lot of thought to what might have happened if she hadn't gone past Libri di Luca at just the right moment on that day when Luca was reading aloud from *The Stranger*. Katherina was convinced that if she had walked past either before or after Luca gave the reading, she never would have met Luca or Iversen or the receivers, and as a freelance she might have even gone insane or taken her own life.

That was why, afterwards, she appreciated the fact that Jon picked her up when he did, and not ten minutes later.

They met at the bookshop, where the glazier had just finished installing the new windows. After having so little daylight inside the shop, everything seemed transformed when the afternoon sun found its way through the new panes of glass. Columns of illuminated dust motes fell across the floor, and the letters of the shop's sign cast sharply delineated shadows on the exposed floorboards.

It was mid-afternoon, and Jon told her he'd decided to take a couple of days off, which had not been well received at the office. Even though the lawyers were entitled to do so, it was apparently frowned upon if they took time off in lieu of overtime pay. Extra hours were not regarded as time they could actually draw on; rather they were considered a status symbol, useful only for bragging rights or to substantiate their martyrdom.

Katherina listened in silence to Jon's description of the law office environment as they drove out to the State University Hospital. He talked non-stop until they reached the hospital, but he seemed to sink back in his seat the moment he turned off the engine and stopped his complaints. He looked as if he'd just awakened from a dream and needed time to figure out where he was before he could continue. They sat in the car for a moment, staring through the windscreen at the grey hospital building, before Katherina got out and Jon followed.

'He's been moved to a private room,' explained the nurse behind the counter.

'Is he all right?' asked Katherina in alarm.

'Yes, yes,' the nurse assured them. 'He's fine. We just thought it was better for him to have his own room, considering his condition. He's had quite a shock, but he's getting better, especially after that young man brought some books for him.' She smiled.

'Pau?' asked Katherina.

'I didn't get his name. He was here yesterday, a young man, he was bald, and wearing those baggy trousers that seem to be in style these days.'

Katherina nodded.

'You'll find Svend Iversen in room five-twelve,' the nurse said, pointing down the hall to her left. 'He's alone now.'

They thanked her and walked down the corridor she'd indicated.

'How thoughtful of him,' said Jon in a low voice.

'Yes, it's not like Pau,' replied Katherina.

They stopped at the door to room 5-12, and Jon knocked. There was no response, so Jon knocked again, this time louder. Katherina thought she heard a rhythmic banging from inside the room, like two pieces of metal being slammed together.

'Iversen?' said Jon, pushing open the door. 'It's us, Katherina and . . .'

From the doorway they both had a full view of the small private room, which had space enough for only the hospital bed and a couple of visitors' chairs. The curtains were open and light was streaming in through the window and onto the white bedclothes, almost blinding them.

Iversen was sitting in the bed, his back erect and his right hand gripping the bed rail, which was rattling frantically because his whole body was shaking so violently. He was foaming at the mouth, and a disturbing hissing sound was escaping from his lips as saliva sprayed out with each spasmodic breath. Even scarier were his eyes, which were open wide and staring down at the duvet in front of him without seeing a thing.

'Iversen!' shouted Katherina and ran over to the bed, followed by Jon.

When they got closer, they could see that a book lay open in Iversen's lap. His left hand was holding the volume, gripping it tightly in spite of all the shaking. Jon reached for the book, but Iversen had such a grip on it that he couldn't wrest it from him. His body shook even harder, and Jon had to let go. He promptly grabbed the pillow from behind Iversen's back and pressed it down over the book, hiding the pages from the man's wild eyes.

As if Jon had turned a switch, the shaking stopped and Iversen's eyelids slowly closed as his old body sank back against the bed. His breathing was still fast and irregular, but the awful wheezing sound was gone.

'Go get the nurse,' said Jon as he removed the pillow and tore the book out of Iversen's hand.

Katherina dashed out into the hall and headed for the nurses' station, which suddenly seemed very far away.

'Help!' she cried loudly as she ran. She was quickly out of breath from running and shouting at the same time, but she didn't stop, even when the nurse came into view. She shouted again, motioning to the woman.

'Iversen,' she gasped, pointing back towards the room. 'He's had . . . he's had an attack.'

The nurse started running while Katherina stayed where she was, bending over and supporting herself against the wall to catch her breath. The blood was roaring in her ears as she gasped for air and her fingers began to tingle. Slowly she straightened up and stared in both directions. Patients were peering inquisitively from the doorways, some in wheelchairs, others wearing robes or hospital gowns. A doctor came running past her with a stethoscope bouncing round his neck.

Katherina clung to the railing along the wall as she walked back. With each step she looked around, studying the faces of the people who had begun to crowd into the hall. Everyone wore expressions of surprise and concern. Some whispered to each other as she passed, but no one was behaving suspiciously or tried to slip away.

Back at Iversen's room, they had hooked him up to an ECG, and the sound of his heartbeat cut through the room like a knife. The doctor was bending over the patient while the nurse adjusted the dials on the machine. Jon stood a few steps away from the bed, studying the scene with a worried look. In his hands was the book that Iversen had held on his lap.

Slowly the patient's heartbeat began to slow, and the doctor straightened up so that Katherina could see Iversen lying in bed. His face was white and his eyes were closed. His right hand was still holding the bed rail, but as she watched, it released its grip and dropped onto the bed.

'He's okay now,' said the doctor with relief.

Katherina went to stand next to Jon with her hands pressed to her cheeks. He put his arm round her shoulder and gave her a brief hug. It felt nice, and she leaned against him.

'I've given him a sedative,' explained the doctor, casting a quick glance in their direction and then looking back at his patient. 'He'll sleep for the next five hours. But he seems to be stable now.'

'What happened?' asked Jon.

'It was probably a panic attack,' said the doctor, sounding as if he believed it. 'It happens sometimes with patients who have gone through a traumatic experience. They relive the event, which can provoke a panic attack like this. It can be dangerous for a man his age.' The doctor nodded at them. 'It was lucky you were here, otherwise it might have ended with a heart attack.'

'And there's nothing else that might have provoked it?'

The doctor shook his head. 'That's very unlikely. The patient suffered no serious physical injuries in the fire, he has no lesions or any sign of a concussion, so I would rule out any other causes.'

Jon and Katherina exchanged glances.

'Can we stay with him?' Katherina asked the nurse.

'If you like. But as the doctor told you, he won't wake up for at least five hours.'

'We'll stay.'

Jon went to buy provisions while Katherina stayed at Iversen's bedside. She listened to his breathing. It was calm and regular. His face wore a peaceful expression, a sharp contrast to the wild grimace that had frightened her so badly only a short time ago. Of the two of them, Iversen was undoubtedly the one who felt most comfortable being there. Katherina didn't like hospitals, especially hospitals where they couldn't feel safe from attacks by receivers. She couldn't think of any other explanation – a receiver had to be involved, and Jon's expression had told her he'd come to the same conclusion.

It couldn't be a very nice way to die.

The image of Iversen's face, contorted with pain and fear, kept returning over and over again to her mind, and she regretted sending Jon off while she remained here alone.

The feeling of guilt resurfaced. She thought she was over it, but Luca's death and now this incident with Iversen had summoned up unpleasant memories. It was something that had happened so long ago, and for years she had kept the memory at bay, but it was like trying to cover rust with paint – sooner or later it would break through. She discovered that she was sitting there rubbing her chin, the spot where the scar had formed a small cleft.

The door opened, and Jon cautiously tiptoed inside with a plastic bag in his hand.

'How are things going?' he whispered.

'No change,' replied Katherina in a normal tone of voice. 'He's completely out of it.'

Jon set the bag on the bedside table.

'Newspapers, sweets, toothbrushes,' he said. 'We can borrow a bed tonight.' He took off his jacket, hung it on a hook behind the door and sat down in a chair on the other side of the bed.

Neither of them said anything, but Katherina was glad that she was no longer alone.

'Did you see anyone?' asked Jon after a long period of silence. 'I mean, out in the hall, immediately afterwards?'

Katherina shook her head. 'No one I recognized. That's the difficult thing about these powers – you can't see them just by looking at people. It's not like they walk around with a smoking gun behind their backs.'

'What's the range?'

'It varies, depending on the strength of a person's powers. A normal receiver, if you can say such a thing, would have to be in one of the adjacent rooms or on the floor directly above or below.'

'What about someone with your abilities?'

'A little further. Another floor, maybe two.'

'But it's not necessary to see the person?'

'No, but walls reduce the effect.'

Jon nodded once and then kept on, as if lost in his own train of thought.

'So my father's killer could have been standing outside Libri di Luca?' he said at last.

'In principle, yes,' replied Katherina. 'But it wouldn't be easy to sneak up on your father, so I assume the perpetrator was inside the shop in order to achieve maximum impact.' She sighed. 'But Iversen isn't nearly as strong as Luca was.'

'Yet he must represent some sort of threat,' said Jon.

'Or a risk,' said Katherina hesitantly. 'Luca was very focused whenever he read, and it was impossible to pick up any impressions from him, other than what the text conjured up. It was as if he could close out everything else the moment he started reading. Iversen is different. He can be quite unfocused, like most readers, which makes it possible for us to catch glimpses of what he has on his mind.'

'So he's not good at keeping a secret?'

'Consciously he is,' Katherina emphasized. 'But in the presence of a receiver he could give himself away inadvertently.'

'And someone was afraid he had information that we shouldn't find out about?'

'That would at least explain why they went after him, even in his condition.' Katherina studied the man lying in the bed between them. The colour had returned to his face. Only the bandages covering the cuts and burns he'd received in the fire bore witness to the fact he wasn't well. 'The question is whether even he realizes what it is that we're not supposed to know.'

It would take seven hours before they were able to get an answer to that question. Katherina and Jon took turns sitting next to the bed while the other one slept in the room next door. Iversen woke during Katherina's watch, and while the nurse checked his vital signs, she tiptoed out to wake Jon.

The patient seemed remarkably lively and in good spirits, which convinced the nurse that it would be all right for him to have visitors. He was even hungry, so the nurse ordered a couple of sandwiches, which he promptly started to eat.

'I feel as if I've just run a marathon,' he said in between bites. 'My body is completely drained.'

'Do you remember anything?' asked Katherina.

THE LIBRARY OF SHADOWS

Iversen shook his head as he finished chewing.

'The last thing I remember is starting to read Mann.' He nodded towards the bedside table and the book Jon had taken from him. 'I think I'll wait a while before I try that one again,' he added, winking at Katherina.

'Pau brought it for you?' asked Jon.

'Yes, I rang him and asked him to come over with some reading material.' He laughed. 'Isn't it ironic? Every day you collect all sorts of books that you have the best intention of reading when you can find the time – and when you finally do have a chance, this happens.' He shook his head before he took another bite of the sandwich.

'I sure miss pizza,' he said after finishing his meal. The tray in front of him was covered with crumpled food wrapping. 'A good pepperoni with extra mushrooms.' He sighed. 'All right, so tell me what you've been doing.'

Katherina and Jon took turns telling him about what had happened since the fire – about visiting Kortmann, the meeting at the library in Østerbro, Lee's apparent suicide and the meeting with the receivers. During the whole report Iversen listened attentively with a solemn expression on his face. When they were done, he sat there for a moment, shaking his head.

'Pau told me about Lee when he was here. It's terrible.'

'What do you think?' asked Jon. 'Did he commit suicide?'

'If the question is, did he take the overdose, then I think the answer is yes. It's what happened beforehand that's interesting.' Iversen's eyes flickered from Jon to Katherina. 'What clouded his mind to such an extent that he would choose to commit suicide?'

'According to the police, he was a prime candidate: single, a loner and slightly paranoid,' said Jon.

'No doubt,' said Iversen. 'He may have been predisposed in that direction, but he still needed a big push before he would kill himself. What was he reading?'

'Kafka,' said Jon, sounding surprised. 'Kortmann asked the same question.'

Iversen nodded. 'Kafka can be read in many different ways.

Some people read his books as satire, others as nightmarish descriptions of society. You don't have to look very hard to find dejection or helplessness in Kafka's texts, and if the right places are reinforced, it's not difficult to feel rather depressed.'

'Reinforced by a receiver?' asked Jon.

'In principle a transmitter can do the same during a reading,' replied Iversen. 'But that would mean Lee wasn't alone. For a receiver it would be much easier. The person in question wouldn't have to be present in the same room, and if it was done subtly enough, Lee probably wouldn't notice he was being manipulated. He would feel himself becoming exceedingly depressed – so much so that he chose to take his own life.'

'Because of Kafka?'

'In actuality, almost any text could be used, but Kafka has that underlying melancholy that makes it possible to influence the reader in a much less noticeable way than if he were reading *Winnie the Pooh*, say.'

Katherina hadn't said a word during the conversation. She surmised where it was heading, and even though she didn't like to admit it, the discussion confirmed her own suspicions. There was no longer any doubt that a receiver was involved in the events. That had become crystal clear for her when she saw Iversen sitting in bed with no control over his body. With Iversen's theory of Lee's suicide, she had to admit that it pointed in the same direction, which in turn settled any doubts surrounding Luca's death, at least for her. In her mind she listed all the receivers she knew, one by one, and evaluated their motives and ability to pull off something like this, but she came up empty.

'By the way, Clara is mistaken with regard to freelances,' said Iversen, as if he had read her thoughts. 'I know of at least one receiver who was thrown out of the group.'

# 16

Jon could see from Katherina's reaction that this was news to her too. She sat up straight and leaned forward in her chair in order to hear better.

'Who?' asked Jon and Katherina at the same time.

'Strange that I didn't think of this before,' said Iversen, with a slight shake of his head. He closed his eyes for a few seconds. 'Tom,' he said, opening his eyes again. 'His name was Tom. Nørregård or Nørrebo, or something like that. Tom was a receiver, quite a good one, but a bit of a loner, as far as I remember.' Iversen nodded towards Katherina. 'It was before your time. In fact, it must have been around . . .' He opened his eyes wide and looked at Jon. 'I think it was more than twenty years ago. While your mother was still alive, I'm sure about that.'

'What happened?' asked Jon. 'Why was he thrown out?'

'It had something to do with a woman,' said Iversen, shaking his head. 'Sorry, but my memory isn't what it used to be, and it happened a long time ago. As far as I remember, he misused his powers as a receiver to get in bed with a woman. According to rumour, there was more than one, but in any case he got caught and was thrown out of the Society. He was a close friend of Luca's, and Luca was actually the person who exposed Tom and who assumed the heavy responsibility of banishing him.'

'Banishing? That sounds a little harsh,' said Katherina.

Iversen shrugged. 'It was a matter of repeated offences, and in a group like ours it's essential that we trust each other.'

'But wasn't it more dangerous to have him running around loose?' asked Jon. 'What if he gave himself away? What if he revealed his powers, or even put an end to the Bibliophile Society?'

'Luca thought it was best,' replied Iversen. 'And back then no one ever questioned his word. At that time Luca was the head of the Society, and apparently he succeeded in persuading Tom that he was in the wrong. Partly because no one but your father trusted him, and also because, according to Luca, Tom was so embarrassed by how he'd behaved that he could no longer look us in the eye. We never saw him again.'

'It doesn't sound as though he was particularly vindictive,' Katherina pointed out.

'No, that was my impression too,' said Iversen. 'Luca, who was the last person to speak to him, didn't say that Tom was especially angry or bitter, but the timing seems almost too coincidental.'

'So what would he want today?' asked Jon. 'He may have felt disappointed back then, but what about now? Why would he suddenly stop the attacks, only to start them up again twenty years later?'

They looked at each other, but none of them had an answer.

'Nørreskov,' Iversen exclaimed so suddenly that Katherina gave a start. 'His name was Tom Nørreskov.'

'We'll have to see if we can locate him,' said Jon. 'There can't be many guys in Denmark with that name.'

'It's even possible you might recognize him when you see him,' said Iversen. 'He spent a lot of time at Libri di Luca when you were still living with your parents.' He turned to look at Katherina. 'He was gone long before you came into the picture. What surprises me is why Clara didn't say anything about him. She must remember what happened.'

'I've never heard any mention of people being banished,' said Katherina. 'Maybe it's just one of those things that people don't talk about, like the family's black sheep.'

Iversen nodded. He suddenly looked tired as he sat there in bed with his arms crossed on his stomach and his head resting on the pillow. Jon sat up straight.

'Maybe we should let you get some sleep, Iversen.'

He tried to protest but Katherina agreed with Jon and they both stood up.

'We'll be right next door,' said Jon, pointing to the wall.

'Absolutely not,' retorted Iversen. 'Get out of here, both of you. You've got more important things to do than keep watch over a tired old man.' He raised his hand as if swearing an oath. 'I promise not to open a book until you get back.'

Jon knew that even though it was late, Mehmet was most likely still up, and it wasn't far from the State University Hospital on Blegdamsvej to his flat on Stengade. Besides, three hours of sleep and Iversen's new information had left Jon wide awake, so it wasn't difficult to decide to pay a visit.

Mehmet was still up, just as Jon had thought. Wearing headphones and almost motionless, he was sitting in the pale light from his computer screens while the rest of the room was in darkness. Jon and Katherina had to knock hard on the windowpane before he reacted. When Mehmet finally turned to look at the terrace door, he did so reluctantly, as if his eyes had to be forced to follow the movement of his head. When he saw Jon outside, his face lit up with a smile, and he took off the headphones as he got up from his chair.

'Hi, boss,' Mehmet said in greeting after pushing open the door. Only then did he catch sight of Katherina standing behind Jon in the dark. 'And you must be . . . ?'

'Katherina,' said Jon quickly. 'A friend of mine.'

Mehmet's gaze shifted from Katherina to Jon and then to his watch.

'Right,' he said, stepping aside. 'Come on in.'

'You're working late,' remarked Jon when they entered the room. Mehmet had turned on more lights so they could navigate between the teetering stacks of prizes.

'I don't have a slave job in some office that's open from nine to five,' replied Mehmet as he moved a couple of boxes off the sofa so they could sit down. 'My domain is the whole world and all time zones, so I schedule my work hours accordingly.'

'So it's a twenty-four-hour slave job?'

'Something like that,' admitted Mehmet, with a brief laugh. 'What about you, Katherina? How do you pass the time?'

'Books,' replied Katherina, adding: 'I work in a bookshop.'

'Really?' exclaimed Mehmet, his gaze flying over the boxes in the room. 'I just happen to have—'

'We're not here to buy anything,' said Jon, holding up his hands. 'Katherina works in my father's antiquarian bookshop, which I've now inherited.'

Mehmet gave Jon a searching look. 'I didn't really think you wanted to buy romance novels at three in the morning. You're here about the nerd's PC, right?'

Jon nodded.

Mehmet looked from one to the other of them. 'Was he a close friend of yours?'

'No,' replied Katherina and Jon in unison.

'I only met him once,' Jon went on. 'He was just an acquaintance.'

'Okay,' said Mehmet, relieved. 'Actually, it's wrong to call him a nerd. There's nothing wrong with nerds. At least they have a passion for something, whether it's stamps or aeroplanes or computers – and that's cool. Your . . . acquaintance, Lee, was a nerd-wannabe. A guy who may have worked with computers, but didn't have the abilities or the stamina to be a real nerd, though he did try to hang out with them by using the right buzzwords and references.' He cleared his throat. 'Lots of people think that nerds are losers, but the real losers are the wannabes, the pretenders, who think they can cheat their way to respect – very uncool.'

'But he had an IT job,' said Jon. 'He couldn't have been completely hopeless.'

'Well, you don't have to be a nerd to get an IT job,' Mehmet pointed out. 'Far from it. Wannabes can be smart enough at their jobs. Nerds are more difficult to control. They want to do their own thing, and they have a hard time taking directions about how to do their work.'

For a long time Jon had thought a nerd was merely someone who spent all his time at a computer – someone who was scruffy and ate pizza and drank Coke and had problems with the opposite sex. For him there was no measure of quality, other than that a nerd could do more than start up a word processing program. It was only lately that 'nerd' had increasingly replaced terms like 'eccentric' or 'fanatic' to express the fascination and mania that infected even stamp collectors. In that sense, Luca and the customers who came to Libri di Luca could be called 'book nerds', though they would undoubtedly prefer 'bibliophiles'.

Meeting Mehmet had expanded the boundaries of what Jon associated with nerds. Mehmet was well groomed and socially adept. He had a large circle of friends who were interested in things besides computers. More overtly, he was the son of Turkish parents, which meant that he looked significantly more healthy than the nerd stereotype, usually a pale, pimply teenager wearing glasses.

'I don't think of myself as a nerd,' said Mehmet, as if Jon had been thinking out loud. 'But I don't try to present myself as one either.' He went back to his desk to get a stack of printouts. 'Lee, on the other hand, did. He subscribed to various "nerdy" blogs on the Internet, and it's obvious he was trying to hustle himself a chance to get down with the cool guys. The answers and the pieces he wrote are banal and show that he didn't really get the terms he threw around.'

'What sort of blogs did he participate in?' asked Jon.

'Mostly computer-related,' replied Mehmet, scanning a piece of paper he was holding. 'Databases, networks, OOP and other programming areas. Plus some bizarre offshoots like brain research, literature and antique books.' He glanced up at Katherina. 'Is that anything you can use?'

'Maybe,' replied Katherina with a shrug.

'He wasn't especially active in the last three groups I mentioned.

It was like he just lurked and read the blogs without taking part in the debate himself.' He waved the papers. 'I'll give you the list so you can see what you can work out for yourselves.'

'Okay,' said Jon. 'Is there anything else you can tell us?'

'I looked at what he was doing on the Net lately,' replied Mehmet. 'It follows the same trend as the blogs. He looked at a lot of web pages with computer-related subjects, a number of libraries and literature pages. He also visited various porn sites and a few travel agencies.'

'Travel agencies?' Katherina said.

'Yes, he was looking at trips to Iraq and Egypt, but he didn't buy any tickets.' Mehmet stood up and handed them the stack of papers. 'But that's all in here too.'

Jon took the pages and leafed through a few of them.

'So that's your man,' Mehmet concluded. 'A slightly pathetic loner wannabe without many friends or social skills. Probably in his mid-twenties with a steady but not particularly demanding job in the IT field. Plus a couple of interesting deviations from the profile, which lean towards a romantic fascination with literature and exotic travel destinations.'

'Impressive,' said Katherina.

Mehmet shrugged. 'Do you know the saying: Show me your rubbish bin and I'll tell you who you are? The same can be said about a PC – but it's really much easier. The way we move around when we're surfing the Net says a lot about us, and the tracks are easy to follow if you know where to start.' Mehmet was leaning against his desk with his arms crossed and a satisfied smile on his lips.

'There's something else we'd like your help with,' said Jon, his eyes still fixed on the papers. 'We're looking for a man by the name of Tom Nørreskov. Can you find us his address?'

'If you can spell his name,' said Mehmet with a grin.

While Mehmet went to work behind his three flat-screens, Jon started going through the printouts from Lee's computer. Katherina sat next to him on the sofa and glanced around the room while he read. He sensed that she was receiving, but he wasn't worried. On the contrary, he found it reassuring, certain that she would pick up on anything he happened to miss. And at the same time, she could sense what information he thought was relevant even if he didn't say so out loud. The idea that she might be able to perceive more than he cared to reveal did cross his mind a couple of times, but he dismissed the thought, realizing that even if she did, it didn't really bother him.

Every once in a while Mehmet poked his head out between the monitors and asked them questions about Tom's age, job, education, known hangouts, and they made the best guess they could.

'Bingo!' exclaimed Mehmet after half an hour when the only sounds coming from him had been the clacking of the keyboard and a few outbursts that were impossible to comprehend. 'What do you want to know?'

Both Katherina and Jon got up and went over to the desk where Mehmet was leaning back in his chair, looking at the three screens with satisfaction.

'First of all, where does he live?' Jon asked.

'Vordingborg,' replied Mehmet. 'On a farm outside of town, as far as I can tell from the map. Twenty years ago he lived in Copenhagen, just as you thought, specifically in the suburb of Valby, but he moved to southern Sjælland fifteen years ago after getting divorced.'

'Divorced?' Katherina repeated.

'Yes, sixteen years ago. But then he does something strange,' said Mehmet, pausing for dramatic effect. 'First he gives up custody of his children, and then he changes his name to Klausen – that's why it took so long for me to find him. Only then did he move to Vordingborg, where he's lived ever since, according to the national register.'

'So he's a farmer?' asked Jon.

'I don't really think so,' said Mehmet. 'He's made enquiries with the local authorities about the leasing of land, so my guess is that he has rented out his fields. Plus there's a T. Klausen employed by the local rag as a freelance book reviewer.'

Jon nodded. 'That must be him.'

Katherina agreed. 'Is there anything else?' she asked.

'He doesn't have a phone and doesn't pay for a TV licence . . . What the hell does anyone do out in the sticks without a phone or a TV or a woman?'

'Read books?' Jon suggested.

'Ha! Yeah, well, I guess that's the only thing left.' He gave Jon a searching glance. 'Books again, huh?'

Jon didn't answer. 'Can anyone tell you've been searching for him?'

'If they swipe my computer, they can. Or if there's someone in Vordingborg Municipality who's in charge of watching for exactly that type of search and also has a contact with my Internet service provider.' Mehmet threw out his hands. 'I don't know what you're mixed up in, and I don't want to know either, but it would be very strange if those kinds of forces are in play just because of a bookworm.'

'Even so, make sure you remove any traces you can.'

'No sweat. You know me. I'm caution itself.' Mehmet nodded towards a spot on the ceiling behind them. 'I've even got security.'

They turned around. On the ceiling, just over the door to the garden, was a camera the size of a box of kitchen matches.

'I need to look out for myself, if the police aren't going to do it,' Mehmet explained with a touch of bitterness in his voice.

'Okay,' said Jon. 'But erase the tape of the last couple of hours, all right?'

'Tape?' Mehmet burst out laughing. 'You're a dinosaur, Jon.'

'I know, I know. Just erase it, okay? We've got to go.'

Mehmet shook hands with them.

'And thanks for your help,' Katherina added.

'No prob,' replied Mehmet, opening the door for them.

Jon was extremely happy with the visit. For the first time since he'd agreed to handle the investigation, he had the feeling they'd taken a step forward. He could sense that Tom Nørreskov had played a role in the whole thing, and they'd been lucky enough to track him down in spite of his attempts to hide. But Jon also suspected that this breakthrough was going to be short-lived.

They had to follow up on the lead while it was fresh, and that meant a trip to southern Sjælland. They decided that Jon would pick up Katherina the next morning around ten. They both agreed not to take anyone else along. Pau wouldn't be any use; on the contrary, his attitude might ruin the whole trip, and besides, someone had to watch the shop.

This probably wasn't the most convenient moment for Jon to neglect his career, but the sooner he resolved this matter, the faster he could get back to focusing one hundred per cent of his attention on his work.

Jenny sounded worried when he rang in to check for news.

'I don't think they're very happy that you're spending so much time out of the office,' she whispered. 'There are rumours they want to take you off the Remer case.'

'Nonsense,' said Jon. 'As long as Remer doesn't answer my queries, I can't do anything anyway. Halbech knows him. He knows how difficult Remer can be.'

'Maybe. But promise me you won't take any more time off after this.'

'No reason to be nervous on my behalf.'

'Take care of yourself, Jon,' said Jenny and rang off before Jon could reply.

Maybe he was mistaken about Halbech's patience, but there would be plenty of time to make amends – there was nothing like unpaid overtime to smooth things out with his boss.

In a strange way, the meeting with Tom Nørreskov, Klausen, or whatever he wanted to call himself, seemed far more urgent, as if the trip to Vordingborg were a race. Although Jon didn't know whether there was a prize, or whether he even wanted to win.

# 17

'How about if I come along and keep an eye on you?' asked Pau.

Katherina shook her head. 'Someone has to keep the bookshop open.'

An hour earlier she had got hold of a sleepy Pau on his mobile. He answered in monosyllables and with unhappy grunts, but after she told him about their visit to the hospital, his tone changed. When she explained they were going to visit a freelance, he finally allowed himself to be persuaded, and a short time later he showed up at Libri di Luca with rumpled hair and wrinkled clothes.

'But he might be dangerous,' Pau insisted.

'It's not even certain that he has anything to do with this,' she replied. 'Besides, I never said it was a man, did I?'

Pau shrugged and muttered something unintelligible.

Katherina took out her key ring and removed the key to the shop. 'You can close up at five if there aren't any customers. Here's the key to the front door.'

'I have a key,' replied Pau, sticking his hands in his pockets. 'I'll take care of things, don't worry.'

At that moment Jon's Mercedes pulled up at the kerb outside the shop. Katherina grabbed her jacket and bag and headed for the door.

'Have fun working,' she called, giving Pau a wry smile.

'Very funny,' he said, raising his hand. 'Now get out of here.'

Katherina went over to the car. Jon had climbed out and was standing there looking at the cloudless blue sky above the buildings. His nostrils flared and contracted in time with the deep breaths he was taking, as if he wanted to savour the city air one last time before their trip out to the country. It was the first time Katherina had seen him wearing something other than a suit. Instead, he had on jeans and a heavy woollen sweater. He looked good.

'How long will it take to get there?' Katherina asked after a slightly awkward hug.

'An hour, maybe an hour and a half,' replied Jon as he started the car. 'I don't think there's anything but tracks through the fields where his farm is located, so we'll probably have to take a roundabout route.'

Katherina waved to Pau, who was watching them from the new windows of Libri di Luca. He didn't wave back but instead turned round and disappeared further into the shop so she couldn't see him. The Mercedes pulled into the street, and they slipped into the flow of traffic.

Neither of them said anything until they got out of the city. Without the shadows from the buildings, the sharp autumn sun made them both squint.

'Do you think he's the one?' asked Katherina.

'It's possible, though I don't really see what his motive would be, twenty years after he was banished.' Jon paused. 'Unless Mr Nørreskov has gone insane from being alone. Maybe one day he just snapped, and he turned his anger towards the event that started his whole downward slide – his banishment.'

'But why did he stop, back then?'

'It could be that he was satisfied with splitting up the Society,' Jon suggested. 'It was Luca's project and an effective way to hurt him.'

Katherina thought about Pau's warning. He'd probably only meant it as a joke or as a means of getting out of being a bookseller for the day, but if Tom had gone crazy out on his farm, so isolated from other people, it suddenly didn't seem so implausible that he might react violently to being disturbed. If he really was the one, then he'd already committed murder.

'But this time merely hurting Luca apparently wasn't enough,' Jon went on, sounding bitter. 'This time Luca had to die.'

'Could it have been an accident? Maybe he just wanted to give Luca a scare, but he didn't stop in time.'

'You could answer that better than me. Are receivers capable of killing by accident?'

Katherina stared out of the windscreen at the road ahead. The sunlight made the surface gleam, giving it a raw, metallic sheen. All the guilt resurfaced and she felt her throat close up. The seatbelt seemed to tighten and the interior of the car suddenly felt very cramped. This time she couldn't disappear or evade the issue as she had been lucky enough to do many times before.

'Are receivers capable of that?' Jon repeated.

'Yes,' she replied reluctantly. 'I've killed someone myself.' She noticed that Jon gave her a sidelong glance, but she kept her eyes on the road and resisted the temptation to rub the scar on her chin.

'It was my Danish teacher,' she began. 'My favourite teacher. Her name was Grethe. I don't remember how old she was. You don't pay much attention to things like that when you're a kid – that's when adults have only two ages: grown-up and old. I was twelve. My problems with reading had begun to show up for real and I was often sent to the remedial class, separated from my class-mates. But not on that particular day.' She paused, shifting in her seat to find a more comfortable position.

'As usual, everyone was begging Grethe to read us a story. I was one of the most eager because I loved hearing stories read aloud. It made me forget my own reading problems. When Grethe read to us, we were all equal. That day she had brought a new book to school. *The Brothers Lionheart* by Astrid Lindgren. One of the other girls had brought a cake – you know the kind that's coloured bright green and covered with a thick layer of brown frosting that gets stuck in your throat? It took time to cut the cake into equal-sized pieces and hand them out to everyone in class. When we all had a piece, Grethe took her glasses out of a worn leather bag and put them on, pushing them into place on the bridge of her nose. As soon as she put on her glasses we were all as quiet as mice. She started reading. We'd already heard her read the Emil books and *The Children of Noisy Village* and other stories by Lindgren, but we weren't at all prepared for the sad beginning of *The Brothers Lionheart*. I was instantly gripped by the story. From the very first page I was so enthralled that I even forgot to eat my cake.'

Katherina fell silent. Jon turned his head to look at her for a moment as his way of urging her to go on.

'Grethe was incredibly good at reading aloud. Since then I've often wondered whether she had the powers, or whether it was just a natural gift. Whenever she read, we would be instantly hypnotized by her voice and cadence. As I sat there in class, I had the feeling that this book was something special and I didn't want the reading ever to stop. I wanted to hear the story all the way to the end, without any unnecessary breaks or disturbances. The book had such a beautiful voice, gentle and patient like a loving grandmother. Without knowing what I was doing, I clung to Grethe's presentation of the story, almost pulling her through it. The strong feelings that the brothers shared in the beginning hit me so hard that I must have unconsciously reinforced them and sent them back to Grethe.'

Katherina clasped her hands in her lap.

'The bell rang, but I didn't want the story to stop there and I refused to let Grethe go; I forced her to keep reading. The other kids in class started looking at each other in bewilderment. They'd never experienced anything like this before, but everybody was happy that the story was continuing because we'd reached the section where Jonathan is reunited with his brother. But Grethe had started to shake. You couldn't hear it in her voice, but her hands were trembling, and there was a hint of fear in her eyes behind her glasses. I didn't notice much, because I was so happy. I wanted to hear the whole story, know everything that happened, so I greedily forced Grethe to go on.' Katherina sighed heavily. 'It was only when one of the girls in the class started screaming that I realized something was wrong. Blood was running out of Grethe's nose and ears, pouring down over her lips and chin and neck. The spell was instantly broken. I was terrified and covered my mouth with both hands so I wouldn't scream. Grethe's voice stopped. Her body collapsed and toppled over onto the floor, making her glasses fly across the linoleum. Everybody else jumped up to help her. Some kids ran for help while one of the boys, whose father was a fireman, put Grethe in a first-aid position. But I stayed in my seat. I couldn't take my eyes off the body on the floor. Grethe's eyes were staring blankly at the linoleum and I didn't doubt even for a second that she was dead. I knew I had killed her.'

Katherina looked out of the side window, away from Jon.

'You didn't know what you were doing,' he said. 'How could you know?'

The feeling of guilt was back, full force. Hadn't she known? The incident in the classroom had taken place after she had first met Luca, who had warned her at the very beginning not to focus her powers too intensely. And even though she'd been totally immersed in the story, she had still picked up tiny danger signals, such as the fact that Grethe's body was shaking and the nervousness of the other kids. Yet in spite of everything, she had kept on going until it was too late.

'They said she had a cerebral haemorrhage. In biology class they showed us how something like that can happen. They went over the model of the brain and explained how blood pressure, veins and blood flow are all connected.'

'You didn't tell anyone about this?'

Katherina shook her head. 'Not until much later. Then I told Luca and Iversen and a couple of others in the Society. They were the only ones who would be able to understand.'

'What about your parents?'

'I'd already subjected them to enough, with my dyslexia and the voices I claimed to hear.'

Jon turned off the motorway and they began a lengthy drive along country roads through villages and woods and over hills. After a while, as they were driving past green fields, Jon slowed down. He pulled out a piece of paper from between the seats.

'There's supposed to be a turn-off on the left somewhere around here,' he said, leaning forward to peer out of the windscreen. A few hundred metres further along, he stopped the car. On the left a muddy, rutted track led across the field and disappeared into a grove of trees. Next to the track was a sign with the number 59 on it.

They looked at each other.

'Ready?' asked Jon.

'Ready.'

Jon turned the wheel and slowly drove along the rutted track. Even at that slow pace they were tossed about in their seats.

After twenty metres a sign appeared at the side of the road.

'"No trespassing",' Jon read.

Ten metres further on there was another sign.

' "Private property" and "Trespassers will be reported to the police",' Jon quoted. 'Not especially hospitable, is he?'

'He knows we're coming,' said Katherina calmly.

'What do you mean? Have you seen him?'

'No, but he can hear us.'

'Are you sure? We can't even see the farm yet.'

'The signs,' Katherina said. 'They're not just there to keep people away.'

Jon gave her a look of surprise.

'They act as a warning system,' she explained. 'He "heard" you read them.'

Jon stared at her for a couple of seconds in disbelief, until he realized what she meant.

'Now I get it.' He looked embarrassed. 'Sorry.'

'That's okay,' said Katherina. 'Such brief texts can't tell him anything about us except that we're on the way.'

They followed the track through the small grove of trees. More signs stood along the road. Others were fastened to tree trunks, and even though Katherina sensed that Jon tried not to read them, she still received their text: 'No admittance', 'Guard dogs', 'Private property'.

After a hundred metres they arrived in a big clearing, and there stood a white-painted farm building with three wings and a thatched roof. In many places the paint was peeling off the walls. Big green patches of moss covered the straw on the roof. One window was covered with plywood and the rest looked as if they hadn't been washed since they were installed. The perimeter of the clearing was filled with rusty farm implements that had long since served their purpose and had been left to fall apart.

Jon drove his Mercedes into the farmyard where grass and weeds had taken over most of the area from the gravel. A grey Volvo estate car was parked next to one wing of the building.

'That must be the main building,' said Jon, pointing to the one behind the Volvo. He parked in front of the estate car, and they got out.

After the echo from the closing doors had faded, the place was utterly quiet. Katherina savoured the silence as she looked around. The house they had decided was the main building was about a hundred square metres with windows a metre and a half off the ground. She couldn't see in, either because of the thick layer of dirt on the panes or because something was covering them on the inside. The two other wings were in worse shape. On one, half the roof had caved in; the other lacked both windows and doors.

Jon went over to the front entrance. A big sign with a lot of text was fastened to the heavy oak door.

'Don't read it,' Katherina warned. 'It's too long – it'll just make things easy for him.'

Jon nodded and looked the other way as he fumbled with the door knocker. The pounding sound echoed over the farm. Jon leaned close to the door to listen. Nothing happened. He glanced at Katherina and shook his head. He knocked again, this time a little harder.

Katherina went over to one of the windows and tried to peer inside, but a dark cloth prevented her from looking into the room. She tried the other windows facing the yard, but they were all covered with curtains, furniture or plywood.

'Hello! Anybody home?' shouted Jon at the door.

Katherina thought she saw a shadow in one of the empty

windows in the building with the collapsed roof. She slowly strolled towards what must have once been the stable. Again she saw a shadow, this time behind a windowpane that was so filthy it was impossible to tell what or who the shape was.

'Jon,' she called in a low voice as she kept walking towards the stable.

Jon stepped away from the front door and went over to her. 'Yes?'

She pointed at the stable without speaking.

The door was in the middle, facing the yard. It had once been blue but dry rot and wear and tear had turned it almost completely grey and it hung wearily from its hinges. Katherina gave it a shove. With a long-drawn-out screech the door reluctantly opened.

'Hello?' she called. 'Anyone here?'

She stepped inside with Jon right behind her. The space had not been used as a stable in a very long time. The stalls were filled with rubbish, the remains from the collapsed roof or crates and furniture.

'Over there,' said Jon, stepping past her.

At the other end of the stable, closest to the main building, a door opened and they saw a silhouette run out, slamming the door. Jon raced for the door, having to jump over crates and old junk blocking his way. Katherina instead turned on her heel and ran out into the yard and then over to the main house. She reached the corner of the building just as Jon came bursting out of the door. They continued on together to the gable end and then around to the back of the house. They didn't see anyone, but they did hear a door slam. Banging and pounding sounds revealed that the door was being emphatically bolted.

They slowed down and stopped outside a dark, solid-looking door with black metal hinges.

'We just want to talk to you,' shouted Jon, out of breath.

There was no reaction from inside the house.

'Tom?' Katherina ventured. 'We need your help.'

Jon knocked on the door.

'Tom Nørreskov? We know you're in there.'

They listened tensely.

'Go away,' they suddenly heard from behind the door. 'You have no business being here.' The voice was low and hoarse.

'We just want to talk to you, Tom,' said Katherina.

'I have nothing to say to you. Get out of here, or I'll call the police.'

'Won't you at least confirm that your name is Tom Nørreskov?' asked Jon.

'There's no Nørreskov here. My name is Klausen. It says that on the door. Now go away.'

'We know that you changed your name in eighty-six,' said Jon. 'We know that you were thrown out of the Society, and we know why.'

For several seconds there was no response from behind the door. Then they heard a faint muttering. Katherina and Jon looked at each other.

'It sounded like he repeated the words "thrown out",' whispered Jon.

'What are you whispering for?' yelled the man behind the door. 'Who are you? What do you want?'

'We just want to talk to you,' Katherina repeated. 'My name is Katherina, and Jon Campelli is with me.'

Again a couple of seconds of silence behind the door.

'Campelli?'

'Jon Campelli,' Jon confirmed. 'I'm the son of—'

He was interrupted by the sound of bolts being thrown. Slowly the door opened a crack and a head came into view. The face was almost completely hidden by hair and a beard. A pair of wide-open blue eyes looked Jon up and down.

'Campelli,' said the man again, nodding to himself.

'We just want . . .' Katherina began, but stopped when the man pulled the door wide open and took a step back.

'Come in, Jon, come in. I have a message from your father.'

# 18

Jon's feet suddenly felt very heavy. He couldn't lift them but just stood there staring at the man in the doorway. A tall, smiling man with a mass of hair, a lean body, probably even skinnier than his loose dark-green sweater and baggy cords intimated, and a slightly bowed back. His big beard was grey at the ends, and in several places it was matted and knotted.

'Come in,' said the man again, motioning them eagerly inside with bony fingers.

Jon felt Katherina's hand on his shoulder, and he slowly stepped through the doorway into the house. When they both stood inside a small dark hallway, Tom Nørreskov slammed the door behind them. They stood still in the dark, listening to him carefully locking the door. The air was rank and heavy.

'Excuse me,' said Nørreskov as he slipped past them. 'Just let me turn on the light.' A dim lamp in the ceiling came to life, casting a yellow glow over a cramped hallway cluttered with cardboard boxes of various sizes. 'I don't use it much myself. The light, I mean.'

He disappeared through an opening between the boxes, which led to another room, and there too he turned on a light. Katherina and Jon followed him into a big room. All four walls were plastered with newspaper clippings, pictures and countless little yellow slips of paper with hand-written notes. Multi-coloured strings were stretched between many of the pieces of paper, so the whole thing looked like a web of information, a paper version of the Internet. In the middle of the floor, right underneath the glare of a bare bulb, stood a big, worn leather chair, and in front of the chair was a Morocco ottoman that looked as though it had been punctured. All around the chair were stacks of books, in no apparent order.

Tom Nørreskov ushered them onwards into the next room, which was filled with bookshelves as well as a large sofa which, judging by the bedclothes, also functioned as a bed. In front of the sofa was a low coffee table covered with countless leather-bound volumes. He quickly gathered up the bedclothes and tossed them behind the sofa. After giving the cushions a cursory brushing with the palm of his hand, he motioned for them to sit down.

'We have a lot to talk about.'

Jon and Katherina sat down on the leather sofa while their host went to get the Morocco ottoman from the other room and placed it across from them. He kept his eyes fixed on Jon the whole time, with a little satisfied smile playing over his fleshy red lips.

'You said that Luca left me a message?' Jon began.

Tom nodded eagerly. 'You see, your father had a feeling that they were going to make a move soon, and in case something happened to him, and you turned up, I was supposed to give you this message.'

'Which is?'

Tom shook his head and broke out in a big smile. 'I'm so glad to see you again, Jon. You probably don't remember me, but I visited Libri di Luca many times when you were a boy.' His smile disappeared. 'I was very fond of your father. We were close friends, and he's the only one who ever visited me for all these years.'

'He came here?' said Katherina with astonishment.

'Once a month, I'd say. Usually on Sundays, when the bookshop was closed.'

'He never mentioned anything about that,' said Katherina.

'No, of course not,' replied Tom, a bit annoyed. 'That was all part of the plan.'

Jon had so many questions that he didn't know where to start. Even though he hadn't seen his father in years, this place and this man didn't fit at all with the image he'd had of Luca. And it seemed even less plausible that Luca would have made plans with a banished member of the Bibliophile Society, of which he was such a faithful defender. And to top it all off, Jon's own arrival was supposed to have been predicted, like some sort of resurrection.

'What's the message, Tom?' Jon insisted.

Tom regarded him with his clear blue eyes as he made a tent with his bony fingers. He was no longer smiling.

'Stay away,' he said finally.

'What?' exclaimed Jon and Katherina in unison.

'Forget what you think you know, sell the shop and get on with your own life,' said Tom, clasping his hands with his fingers interlaced. 'Turn around, get going and don't look back.'

'But—' Jon began.

'It's for your own good. Your father loved you more than anything on earth. He was so proud of you – your success in school, your travels, your career. He talked about you for hours, how smart you were, how you'd made a success of everything. Did you know that he went to a lot of your court appearances?' He shook his head. 'Probably not, but he did, and he was damn proud.'

'Then he had a strange way of showing it,' said Jon, crossing his arms. 'Why didn't he ever say anything?'

'Haven't you figured that out?' said Tom impatiently. 'He wanted to protect you. Luca preferred to be a terrible father than a childless one.'

Jon got up from the sofa and paced around the room with his eyes on the floor and his hands on his hips. He felt nauseated, no doubt because of the stale air in the house. How could anyone stand to live like this? It was impossible to think. The questions he'd been burning to ask only moments ago had now disappeared to be replaced by others, and he wasn't sure he wanted to know the answers.

'You mentioned a plan,' said Katherina as Jon kept pacing.

'I'm sorry,' said Tom, 'but I can't tell you any more. I promised to convey Luca's advice to his son, but I don't think it would be appropriate to involve him any further.'

Jon stopped and turned to face Tom. 'And what if I choose not to follow his advice?' he said angrily. 'I'm already involved. There are people who expect something of me, and other people who have tried to scare me off. So don't tell me I should just turn my back on everything and go on as if nothing ever happened, no matter how much I might want to.'

'I can see that,' Tom admitted. 'But I think you should—'

'I'm tired of being kept in the dark. Tell Katherina what she wants to know. What sort of plan was it?'

'Okay, okay.' Tom turned to Katherina. 'The plan. Yes, all right,' he began, nodding to himself. 'The plan was that we'd make them show themselves, or at least we'd find proof of their existence.'

'Who?' asked Katherina, casting a glance at Jon, who had resumed his pacing.

'We called them the Shadow Organization,' said Tom with a smile.

'Maybe you'd better start from the beginning,' Katherina suggested.

Tom hesitated, glancing at Jon.

'Go on,' Jon commanded.

Tom sighed. 'It all started with an obsessive idea,' he said. 'It was almost a game we had, Luca and I. I don't remember which of us came up with it first, but one day it occurred to us that there might be another organization besides the Bibliophile Society, a group that operated in secret, in the shadows. An organization different from the Bibliophile Society in that the members consistently used their powers for criminal activities or at least for selfish purposes.' He cleared his throat. 'It was mostly for our own amusement, a sort of in-joke. Soon we started looking through the newspapers for events that might support our theory. We'd show them to each other with a glint in our eyes. "The Shadow Organization has struck again," Luca used to say when he triumphantly presented a newspaper clipping about a politician who had suddenly changed his opinion, or a businessman who had done something unexpected.' Tom smiled to himself. 'It was of course nothing but our wild imaginations. We were younger back then, and our imaginative powers weren't nearly as ossified.'

Tom cleared his throat again, and Jon surmised he hadn't used his voice in a long time.

'The examples of events and coincidences began to pile up,' Tom went on. 'And finally we could no longer ignore the fact that there was a strong possibility that what we had invented as a private joke might be a reality. For a long time we dismissed the idea, but our eyes had become trained to see possible connections in the stories, and we found more and more events that indicated the existence of such an organization.

'What did the others say?' asked Katherina.

'We kept it to ourselves,' said Tom with regret in his voice. 'I suppose we were seized by some sort of persecution complex. One of our assumptions was that if such an organization had been kept secret from the Society, that must mean only one thing: that we had spies among us.'

'Who?' asked Katherina.

Tom shook his head. 'There were several candidates, but we never found any concrete proof. That was why we devised "the plan" to flush them out.'

Jon stopped pacing back and forth across the uneven floor and once again sat down on the sofa next to Katherina. Tom shifted his glance to Jon. There was sorrow in his blue eyes.

'The plan was that if one of us was thrown out of the Society for sufficiently unpleasant reasons, that person would end up being recruited by the Shadow Organization shortly afterwards.' Tom sighed. 'Simple and straightforward.'

He looked away from Jon and began surveying the room. His eyes scanned the ceiling, moved down the bookshelves and then across the worn floorboards. He seemed to be reorienting himself after a sudden awakening. He looked down at his hands.

'The first part of the plan was a resounding success,' he went on with a little smile. 'My supposed crime was so repulsive that everyone distanced themselves from me, and I think they were privately grateful that Luca was the one who took responsibility for banishing me. No one questioned the authenticity of the cover story, because who would make up something like that?' He let the question hover in the air for a moment. 'Then it was just a matter of waiting,' he continued, throwing out his hands. 'So that's what we did. And something happened all right, but it wasn't anything that even in our wildest imagination we would have—'

At that moment both Katherina and Tom got to their feet. They tilted their heads and looked up at the ceiling, as if they were listening for sounds on the roof.

'What?' asked Jon, looking from one to the other. Tom closed his eyes, his forehead deeply furrowed.

'No trespassing,' whispered Katherina, putting a finger to her lips. 'The first sign.'

Jon discovered he was holding his breath. Even though he couldn't hear anything, he could tell how tense the other two were. Katherina had closed her eyes, and very slowly she raised her hand towards Jon, to indicate he should stay seated. He didn't move.

'They're gone,' said Tom after more than a minute. He opened his eyes at the same moment as Katherina did, nodding in agreement.

'They?' said Jon.

'There were at least two people who read the sign,' Katherina explained. 'After that, nothing.'

'It happens often,' Tom reassured them. 'Folk get lost or try to take a short cut. Most of them turn round when they see the first sign.' He sat down again, and Katherina followed his example.

'I don't know many who can receive from such a distance,' said Tom, giving Katherina an appreciative nod. 'Luca told me about your powers.'

'He deserves all the credit,' said Katherina.

'That's one thing we have in common,' said Tom with a smile. 'I was his pupil, just like you. But we all have a natural limit, beyond which we can't go, no matter how zealously we train. For some people the limit is set much lower than what you've just displayed.'

'Can we get back to what we were talking about?' asked Jon impatiently.

'Yes, of course,' said Tom, but then he stopped.

'You were saying that something happened after you were banished,' said Katherina.

Tom nodded solemnly. 'Several things happened. First of all, the number of events increased. They were now so obvious that others in the Bibliophile Society also realized that something was wrong. But instead of looking outside the Society, they turned their attention on their own ranks. The accusations became rampant, and distrust grew between the two divisions of transmitters and receivers.' He fixed his eyes on Jon. 'Luca tried to keep the whole thing together, and he succeeded for a long time, even though factions arose, wanting to split the Bibliophile Society in two.'

'Kortmann?' Jon interjected.

'He was the spokesman for the transmitters, yes,' Tom confirmed. 'Kortmann was an ambitious man, but as long as Luca was at the helm, the group stayed together, however tenuously.' He stopped again and looked down at his hands.

'Then what?' asked Jon.

'Then . . . then your mother was murdered,' said Tom quietly.

In the back of his mind Jon had somehow known this would come. Ever since the reason behind Lee's suicide had been suggested, the possibility had been nagging at his subconscious. But he'd managed to suppress it. Now Tom's dry statement that the same thing had happened to Marianne struck Jon like a blow to the chest. He gasped for air and bowed his head as he concentrated on his breathing. Next to him Katherina shifted position. He nodded to indicate that he was okay.

'Luca was devastated, of course,' Tom went on. 'He blamed himself for what happened, as if he were the one who had pushed her from the sixth-floor window. Of course he knew that in a purely physical sense he hadn't had anything to do with it, but he was convinced that it was our investigation of the Shadow Organization that had provoked the murder. He couldn't use the knowledge. He didn't have the resources to do anything with it. Instead he opted out. Out of the Bibliophile Society, out of his family, out of life beyond the walls of Libri di Luca. The bookshop became his refuge during all his waking hours.'

'Yes, I know,' said Jon tersely. 'That part I remember very clearly.'

'He sent you to a foster home to protect you,' said Tom earnestly. 'He knew they wouldn't go after him; they'd go after the ones he loved. Marianne and you. After losing your mother, he wanted to do everything he could to protect the family he had left, even if it meant never seeing you again.'

Jon's feeling of nausea was getting worse. He heard what Tom Nørreskov was saying, registered the words and attempted to assign some meaning to them. In the world that Luca found himself in back then, there was probably some degree of logic to what he'd done. But compared with Jon's own memories from that period, the whole thing made no sense. The leap was too great from believing that his father hadn't wanted anything to do with him to accepting that he had practically sacrificed himself for his son's sake.

'Why didn't he ever say anything?'

'Out of fear. He didn't dare say anything to anybody. The risk that the Society had been infiltrated kept him from seeking help from the group. For a long time after Marianne's death he didn't even come to visit me. Where was he supposed to turn?'

'What about Iversen?' said Katherina. 'Couldn't he help?'

'He certainly did,' replied Tom. 'More than he knows himself, but only by offering support, as a friend and assistant in the bookshop. He made sure that Luca remembered to eat, and he kept him updated on what went on in the Bibliophile Society. The break between transmitters and receivers quickly became a reality after Luca resigned, and apparently that helped. The events stopped, or at least they were no longer as blatant for those who didn't know what to look for. Kortmann became the head of the Society on the transmitter side, while Clara took charge of the receivers. There was an idyllic sense of peace for a while.'

'So Iversen doesn't know about the Shadow Organization?'

'No,' said Tom firmly. 'It's not that we didn't trust him, but in some ways he's like an open book, if you'll excuse the expression. He would have ended up giving away what we knew about the Shadow Organization, completely inadvertently, of course, if he had found out what we knew. That's why we decided very early on not to involve him. For his own good.'

'What happened with the plan?' asked Katherina. 'Were you ever contacted by the Shadow Organization?'

Tom shook his head. 'Never.' He clasped his hands in front of him. 'But they might have had a hard time finding me. During that time I was pretty paranoid. Truth be told, Marianne's suicide nearly scared the life out of me, and I tried to protect myself as best I could. After a while I left everything behind and moved out here.' He let his gaze slide over the room. 'Only Luca knew where I was, or at least so I thought.' His red lips opened in a big smile. 'Until today.'

'Shh,' said Katherina suddenly, raising her hand.

Tom tilted his head to the side and closed his eyes. As he sat there on the ottoman with his hands clasped, he looked like a meditating monk. Jon turned to face Katherina, sitting beside him.

'No trespassing,' she whispered.

Jon nodded that he understood and leaned back against the sofa. Right now he wished he could hear what they heard so that he could at least participate.

'Private property,' said Katherina.

'The second sign,' Tom interjected.

Jon looked from one to the other. They both had their eyes closed and were sitting in the same position as when it started, concentrating and not daring to move.

'Trespassers will be reported to the police,' growled Tom. 'They're in the woods.'

'Three people,' Katherina added.

If he hadn't been afraid of breaking their concentration, Jon would have jumped up and run outside to see who was approaching. But he didn't dare do anything except sit motionless on the sofa. Jon let his eyes scan the room. The mosaic of book spines made the room seem less empty than it actually was, maybe because the books were apparently so randomly placed. He leaned forward towards the nearest bookshelf.

'No, Jon,' exclaimed Katherina loudly.

# 19

'MichelFoucaultGünterGrassWordsAndThingsLullabyThomas
PynchonMason&DixonRichardFordSusanSontagFinnCollinThe
AnatomyOfHatredTheLastValkyrieSonOfTheWindArturoPérez
ReverteMarcelProustSnowFalling . . .'

The flow of titles and author names that Jon was reading
drowned out the reception of the individuals who were on their
way to the farm.

'Stop it,' Katherin commanded.

Jon glanced at her in surprise, but his expression quickly
changed to remorse. He fixed his eyes on the floor.

Katherina closed her eyes and again focused on receiving, but
she couldn't pick up anything more. What did that mean? Had they
stopped, or were they in between two signs? Even though it was
convenient to receive from a distance, it was also frustrating not to
be able to see what was really happening.

She jumped up from the sofa and ran through the rooms to the
door. There she fumbled with the three bolts that were preventing
her from exiting. When she finally flung the door open, the other
two were right behind her.

Outside all three of them ran towards the track. Jon was faster
than the others, so he went on ahead until he reached the first turn.
There he came to an abrupt halt. When Katherina and Tom caught

up to him they saw a grey Land Rover backing down the track away from them. The shadows of the trees made it impossible to see who or how many people were in the vehicle. Katherina was about to run after it when Jon stopped her.

'They picked somebody up,' he explained. 'A guy came out of the trees on the left. There might have been more.'

Katherina peered through the tree trunks but the dense firs prevented her from seeing more than a couple of metres into the woods. The car had disappeared from sight but they could still hear the engine. It was driving away at a great speed.

'Did you get the number?' asked Katherina.

Jon shook his head. 'TX or something like that.'

'I'll get my shotgun,' said Tom and ran back to the house before the others could react.

'What did the man look like?' asked Katherina. 'Did you recognize him?'

'No,' replied Jon. 'He was short and thin, wearing hunting gear, with a hat and all the rest.'

'And a rifle?'

'Maybe. But I didn't see it.'

Jon took several steps forward, peering into the woods. They stood there for a couple of minutes and listened without hearing anything but the wind in the treetops.

'I'm sorry I ruined things,' he said without taking his eyes off the trees. 'I'm still not used to the idea that reading can be so revealing. All my life I've thought that reading silently was a private matter, a sort of personal space I could enter and be in all alone. But in reality I've been broadcasting like a radio station.'

'A radio station with an imperceptibly small number of listeners,' Katherina pointed out. 'Most people can spend an entire lifetime reading and never run into a receiver.'

'They do conceal themselves well,' said Jon with a smile. He nodded towards the farm. 'Yes, I know, Tom is a special case.' His smile vanished, and he gave her a searching glance. 'Very special. The question is, can we trust him?'

'Do we have any choice?'

'I've heard so many incredible things during the past week that this almost makes sense.' Jon once again fixed his eyes on the trees. 'At least it explains a lot of what has happened, to Luca in particular. I sure could have used that information a little earlier.'

Katherina noticed that his hands were clenched and his knuckles were white.

'The most unbelievable thing for me is that Luca never said anything,' she said. 'Not even to Iversen.'

Jon raised his hand to signal her to be quiet. In among the trees they could hear branches snapping and the sound of footsteps in the underbrush. Jon took a few more steps along the track and Katherina followed. Now they could make out a figure heading straight for them, and they could hear panting from the exertion required to push aside the intertwined branches.

Out of the shadows stepped Tom, red in the face and gasping for air. Under his arm he carried a shotgun adorned with twigs that had been torn off as he made his way through the woods.

'Nothing,' he told them after catching his breath. 'If anyone was here, he's gone now.' He handed the gun to Jon so he could brush the twigs and leaves out of his hair and beard.

Neither Katherina nor Jon had much desire to return to the dark farmhouse. Tom fell behind as they strolled up to the yard where the cars were parked. It was cold, but Katherina enjoyed the fresh air after the stuffy atmosphere inside the house.

'Who do you think it was?' asked Jon after they reached the yard and Tom had caught up.

'If it was the Shadow Organization, that's the closest I've ever been to them,' said Tom, reaching for his shotgun. Jon returned the gun to its owner, who carefully wiped off the dirt and dust from the barrel and butt.

'Did anyone follow you here?' asked Tom without taking his eyes off what he was doing.

Jon shook his head. 'I didn't notice anyone.'

'Seems a little odd that they'd show up on the very same day that you turn up here,' said Tom, casting a sidelong glance at both of them. 'Who knew where you were going?'

'Iversen and Pau,' replied Katherina.

'And my computer guy,' added Jon.

'Do you trust them?'

Katherina and Jon both nodded.

Tom scanned the buildings around them and gave a little sigh. 'I'd like you to leave now,' he said calmly.

Katherina and Jon exchanged glances.

'Shouldn't we stay for a little while, in case they come back?' asked Jon.

'No thanks,' said Tom, taking a step back. 'I can take care of myself. I've been doing that for twenty years. Please just leave me alone.'

As he stood there facing them with his shotgun under his arm, Katherina couldn't help feeling that his words were more than just a polite request. Even though his voice was controlled, Tom's body seemed tense, and his eyes kept shifting from one of them to the other.

'Let's go,' Katherina said softly, before Jon could object. 'Thanks for everything, Tom. You've given us some important information today, and we'll do our best to make good use of it. Of course, we hope to see you again. If the Shadow Organization really does exist and it's launching some sort of offensive, we'll need everyone's help.'

Tom nodded, though he had a slightly dubious look in his eyes. He watched them carefully as they got into the car. As they drove away, Katherina studied him in the mirror. Nørreskov stood in the farmyard and watched them for a moment, then he turned round and quickly walked towards the main building.

'A little paranoid, don't you think?' said Jon after they'd come out on the other side of the woods.

'All those years alone in this place would make me a bit odd, too,' said Katherina, hurrying to add: 'Even odder, I mean.'

They drove back to Copenhagen in silence. Katherina sensed that Jon would prefer to think through the new information on his own, and she spent the time looking for cars that might be following them. But they reached Copenhagen without seeing any Land

Rovers or other suspicious vehicles, and their mood lifted significantly when they drove in among the tall buildings of the town centre.

Jon turned off the engine in front of Libri di Luca, but he made no move to get out of the car.

'I think I need some time to think about all this,' he said, giving her an apologetic look.

'Of course,' said Katherina. 'Take your time. Let me know if there's anything I can do.' Through the shop windows she could see Pau walking around inside. 'What do we tell the others?' she asked, nodding towards Pau, who had taken up position in the window with his hands on his hips and his eyes fixed on them.

'I've been thinking about the same thing,' said Jon. 'All my father's secrecy certainly didn't do him any good – on the contrary. So maybe we should just lay our cards on the table and tell them everything.' He shrugged. 'Maybe that would make someone give himself away, if there really is a mole in the Bibliophile Society.'

Katherina nodded. 'This evening I'm going over to the hospital to visit Iversen,' she said. 'So I'll tell him what we found out. I think we owe it to him to be the first to know.'

'Good. Then I'll tell Kortmann tomorrow.'

Katherina said goodbye and got out of the car. Jon started up the Mercedes, but she noticed that he didn't drive off until she was safely inside.

'Well?' said Pau even before she had shut the door. 'What happened down there?'

Katherina glanced around the room to make sure no customers were present.

'He's not the one behind it all,' she said. 'I can't tell you anything more right now.'

'Arghh! Come on, Katherina,' exclaimed Pau, disappointed. 'What was he like? Tell me. I dropped everything, you know, to take your shift.'

Katherina sighed. She told Pau about Tom Nørreskov's solitary life and about the farm, but nothing about the Shadow Organization or his connection with Luca.

'What a weirdo,' muttered Pau when she was done talking, but she refused to be pressured by Pau to say anything more. 'I wonder what he's really doing out there on a farm in the middle of nowhere.'

Katherina escaped commenting because at that moment a customer came in.

For the rest of the day she evaded Pau's questions and then sent him home before closing time so she could be alone. After locking up, she got on her bicycle and rode over to the State University Hospital. On the way she bought a pepperoni pizza, and the aroma made everyone in the hospital turn to look at her with a pleading look in their eyes.

Iversen looked as if he'd fully recovered. The small man was sitting up in bed, and his face lit up with a big smile when she came into his room. He laughed out loud when he saw that she'd brought him a pizza.

'I actually just ate,' he said. 'If you can call it eating, considering the food in this place.' He patted the bedclothes covering his stomach. 'But there's always room for a pepperoni pizza.'

With great joy he bit into a slice of pizza as Katherina told him what she and Jon had been doing. She recounted everything Tom Nørreskov had told them. Several times Iversen was so surprised by what she said he almost choked on his food. But he let her talk until she was done and he had finished his meal.

'I've always known that Luca was harbouring a few little secrets, but this goes way beyond my wildest imagination.' Pensively he wiped his mouth. 'Is it really true that I can't be trusted?'

'Of course you can,' said Katherina. 'You might say that it's your open heart that gives you away.'

Iversen shook his head. 'If I'd only known, I would have paid closer attention, and maybe I could have helped.'

Katherina took his hand. It was warm and dry.

'You did help him, as a friend and colleague. That was what he needed.'

Iversen shrugged. 'We'll never know now,' he said with a sigh. 'I'm glad you told me. But do you think it was wise? What if I happen to give away the fact that we know about the Shadow Organization?'

Katherina squeezed his hand. 'Everybody in the Society is going to know about it now,' she said solemnly. 'We're going to need the help of every single person if we want to fight back.'

They sat together for a couple of minutes, holding hands and not saying a word.

'How blind I've been,' Iversen then said bitterly. 'So many pieces of the puzzle are suddenly falling into place. Tom's banishment, Luca's reaction to Marianne's suicide, Jon being sent to a foster home. It's incredible how that little man could have kept such big secrets to himself.'

'Luca probably found support with Tom,' Katherina suggested.

'Tom,' said Iversen to himself, shaking his head. 'They sure pulled the wool over our eyes.'

'But they paid a high price,' Katherina pointed out.

'We have to take Tom back,' said Iversen firmly. 'After the way we treated him, we have to make it up to him somehow.' He slapped the bedclothes. 'And we need him. Who better to help us against the Shadow Organization? He's the expert.'

'I don't think you should count on him wanting to leave his farm,' said Katherina. 'All Tom seems to be interested in is looking out for himself. Not that I blame him, after what he's been through.'

'There must be something we can do.'

'It would probably be best to leave him in peace.'

'That'll be difficult if we're going to convince the others. Will Kortmann – or Clara, for that matter – accept this explanation without having Tom here to confirm your story?'

'They'll have to. And they'll listen to Jon. He's the one who has been most affected by what happened. Tom chose his own fate, in a way. While Jon was cheated out of his. But who knows what would have happened if he had stayed with Luca?'

'How did Jon take it?' Iversen asked with concern.

'Considering the circumstances, he was surprisingly calm,' said Katherina. 'It's hard to say what he's feeling. In that sense, he resembles Luca – he's much too good at keeping secrets. I think he's bitter that he was never told the truth.'

'I suppose we all are, to some extent. Whether it was justified or not, it's never fun to be kept in the dark. Maybe this will present an opportunity for reuniting the Bibliophile Society – which was always Luca's dream.'

'There might still be traitors among us,' Katherina pointed out.

'True enough. It could be more true than ever, in fact, but it's time to smoke them out, and for that we'll need everybody's help. Especially Jon's.'

'And Kortmann?'

'Kortmann and Clara are just going to have to bury the hatchet,' exclaimed Iversen furiously. 'Even if I have to force them to pick up the spade to do it.'

Katherina noticed that the ECG, still hooked up to Iversen's body, was making some rapid upswings. She patted his hand.

'Take it easy, Iversen, or you're going to bring the whole hospital running.'

The next day was the first time Katherina opened the bookshop with the knowledge that the contents of the numerous shelves were not always used for a good purpose. Until then she had regarded the job of selling books as honourable – an occupation whose intention was to enlighten people and provide them with valuable experiences. Now she had the feeling that she might as well be working in a gun shop. There were individuals who would use the books she sold them to hurt others. She'd known for a long time, of course, that the risk existed, but this was the first day that she realized it was being done deliberately, and in an organized manner.

Her new insight made her involuntarily study the customers who turned up, and she caught herself slinking after some of them in order not to let them out of her sight. She also used her powers to gather all the impressions that she could, and if she found any of the customers to be suspect, she made sure that they lost any desire to read and then quickly left the shop.

In mid-afternoon, Jon rang. In her hypersensitive state, Katherina could hear at once that something was wrong.

'How's Iversen?' he asked.

'He's going to be discharged today or tomorrow,' said Katherina, and then went on to tell him about her visit to the hospital the previous evening. But judging from Jon's brief comments, she gathered his thoughts were elsewhere.

'Is anything wrong?' she asked after a pause in which neither of them said a word.

Jon gave a curt laugh on the other end of the line.

'Yes and no,' he replied. 'I've come to . . . or rather I should say that I've been forced to make a decision.'

'Yes?' Katherina held her breath. Her brain was swiftly summoning up one horror scenario after another. A decision about what? Libri di Luca? Was he going to sell the shop after all when faced with the prospect of landing in the middle of a battle with the Shadow Organization? Had he been threatened? Bought?

Jon cleared his throat before he went on.

'How does a person go about getting activated?'

# 20

After Tom Nørreskov told them about the Shadow Organization and Luca's involvement, Jon had tried to reprogram his brain with the new information. After spending twenty years feeding it with speculations, allegations and anger, it felt as if he now had to switch the two halves of his brain around in order to find the true meaning. It was something he had to do alone, and after dropping Katherina off in front of Libri di Luca, he went straight home to his flat.

He unlocked the door, took off his jacket and went into the living room. The cleaning woman had been there, judging by the scent and the way the lifestyle magazines were stacked neatly on the black coffee table. The afternoon sun was shining through the newly washed windows, making him squint as the light reflected off the white floorboards and white walls. He went over to the black leather sofa and sat down with a sigh. The only other piece of furniture in the living room was a low grey bookcase along the opposite wall. On top stood a wide-screen TV and surround-sound system, taking up most of that wall. The wall behind him and the spaces between the windows were dominated by small black banners printed with Chinese characters in silver and red.

Jon leaned forward, picked up the stacks of magazines and set them on the floor. He then shoved them under the sofa without looking at them. The last thing he wanted to do right now was read.

As Jon sat on the sofa with his eyes fixed on the blank TV screen, the sun sank behind the rooftops and softer light filled the room. He found himself immersed in a swirl of questions and theories that refused to let him go. He went back and forth endlessly between his own childhood experiences and Tom Nørreskov's story. Hunger finally made him get up from the sofa and go out to the kitchen, where he threw together a meal from food he found in the cupboards. Then he dragged himself off to bed.

After a sleepless night Jon decided to go to the office. Partly so he could think about other things, and partly to re-establish contact with his former life, which now seemed so distant that he needed to see whether it really existed or was just a dream.

Jenny gave him a friendly nod when he arrived, but she didn't say anything, and Jon thought he glimpsed a mixture of relief and concern in her eyes. He found out the reason for her concern an hour later when he was summoned to Halbech's office.

'Hello, Campelli,' said Frank Halbech in a businesslike tone after Jon had closed the door behind him and sat down on a chair in front of his boss. 'Nice of you to show up.'

Jon, who was prepared to defend himself for taking time off, nodded. 'Yes, there were still some things to take care of following my father's death, and since the Remer case can't move forward as long as the main player won't give us the information we need, I thought it would be okay.'

Halbech's expression didn't change, but he gave Jon a searching glance.

'I've tried to get him to answer my queries,' Jon went on. 'But he's always either unavailable or he keeps mixing up other things in the case that have nothing to do with the charges.'

'That doesn't match up with what he told me,' said Halbech, leaning back in his office chair with his arms crossed. 'I spoke to him yesterday, since you weren't here. He wants you off the case.'

Jon did his best to hide his surprise.

'Remer claims that you seem uninterested, lazy, that you're not taking the case seriously. According to him, he's been available the whole time, and he was the one who had to contact you to get some sense of what was going on.'

Jon shook his head. 'That's not at all what happened. Remer's the one who's been impossible to reach. He doesn't even answer his emails.'

'Well, you've done something to piss him off, Campelli,' said Halbech, leaning forward. 'Remer puts a lot of money into this firm. So much that we can't afford to lose him because of the family matters of one of our co-workers. Of course it's regrettable that your father died, but you can't let that affect your work.'

'And I don't think I have,' said Jon. 'I can show you the correspondence that—'

'Right,' Halbech cut him off. 'I'm familiar with the correspondence. Remer read some of it to me, and I have to admit that I had expected you to use a more professional tone with our best client.'

Jon looked at him wide-eyed.

'He *read* it to you?' he asked.

'Yes,' Halbech confirmed, sounding annoyed.

'On the phone?'

'No,' replied Halbech, clearly annoyed now. 'I told you that he was here yesterday. He had copies of your correspondence, and he gave me a few examples, and I must say that . . .'

Jon was no longer listening; a shocking realization forming in his mind. He pictured Remer sitting in the same chair where he now sat, reading aloud to Halbech, the co-owner of the law firm, who would have listened carefully and receptively to what the firm's notorious cash-cow had to say. Jon could guess how the tone of the text might seem, given his absences from work this last week, but what if Remer was a transmitter? Halbech wouldn't have had a chance.

As he sat there explaining how Remer had reviewed the material for him, Halbech seemed genuinely convinced that he was spouting his own appraisal, as if he had in fact formed an opinion about the material and had independently drawn his own conclusions.

'. . . and so we've decided to take you off the case,' Halbech finished saying.

'Okay,' said Jon with resignation. He started to get up.

'In fact,' said Halbech, raising his voice, which made Jon stay in his chair. 'In fact, we've had to take another look at your employment with the firm.'

Jon stared in shock at the man behind the desk.

'This office has no use for individuals who don't take our clients seriously,' Halbech elaborated without blinking. 'The clients come to us because they're in a bind, in one way or another, and it's our bloody obligation to treat them professionally. If word gets around that we're not serious about our work, whether it's true or not, we're finished in this business.'

'What is it you're trying to say?'

'That you're fired,' said Halbech curtly without taking his eyes off Jon. 'Relieved of your duties. Pack up your personal possessions and leave the building immediately.'

Jon knew there was nothing to be done. It wouldn't do any good to try to argue or explain. Remer had won this round, that much was clear. Jon looked down at his hands, as if they were what had prevented him from working. He noticed a rage growing inside him. Halbech was not the enemy here – he merely thought he was protecting his business. Jon nodded.

'Fine,' he said and got up.

'Jenny will escort you out,' said Halbech with a nod towards the door. 'Goodbye, Campelli.'

Jon turned on his heel without saying goodbye and walked over to the door. Outside Jenny was waiting, tears in her eyes.

'I'm so sorry, Jon,' she said at once.

'It's okay,' said Jon, giving her a hug. She was trembling, and she held onto him for a long time until Jon gently cleared his throat.

Jenny reluctantly released him. 'I have to ask you for your mobile and car keys,' she explained, stifling a sob and giving him an apologetic look.

Jon nodded. 'Let's get it over with.'

Ten minutes later he stood out on the pavement with no job or car or phone. He hardly knew which was the greatest loss. His job had secured him a certain standard of living, and the car had allowed him to get around, but without a mobile he felt very alone, cast out from the flow of information and unable to reach anyone who might help him. That was of course a load of crap, he persuaded himself. But it still took a long time before he found a public telephone that was functioning, and when he did find one, he decided to forget it. Partly because he didn't know what number to ring – all his phone numbers were stored in the mobile that he had just turned in – and partly because it suddenly seemed much too public to be talking on a pay phone in the middle of Strøget, the pedestrian street – much worse than if he'd used his mobile in the same place.

Jenny had slipped him a taxi voucher, but he left it in his pocket and walked home instead. On the way he had an opportunity to gather his thoughts. The rage was still hovering inside him like a stomach-ache, but it gave him a sense of satisfaction to know where he should direct his fury: at Remer and the Shadow Organization. They had succeeded in destroying Luca's life, and they were well on the way to doing the same with him. They had taken what he loved most – his work – or so they thought, at least. But Jon had actually begun to have his doubts. The events of the past few days had pushed his law career into the background, and he was no longer sure it was where his passion lay. But under no circumstance was he about to let this all just pass.

Back home in his flat, he rang Katherina.

After that everything happened very fast. Katherina rang him back in less than ten minutes. She had spoken to Iversen, who was going to be discharged that same day, and he had immediately suggested they should carry out the activation – or seance, as they called it – the following day. Jon asked if there was anything he needed to do to prepare, but the only advice Katherina could give him was that he should relax. So that was what he did, along with a bottle of red wine. The day ended with him falling asleep on the sofa, which was where he awoke the next morning.

In the sunlight, everything looked different. A couple of times he considered ringing Frank Halbech to explain the whole matter, but each time he tried to imagine the conversation that would result, he gave up. Besides, he had a terrible headache that prevented him from thinking clearly and reminded him how long it had been since he'd drunk a whole bottle of wine by himself.

The seance wasn't going to take place at Libri di Luca until after closing time, so his hangover had time to subside over the course of the day. In the evening Jon ate a solid meal of beef stroganoff, which for once he prepared from scratch in his kitchen. After that he took a cab to Libri di Luca, where Iversen was waiting.

Aside from a couple of cuts on his face, the old man looked like his old self, and he didn't even show any sign of fatigue after spending all day in the shop for the first time since his hospital stay.

'It's so wonderful to be back here again,' he said, smiling happily as he looked around the room. 'She's taken good care of the place, Katherina. I gave her the day off, but they'll be here for the activation – both Katherina and Pau.'

'Is that necessary?' asked Jon, who was beginning to feel uneasy.

'The effect is better the more participants there are,' Iversen explained. 'Katherina is especially important. As a receiver, she has the ability to guide your powers if it should turn out that you're a transmitter like your father.'

'And if I'm not?'

'If you're a receiver like Katherina, we'll need to proceed more cautiously. Not because there's any danger for you, but there could be some risk for me, as the reader of the text we're using. When you're activated, you won't know how to control your new powers.'

'And what if it turns out that I don't have any powers at all?'

'I'm sure you do, Jon. I've already noticed something about you. The Campelli tradition suggests that you're a transmitter, but it won't be possible to tell until the seance is over.'

'Does it hurt?'

'Not if you're relaxed and open,' replied Iversen. 'But if you try to fight it, there might be some pain associated with the activation. If you block it completely, we won't be able to carry it out, no matter how much we pressure you. Most people are naturally a little nervous in the beginning and have a hard time surrendering, but once they realize that it goes easier if they relax, the rest usually proceeds painlessly.'

'It sounds as if you've taken part in quite a few seances.'

'Actually only three.' Iversen smiled with embarrassment. 'And one of them was my own activation.'

Jon laughed. 'I feel much better now.'

Iversen studied Jon intently. 'I didn't mean to make you nervous, but the truth is that it's not an exact science. There are plenty of things we don't yet understand. But you're in good hands, Jon. If we sense that the slightest thing is going wrong, we'll just abort the whole process.'

'I hope you're not going to stop the whole thing just because I might happen to frown. I'm ready to do whatever's necessary, even if it does hurt a little.'

'Let's wait and see, Jon. Wait and see.'

At that moment there was a knock on the door and they both turned towards the sound. Katherina came in wearing a long dark coat. She gave Iversen a hug and then, smiling, held out her hand to Jon. He took her hand and pulled her close for an embrace. It was nice to see her again, so nice that he had to divert his eyes as their bodies separated.

'So, are you ready?' asked Katherina as she took off her coat and draped it over the counter. Underneath she was wearing a blue sweater, a pair of snug jeans and short black boots.

'As ready as I'll ever be.'

'Don't worry, we'll get you through this in one piece,' she said.

'Yes, well, that's what you all keep telling me.'

Katherina went downstairs while the two men stayed at the counter.

'So we're just waiting for Pau,' said Iversen, peering out of the window.

They didn't have to wait more than a couple of minutes before Pau came rushing through the door, making the bells dance.

'Hi, Svend. Hi, Jon.'

Both returned his greeting.

'Great night for an activation, huh? I mean, wind, rain and maybe if we're lucky we'll even get some thunder.'

Iversen smiled. 'So maybe we should move it outdoors?'

'No, that's okay, Svend,' said the young man, tossing his leather jacket on top of Katherina's coat. 'The princess here?'

'She's downstairs,' replied Iversen. 'We're just waiting for you.'

Pau seemed to think about that for a moment, but then he clapped his hands together and looked at Jon. 'Well, let's get started then.'

Jon and Pau went on ahead while Iversen locked the door and turned off the lights in the shop.

'How many activations have you participated in?' asked Jon when they reached the stairs.

'Just one,' said Pau. 'My own. But I wasn't really conscious during it. I was run down by a psychopath on Strøget and hit my head on the cobblestones, and when I woke up from a coma three weeks later' – Pau snapped his fingers – 'bam! That was it.' He started down the stairs. 'It took a while before I figured out what it was all about, even though I could tell right away that something was wrong. But you'll soon see what I'm talking about. Just wait.' He laughed.

They had reached the bottom of the stairs and continued on down the dark corridor to the oak door that led to the library. A faint light came from the doorway.

'Hi, Kat,' said Pau as he stepped inside.

Jon followed Pau into the room. The electric lights were dimmed and the room was almost entirely lit by candles on the table and the few shelves not holding books.

'It's just for atmosphere,' Katherina told Jon. 'It doesn't have any importance for the activation.' She smiled.

'But it's damned cosy,' exclaimed Pau as he dropped into a chair. 'All we need now is some incense and herb tea.'

Katherina ignored him and pulled a book from the glass case in front of her.

'Have you read this?' she asked, handing the volume to Jon.

He took the book and studied it. It was bound in black leather, and even though he didn't have much understanding of such things, he could tell that it was high-quality workmanship. When he turned the book round to look at the title, he saw that it was *Don Quixote*.

'No,' Jon said at last. 'I've never got round to reading it.'

'That's a shame,' she said. 'It's a classic. Iversen has read it to me several times.'

Jon nodded and leafed through the book. The paper was thick and pleasant to the touch. It was obvious that someone had put some love into this edition.

'We're going to use it for the activation,' Katherina said casually as she took out another book and then closed the glass case.

'This one?' said Jon in surprise. 'I thought it would involve all sorts of oaths and magic formulas.'

Katherina smiled. 'It's not the words that are important. It's the energy and the emotions that the text conjures up that mean something.' She placed her free hand on the book Jon was holding. 'This one is strong. Can you feel it?'

Jon placed his palm on the book, brushing against Katherina's fingers, which she quickly removed. He closed his eyes and tried to sense the energy she was talking about.

Pau laughed behind them.

'Can you feel anything, Jon?' he asked sarcastically.

'Not the slightest,' Jon decided, opening his eyes.

Katherina shrugged. 'Well, you haven't been activated yet. That usually helps, but even people who are activated can't always feel it.' She cast a glance at Pau, whose smile instantly froze.

'So, is everyone ready?' they heard Iversen say as he came into the room. They all confirmed they were, and Iversen closed the door. Katherina handed the book to Iversen, and they all sat down in the chairs around the table. There was a moment of silence. The flames from the candles slowly stopped flickering. Jon's heart started beating faster, and sweat made his hands damp, as well as the book he was clutching. Across from him sat Iversen. Katherina was on his right, and Pau on the left.

Iversen picked up a book. It was bound in leather, like the one that Jon was holding, but a white bookmark was sticking out of it.

'This is the text we're going to use for the activation. It's the same as the one that you have in your hands, and the whole process really just involves us reading together. I'll start by reading aloud, and then you join in. It's important that we read at the same pace, but that's usually not a problem, once we get going.'

Iversen fell silent and looked expectantly at Jon, who with a curt nod acknowledged that he understood.

'It's been a long time since I read anything aloud,' he said uncertainly. 'At least from a work of fiction.'

'You'll do fine. Katherina will help both of us keep the right tempo,' Iversen explained. 'As we get further along, she'll reinforce or mute the emotions that come up. Don't be afraid, just relax and concentrate on the reading and the rhythm. Immerse yourself in the story and the mood of the book. The more relaxed you are, the easier the activation will be.'

Jon nodded again and took a deep breath. 'I'm ready.'

Iversen opened the book at the place where the bookmark stuck out.

'Page fifty,' he said.

Jon turned to the right page in his copy.

Iversen started reading. His voice was clear and the pace was slow. Jon followed along in the text, and after a couple of paragraphs joined in. He cleared his throat a few times during the first section, and he really had to concentrate to match Iversen's voice. The next section went more smoothly and he had an easier time keeping up. Together they picked up the pace a bit so it didn't seem as artificially slow as when they started. As they turned the page, Jon cast a quick glance at Iversen. He was leaning back in his chair, focusing all his attention on the book. His whole face radiated a tense concentration that made him frown and hold the book closer to his eyes.

The reading continued and Jon noticed how the rhythm and tempo had stabilized; he no longer had to concentrate as much to keep it going. The type and the words before his eyes practically invited his voice, enticing him to pronounce them, as if they had been waiting years for this moment. Little by little Iversen's voice grew fainter until finally Jon didn't hear it at all. He heard only his own voice. It felt as if he were lying in a canoe, low in the water, floating along a river at a comfortable and even speed. The surface was broken only by the boat, while an invisible undercurrent carried it along. He didn't hesitate even when he turned the page. He felt as if he could see what was on the next page so that he could continue reading without interruption.

The letters of the words seemed sharper and more distinct in relation to the white background, which also appeared to have changed character. It was no longer the thick, white surface in which the structure of the paper pulp could be glimpsed; instead, the background was more even, with a glossier surface, as if it were a frosted white windowpane on which the type had been embossed. Behind the pane he could suddenly discern silhouettes appearing and disappearing like a shadow play that was out of focus.

Jon hardly noticed any more that he was reading aloud. The reading itself proceeded almost mechanically and he was able to admire the interplay between the type and the background. He focused on the shadows as they appeared, and after a while he had the feeling that they were following along with the story. When the text mentioned two men on horseback, he could sense there were two figures on horseback behind the white pane, and when the text described a windmill, he could make out its rotating sails cleaving the air behind the white fog.

This discovery made him concentrate even more on the shadows as he read, and just as the main character lunged at a sail of the mill, the white pane shattered and thousands of shards of glass fell away, revealing the scene behind.

Jon gave a start, but the reading continued at the same tempo, even though the words were now hovering mysteriously in the air in front of the scene with the main character and the windmill. They looked like subtitles for a film, but in this case the reading of the words drove the images forward and not vice versa. He could feel his heart beating faster again, his pulse rising.

The reading continued inexorably, as if he were no longer in control of it and he could enjoy the images it was creating. They became clearer and clearer the more he read until he felt he could almost step into the landscapes visible behind the text. The colours of these images were strong and clear, but they seemed artificial. It was as if the colour control on a TV was broken and the result was colour-saturated images that threatened to flow together. The outlines of the people and surroundings seemed blurred, and he tried to freeze the boundaries by intensely focusing on the hazy border areas. He felt a slight resistance, as if he were turning a rusty door handle, but suddenly he broke through and discovered he was able to adjust the sharpness of the images. Astonished, he played with this new tool. He let the scene flow all the way out, so it looked as if it were taking place in a thick fog, and then he adjusted the focus so sharply that the characters looked as if they'd been cut out of cardboard with a scalpel. He could also adjust the colour balance. The scene could be made brighter or darker, and he could control how warm it felt by bathing it in soft yellow light. He experimented with all the adjustments, finding the outer limits and the possibilities for combinations. He noticed that some adjustments offered resistance, but if he focused very hard, he could break through that threshold too and force the precise mood he wanted on the scene.

The speed at which he read also had an effect. If he read slowly, he had more time to fill the scene with emotions and mood, while a rapid reading speed was not nearly as nuanced and restricted the impact to a few powerful emotions. Jon noticed that when he read quickly, his heartbeat was faster and not entirely regular and he began to sweat, as if he were exerting himself physically. He tried to figure out how fast he could read, but again something seemed to be holding him back, some sort of brake that prevented him from exploring the rest of the scale. Slightly annoyed, he began reading spasmodically, like a pile driver, to remove this obstacle, but he noticed his body lurch and he felt a huge hand grabbing hold of him and holding him tight. He tried to get free, but the more he struggled, the more the grip tightened, and he had no choice but to slow his reading down. The grip still didn't loosen, and he felt as if his lungs were no longer able to get any air.

Jon stopped reading.

Incapable of taking in anything around him, he closed his eyes and his head fell forward towards his chest. Only a few seconds passed before he began taking in impressions from the basement again.

It was his sense of hearing that returned first, very slowly, as if someone were turning up the volume. He could sense commotion around him, the sound of footsteps and furniture being moved. Nervous voices conversed, though he couldn't hear what they were saying, and a crackling sound sliced through the air above his head. Then he smelled smoke; the sharp odour of burning wool and plastic found its way into his nose, tearing at his nostrils. Then Jon opened his eyes.

The sight he encountered was so unreal that his first thought was that it had to be a dream, or that he was still immersed in the story. The room was almost completely filled with smoke, several of the candles had toppled over, the chair on his left had fallen backwards, and sparks and electrical discharges were flying out of the light fixtures. Iversen and Pau were running around putting out the flames that had taken hold on the carpet and furniture. Pau was using his sweater while Iversen was armed with a rug.

Katherina was sitting to Jon's right, staring at him with a blank expression in her eyes. Two thin streams of blood were coming out of her nose, collecting at her lips, and running down her chin. Her hands were clutching the armrests of her chair so hard that her knuckles were white.

Jon's next thought was that the bookshop had been attacked again.

'Who was it?' he managed to stammer, noticing how dry his throat was.

Pau cast a glance at Jon on his way over to a switch near the door where a burst of flame had just ignited the door frame.

'Hey, he's back,' shouted Pau to Iversen, flinging his sweater with his left hand at the flames coming from the electrical outlet. 'She did it.'

Jon noticed that Pau's right arm hung limply at his side.

'Jon?' Iversen came over to him. 'Jon, close the book. Do you hear me?'

Jon turned his head towards Iversen, who came closer with the rug slung over one arm. Jon was about to look down at the book when Iversen began shouting at him.

'Jon, look at me! Just close the book, Jon. Look at me, and close the book!' There was fear in Iversen's voice.

Jon kept eye contact with Iversen as he slowly closed the book. An obvious expression of relief spread over Iversen's face.

'Who was it?' Jon asked again.

'It was you, Jon,' said Iversen. At the same instant he caught sight of new flames leaping up behind Jon's chair. He immediately went over to slam the rug at the fire until the flames died out. In the meantime, Pau had put out the fire at the electrical outlet and was now standing at alert, keeping an eye on the room in case any new fire should break out. The sweater he was holding ready in his hand was smoking faintly.

Katherina had bowed her head so her chin rested on her chest. Her hands were clasped in her lap, as if in prayer. They were trembling ever so slightly.

Jon tried to stand up, but was immediately seized with dizziness and dropped back into his chair. He felt Iversen's hand gripping his shoulder.

'Just stay where you are, Jon. It'll be over soon.'

He wanted to turn round to face Iversen to ask for an explanation, but before he managed to turn his head, he blacked out.

# 21

'That was crazy!'

Katherina heard Pau's excited voice as if it were a radio that had suddenly been switched on, much too close. It sounded as if she were in the bookshop. Judging by the leather underneath her, she must be sitting in the armchair behind the counter, with her head tilted to one side.

Why was she sitting here? She felt so exhausted that she couldn't even open her eyes. What had happened?

She heard Iversen answer Pau in a somewhat more subdued tone, his voice extremely grave.

'Things could have gone terribly wrong,' he pointed out. 'And we still don't know how they're feeling. What about you? How's your arm?'

'It's okay,' replied Pau casually. 'It just tingles a bit, like it's asleep. But holy shit, it sure hurt when he zapped me. How'd he do that?'

'I don't know, Pau,' said Iversen wearily.

'If that's what activations are like, we should have more of them,' said Pau firmly.

'That was absolutely not normal,' Iversen emphasized. 'I've . . . I've never seen anything like it.'

Katherina could hear a trace of nervousness in Iversen's voice.

He was scared. Why? She tried to think back. They'd been down-stairs in the basement. Jon had been there too. The activation.

She gave a start when she remembered.

'Is she awake?'

Katherina felt someone bending over her.

'No,' said Iversen very close. 'It was just a spasm.'

She wanted to shut them out for a little while longer. First she had to work out what had happened.

All four of them had been in the basement for Jon's activation. She herself had made all the preparations, with candles and every-thing. It was supposed to be pleasant, like adopting a new family member, but something had gone wrong.

At first everything proceeded according to plan. Iversen started reading, and Jon quickly fell into the rhythm, helped along by Katherina's efforts to focus his attention on the text. Pau had just sat there, gawking, with a silly smile on his face, as if he were wait-ing for a chance to tease the new boy in class.

After a couple of pages Iversen had glanced at her and nodded. She closed her eyes and concentrated on Jon's reading as she shut out everything else. Slowly she reinforced his attempts to accentuate the text he was reading, and she made sure his attention continued to be directed at the book. The images he created became more and more rich and detailed, until she held him back a bit. She sensed him trying to override this sudden obstacle, like a mass of water that had been dammed up.

Then Katherina opened her eyes. Iversen had stopped reading, and again he nodded to her. She closed her eyes again and removed the barrier to Jon's progress, as if she were uncorking a bottle. At the same time she enhanced what he was accentuating so the result was an explosive leap forward, filled with colours and a rapid flow of pictures. The activation was achieved, and she was sur-prised at the richness of detail and depth in Jon's interpretation of the text. The images he had created as an ordinary reader seemed like blurry black-and-white pictures in comparison to these, which were saturated with colour, clarity and nuance. It was like the difference between watching a film on TV and on a cinema screen.

Gradually she reduced her own influence. Jon now had no trouble maintaining his concentration, and she even sensed how he was experimenting with his new instrument. When she opened her eyes, Iversen was sitting there with a big grin on his face, while Pau was so immersed in the story that he paid no attention to anything else around him.

'What did I tell you?' whispered Iversen, giving Katherina a wink. She smiled back.

It was hard not to get caught up in Jon's gripping storytelling technique. The images and associations he created kept enticing the listeners to go along on a fantastic journey. Katherina, who had heard *Don Quixote* many times, didn't remember ever being so tempted to immerse herself in the story as she was now. The hair on her arms stood on end, and she felt a slight tickling in her stomach.

Katherina again turned her attention to Jon's discovery of his powers. She directed his focus to the various means at his disposal, and each time he surprised her by going further than she thought possible.

It was during these breakthroughs that physical phenomena began to manifest themselves. The candles were blown out. The lamps pulsed with shifting voltage, the furniture began to shake.

Iversen asked Katherina to bring Jon back. There was a trace of nervousness in his voice. Jon didn't notice anything, but sweat was pouring down his face and little blood vessels had burst in the whites of his eyes. But he kept on reading in a loud, clear voice and all of Katherina's attempts to subdue him were in vain. The bookcases began to shake violently. The books came toppling off the shelves and fell to the floor.

The commotion brought Pau out of his trance. He got up to take hold of Jon but before he could touch him a blue spark leaped from Jon's elbow and through Pau's outspread fingers. Pau was slammed back into his chair, which fell over backwards. He quickly got to his feet but he was holding onto his right arm and moaning loudly.

Katherina continued her attempts to mentally put the brakes on Jon but the discharges got even stronger. Little flashes of lightning danced out of Jon's body and over to the electrical fixtures, which sprayed sparks into the room. Pau and Iversen were fully occupied stomping out the embers and flames, while the furniture started shaking more violently and jumping about. At one point a bookcase fell on top of Iversen and Pau had to come to his rescue.

Katherina tried to follow the pulse that she sensed lay behind the bursts of energy coming from Jon. They occurred spasmodically, at regular intervals, and when the next pause came, she directed all her powers at breaking Jon's concentration. Her chair was shoved a metre away from him, but the reading stopped, and he raised his eyes from the book to stare at Katherina. His bloodshot eyes were filled with confusion and fear.

After that she remembered nothing more.


'Katherina?' Iversen's voice was very close.

She opened her eyes and looked up into Iversen's worried face. He smiled.

'Are you feeling all right?'

Aside from a sluggishness in her whole body and the feeling that she hadn't slept in a long time, she was fine. She nodded.

'What about Jon?' she asked.

'The master of fireworks?' said Pau, poking his head into her field of vision. 'He's totally out of it. But still alive.'

The two men straightened up and looked behind them, where Jon was lying on a camp bed. From what Katherina could see, he was sleeping peacefully.

'We lugged the two of you up from the basement,' Iversen explained. 'It's still being aired out. I don't think the electrical switches are ever going to work again. They're completely melted.'

'How could that happen?' asked Katherina, her voice hoarse.

Iversen shrugged. 'It's beyond me,' he admitted. 'We were hoping you could tell us something.'

'Nothing except that he was incredibly strong,' replied

Katherina. 'Stronger than any transmitter I've ever encountered before.'

Iversen nodded pensively.

'But lightning?' Pau interjected. 'Was that wild enough for you?'

'It does seem very extreme,' Iversen acknowledged. 'But we activated latent areas of his brain. Who knows how much is hidden away up there?' He tapped his index finger on his temple. 'Maybe we flipped a couple of extra switches.'

'Or blew a fuse,' suggested Pau cynically.

All three of them fell silent as they exchanged worried looks. Even Pau seemed to have grasped the seriousness of the situation. A hint of nervousness had slipped into his eyes. From the camp bed they could hear Jon breathing evenly.

Katherina looked down at her hands. It had been her job to control the seance. Of course no one could have predicted how things would go, but she was the one who should have stopped Jon earlier and prevented everything from getting out of control. Maybe she had put too much pressure on him. Her fascination with how his powers were unfolding had made her hesitate when she should have intervened. The electrical switches might not be the only things that had melted. Even though Jon was breathing all right, they couldn't know whether he was nothing more than a vegetable behind his closed eyes.

'Maybe we should have someone take a look at him,' said Katherina.

'We've discussed that,' said Iversen with a sigh. 'But who would we get, and what should we tell them?'

Katherina had no answer.

'Whatever else we do,' Iversen went on, 'we'll have to contact Kortmann.'

Katherina gave a start. During all the preparations for the activation and Iversen's homecoming from the hospital, they had completely forgotten to inform Kortmann about their meeting with Tom Nørreskov and what he'd said about the Shadow Organization. To top it all off, they had thrown themselves into an activation that Kortmann had specifically advised against.

With a nod she gave her assent.

'I think we should call in Clara too,' she added firmly. 'The receivers have just as much right to know what's going on as the transmitters.'

After an hour Clara turned up, the first to appear of those they had summoned. Jon was still asleep. Katherina had been sitting at his side most of the time, and apart from a couple of grunts and incomprehensible sounds, he had remained calm. Clara greeted everyone and then leaned over Jon as if to assure herself that he was actually sleeping and not just pretending. She squatted down next to the bed and grabbed his wrist to take his pulse.

'And he's been like this ever since the activation?' she asked perfunctorily.

Iversen confirmed that Jon's condition hadn't changed and then recounted in rough outline what had happened during the seance. When Clara heard about the physical phenomena, she opened her eyes wide and let go of Jon's wrist, as if she'd burned herself.

'Very interesting,' she said and stood up. Her eyes met Katherina's, as if looking for an answer, but Katherina could only shake her head weakly.

At that instant the door to the bookshop opened and a young man came in. It was Kortmann's chauffeur. Without looking at them, he held the door open for Kortmann, who with some difficulty rolled his wheelchair over the threshold. He hesitated for a moment when he saw Clara, but then he turned to his assistant and nodded. The young man left Libri di Luca, closing the door carefully behind him.

'Clara,' he said loudly. 'I didn't expect to see you here. It's been a long time.'

'Same here, William,' said Clara, going over to the man in the wheelchair and holding out her hand.

Kortmann grimaced and shook her hand briefly.

'And Iversen is up and about again, I see.'

Iversen smiled and nodded. 'I'm fine.'

Kortmann moved closer to the bed and studied Jon's face.

'That's more than can be said for our young friend here,' he said, shifting his gaze to Katherina. She could see his jaw muscles tighten. 'How could you even think of carrying out an activation without telling me?' Kortmann abruptly turned his head to look at Iversen.

Iversen looked terrified and had to search for words. 'We didn't think it was necessary,' he managed to stammer. 'And he insisted on doing it as soon as possible.'

'So what happened?'

For the second time Iversen described the seance. Kortmann didn't visibly react to what he heard, but he kept his eyes fixed on Iversen.

'Let me see the basement,' Kortmann demanded. 'You,' he said, pointing to Pau. 'If your arm is all right now, you can carry me downstairs.'

Pau nodded eagerly and then struggled a bit with the man's frail body until he got a proper grip and lifted him out of the chair. Katherina thought Pau looked like a ventriloquist with Kortmann as the well-dressed dummy. While the others went down the spiral staircase to the basement, she stayed behind with Jon. It was impossible to tell just by looking at him that only a few hours ago sparks had flown out of his body. His eyes moved behind his eyelids, and his breathing was calm. Cautiously she placed her hand on his forehead. It was warm and slightly damp.

After ten minutes the others returned. Pau put Kortmann back in his wheelchair and wiped his brow with the back of his hand.

Kortmann moved closer to the bed and studied the unconscious Jon with renewed interest.

'Young Campelli is full of surprises,' he said to himself. 'Have any of you ever seen anything like this before?' he asked Clara, who was standing on one side of the bed.

She shook her head. 'Never. There's never been anything that even resembled physical phenomena, energy discharges or whatever you want to call it.'

'So we don't in fact know what we're dealing with here,' said Kortmann. 'It could be a new sort of Lector power that we haven't yet seen, or it could be a separate phenomenon – an area of the brain that became activated by accident and has no relation to our powers.'

Katherina cleared her throat. 'I think it has something to do with his powers.'

'Can you explain?' asked Kortmann, sounding annoyed.

'When we use our powers on transmitters, we can feel a kind of pulse in the accentuations or energies they emit.' Clara nodded agreement. 'And I sensed that the phenomena followed the beat of Jon's heart,' Katherina explained. 'It's true that the frequency was irregular, but the phenomena occurred and were reinforced with every pulse – I'm sure of that.'

'And this . . . pulse. Is it something that only transmitters have?' The tone of Kortmann's voice was gentler but his eyes were cold. Katherina shifted her glance to Clara, who was smiling at her like a proud mother.

'Yes,' replied Katherina. 'It has nothing to do with a normal pulse. It only occurs when transmitters use their powers.'

'That's how we, as receivers, can determine whether someone has transmitter powers and is using them or not,' Clara added.

Kortmann rolled his wheelchair a short distance away from Jon's bed.

'So that means he's not dangerous as long as he's not reading. Is that right?'

'That seems to be the conclusion,' said Clara.

Kortmann cast a glance at the bookshelves surrounding them.

'But when he reads . . .' he said slowly, as if he were working out a maths problem. 'We have to assume he didn't do it deliberately. Is he at all able to control these energy discharges?' Kortmann fixed his eyes on Iversen, who was leaning against the counter.

'As far as I could tell, he had no idea what was happening around him,' said Iversen.

'He was totally out of it,' Pau added.

'My sense was that he was able to control the force of the energy discharges,' said Katherina, 'exactly the way you can accentuate the text with more or less force. The range he has at his disposal is simply much greater.' The others had all turned to look at her, but they didn't seem to have understood the implications of what she was saying. 'If the phenomena occur during the very violent discharges, as I felt they did, he is also capable of preventing them from happening.' She raised her index finger before the others could say anything. 'On the other hand, I don't think he can control the energy once it's been set loose.'

No one said anything for a couple of seconds. Then Kortmann threw out his hands.

'Pure guesswork,' he exclaimed. 'It's nothing but guesswork right now. The only way we're going to get answers to these questions is by asking him when he wakes up.'

Iversen nodded in agreement.

'You said there was something else you wanted to tell me,' Kortmann indicated, crossing his arms.

'We paid a visit to Tom Nørreskov,' said Katherina, getting straight to the point. She studied Kortmann's and Clara's reactions. Kortmann frowned for a moment but then his eyes grew wide and he opened his mouth. Clara seemed to have recognized the name at once, and she looked at the floor.

'Wasn't he . . .' Kortmann began.

'Yes, he was banished from the Society more than twenty years ago,' Iversen confirmed.

Katherina and Iversen jointly described the meeting with Nørreskov and his theory about the Shadow Organization. It took almost an hour, in which Katherina explained how she and Jon had found Tom and described their conversation with him. Along the way Iversen was able to supply observations and descriptions of events that supported Tom Nørreskov's story. During the entire presentation, Kortmann sat in his wheelchair with a sceptical look on his face, listening without comment. Clara moved about the bookshop, nodding several times. Pau had sat down on the floor in a lotus position, looking offended, probably because he hadn't been let in on this information earlier.

Both Iversen and Katherina recounted the facts eagerly, and as the account progressed, Katherina's hunch that they had uncovered the real reason for the events of both twenty years ago and more recently was reinforced. Any gaps she found in the story, Iversen was able to explain, based on his knowledge of what Luca had done or said.

Afterwards there was a long pause; no one said a word. Clara had stopped pacing back and forth, and Pau had bowed his head to the floor.

'Where is Nørreskov now?' asked Kortmann.

'Most likely still on his farm,' replied Katherina. 'He seemed almost paralysed with paranoia, and he'd probably be unwilling to leave his hiding place.'

Kortmann shook his head. 'Now that Luca's dead, the only thing you can base your theory on is the imagination of a recluse,' he said sarcastically.

'But—' Iversen protested.

'It may well be that your theory fits certain isolated events. But I was *there*, twenty years ago. There were no signs of secret conspiracies. And that's your proof.' The man in the wheelchair nodded towards Clara, who was standing with her arms crossed, regarding him coldly. 'As soon as the Bibliophile Society split up, the attacks stopped.'

'But that just shows the Shadow Organization got its way,' Iversen ventured. 'They wanted to weaken the Society by splitting it apart, and they were successful beyond their wildest expectations.'

'That's totally unreal,' said Pau. 'A Shadow Organization? Wow, I'm really scared.' He shook his head. 'You guys had better get hold of yourselves.'

For once Kortmann seemed to agree with Pau, and he gave him a nod of approval.

'And where is the evidence that unequivocally points in the direction of this Shadow Organization? Quite an imaginative explanation, to put it mildly, with no proof that it exists – as opposed to a group of receivers, and we already know they have the potential. How are we supposed to find such an organization, if it even exists? Where are we supposed to start looking?'

'I know where,' said a hoarse voice behind them.

They all turned around to stare at the bed where Jon had propped himself up on his elbow.

'I know exactly where to start.'

# 22

The thirst was the worst part.

Jon felt as if his throat were lined with insulation material, that awful glass wool, and it hurt every time he swallowed. A listlessness had also overtaken him, and even propping himself up on one elbow took a great effort. That's why he had lain there listening to the others for a while before drawing attention to himself. He had awakened as Katherina was in the midst of describing their visit to Tom Nørreskov, and he hadn't felt it necessary to intervene until now.

Jon's arm began shaking underneath him and he dropped down onto his back again. The others came running over. Katherina was the first to reach him. He gave her a smile. He was glad to see her safe and sound.

'It's okay,' he said. 'I'm just a little tired.' He felt her hand on his forehead and closed his eyes.

'Does it hurt?' asked Iversen.

Jon shook his head.

'Could I have some water?'

Iversen sent Pau downstairs to get water – a task that obviously did not please the young man, because they could hear his disgruntled muttering as he descended the stairs.

'Do you remember anything?' asked Kortmann impatiently.

Jon raised his arm, pointed at his throat and shook his head.

'You've been activated,' Iversen explained. 'That's when you fainted, during the seance. We were afraid you might not wake up again.'

Jon opened his eyes and smiled. He didn't feel anything special other than fatigue and thirst. There was no sign that he had changed, and for a moment he wished he didn't have the powers but was just a normal person who could resume his old life.

'You're a transmitter, like your father,' said Iversen with pride in his voice. 'And a bit more than that, I must say.'

Pau came back with a glass, and Jon propped himself up again and greedily drank the lukewarm water. He handed the glass back and gave Pau a grateful nod.

'You'd better get some more,' suggested Katherina, and Pau trudged off.

'I don't feel any different,' said Jon after clearing his throat vigorously. 'Are you sure it worked?'

'I'll say it did,' exclaimed Iversen, laughing with relief. 'Far beyond our expectations.'

'Don't you remember anything at all?' asked Kortmann again.

Jon tried to concentrate, but he was much too exhausted.

'I remember watching a film,' he began hesitantly. 'And there was lots of smoke and fire.' He looked enquiringly at Iversen. 'You said I did that?'

Iversen nodded. 'Apparently your powers can manifest themselves as energy discharges of one sort or another, most likely electrical. In any case, you shortcircuited the electrical fixtures in the basement, causing fire to break out.'

Jon peered at the others. None of them laughed; on the contrary, Clara and Kortmann seemed uncomfortable at even being in the same room with him. Clara was standing at the foot of the bed, wringing her hands, while Kortmann sat a short distance away with his hands on the wheelchair handrims, ready to roll away if it proved necessary.

Pau came back with another glass of water; he too seemed scared to come too close to Jon. After delivering the glass, Pau gripped his right arm with his left hand and backed away from the bed. Jon drank the water.

'You mentioned that you knew where we would find the Shadow Organization,' said Kortmann.

Jon nodded.

'A client,' he said curtly. 'Someone who has shown a suspicious amount of interest in taking over Libri di Luca.'

Kortmann and Clara exchanged puzzled glances and then looked at Jon. He didn't feel like giving them any more details at the moment. Partly because he was too worn out for a major inter-rogation, and besides, he was still bitter about what Remer had cost him – a bitterness that might give the wrong impression to his listeners, who were already sceptical.

'I don't buy it,' declared Pau. 'He could just be a zealous book pusher. If there really is a Shadow Organization behind everything, what would they want with Libri di Luca?'

'I think I can answer that,' said Iversen. 'Libri di Luca is one of the oldest antiquarian bookshops in Copenhagen. The books up there on the balcony and downstairs in the basement don't just have sentimental value for a bibliophile. They have been charged. For years Lectors have been reading these books in this very location. For reasons we don't fully understand, a book becomes charged with each reading. Luca even had a theory that this energy could be accumulated in the building itself.' Kortmann was about to protest, but Iversen raised his hand for permission to go on. 'Perhaps it's no coincidence that it's easier to conduct an activation here than in other places,' he continued. 'Perhaps it's because of the books themselves, but it could also be because the walls contain the energy of generations.'

'And it's that energy that Jon released?' Katherina asked.

'Yes. Or he was able to link to it in some way,' replied Iversen. 'At least that would explain why the Shadow Organization isn't just interested in the books but in the space itself.'

'But then why did they try to burn the shop down?' asked Pau stubbornly.

'It could have been just a warning,' replied Iversen. 'Or perhaps the energy doesn't disappear with fire.'

Jon had lain down again. He didn't feel he had tapped into any outside energy source; instead it felt as though he himself had been drained so effectively that he could hardly keep his eyes open. The voices around him merged together into a humming sound, and he tried hard not to fall asleep. He thought he heard Katherina calling him, but he no longer had the strength to open his eyes.

Jon savoured waking up in his own bed. He could hardly remember the last time he was able to stay in bed in good conscience and take a snooze. There was nothing he had to do, no piles of work tugging at his conscience or meetings he had to attend. On the nightstand was a glass of water, which he downed in one gulp. It was daylight outside. The clock radio told him it was early morning.

He didn't remember how he'd managed to get home, and it was his curiosity about this question that finally made him get out of bed. He was wearing a T-shirt and boxers, which seemed to indicate that he hadn't undressed on his own. Normally he slept in the nude.

In the living room he found Katherina sleeping on the sofa. She was covered with a grey blanket, a paltry counterpoint to her red hair and pale complexion. A pair of jeans and a sweater were neatly placed on the coffee table next to a glass of water.

He stood there studying the sleeping woman. The flickering of her eyelids revealed that she was dreaming, and for a moment he wished to be there, to see the pictures she was seeing, just as she was able to see the ones his reading had produced. He smiled as he tore himself away and tiptoed out to the kitchen. There was nothing in the cupboards that he would want to offer a guest for breakfast, so Jon slipped quietly back to the bedroom to put on his clothes and shoes.

It was foggy outside, a thick, almost creamy mist that made it difficult to see more than twenty metres ahead. With his hands in his pockets, Jon strolled the few hundred metres over to the bakery.

It was in the bakery that he first noticed it.

Jon was standing in the queue behind two other customers. An elderly woman was in front, fumbling with the coins in her purse, and behind her stood a middle-aged man in a suit, trying to control his impatience. He was presumably on his way to work, and judging by the clock, he was running late. Jon's gaze scanned the interior of the shop, looking from the customers to the bakery assistant to the newspaper rack.

As he focused on the morning paper, he felt a slight jolt that made him wince. The story on the front page was a relatively ordinary article about a new school reform the government had in the works, but as Jon began reading the opening paragraph he felt the text reach out towards him, as if it were elastic and almost insisted on being read aloud.

Alarmed, Jon shifted his glance away, but no matter where he looked, he felt words and messages forcing themselves on him from signs, posters and brochures hung up around the shop, enticing him to pronounce them and shape them.

He looked down at his shoes and kept his gaze there until the bakery assistant asked what she could get him. He ordered and paid without looking up and then hurried out of the shop as soon as he had the bakery bags in hand.

On his way home, Jon kept his gaze on the pavement and walked quickly until he reached the front entrance. He took the stairs at a run, because when he glanced at the nameplates on the doors, it was as if they were reaching out for him, trying to stop him or trip him.

Jon hastily let himself into the flat and slammed the door shut. Out of breath, he stood there for a moment, leaning against the door frame.

'Jon?'

He heard Katherina's worried voice from the living room. He wiped the sweat from his brow and went into the flat. There he was met by Katherina, who had put on her sweater and wrapped the blanket round her waist. She came towards him.

'Are you okay?'

'I went to the bakery,' he said, holding the bags out in front of him. His hands were shaking so hard that the bags rustled.

'What happened?' Katherina asked with concern.

Jon sat down at the kitchen table and told her about his experience at the bakery. Only afterwards did he discover he was still clutching the bags and still wearing his jacket.

'I think that's perfectly normal,' said Katherina. 'Iversen likes to tell the story about when he was first activated; he felt as if he were being attacked by all the books that had previously been his best friends.' She took the bakery bags out of his hands. 'It only seems like that in the beginning. After you get used to it, you'll feel more in charge.'

Jon's breathing had returned to normal, but he stayed sitting in the chair as he took off his shoes and jacket. Katherina went back to the living room. He rubbed his palms over his face. What would have happened if he'd actually read that newspaper? Would it be safe for him ever to read anything again, or was it only in Libri di Luca that he was a danger to those around him?

'How did we get back here yesterday?' Jon called loudly.

'You mean the day before yesterday,' Katherina shouted back. 'You've been asleep for thirty-six hours.'

She came back to the kitchen, fully dressed now.

'Kortmann drove us here. His chauffeur carried you all the way upstairs. We couldn't get you to wake up.'

'And you've been here the whole time?'

'I didn't have anything else to do,' she said, smiling with embarrassment.

Jon fixed her with his gaze. He could see she hadn't had much sleep, and he pictured to himself how she might have sat by his side as he slept. Maybe she had stroked his forehead lightly with her fingertips with a worried look in her green eyes.

He cleared his throat and looked down.

The news that he'd slept for a full day and a half woke up his stomach and he suddenly felt very hungry. He got up to make coffee.

As they ate, Katherina told him what had happened in the

bookshop after he fell asleep again. They had mostly spent the time discussing whether the Shadow Organization existed or not, and they hadn't come to any sort of consensus. Clara was convinced and called for a meeting of the two factions, while Kortmann and Pau refused to believe in it. The discussion had ended with a compromise. Jon was going to have to seek out Remer to establish or refute his affiliation with the Shadow Organization, and after that they would decide what to do next.

'So how are we going to find him?' asked Katherina cheerfully.

Jon rummaged through the pockets of his jacket, which was still draped over the back of his chair.

'We'll have a little help from this guy,' he said, placing a key ring on the kitchen table.

Clever Smurf stood among the keys with a pensive look on his face.

'Our entrée to the Remer case. I forgot to turn in the keys when they fired me.' He stood up. 'But first I'm taking a shower. I think I need it.'

The fresh baked goods and coffee had done the trick. Jon was no longer hungry and the coffee had given him a buzz. As the water from the shower sprayed over him, he couldn't help smiling because he felt rested and content, and soon he would also feel clean. He enjoyed the feeling of the hot water on his skin. He closed his eyes and turned his face up towards the spray.

Maybe that's why he didn't notice Katherina come in until she wrapped her arms around him and pressed her body against his back. She was hot, hotter than the water. He hummed contentedly and let his hands slide over hers. She kissed his back and caressed his chest and stomach. When he tried to turn round, she stubbornly held him tight. He let her have her way, leaning forward with both hands on the wall in front of him. Her hands slid down across his stomach and out to his hips, then down his thighs. She moved her hands back the same way, touching him only with her fingertips, just as he had seen her stroking the spines of the books the very first time he saw her in Libri di Luca. Then she rested her hands on his hips and turned him round to face her. Jon opened his eyes and looked into hers. The sight of her red hair, those green eyes and the white skin made him catch his breath. He leaned forward and carefully kissed the scar on her chin. She sighed, and he moved his mouth to her lips. With a slightly sharper tug she pulled him closer and returned his kiss.

They spent the following day alternating between making love, sleeping and eating. They shut out everything else; not even Iversen's worried messages on Jon's voicemail could make them show any interest in the world outside the flat. As reserved and wary as Katherina had seemed to Jon when he first met her, she now seemed open and warm, and it felt unreal that only two weeks ago they hadn't even known the other existed.

They both knew they couldn't isolate themselves forever, but they postponed it as long as possible and kept finding new excuses, mainly sex, for blocking out the world. Aside from the fact that it was wonderful hiding out with Katherina, Jon was also concerned about how he was going to function outside, where his new powers might manifest themselves. Katherina was sure he would be able to control them now that he was aware of the consequences, but he wasn't convinced. The activation should have been only a matter of form. They had meticulously avoided any reading since he'd come back from the bakery, but at some point he would have to leave the flat. Katherina suggested they start with some controlled reading.

For safety's sake Katherina rang Iversen, who was relieved to hear they were okay. He also thought it was a good idea to do a little training before Jon was let loose.

Jon had never in his life bought a work of fiction. The breach with Luca had made him hate books to such a degree that he read only non-fiction, but he did own a couple of detective novels that had been given to him as presents. They were stuffed away in the bottom of the wardrobe. As Katherina brushed off the dust, she decided there was no danger of them being charged. They most likely never been read, and so they were 'dead' in the Lector sense.

'First you need to familiarize yourself with your powers,' said Katherina, trying to sound serious even though they were lying naked in Jon's bed. 'As you've already noticed, a text can fill up a lot of space in your consciousness. You can't ignore your powers, but you can learn to mute them when you aren't using them.'

'So what exactly do we do?' asked Jon.

'You start reading, and I'll jump in if it begins to get out of hand,' she replied. 'The most important thing is that you take it easy and don't try to force the powers or make any big deviations. I have to be able to follow along the whole way.'

'In a minute you're going to tell me that it's just like riding a bicycle,' said Jon.

Katherina laughed and blushed. 'Just start whenever you're ready,' she said, handing him one of the books. 'If you sense an obstacle, that's me holding you back, and that means you should stop.'

Jon nodded and studied the cover. He gave a start when the title rose up towards him like a three-dimensional advert. He observed the phenomenon for a while, getting used to the way the type was pulsating in both colour and size.

'You doing okay?' asked Katherina.

He nodded and opened the book. Suddenly all the symbols on the page came rushing at him and he had to look away. He felt sweat break out on his forehead. Stubbornly he forced himself to look at the page again and started to read. His impression of the book pages instantly changed. It felt as if the words and letters were now behaving themselves, waiting for their turn to be read, instead of having all the sentences on the page creating one big confusion like before. Relieved, Jon quickly found a comfortable reading pace, but he still didn't dare put any emotion into his reading, and occasionally he cast a glance at Katherina. She was lying on her stomach, resting her head on her arms, with her face turned towards him. There wasn't a trace of concern in her expression.

This time he sensed right from the start that he was sitting in front of a multitude of invisible knobs that he could adjust in order to put life into the story. Slowly he began adding more feeling to his reading; he gave the characters more personality and lent more colour to the descriptions. Just like during the activation, the background became glass-like and the type more distinct, but Jon hesitated to break through the white surface. He determined that his perception of the white surface and the images he created from the text were two different things. The images were formed from his knowledge and the interpretation of the text, and they were a product partly of his own experiences and also of the accentuation he was able to give to the scene by virtue of his new powers. The story took place in Copenhagen, which made it possible for him to add details that weren't in the text but that resulted from associations he made.

Jon experimented with colouring the mood of the images, and he discovered that when he really concentrated, shadows began appearing behind the glass surface. Those images approached the images created by his subconscious. But whenever he got that close, he was stopped, and he didn't try to force his way any further. In this way he tried out various effects for a while, until he heard Katherina calling him.

He looked away from the book and discovered her sitting astride him.

'How'd it go?' he asked, tossing the book aside.

'It was beautiful,' she said. 'You're very talented.'

'Thanks. But I have to be honest and admit I have no idea what I'm doing.'

'You'll get there,' said Katherina with conviction. 'I think it went fine. There are two things you need to take into consideration. First, the listeners. Everyone perceives a story differently, partly because of their experiences but also because on that particular day they might be either especially vulnerable or thick-skinned. That's why the tone should be within a certain margin of safety, so you don't have too violent an effect on the weakest of your listeners.'

'How do I know what the listeners can tolerate?'

'Over time you'll learn to sense how the reading is being received. That's why we need to practise.' She pressed her belly against his and smiled shamelessly.

'What sort of practice are you thinking about now?' Jon asked with a laugh. 'But you said there were two things.'

'The second thing is more difficult,' said Katherina solemnly. 'Because we don't know how it happens – the physical phenomena that you're apparently able to produce. It's important that we find out exactly under what circumstances they occur and how far you can go before they appear. Otherwise we can't stop you before it gets serious.'

'Thanks a lot.' He told her about his perception of the glass surface and how he had broken through it during the activation.

Katherina nodded.

'That could very well be the boundary,' she said.

'So, have I earned a break?' Jon asked, placing his hands on her hips.

'You've earned more than that,' she said with a smile and leaned towards him.

# 23

'Why don't we use Mehmet?' asked Katherina.

They'd gone out to rent a car, a Suzuki minivan, and then driven home to Katherina's place, where she threw together some clothes. Now they were on their way through rush-hour traffic to Libri di Luca. The vehicle was poorly insulated, and they had to talk loudly to hear each other.

'Couldn't he find out what we want to know?' Katherina wasn't wild about the idea of breaking into Jon's former workplace in order to look for information on Remer.

'I'm sure he could,' replied Jon. 'But it would take him a long time. Unlike Tom Nørreskov, Remer is a master at covering his tracks. The files will at least give us a starting place. Everything the firm knows about him has been collected there – information about his business empire, his properties, addresses, investments, everything.' He clenched his teeth as he shifted gears with unintentional roughness in the unfamiliar vehicle. 'Besides, I want to keep Mehmet out of this for as long as possible.'

They had spent most of the day exploring Jon's transmitter powers. Even with the rather limited selection of literature in his possession, he had still managed to get a sense of his capabilities. Katherina could tell that he now had his powers under control, but they didn't venture outside unless he said he felt confident. She wanted to train him on some of the charged books from the shop, but didn't want to pressure him too much. It was difficult. She wasn't sure whether it was because she'd fallen in love with Jon or because of his powers in general, but when he read, it was as if an unbreakable barrier surrounded them, shutting out everything else. With the right texts, he would be impossible to withstand, at least for her.

Jon himself was more preoccupied with catching Remer off guard. His expression turned cold whenever he spoke of his former client; he reproached himself for not being more suspicious from the start. In his eagerness to pay Remer back, he had decided to carry out the break-in that very night. Katherina had insisted on coming along, even though she knew she wouldn't be able to help him much.

They parked a short distance away from Libri di Luca and hurried through a cloying drizzle to the bookshop. Even though it was more than an hour past closing time, the door was still open, and Iversen was strolling among the bookcases, humming. He popped into view at the sound of the door.

'Oh, it's you two,' he exclaimed, rushing up to Katherina to give her a warm hug. 'How are things?' he asked, studying Jon intently. 'Any problems with . . .'

Jon shook his head. 'It's going fine,' he said. 'Though I feel a little like I'm back in school.' He nodded towards Katherina. 'Sitting in front of the stern teacher.'

Iversen laughed and then looked from one to the other. Katherina felt heat rising in her cheeks. The old man smiled approvingly and nodded.

'You're in good hands, Jon. You can be sure of that.'

'We need some books that are more suitable for training,' said Katherina. 'Jon's collection of detective novels doesn't offer much finesse.'

'I can understand that,' said Iversen. 'Let's find some . . .'

The lights in the shop flickered violently a couple of times, then dimmed, only to return to a normal voltage.

'Oh no,' said Iversen. He went over to the stairs leading to the basement. 'Pau is having a look at the electrical fixtures downstairs. He said he'd done it before, but so far he hasn't accomplished much other than blowing a few fuses.'

Jon and Katherina followed him down to the basement.

'Shit,' yelled Pau from the library.

'Did something happen?' called Iversen.

Pau stuck his head out into the corridor.

'No, I'm okay,' he muttered. 'It's these fucking switches that are giving me a hard time.'

'Maybe you should turn off the power in the meantime,' suggested Jon.

'That won't matter – 220 volts doesn't really hurt.' He nodded to Jon. 'The zap you gave me was worse.'

'Well, it looks like you've managed to fix a few things,' said Iversen, stepping past Pau into the library. The lamps above the bookshelves were on, lighting up the multitude of leather-bound spines with a soft, yellow glow.

'What about you?' said Pau, looking at Jon. 'You okay, or what?'

Jon nodded. 'I feel fine.'

'Have you come to your senses?' asked Pau.

'What do you mean?'

'You know, all that stuff about the Shadow Organization,' said Pau. 'Somebody's got to bring the old man back down to earth.' He pointed over his shoulder at Iversen, who was walking along the shelves, gathering a big stack of books in his arms.

'We're going to get the proof tonight, Pau,' said Jon firmly. 'Then we'll see who comes to his senses.'

'Tonight?' asked Pau with interest. 'Wouldn't you like me to go with you?'

'No, thanks,' replied Jon. 'The fewer people, the better, I think.'

'You sure? I'm good at night exercises,' said Pau, grinning at Katherina.

She sighed. 'I think we can manage on our own, Pau. But thanks anyway.'

'Oh well, I'm probably going to be fiddling with the electricity for most of the night.'

Iversen came out into the hall and handed Katherina a stack of books.

'I'll just get you a couple more,' he said and disappeared back into the library.

Katherina noticed the familiar buzzing sensation emanating from the volumes in her arms. It was a completely different experience from holding a mass-produced book, like the ones they had used back at Jon's flat. These were alive.

'Try to feel it,' she said, holding out the stack to Jon.

He resolutely placed his hand on the top book. His fingertips barely touched the surface before he yanked his hand back in surprise, as if he'd received a shock.

'What the hell?' he exclaimed, rubbing his hand on his thigh.

Pau laughed. 'That will teach you,' he said, laughing even louder.

Katherina ignored him. 'These books are charged,' she explained. 'There's a difference in how powerful they are. Most Lectors can feel the energy just by touching them.' She cast a glance at Pau. 'Others have to stick their fingers in an electrical outlet to achieve the same sensation.'

Pau's eyes flashed, but he didn't say a word. He turned round to go back to his work.

'Did it hurt?' asked Katherina.

'No,' replied Jon. 'I was just surprised. It felt like static electricity.'

Iversen appeared with more books, which he handed to Jon. Jon hesitantly took them.

'You can always borrow more,' said Iversen. 'But these will be a good start. There's a little of everything, with varying degrees of power.' He gave Jon a wink. 'But I think we'll save the more powerful ones for a while.'

'Good idea,' said Jon. 'At least I need to be able to hold on to them.'

Upstairs they put the books on the counter, and Katherina told Iversen about the progress they'd made so far with Jon's training.

Iversen nodded pensively. 'Every transmitter has his own way of perceiving his powers,' he said. 'But most have the feeling they have some sort of toolbox or palette at their disposal, which they can use to influence their listeners.'

'For me, it feels as if I'm standing in front of a big mixing console that has endless ways of being tweaked,' said Jon, with a smile. 'It gives me a real feeling of . . . power. I think I could get used to this.'

Iversen looked at him intently.

'Be careful,' he warned. 'In the beginning you're only allowed to use your powers on other Lectors, and preferably when Katherina is close by.'

Jon nodded.

'Many people are tempted to overdo it the first couple of times,' Iversen went on. 'In your case, it could be downright dangerous, but even for an ordinary transmitter it can have unfortunate consequences. Aside from the emotional effects the text may evoke, the listeners can get headaches or feel nauseated if the transmitter doesn't dole out the accentuation carefully, and always in keeping with the message of the text.'

On a few occasions Katherina had witnessed a transmitter who had carried out such distortions, as they were called. It typically happened if an inexperienced transmitter tried to force the message of the text or actually tried to twist the meaning too far from the original intent. Pau had been one of the worst offenders when he first came to Libri di Luca. Since he'd never been trained, he didn't know the strength or limitations of his own powers, and he had distorted most of his readings, out of either ignorance or impatience. Fortunately his powers were limited – a fact he didn't like being reminded of – so not much happened. After a couple of months of instruction under Luca's supervision, Pau was able to get the distortions under control, but he'd never become a particularly skilful transmitter, like Iversen, nor was he nearly as powerful as Jon.

'We're going to get the information on Remer tonight,' Jon told him. 'Can we meet here tomorrow, before you open?' He stacked up the books on the counter and then stuck them under his arm.

'Of course,' said Iversen. 'I'll be here an hour early.' He gave Katherina a hug. 'Be careful,' he whispered in her ear.

The law firm of Hanning, Jensen & Halbech was located on Store Kongensgade in an old building with a majestic facade and a view of the Nyboder district. It was two a.m., but lights were still visible on the floor where the Remer office was located.

'What now?' asked Katherina, both disappointed and relieved at the prospect of having to give up the break-in.

'It could be someone working late,' Jon admitted. 'Or maybe someone forgot to turn off the lights. Or it might be the cleaning staff.' He looked in both directions. At this time of night there was no traffic and only a few windows had lights on. 'Let's find out,' he said.

They crossed the street to the redbrick building. They stopped in front of the heavy oak door, and Jon took another quick look around. Then he took out the key ring with Clever Smurf and unlocked the door.

Silently, and without switching on any lights, they climbed the stairs. At each landing a glass door led to exclusive corporate offices, but the lights were out everywhere until they reached the third floor, which belonged to Jon's former employer.

He peered round the corner through the panes at the reception area, then swore under his breath.

'Anders Hellstrøm is here,' he whispered, letting Katherina see for herself.

Beyond the window was a big, open-plan floor with grey desks and flat-screen monitors at every station. At one of the desks sat a man in his shirtsleeves. He had his back to them, and the desk was covered with ring-binders and piles of documents that threatened to topple to the floor if anyone happened to slam the door too hard.

Katherina concentrated on what the man was reading. She noticed that he was tired – his reading was uneven and unfocused. Images of a bedroom and a comfortable-looking sofa kept popping up in the flow of legal terms, and several times he had to start over on a passage he had just read.

'Where do we have to go?' asked Katherina quietly.

Jon pointed at one of the doors at the very back of the room. There was no way to get there without being seen by the man sitting at the desk. All he had to do was glance up.

'I can distract him,' Katherina suggested.

Jon gave her a look of astonishment but then nodded and selected a key from the key ring.

Katherina again focused on what the lawyer was reading. This time she helped him to concentrate, reinforcing the printed text as she shut out irrelevant images. She sensed the man's feeling of relief and a rising interest in the document lying in front of him. Soon he was so absorbed that she only needed to give him a slight nudge to maintain his focus.

'Now,' she whispered. 'But we have to be very quiet and walk close to the wall.'

Jon nodded and coaxed the key into the lock. The man didn't notice, so they stepped into the room, closing the door behind them. Katherina enhanced the pull of the text even more as they tiptoed along the wall, as she had suggested. Meanwhile, the lawyer kept on reading, paying no attention to anything around him. As they passed the man, Katherina could see his florid face with obvious black circles under narrow eyes fixed on the text. It was apparently a case about a conflict between neighbours, and the documentation he was reading was dry stuff about the home-owners' association's easements and plans.

When they reached the far side of the room, Jon let them into a small office filled with filing cabinets. Only after they had closed and locked the door behind them did they dare speak.

'Whew,' whispered Jon. 'That was certainly effective.'

'In reality he should be thanking us,' said Katherina, smiling. 'He'll never forget what he read here tonight. And hopefully he'll get to bed earlier.'

'I could have used you when I was studying for exams,' said Jon, giving her a wink. 'But he's a good guy, that Anders. So just keep it up.'

Katherina nodded.

Jon began looking through the filing cabinets and studying documents. His scanning of files, summaries, excerpts from reports and rulings in the Remer case got mixed up with Anders Hellstrøm's case, but Katherina muted Jon's reading so she could keep focusing the other lawyer's attention.

There were many filing drawers in the room but Jon seemed to know where to find what they were looking for. He swiftly moved from one cabinet to another, plucking documents from folders.

Maybe he was getting a bit too eager, because suddenly he slammed shut one of the metal drawers with a loud bang.

They both froze, and Katherina noticed that Hellstrøm also stopped reading. She pictured him staring at the door of the room where they were hiding. Holding her breath and closing her eyes, she concentrated exclusively on what was happening inside the main office.

For a couple of seconds she received nothing, but then texts began turning up, words that could be notices on a bulletin board or product names. They appeared in brief flashes, and she tried as best she could to pique his interest in everything he was reading unconsciously. She noticed that he hesitated but also that the little flashes kept changing, new words and sentences showed up, which meant he was either shifting his glance or he was on the move.

Katherina caught Jon's attention and pointed anxiously at the door. Jon nodded and cautiously stepped towards it to switch off the light. The next second the door handle rattled and the door shook. After a moment of silence, they could hear the lawyer mutter to himself outside the door and then move away.

Only when Katherina began receiving images from Hellstrøm reading yet another summary from a general meeting did she whisper to Jon that he could continue his search. The light came on again, and Jon histrionically ran his palm over his forehead.

'That was close,' he whispered, giving her a quick kiss before he went back to looking through the filing cabinets.

After half an hour Katherina noticed that the lawyer outside their door was so tired even she couldn't hold his attention any longer. If she pressed him any harder, he might faint, and he wouldn't wake up until the next day with the worst headache of his life.

'He's almost worn out,' she whispered to Jon.

He nodded and tossed a few more pages onto the stack of documents he'd collected on the desk.

'Are we just going to take them with us?' asked Katherina softly.

'They'll never notice anything's missing,' Jon whispered back. 'This case is so massive that a couple of pages here or there isn't going to make any difference.'

Katherina estimated there were more than five hundred pages in the pile Jon had gathered.

'Besides, he deserves it. I think we have what we need. Let's get out of here.'

Katherina made sure the exhausted lawyer kept his attention fixed on his papers as they left the office and sneaked back through the main room along the wall. Anders Hellstrøm's eyes were staring with obvious strain at the documents, and Katherina and Jon could see that his hands were trembling ever so slightly.

After they had passed him they picked up their pace, moving as fast as they dared across the last section of the office to the door. Jon locked up as Katherina released her hold on the lawyer's attention. She saw his body crumple in his chair, but then with a jolt he straightened up and looked around. He rubbed his eyes, stood up and stretched, at the same time yawning so loudly they could hear it outside the door.

'Sleep tight,' said Jon.

The next morning they arrived at Libri di Luca just as Iversen was unlocking the door.

'How'd it go?' he asked.

'Fine,' replied Jon. 'I think we have what we need.' He held up the plastic bag containing all the documents.

'I don't want to know how you got those,' said Iversen, shaking his head. 'We can sit in the basement. Pau fixed all the lights yesterday.'

They went inside and headed down to the basement. In the

library Jon and Iversen divided up the pile of papers. Jon took the ones dealing with Remer's extensive corporate structure while Iversen went through the press clippings and background information dealing with the man himself.

Katherina felt useless as she roamed around among the bookshelves while the others worked. She was receiving their perusal of the documents, but it was mostly lists of companies and personnel, so she quickly lost interest. Instead, like so often before, she used the time to admire the countless books in the library. She never tired of studying all the exquisite illustrations and the workmanship that had gone into each volume. A few books had been so damaged by Jon's activation that they had been unsalvageable, but the quick action of Iversen and Pau had prevented the major disaster that might otherwise have resulted.

Next to the light switch inside the door was a big scorched patch, and charred sections of the carpet bore witness to the violent event several days earlier. There wasn't much chance that anything would go wrong by reading the papers Jon was now looking at, but with his activation in mind, Katherina directed all her attention to what Jon was reading. Everything proceeded without drama. Jon read the lifeless texts without adding any emotion, and judging by the images that occasionally turned up, he wasn't especially focused. Katherina blushed when she discovered some of the images were of herself.

'Stop,' she exclaimed suddenly, pointing at Jon.

The two men looked up at her in surprise.

'What are you reading?' she asked.

Jon looked down at the documents. 'A list of board members at one of Remer's companies. Why?'

'Read the names again,' said Katherina.

Jon looked again at the page and slowly worked his way down the list. About halfway he opened his eyes wide.

'W. Kortmann,' he said in astonishment.

# 24

In the sunlight Kortmann's villa looked even more grotesque than on the night when they last visited. The huge building with the gleaming red bricks looked like some sort of cake, even though the impression was seriously marred by the rusty tower for the lift, which was leaning against the house like an old hollow tree. The sky was a deep blue, and the lawn surrounding the villa still had a lush green colour, even though they were well into October by now.

Jon wondered if it was because of the good weather or because Katherina had come along that Kortmann received them in the driveway instead of in his library. He was sitting in something that resembled an antique wheelchair with a curved black metal frame and a seat covered with red leather. A thick blanket hid his legs, and a pair of sunglasses concealed his eyes.

They had rung Kortmann several hours earlier, explaining that there was something they wanted to show him. He had sounded neither surprised nor particularly curious, merely suggesting that they meet that same afternoon. Both Iversen and Katherina insisted on going along – for different reasons, Jon suspected. Iversen was convinced that just because Kortmann was on the board of one of Remer's companies, that didn't necessarily mean he was part of the Shadow Organization. On the contrary, he might know nothing and was being used without his knowledge. Jon sensed that Katherina was of a different opinion. She pointed out that it was Kortmann who had constantly put up roadblocks to meetings of the two groups, and he was the one who was chiefly responsible for the split twenty years earlier. Who could possibly be a better mole?

Jon tried to stay neutral. Remer's corporate structure was so vast and complex that it might well be a coincidence, but he still couldn't get the idea out of his head that Kortmann was Remer's mysterious bookseller friend. Kortmann was no book dealer, but he knew enough about Luca, Jon and the bookshop to explain Remer's knowledge and interest.

'Welcome,' Kortmann declared in a friendly tone as Katherina, Iversen and Jon got out of the car. Jon was carrying an envelope with the documents pertaining to the company in which Remer and Kortmann had mutual interests.

They greeted Kortmann and took turns shaking his hand. He then rolled his wheelchair ahead of them, leading the way along a path that went round to the back of the house.

'I thought we might sit outside and enjoy the weather,' said Kortmann.

He led them over to a big terrace at the bottom of the garden. The wall surrounding the property and the tall, old trees gave the impression that they were totally isolated from the outside world.

A black-clad man was busy moving refreshments and glasses from a silver tray onto a patio table surrounded by mahogany chairs. The man, whom Jon recognized as Kortmann's chauffeur, gave them a polite nod and then walked back towards the house.

'Have a seat,' Kortmann invited them, gesturing towards the chairs. 'Let's hear what you've found.'

They sat down as he requested and Jon took the documents out of the envelope. Kortmann didn't react.

'We've managed to find some information about the individual we think is a member of the Shadow Organization,' said Jon, pushing to the middle of the table the paper with Kortmann's name on the list. His name had been highlighted in yellow.

Kortmann turned to look at Katherina, then at Jon. 'What is this?' he asked without deigning to give the document a glance.

'A list of the board members for the Habitat development,' explained Jon. 'Your name is on the list.'

'I'm on so many boards,' said Kortmann wearily. 'What's so special about Habitat?'

'The majority shares are owned by Remer, and we're positive that he's part of the Shadow Organization.'

'Remer?' Kortmann repeated, glancing away for a moment. Suddenly he burst out laughing. 'Remer is supposedly in your Shadow Organization? No, come on now. I know that at times Remer can be very creative in his interpretation of the law, but the idea that he's behind a secret plot . . .' He laughed again.

'We're not saying that he's the leader,' Katherina emphasized. 'Just that he's part of it.'

Kortmann looked at Katherina, and his smile disappeared. He turned to Jon. 'I must admit that I'd expected more from you, Campelli. First this insane theory, devised by an eccentric like Tom Nørreskov, about a Shadow Organization, even though it's impossible to prove its existence, and now the idea that Remer, of all people, is supposed to be part of the conspiracy.'

Jon could feel his anger growing. Making a great effort to keep his voice neutral, he described the entire chain of events concerning Remer, his interest in Libri di Luca and how Jon had been fired from his job.

'That sounds more like Remer,' said Kortmann when Jon was done. 'You can call him a hard, calculating and opportunistic man, but he's no leader of some sort of sect.'

Katherina shifted uneasily in her chair, but Iversen placed his hand on her arm to keep her from exploding.

'How well do you know him?' asked Iversen in a placatory tone of voice. 'Does he have a different relationship with you than with the other board members?'

'I don't think so,' replied Kortmann. 'There's a congenial and professional atmosphere, and we happen to agree on many issues – that's all.'

'Has he ever read anything aloud for you?'

Kortmann shrugged. 'We've occasionally read things to each other. The minutes of meetings, drafts for press releases – that sort of thing.'

Kortmann fell silent, turning his face up towards the blue sky. Jon could almost see him thinking through the consequences of the question: 'What if . . .'

'Can you deny he's a Lector?' asked Katherina impatiently.

'Of course not,' snapped Kortmann. 'Only a receiver can do that.'

'So that's one time when you could have used our help,' she concluded.

Kortmann didn't reply.

'There's another name on the list,' said Jon. 'A Patrick Vedel. Do you know him?'

'Not outside of our work together on the board,' said Kortmann. 'Why?'

'He's on almost all of Remer's boards,' Jon explained. 'We think he's a receiver. A team consisting of a transmitter, Remer, and a receiver, Patrick Vedel, would be a strong combination on a board. Wouldn't you agree?'

'If I bought your theory, yes,' replied their host. Even though Kortmann had sunglasses on, Jon could still feel his sharp gaze aimed at him. 'But I don't.'

Maybe they'd made a mistake by coming here so soon without concrete evidence, but Jon doubted whether Kortmann could ever be convinced, either because he simply refused, or because he was part of the whole thing.

'Why exactly have you come here?' asked Kortmann, turning away from Jon. 'Iversen, why don't you tell me why you're all here?'

Iversen cleared his throat and nodded at the paper in the middle of the table. 'We found your name,' he said without looking at Kortmann.

'Am I on trial here?' The man in the wheelchair clenched his fists, and the tone of his voice was anything but friendly.

'We've proved that there was a connection between you and the Shadow Organization,' said Katherina.

'There is no Shadow Organization!' he shouted, making Iversen jump. 'It's a figment of your imagination, a smokescreen fabricated by the only people who have something to gain by diverting attention from themselves.' He pointed at Katherina. 'Who thought this up in the first place? Tom Nørreskov, a receiver. And who has been deeply involved in the investigation? And whose opinion has been given a suspicious amount of weight? A receiver.'

Kortmann took off his sunglasses and stared straight at Jon. 'Can't you see it yourself?'

Jon calmly regarded the man in the wheelchair. His reaction was convincing; his eyes were fierce, his nostrils flaring. If he was play-acting, he was good at it, but Jon had enough experience of powerful people to know that they were often successful precisely because of their ability to appear convincing, even when there was no substance to their claims.

'I see a man who's afraid of losing power,' Jon said calmly.

The man in the wheelchair studied Jon for a moment and then put his dark glasses back on.

'I'm sorry to hear that,' he said firmly. 'I was counting on you, as a Campelli, to work with the Bibliophile Society.' He sighed. 'But as things now stand, that's impossible.'

'But he's been activated,' Iversen objected. 'Jon is the strongest Lector I've ever seen.'

'And for that reason he's much more dangerous to us, Iversen.'

'Us?' Iversen repeated.

Kortmann pressed a brass button on the armrest of his wheel-chair.

'I'd like you to leave now,' he said calmly. 'Iversen can stay, of course. But you two must leave my property immediately.'

They heard a door slam in the house and the chauffeur came walking towards them. Jon and Katherina stood up. Iversen hesitated for a moment, but then got up as well.

'Iversen?' said Kortmann, leaning forward in his chair. 'Don't be stupid. Don't do something you'll come to regret. I can get you another job. The Society is your life. Why throw it away for the sake of a lie?'

Iversen looked at Jon and Katherina for a moment and then turned to face Kortmann.

'I'm not doing this for myself, for them or for the Society,' he said firmly. 'I'm doing it for Luca.'

He turned and headed for the driveway, taking deliberate strides. Jon and Katherina followed.

'Are you okay?' asked Jon as they drove away from the suburb of Hellerup.

Iversen sat in silence in the back seat, staring out of the side window. He gave his head a brief shake and then smiled at Jon.

'I'm fine,' he said. 'Just disappointed, that's all.' Again he turned his gaze towards the houses slipping past. 'We need to get hold of the others,' he said. 'Preferably before Kortmann does. We have to know how many are with us.'

Jon nodded. They had no idea how big the Shadow Organization might be, but it was guaranteed that three people were too few to do anything about it. 'Kortmann gave me a list of all transmitters,' he said. 'We can start at the top.'

'Excellent,' said Iversen. 'I was afraid I wouldn't be able to remember all the names.' He caught Jon's eye in the rear-view mirror. 'But I think it would be best if I was the one who contacted them.'

'Okay,' said Jon.

'How many do you think we can count on?' asked Katherina.

'I have no idea,' replied Iversen. 'Each person is going to make up his own mind. We can't expect everyone to believe this sort of story, but that's probably not the only factor that will come into play. Some people are already unhappy with Kortmann, but there are no doubt others that are going to give us problems.' He sighed. 'Pau is one of them, I'm afraid.'

'Him I can live without,' muttered Katherina.

'What about the receivers?' asked Jon. 'Can we count on them?'

'I'm sure we can,' replied Katherina. 'Of course there are going to be a few sceptics, but I think they'll support us. I'll get Clara to call a meeting as soon as possible.'

'Is there anything I can do?' asked Jon.

'You can keep training,' Katherina suggested, and smiled.

It felt as if several years had passed since Jon had met Iversen at the Assistens Cemetery. At that time he'd had a career and was in a blessed state of ignorance. He'd also harboured a burdensome anger against the father whom he believed had abandoned him. The anger was now gone, Jon realized, or at least it had changed character. What remained was bitterness at being kept in the dark, but the anger itself was now directed at other targets: the reasons for his parents' deaths.

Luca had been buried next to Arman, but it had been a very long time since Jon had visited his paternal grandfather's grave, so it took some time to find the right place. The two gravestones stood next to the outer cemetery wall, and around them stood a solid-looking wrought-iron fence about half a metre high. Many of the other graves along the wall were covered with ivy, but the Campelli plot had recently been cleaned and the dark granite stones rose proudly from the white gravel as if it were a Japanese garden. A single withered bouquet lay in front of Luca's headstone.

The inscription on the headstone had been etched with gilded letters, soberly listing Luca's name, birth date and date of death. The 'L' of his first name and the 'C' of his surname were shaped like little pictograms with curving lines, like the initial capitals in old books.

The sun was shining in a cloudless sky and it was cold. Luckily the wall offered protection to the surrounding trees and bushes from the wind, but it was still very cold – most likely the reason why there was no one else to be seen in the cemetery.

Jon stood there for a while, looking at the grave in silence. He wasn't entirely sure why he had chosen this place for his training. His flat felt too confined, and now that he was supposed to read on his own, he felt a little calmer about being in a place where there were no electrical fixtures. Maybe it was to prove something to Luca. He didn't really know, but now that he was here, it felt right.

He sat down on a rock in the sun and reached into his coat for the book he'd taken from the stack Iversen had given him. It was

*The Divine Comedy*, supposedly one of Luca's favourite books, and even though it was a small travelling copy, there was no doubt that it had been lovingly bound. The leather was a deep burgundy and the title had been stamped in black type.

Jon opened the book at random and began to read. It was a strange feeling to be reading aloud among the graves, but he had a sense of security sitting there among the trees and bushes and heavy stones. Here he was not afraid of being overheard or observed. He was alone and could focus on his reading.

Gradually he worked out how far he could go, but it took a while for him to find his way into the verse form, which made it difficult to inject any emotions. After three or four pages he finally found the rhythm and level of concentration that gave the paper its glassy appearance, and the shadows behind it began to appear like figures in a morning fog. He focused on them until they became as sharp as silhouettes cut from paper.

Iversen and Katherina were most likely gathering supporters at this very moment – and apparently Jon's help wasn't needed. He'd felt that he was in the way. In that sense it was nice to get away for a while, partly so as not to ruin anything for them, and partly just to spend some time alone. Yet it was frustrating not to be able to do anything.

After a few more pages, he began urging his powers to go further, shattering the glass surface on which the images had moved. He had the same feeling of power he'd noticed during his activation. The reading proceeded on its own; he could concentrate on adding colour to the story. Slowly he began to embellish the character descriptions and the dreary settings in which the people found themselves. There was no resistance, but the whole time he held himself back a bit. Like a film editor, he tried to create slow, smooth segues between the scenes instead of abrupt shifts.

He had no idea how long he'd been reading, but when he put the book aside, he was sitting in shadow. His throat was dry and his fingers, which had been holding the book, were cold and almost numb. He held them up to his lips and blew warm air on them. Everything around him was in shadow, and it was difficult to make out any details, but when his eyes fell on Luca's grave, he froze and held his breath.

The bars of the fence around the plot, which had previously been straight and vertical, were now bent, stretched out, and coiled, forming patterns that looked like eddies and waves. Anyone who hadn't seen the grave before would most likely not have noticed anything unusual, other than the artistry it must have taken to bend the metal bars in such a mesmerizing way.

Jon glanced around, almost expecting to see a team of black-smiths standing there and having a good laugh at his expense, but the only things moving were the treetops, swaying in the wind.

When he stood up, he noticed an overwhelming sense of fatigue, but he felt well enough to go over to the fence and study it close up. There was nothing visible on the metal itself. It seemed as if it had always looked that way, corroded by wind and weather.

Cautiously he leaned down and touched the iron bars with his fingertips.

The metal was ice-cold.

# 25

Even though there were more than thirty people present at the Centre for Dyslexia Studies, it was still so quiet that Katherina was convinced everyone could hear her heart pounding. She had just finished explaining about their discoveries regarding the Remer material and about Kortmann's definitive dismissal. Now she was awaiting the opinion of the receivers. There weren't many friends of Kortmann present, but her credibility depended on whether or not they bought the theory about the Shadow Organization. It was rare for her to talk for such a long stretch without interruption, and along the way she'd been forced to drink some water several times to get rid of the dry feeling in her mouth.

Clara, who as usual had managed so efficiently to gather the receivers for a meeting, now cleared her throat and was the first to speak.

'How sure are you that this Remer is a transmitter?' she asked, giving Katherina an intent look.

'For us there's absolutely no doubt,' she replied.

'But you haven't tested him?'

'No.'

Clara nodded. Several of those present put their heads together to whisper to each other.

They hadn't tested him for the simple reason that Jon was the only one who'd had any contact with Remer, and that was before Jon was activated, so he hadn't had the chance to discover Remer's powers. Besides, a receiver was required to confirm beyond any doubt whether an individual was a Lector or not.

'I was hoping for a little more concrete proof,' said Clara, letting her eyes scan the dubious faces all around them.

'And I was hoping that I could give you that proof,' Katherina admitted. 'But we thought it was better to present the information to everyone as quickly as possible, also to the transmitters.'

Her body felt tense and her eyes searched for allies in the room. Most cast their eyes down when she glanced at them; others stared back with expectant expressions, as if they thought that any minute she might break down or hand over the definitive proof. She pondered how she herself would have reacted if someone had told this story to her. Probably in much the same way. It wasn't so strange that they were sceptical, so she couldn't really allow herself to be bitter.

'I think,' Clara began, raising her voice to be heard above the murmuring that had started up. 'I think we can't afford to sit around and ignore this.' Everyone fell silent. 'If there's any truth in the existence of this Shadow Organization, then we have to respond. I'm not sure how, but we can't pretend nothing's going on.'

Katherina could have jumped up and danced with that lovely woman. For a moment she had thought they would all turn their backs on her, as seemed to be happening to Iversen, but she'd been foolish to think that these people, who had helped each other in so many situations, would desert her now when she needed them most. She felt a lump in her throat and drank some water to hide her own reaction.

'So, what now?' said Clara.

Katherina cleared her throat. 'Iversen is in the process of finding out which transmitters are on our side,' she said. 'We're all supposed to meet later at Libri di Luca.'

Clara nodded.

'Luca would have wanted it that way,' she said. 'A reunion in his own bookshop.'

'It's probably not going to be so much a reunion as a meeting of an entirely new group,' said Katherina gloomily. 'I'm not sure that Iversen will have much luck at getting the transmitters to join us. Many of them are loyal to Kortmann and wouldn't be convinced even if the Shadow Organization handed out business cards.'

'They've always been divided in William's group,' said Clara sadly. She scanned the faces of the receivers. 'We need to make them feel welcome. This is our chance to finish the work that Luca started so long ago.'

Iversen was setting up chairs at Libri di Luca when Katherina returned from the meeting with the receivers. It was after closing time but the door was not locked and all the lights were on in the shop.

'How many do you think we'll need?' asked Iversen, casting a worried glance at the stack of chairs that hadn't yet been set up.

'All the receivers are coming,' said Katherina proudly.

Iversen gave her a grateful look and smiled with relief.

'Well done, Katherina. Was it difficult?'

'Not really, but they're still sceptical. How did it go with the transmitters?'

The smile on Iversen's face vanished and he looked down at the floor.

'Rotten. Kortmann had already spoken to a lot of them.' He sighed. 'Five of them should show up, maybe a couple of others who haven't yet made up their minds.'

'What about Pau?'

Iversen looked distressed and shook his head.

'We shouldn't count on him.'

'Why not?' exclaimed Katherina. Even though she didn't always get along with Pau, she was still surprised that he would desert the ones who had taken him in when he most needed help.

'He was angry,' said Iversen. 'You know how he is. Always short-tempered and self-righteous. He claimed the receivers were to blame for the whole thing and that you had manipulated us all.'

Katherina gritted her teeth. 'We can get along just fine without him.'

'Of course we can,' said Iversen. 'I was just hoping that . . .' He didn't complete the sentence.

'Maybe he'll come back. Maybe they'll all come back, once we have proof.'

'I hope you're right.' He grabbed the next chair in the stack.

Katherina helped set up the rest of the chairs. There was room for forty people in the front part of the shop, approximately the same number that normally attended the evening readings at Libri di Luca. They weren't exactly comfortable chairs, but the readings were always so compelling that after a while the audience would forget about their discomfort. Only afterwards would they notice how sore their bodies were, a strangely pleasant soreness that everyone shared and that made them all smile at each other as they stretched their limbs during the breaks.

One by one the Lectors began to arrive. They nodded to each other in greeting and started wandering among the shelves, studying the books. Katherina stood on the balcony, receiving the stream of titles, author names and excerpts that emerged. They quickly became mixed in an incomprehensible babbling, like a shop filled with radios all tuned to different stations. She muted the reception and concentrated instead on the facial expressions of those present. Most were nervous, their eyes flitting over the spines of the volumes without taking in what was printed on them. Those who tried to read passages from the books did so without any real involvement or concentration. Katherina recognized Henning from the transmitter meeting. He had arrived early, wearing a grey suit and white shirt, and his hair seemed a good deal darker than she remembered. When he caught sight of her, he nodded politely, and she sensed he was making sure to keep her in sight, casting a glance at her no matter where she happened to be in the shop. Maybe she was just being paranoid.

Jon came into the bookshop with a pensive look on his face. He glanced around and quickly caught Katherina's eye. The smile he gave her made her gasp for breath, and she couldn't help breaking into a big grin herself. On his way over to the stairs, Jon was stopped several times by people who wanted to say hello, curious to hear about the activation. When he finally reached her, Jon hugged Katherina without hesitation, and they kissed for a long time, ignoring the fact that everyone had a good view of them up on the balcony.

Katherina blushed bright red when Jon finally released her, and she noticed people casting embarrassed glances in their direction. Henning's eyes were blinking even more rapidly than usual and an amused little smile appeared on his lips.

'Did you do any training?' asked Katherina after catching her breath.

Jon nodded and was about to say something but was interrupted when the shop door opened and a group of about ten receivers came in. Behind them was the couple from the meeting at the Østerbro Library. In addition to them and Henning, Katherina had recognized a middle-aged man she remembered seeing at the evening readings. Including Iversen and Jon, she counted a total of six transmitters – not impressive in comparison to the twenty-five receivers who had shown up so far.

When she pointed this out to Jon, he nodded solemnly.

'Is Pau coming?'

'He's backing Kortmann,' said Katherina.

Jon didn't seem either surprised or annoyed by the news.

'What about the librarian?' he asked, leaning over the railing and scanning the people down below.

'I don't think she's coming either,' replied Katherina. 'But Iversen mentioned that some people still hadn't taken sides.'

Jon nodded. 'Let's hope that she changes her mind. We could really use a historian.'

Katherina was about to ask him what he meant by this when Clara came in, to be greeted by an effusively friendly Iversen.

'We'd better join them,' said Jon, pulling her gently towards the stairs.

Down below people were settling into the chairs. The separate grouping of transmitters and receivers was obvious, and nervous glances were cast back and forth between the two factions. Katherina and Jon found seats in the front row. In the meantime, Clara and Iversen stood behind the counter, talking in low voices. From their position, Katherina and Jon heard Iversen telling Clara about his attempt to persuade the transmitters to show up. She looked both tired and resigned.

Iversen went over to the door and looked out before he locked up.

'I don't think anyone else is coming,' he said, turning to face the gathering. 'You all know why we're here,' he began. 'But just to sum up: we're convinced that there exists a Shadow Organization of Lectors who are behind the latest attacks on our members. There are strong indications that this same organization was also behind similar events twenty years ago, events that led to the break-up of the Society into transmitters and receivers. We have reason to believe that a certain Otto Remer plays a leading role in the Shadow Organization, and we have proof that he's had contact with Kortmann.' Scattered murmuring broke out in the room, making Iversen raise his hand in a calming gesture. 'It's not clear how serious that contact was. Kortmann may not have been aware of Remer's agenda, and it's not certain that Kortmann was exploited at all.'

'In the worst case, Kortmann is part of the Shadow Organization,' Clara interrupted him. 'But until we know more, we ought to regard him as a victim.'

Katherina shifted uneasily on her chair. She had difficulty picturing Kortmann as an innocent victim. His whole attitude towards her and other receivers had been laced with distrust and arrogance. He'd used every opportunity to make the distance between the two groups even greater, showing no desire for reconciliation. Even Luca, who never had a bad thing to say about anyone, had fretted over Kortmann's negative attitude.

'Kortmann doesn't believe the Shadow Organization exists,' Iversen went on. 'That's why he's not here tonight. Just as twenty years ago he put the blame for events on the receivers.' He nodded towards the group of receivers, whose murmuring expressed their dissatisfaction. 'It could be sheer stubbornness or vanity. Admitting that he was wrong back then, and now as well, would be a great loss of face for him. And those of us who know Kortmann well know that this is something he tries for all the world to avoid.'

Henning raised his hand and Iversen gave him the floor.

'No matter whether we assume that Kortmann is the mole or he's innocent and is being used without his knowledge by this Shadow Organization, it means only one thing.' He paused dramatically. 'It means that they've been able to get very close to Kortmann, and of all of us he is the most protected and isolated, with his private chauffeur and everything. So what's to stop more of us being part of the conspiracy?'

'Nothing,' Iversen admitted. 'It's highly probable that one or more of us sitting here in this room is working for the Shadow Organization, either actively or unknowingly.'

Henning grimaced. 'So how do we make sure there aren't any spies?' he asked, sounding defeated.

'We have to admit that we don't have an answer to that question,' said Clara. 'A polygraph test might be a possibility, but if the individual doesn't even know he's passing on information, it would be useless. All the Shadow Organization needs is for a receiver to be in the vicinity of one of our members whenever he or she is reading.'

'If that person doesn't manage to focus his thoughts,' Iversen interjected, with regret in his voice.

'It could happen to any of us,' said Clara. 'It could be one of your colleagues, a neighbour or a lover. We're not used to taking those kinds of precautions – it would seem too vain. In that sense we've been very vulnerable.'

A lengthy discussion ensued as to how any moles might be uncovered. Some suggestions bordered on resorting to torture by using truth serum. Someone else proposed that each person should read a sufficiently long text under the careful observation of a committee of receivers who, in theory, would be able to receive any incriminating thoughts or images. But this idea was rejected when

Katherina pointed out that Luca had been capable of focusing his attention to such a degree that none of his private thoughts could be intercepted. Besides, the method wouldn't be able to catch those who were unaware of their own inadvertent disclosures.

Even though a mood of despondency was beginning to spread through the room, Katherina could sense that those present were still prepared to cooperate. No accusations of blame were exchanged between the two groups; everyone realized that this was a shared problem and offered suggestions for a solution. Yet none of the proposals seemed convincing and they soon ran out of ideas.

For a moment no one said a word, until Iversen cleared his throat.

'The only person we are pretty sure is part of the Shadow Organization is Remer,' he said.

'So let's start there,' said Clara. 'Do you know where to find this Remer?'

'He's on the move a lot,' said Iversen. 'We've found three private addresses and multiple company addresses.' He sighed. 'He could be at twenty different locations, at least – and that's just in Denmark.'

Clara looked around and threw out her hands. 'Twenty locations? There're plenty of us here to handle that. How about monitoring each place?'

'And we do have a photo of him,' Katherina added eagerly.

'And it should be possible to get a sufficient number of vehicles,' Clara interjected. 'All it takes is a little patience.'

Henning raised his hand like a polite schoolboy.

'I'm sorry to point this out,' he began, looking as if the discussion amused him. 'But none of us is exactly a private detective. I may be mistaken, of course, but I don't think that anyone here has ever tried to follow a man or a car, and if this Remer has villainous intentions, as you claim, we have to assume that he's much better at that sort of thing than a bunch of amateurs. I'm sure that he'll see right through it at once and disappear, and we won't be able to do anything about it. What we need is some other way of flushing him out of hiding.'

Clara and Iversen looked at each other. Katherina could see the resignation in their eyes as they realized Henning was right.

'Maybe I can help,' Jon offered.

Everyone fixed their eyes on Jon, who so far hadn't said a word during the entire meeting.

'Of course,' replied Clara, giving him an encouraging nod. 'But how?'

'Hmm, well, I could ring him up.'

# 26

'Remer here. Leave a message.'

Jon recognized the voice on the answering machine as his former client, and he cleared his throat before the tone insisted that he speak.

'This is Jon Campelli,' he began, and then paused briefly. 'I think we should meet. Tomorrow, three p.m., at the Clean Glass pub. Come alone, and don't bring any sort of reading material.' He hung up and studied the faces of Katherina and Iversen on the other side of the counter in Libri di Luca. Iversen nodded with approval. Jon himself was a little surprised that he'd got through to the right number. The business card that Remer had given him at their first meeting could easily have been fake.

'The Clean Glass?' Katherina frowned.

'Not many readers there,' replied Jon.

'I still think it's risky,' said Iversen. 'He'll know that something's up.'

'Maybe,' said Jon. 'But I still have something that they want.' He waved his arm to encompass the space of the bookshop.

Iversen had arranged to have the carpet replaced. The new burgundy floor covering seemed ill suited to the old, worn furniture. But soon dust and footprints would make it a natural part of the room, and all traces of the fire would be gone.

'Besides, what do we have to lose?' asked Jon.

'He hasn't hesitated to kill,' Iversen pointed out. 'Or so we believe.'

Katherina looked worried as she stood there, leaning against the counter with her arms crossed. Jon nodded towards her.

'You'll be there to look out for me,' he said.

'Yes, outside,' Iversen emphasized. 'I'm not so sure we can rule out the possibility of him resorting to good old-fashioned physical violence. What's to keep him from bringing along a gun?'

Jon looked at this man who was usually so cheerful and amiable. Of course he was right, but the methods used so far by the Shadow Organization made it hard to imagine the group turning to conventional weapons. Jon fixed his eyes on the new carpet. In fact, they didn't really know. Maybe physical violence *had* been used. Jon and the others had focused solely on those situations when transmitter powers might have been involved. They had assumed that it was a gentlemanly contest, one group's powers versus another's – but why stop there?

'There will be witnesses present,' said Jon. 'I don't think Remer will try anything.'

Iversen nodded, but he still didn't seem convinced.

There were four customers in the Clean Glass pub. They were all sitting at the bar and didn't even turn round when Jon pushed open the door, letting a little fresh air slip into the tobacco haze. He ordered a draught beer and sat down at one of the tables farthest away from the bar but facing the door. In his inside pocket he had a mobile that he'd borrowed from Henning. The microphone of the attached hands-free set was fastened to the underside of his jacket collar so that Katherina and Henning would be able to hear what was going on when he rang them.

Jon took a gulp of his beer. He'd arrived in plenty of time. Remer wasn't due to show up for another ten minutes, provided that he had taken the bait. Enough time for Jon to speculate about what might happen. The most important thing was that Remer made an appearance, or rather that he drove off from the pub so the others could tail him. Jon hadn't given much thought to the actual meeting, to what he might say or whether he'd be able to control his anger at the role Remer had played in the loss of his job, and maybe even in Luca's murder.

The door opened, and a man in a light trenchcoat came in. Seeing the man's short grey hair, Jon recognized Remer at once. His former client looked around the room and fixed his gaze on Jon for a moment. Then he went over to the bar and placed his order as he cast a cool glance at the four regular customers. Jon used the opportunity to reach into his pocket and press the call button on his mobile.

The bartender set a glass of golden liquid in front of Remer. He paid for the drink, picked up the glass and calmly strolled over to the table where Jon was sitting. Jon's heart started pounding faster and he sensed his anger growing.

'Campelli,' said Remer, nodding at Jon. He turned his chair as he sat down so he would be sitting sideways to the door.

'Remer,' said Jon in greeting.

Remer studied Jon as he took a sip of his drink. He grimaced and cast a slightly offended look at the glass, which he proceeded to swirl, making small circular movements.

'Not exactly a high quality whisky they serve here,' he said, setting his glass on the table. 'I prefer single malt, not these blends.'

'Then you should try the house speciality instead,' said Jon, raising his beer and taking a drink.

Remer smiled briefly. 'I understand you're insisting on becoming a bookseller after all,' he said in a tone of voice that made it sound as if the conversation already bored him.

'You might say that I was given a shove in that direction,' replied Jon. 'But I seem to have a flair for it. My talents in that area have proven to be quite surprising.'

Remer nodded as he examined Jon intently. 'So I've heard,' he said. 'Maybe a man with that kind of talent shouldn't limit himself to a bookshop.'

Jon tried to hide his surprise as best he could. How could Remer already know that Jon had been activated and what the results had been? Was he bluffing?

A small, superior smile spread over Remer's face. 'That sort of skill could be used much better in a larger context.'

'Such as a chain of shops?' asked Jon.

'For instance, yes,' said Remer, taking just a sip of the whisky and swallowing it with lips tight. 'A man with such unique abilities could be useful in many different situations.'

'As a consultant?'

'Problem-solver.'

'He would be expensive,' said Jon.

'It's all relative. If he's worth the cost, it's not expensive. But it would require, of course, that he proved how skilful he really was.'

'A test?'

'Or a check-up,' Remer suggested. 'It just so happens that I have access to facilities that can measure this sort of thing.'

'I wasn't aware that such talents could be measured,' said Jon.

Remer smiled secretively. 'Oh, yes indeed. If someone has the will and the curiosity to achieve the best results, he has to tackle the matter scientifically. Exactly like serious athletes today. Elite sports are not for people who have romantic notions about going for a run out in nature, eating healthy food and getting a good night's sleep. It involves the optimization and total utilization of an individual's potential, and a bit more.'

'And some people are born with a greater potential than others.'

'Precisely,' said Remer firmly, jabbing his finger at the table. 'And those few have an obligation to use their full potential instead of pissing it away on amateur foolishness and trivialities.'

'Such as promoting a good reading experience?'

'Perhaps. Literature has acquired a much too romantic glow these days. Reading has become a kind of distinguished pastime for intellectuals. But it really is nothing more than a means of distributing information, or even a form of entertainment, but first and foremost the transmission of knowledge, attitudes and opinions.'

'That sounds a little cynical to me,' said Jon. 'There are plenty of people who enjoy reading.'

'There are also plenty who play sports for fun,' Remer acknowledged. 'But they'll never be anything but amateurs. If you want to be a professional, you have to have a professional attitude towards the tools in your possession.'

They both took a sip of their drinks.

'Well, Jon?' Remer began after a brief pause. 'Do you want to be an amateur or a professional?'

Jon studied the bubbles rising to the surface in his glass. He'd once heard that beer foamed more in a dirty glass than in a clean one. That didn't bode well for the reputation of this pub, but he presumed it wouldn't make much of an impression on the customers seated at the bar, the professional guests. The conversation had taken a different turn from what he was expecting. He hadn't counted on finding out that *he* was the bargaining chip and not Libri di Luca. That meant, of course, that he wasn't in any imminent danger, but that could also quickly change if he didn't join forces with Remer.

'You don't have to give me an answer now,' said Remer. 'Think it over when you can find some time alone.' His gaze shifted from Jon's face to his jacket, where the mobile was inside his pocket. 'But you should know that we have answers to many of your questions, and we're in possession of facilities that could help you to utilize your potential to the fullest. With us you'll find explanations and the opportunity to use your powers for something substantial.'

Jon nodded. 'I need to give this a little more thought,' he said.

'Of course. But don't wait too long. We can easily become impatient.' Remer gulped down the rest of his whisky and stood up. 'Shall we say three days?'

'Okay, you'll hear from me in three days.'

'Excellent. Talk to you soon, Jon.'

He didn't wait for a response but headed straight for the door and walked out of the Clean Glass without looking back.

Jon pulled up the collar of his jacket and bent his head.

'He's outside now,' he said into the microphone.

'We can see him,' said Katherina's voice on the other end. The sound of a car engine was audible in the background. 'I'll ring when we know where he's going.'

Jon rang off and set the mobile on the table in front of him. Even though it wasn't his, he felt reassured to be once again a member of the communication society. It would have been difficult to carry out their little surveillance action without mobile phones. At that moment Katherina and Henning were setting out after Remer, and they'd be able to report back to him in the pub or notify the other vehicles to take over the pursuit. So they hadn't been able to avoid playing amateur detectives, after all, much to Henning's dismay, but it was the best solution anyone had come up with at the meeting the night before. At least they weren't just waiting around for Remer to show up at twenty different places all over Denmark.

Four vehicles were participating, each with two people, one of whom was a transmitter, the other a receiver. It was a good way to break the ice, in Iversen's opinion, and besides, it might prove useful to have both sets of powers on the scene when Remer reached his destination. Jon hoped they had thought of everything, but they were still amateurs, and he was sure that Remer and his cohorts had much more experience in this line – which marked the difference between amateurs and professionals, as Remer had just mentioned. Their only advantage was that Remer might under-estimate them.

Jon drank more of his beer. A month ago he would have seriously considered the type of offer that Remer had presented – being a consultant to one of the country's richest businessmen was a tempting proposition. As a promising barrister on his way up, he wouldn't have hesitated to change jobs if it would benefit his career. It was a matter of learning from the best and exploiting all available opportunities. Occasionally this meant making use of methods that some would find morally questionable. Not all barristers allowed themselves to take advantage of the errors in procedure made by their opponents, even though it might win the case or lead to a swift settlement. But Jon knew that wasn't all Remer had been asking him.

Jon grimaced. He sensed that he was no longer the same person, and at the moment he couldn't imagine he would ever be able to return to his former life.

The mobile on the table rang. Several of the customers at the bar scowled at him in annoyance and he hurried to take the call.

'It's Katherina,' he heard. 'We're in the Østerbro district, near the embassies.' For a moment her voice was drowned out by traffic noise. '. . . but it looks like he's getting close to where he's going, whatever that may be.'

'Okay,' said Jon. 'Do you think he noticed anything?'

'We've done our best,' replied Katherina. 'We've kept him on a long leash, and we've changed cars a couple of times.'

'Good,' said Jon. 'I'm heading back to the bookshop now. Ring me again when he stops.'

'By the way,' said Katherina before Jon hung up. 'Do you know what kind of car he drives?'

Jon told her he didn't.

'A Land Rover.'

When Jon arrived at Libri di Luca, Pau was standing outside waiting for him. He had his hands stuffed in his pockets and his shoulders were hunched up around his ears. As Jon approached, Pau shifted his feet uneasily.

'Hi, boss,' he said, smiling with embarrassment.

'Hi, Pau,' replied Jon in a neutral tone. Whatever it was that Pau wanted, Jon had no intention of making it easy for him.

'Closed up a little early today, didn't you?' Pau said, giving a laugh. 'What's going on? Did you invent a new holiday or something?'

'Iversen is out,' replied Jon tersely, nodding at the sign in the window that announced the shop was closed.

'When is he going to be back?' asked Pau. It was obvious he hadn't counted on seeing Jon. Iversen was driving around after Remer somewhere in the city, and Jon couldn't answer Pau's question even if he'd wanted to.

'What can I do for you?' asked Jon bluntly.

Pau blinked and nodded towards the door. 'Could we go inside?'

Jon nodded and unlocked the door to the antiquarian bookshop, letting Pau lead the way. He followed and closed the door behind them, without turning over the 'Open' sign.

'Does Kortmann know you're here?'

Pau shook his head. 'He's a psychopath. The only thing he can talk about is how the receivers have ruined everything. Luring everybody over to their side and stuff like that.'

'It was my understanding you shared that opinion,' said Jon, trying to make eye contact with Pau.

'I still don't believe in that Shadow Organization story. But Kortmann is too extreme. He treats us like his private army, that he can order around any way he likes.'

'What about the others?'

'I guess they're going along with it, but I think they're staying mostly because they don't want to make Kortmann mad. Not so much because they believe him.'

'So what can I do for you?' Jon repeated.

Pau looked down at his shoes. 'I'd like to come back,' he said in a low voice. 'I'd rather be with all of you.'

Jon looked closely at Pau. He really did seem to mean it. Maybe they'd been too hard on him. Paranoia had got hold of them and they were seeing spies everywhere, not only from the Shadow Organization but also from Kortmann's rank and file.

'What do I have to do?' asked Pau. 'Do I really have to beg?'

At that moment a mobile rang. They looked at each other reproachfully, until Jon remembered that the unfamiliar ring tone was coming from Henning's mobile in his inside pocket.

'Just a second,' said Jon, moving away from Pau. With his back turned, he took the call.

It was Katherina.

'Remer did stop in Østerbro,' she said. 'Outside what looks like a private school in the embassy area.'

Jon turned so he could keep an eye on Pau as he talked.

'How long has he been there?' he asked. The young man he was watching did his best to look as if he weren't listening, but his fleeting glances in Jon's direction gave him away.

'Since we last talked. About half an hour,' replied Katherina. 'Henning is scoping out the neighbourhood. He wants to find out if there's a way into the building from the other streets.'

'Were you able to pick up anything?'

'Very little,' said Katherina. 'It seems like . . . just a minute, a car is coming.'

Jon listened to Katherina's breathing, and he couldn't help holding his breath.

'A white Polo,' whispered Katherina. 'A man is getting out. He's about thirty, tall, black hair, wearing a suit. He's taking a good look around.' Her breathing stopped. 'I've seen him somewhere before.'

'Where?'

'Oh, no. Now I remember,' she said, aghast. 'It's Kortmann's chauffeur.'

# 27

Katherina was slouched down in the passenger seat so that she could just barely see over the dashboard. Parked fifty metres further down the road was the white Polo Kortmann's chauffeur had arrived in. Even though five minutes had passed since he'd disappeared behind the gates of the building Remer had also entered, she hadn't changed position and her heart hadn't stopped pounding. She could still feel how the man's eyes had scanned the vicinity, like a surveillance camera registering anything suspicious. Had his gaze lingered on the car where she was sitting?

Suddenly the door on the driver's side was yanked open, making her utter a shriek of alarm.

'Hey, what's wrong?' said Henning, as he dropped into the seat beside her. 'I didn't mean to scare you.'

Katherina shook her head, unable to say a word.

Henning slammed the door shut and looked at her with growing astonishment. 'You're really scared, aren't you? Did something happen?'

She nodded, which made Henning shift his glance to the windscreen.

'Did he come out? Did he drive off? No, his car is still there.'

'Kortmann's chauffeur just arrived,' said Katherina finally, after catching her breath. 'In that white Polo. He went inside the school.'

'Are you sure?' said Henning, giving her a searching glance. 'That would mean . . .' He stopped in mid-sentence. 'Well, what the hell would that mean?'

'That Kortmann has sent his errand boy with a message for Remer,' said Katherina, sitting up. She regretted reacting the way she had, and she crossed her arms so Henning wouldn't notice her hands were still shaking slightly.

Henning nodded. 'I think you're right. If it really was his chauffeur, then there can't be any doubt that Kortmann is involved.' He grabbed the steering wheel with both hands and stared out. 'And you're absolutely sure about this?' he repeated.

'I'm telling you, it was him.'

'Bloody hell.'

'Jon's on his way,' said Katherina, but it was clear that her companion was no longer listening. Instead, Henning sat with his eyes fixed straight ahead, looking at the white Polo and muttering angrily to himself.

'All these years,' he said.

Katherina looked at the section of the building that wasn't hidden behind the two-metre-high hedge surrounding the place. It was a two-storey structure made of red brick with a slate roof. Earlier, when they first arrived, they had slowly driven by so that Henning could read the sign attached to the iron gate that opened on to the property. 'Demetrius School' it said, but neither of them knew what that meant.

A fierce wind had started blowing and the sky above was just as grey as the slate roof of the school, making the dividing line nearly invisible. It almost looked as if the roof had been removed from the building, like on a dolls' house. Katherina wished that she could look down inside the rooms and discover whatever secrets the walls were protecting.

The sound of a car engine starting up tore Katherina out of her reverie.

'Now what?' she said, turning to face Henning, who with a lurch put the car in gear and pulled out of the parking slot.

'I have to talk to him,' he said. 'I'll be damned if he thinks he can make fools of us all.'

'Are you crazy?' But Katherina's protests were drowned out by Henning's curses.

'It's the best chance we have. His bodyguard is here, which means Kortmann must be home alone. What is he going to do? Run us down with his wheelchair?'

'Shouldn't we at least wait for Jon?' said Katherina.

'He's not the one Kortmann has been duping for the past twenty years.'

Katherina could see by Henning's expression that she wouldn't be able to change his mind. He was driving fast and shifting gears ferociously, as if it was the car he wanted to punish.

'Let me at least tell him where we're going,' she said, taking her mobile out of the glove compartment.

Henning merely growled in response.

Katherina couldn't start discussing things with Jon while Henning was within earshot. Just before they rang off, Jon said that he would meet them at Kortmann's villa as soon as he could. In the meantime, she had to try to persuade Henning to wait.

'What are you actually planning to do once we get there?' asked Katherina after they'd been driving for several minutes without speaking.

'I want to make him tell me the truth.'

'And if he refuses?'

Henning cast a swift glance in her direction and she thought she saw a trace of doubt in his eyes.

'He won't do that,' he said firmly. 'Besides, I'll be able to tell the truth by looking at him. I've known him almost my whole life.'

'But he's been lying to you all this time,' Katherina pointed out. 'What's going to stop him from continuing to lie?'

Henning didn't answer, but his expression was no longer as fierce, and he had started driving more slowly.

As they approached Kortmann's villa, it started to rain. At first big, heavy drops hammered against the car's windscreen and roof at a slow, intermittent pace. But very quickly the rain started pouring down at such a rapid rate that it sounded like static. The windscreen wipers soon could not keep up, and Henning had to slow down and lean forward to be able to see where he was driving. In a matter of seconds the temperature inside the car dropped several degrees. Katherina shivered.

'The gate!' cried Henning. 'It's open.'

Katherina peered through the sheet of water covering the windscreen. Henning was right. The big wrought-iron gate to Kortmann's property stood open, just wide enough for a car to drive through. They exchanged glances. Henning looked worried.

'I've never seen this before,' he said, driving through the gate. The parking spaces in front of the house were empty. Henning drove as close to the main entrance as he could. After he switched off the engine, they sat there for a moment, listening to the rain.

'It doesn't look like it's going to stop any time soon,' said Henning, reaching for the door handle. 'Are you coming?'

Katherina nodded. They both jumped out and ran for the oak door. A little overhang above the entrance offered some shelter, but after running the few metres from the car they were almost soaked through. Henning pressed the doorbell, and they could hear a muted ringing from inside. They waited half a minute, and then Henning pressed the bell again, this time holding it down longer. Katherina hoped that Kortmann wasn't home after all so they could avoid this impromptu confrontation and disappear without anyone knowing that they'd even been here.

'He's probably upstairs,' said Henning, pressing the bell for another ten seconds. 'He'd better not think we're just going to drive away.'

There was still no response from inside the house and Henning started pounding on the front door with his fist.

'Maybe he's really not home,' Katherina suggested. 'His chauffeur could have driven him somewhere before he went off to meet Remer.'

Henning shook his head.

'He's in there,' he said. 'I can feel it. Come on, we'll take the lift.'

He raced off through the rain and Katherina reluctantly followed. Together they dashed round the house to the lift tower. Even from some distance away, they could hear the rain drumming relentlessly on the huge metal structure. They were drenched by the time they reached the tower door, which Henning yanked open so they could throw themselves inside and get out of the rain.

'What bloody awful weather,' he exclaimed, shaking his head like a dog shaking water off his fur. The floor was splotched with the rain dripping off their clothes.

Inside the tower the sound of the rain was even louder, an uninterrupted hammering on the metal hull that drowned out everything else. Katherina was expecting at any second to hear Kortmann's voice on the loudspeaker near the door, but it remained silent. Henning found the button to start the lift. The huge gears on both sides began to move, and very slowly the platform rose.

'What's that?'

Henning was looking at the floor, so Katherina did the same. At first she couldn't see what he was talking about, but then she noticed a shadow on the floor that couldn't be coming from either of them. The light source was in the ceiling, and they both looked up at it, seven or eight metres overhead.

A shapeless silhouette directly above them was creating the shadow, but they couldn't tell what it was. The lift continued its ascent, and they slowly got closer. Something was hanging from the ceiling of the lift shaft, and Katherina stepped over to the very edge of the platform to get a better look.

'Oh no,' she said when she realized what it was.

Kortmann's lifeless body hung from the ceiling like a piece of meat wrapped in an expensive suit.

'Oh my God,' exclaimed Henning, as he too stepped over to the edge.

The body was coming inescapably closer even though Henning desperately pressed all the buttons he could find. Kortmann's thin legs slowly slid past, followed by his torso, which seemed to be twisted at a strange angle. His face was turned towards Katherina, and she had to look away as they reached eye level. Kortmann's eyes were open wide and his mouth was contorted into a rigid expression of terror.

When Kortmann's feet struck the floor, his body began tipping towards Katherina. She frantically pushed it away. The corpse weighed virtually nothing but it was completely rigid and it fell towards Henning standing on the opposite side. He leaped out of the way, as if the body carried some sort of disease. The corpse calmly came to rest on the floor of the lift, frozen in an awkward position, like a victim of Vesuvius. As they continued upwards, the rope from which Kortmann had been hanging coiled onto the body like a long piece of spaghetti.

With a lurch the lift came to a halt.

Almost simultaneously the rain stopped, just as suddenly as it had begun, and there was utter silence inside the tower. Katherina and Henning looked at each other. Henning's face no longer radiated anger; instead, his eyes were filled with terror. And Katherina knew her expression was similar. Her heart was pounding and she felt nauseated, which made her gasp for air.

'I think we can rule out suicide this time,' said Henning, trying to sound calm. He nodded towards the ceiling. 'It would have been impossible for him to tie that rope himself.'

Katherina followed his gaze to the iron bars overhead where the rope had been tied. It was still more than two and a half metres to the ceiling. She let her eyes run along the rope down to the body on the floor, forcing herself to look at it even though what she most wanted to do was close her eyes or run away. A noose was wrapped round the neck of the frail body and she saw that his hands had been tied behind his back. Henning knelt beside the body and studied the hands as he nodded to himself. Hesitantly he stretched out two fingers to Kortmann's throat and touched him just under the jaw. He yanked his hand away as if he'd received an electric shock.

'He's ice cold,' said Henning, wiping his fingers on his trousers as if he'd touched something contagious.

He stood up, stepped over the corpse and pushed open the door to the house. There lay Kortmann's wheelchair on its side with a checked blanket several metres away. The door at the end of the catwalk stood open, and a light was on inside the house.

They looked at each other.

'Don't you think we should get out of here?' said Katherina.

'Let's just take a quick look,' said Henning, stepping onto the catwalk. Katherina followed. She thought their footsteps echoed much too loudly on the metal flooring and she tried to tiptoe her way forward. Henning didn't seem bothered by the sound and strode towards the door leading into the house.

They entered a hallway with paintings on the walls and a thick carpet on the floor, which to Katherina's great relief muted the sound of their footsteps. Henning continued on to yet another open door at the end of the hall. It led to the library, which Jon had described to Katherina, but she was still surprised by its stylish furnishings and the peaceful atmosphere. She had only experienced Kortmann as a suspicious, power-hungry man and had completely forgotten that they shared a passion for books.

The walls were lined with bookcases filled with volumes bound in beautifully preserved leather. The chandelier hanging from the ceiling sent a soft glow over the reading areas in the centre of the room, while the indirect lighting above the shelves seemed to raise the ceiling, giving the room the air of a museum.

They were no more than twenty metres away from Kortmann's body, but as soon as they stepped inside the room, it felt as if they'd entered an entirely different world of order and refinement. The uneasiness Katherina had felt even before they found Kortmann's body had disappeared, and she now wished they could stay in this room. She went over to the nearest bookshelf and placed the palm of her hand on the spines of several books. They felt warm under her touch.

'Impressive, isn't it?' said Henning, uttering a sigh. 'What's going to happen to all the books now?' There was great sadness in his voice, as if he were talking about small children who had been abandoned. He sank onto one of the leather armchairs and looked around at the surrounding bookshelves. His eyelids blinked rapidly, as if he were greedily taking pictures of a phenomenon that would soon disappear.

With her fingertips lightly touching the books on the shelves, Katherina walked along one wall. There was no doubt they were valuable volumes, and many of them were so charged that her fingers tingled when she ran them over the spines. Henning was right – it would be a great loss if these books were scattered to the winds, but what could they do to prevent it?

'I wish we could take them with us,' said Henning, as if he had read her thoughts.

Katherina nodded. 'We've got to go,' she said, tearing herself away.

Henning reluctantly got up from the chair and took one last look around before they went back to the tower.

In the lift they were once again confronted by Kortmann's body, frozen in the middle of the platform.

'So he was to be trusted, after all,' said Henning with regret in his voice.

'It looks that way,' replied Katherina. She was embarrassed that she'd let herself get drawn into condemning Kortmann without any real proof. But she consoled herself by remembering that he hadn't been especially cooperative either.

'We can't just leave him like this,' said Henning firmly.

'If we move him, we'll become suspects,' Katherina pointed out.

'It's already a homicide case,' said Henning. 'If the police connect us to the case, we'll have a problem explaining things no matter what. I'm taking him to his library. It's where he belongs.' He stood on his toes and stretched his arms up to the ceiling, where he could just manage to reach the knots tied in the rope.

After untying Kortmann, he lifted him up and carried his body inside the house. Katherina stayed where she was. She had a feeling that they were committing a grave mistake, but at the same time she could understand why Henning refused to accept that his mentor for all these years should be left lying in the cold shaft of the lift. When Henning returned, he didn't say a word, just used his sleeve to carefully wipe off the door handle and the buttons in the lift.

It seemed to Katherina that their descent to ground level took forever. All she wanted was to get out of that place as quickly as possible. Ever since their arrival, she'd had a feeling they were being watched. As if the whole thing had been stage-managed and was waiting for them so that they could carry out their roles. Had it been planned that they and not the police should find Kortmann first? Could that be a warning from the Shadow Organization?

The sky outside was still grey; sporadic raindrops were hitting the ground with audible slaps. Even though it was only late afternoon, it was almost as dark as night, and they could hardly see the path in front of them. They hurried through the garden and back to the front of the house, where the car was parked.

Just as they were about to get into the vehicle, they heard the sound of a car engine heading up the driveway. Both of them froze and turned their faces towards the sound.

The next second they were blinded by the headlamps.

# 28

'Something's wrong,' said Jon the moment he saw Katherina's and Henning's expressions in the glow of the headlamps. Behind them Kortmann's villa was in darkness, except for a light in one window on the top floor.

'He must have thrown them out,' suggested Pau from the back seat. 'That would be just like him, the old tyrant.'

Jon had finally been convinced that Pau really meant what he said about being on their side, and so he'd been allowed to come along. It wasn't Jon's decision, after all, whether Pau should be accepted or not into the new alliance. But now Jon regretted bringing him.

Jon drove the car closer. Katherina finally seemed to recognize him and relief spread across her face. She came over to the car the minute it stopped and hugged Jon as soon as he got out. He noticed that she was shaking.

'What happened?' he asked.

'Kortmann is dead,' Henning announced from the other side of the car.

'Dead? How?'

'We found him hanged in the tower,' explained Henning, motioning with his head towards the house. 'It looked as if someone had . . . helped him.'

Jon gently pushed Katherina away so he could study her face. Her eyes were shiny, and she was still shaking. With a nod she confirmed what Henning had said. Jon pulled her close again and wrapped his arms around her.

'Could it have been a break-in?' he asked over Katherina's shoulder. 'I mean, the gate was open, so anyone could have got in.'

Henning shook his head. 'It seems unlikely. As far as I could tell, nothing was missing.'

Jon noticed that Katherina gave a start when Pau got out of the car to join them.

'So much for your theory that he was part of the Shadow Organization, huh?' said Pau.

Henning was just as surprised to see Pau as Katherina was, and he turned to Jon with an indignant look on his face.

'What's he doing here?'

'It appears he has changed his mind,' replied Jon.

'I didn't feel like being Kortmann's errand boy,' Pau interjected. 'But I guess now I won't be.' He shook his head. 'Poor old guy.'

Henning looked intently at Pau but said no more than, 'We can't stay.'

Katherina was shivering. 'Take me away from here,' she said.

'Let's go back to Libri di Luca,' suggested Jon. 'Iversen and the others will be there soon.'

Henning nodded and cast one last look at Pau before he got into his car and drove away.

There were lights on in the windows of Libri di Luca when they got back. Katherina had regained her composure, although she hadn't said much on the drive from Hellerup. Pau hadn't spoken either, merely muttered to himself and sighed.

Henning had already arrived, and he'd obviously told Iversen what had happened, because the old bookseller looked shaken as he sat in the armchair behind the counter holding a glass of cognac. He looked up with distress as Katherina and Jon came into the shop; there was no trace of a reaction on his face when he saw Pau behind them. Clara was there too. She had been Iversen's driver when they were tailing Remer, and she now stood leaning against a bookcase with her arms crossed and a serious expression on her round face.

'I think I could use one of those myself,' said Henning, motioning towards Iversen's cognac. 'Anyone else want one?'

Katherina nodded while the others declined. Henning reached behind the counter and pulled out two glasses, filling each with a generous portion. Katherina accepted the drink gratefully, holding the glass in both hands as if the contents might warm up her fingers.

'You're sure it was Kortmann's chauffeur?' asked Clara after Henning had explained why they'd gone out to the villa in Hellerup.

'Absolutely sure,' replied Katherina in a hoarse voice. She took a sip of her cognac and grimaced as she swallowed the liquor.

Clara nodded solemnly.

'Then there's no longer any doubt,' she said. 'This Remer is somehow involved in what's been happening, and most likely there is some sort of larger organization behind it all. An organization that won't stop at committing murder to reach its goal.'

Everyone except Pau agreed by nodding or murmuring their assent.

'You're all crazy,' Pau declared, taking a step towards Iversen. 'Can't you see this is part of their plan? They're trying to divert attention from themselves. Who's the only person who actually saw Kortmann's chauffeur?' He pointed at Katherina without looking at her. 'A receiver. And who benefits from murdering Kortmann?' He pointed the other hand at Clara. 'The receivers. Can't you see it? They're manipulating us just like they've been doing all along.'

'You're forgetting that Kortmann never would have allowed a receiver inside his house,' Jon pointed out.

Pau raised his arms towards the ceiling. 'Not voluntarily, of course. They could have forced him to do it, caught him by surprise while he was reading and made him open the gate for them.'

'Would that be possible?' asked Jon.

'No,' said Clara firmly. 'We can't steer people by remote control like that; the most we can do is affect their emotions and their attitude towards whatever they're reading.'

Pau had let his arms drop. 'We only have your word for it that it's not possible. None of us knows what you can really do.'

'Rubbish,' said Iversen. 'You're grasping at straws now, Pau. Those of us who have been part of the Society for a long time know that it's true. As Clara said, we need to accept that the Shadow Organization is a reality, and the sooner we do that, the better we can fight back.'

Pau opened his mouth to object but was cut off by Iversen.

'Sit down, Pau. Take a moment to think about what has happened, and you'll come to the same conclusion.'

Sulking, Pau walked over to one of the bookcases and sat down on the floor.

'As I was about to say,' Clara began, casting a quick glance at Pau, 'we must be getting close since they're reacting so violently. It's no coincidence that just as the Society is being reunited, Kortmann ends up murdered. His role was done – they had no more use for him.' She sighed. 'We need to acknowledge that Kortmann was their man, in the sense that he was under the influence of his chauffeur, whom we have to assume is a receiver. So they've known all along what the transmitters were doing, and they were even able to get Kortmann to make decisions that fitted in with their plans.'

'Which first and foremost concerned keeping their own organization secret,' said Iversen. 'But when I think back, I'm sure that Kortmann has had that chauffeur for only seven or eight years. That's still a long time, but it doesn't explain Kortmann's involvement in the break-up twenty years ago.'

No one said anything for a while. Jon could sense a despondent mood. His own emotions were mixed. He too was shocked by the murder, but he and Kortmann had not really cared for each other. From that moment at the funeral when they met for the first time, Jon had felt a certain wariness on Kortmann's part, as if he were sizing up a competitor. In that sense, Jon could have better accepted the situation if Kortmann had proved to be their adversary. But now, when it looked as if he was innocent, things were murkier than ever. What was still worrisome, and what no one was saying out loud even though they were probably all thinking it, was that since the Shadow Organization had been able to get so close to the leader of the transmitters, it was impossible to know who else might be involved, either directly or indirectly. Wasn't it naive to think there were no spies among the receivers?

'So what's left that we need to work on?' asked Iversen, breaking the silence. 'What's the next step?'

Everyone in the shop glanced at each other.

'The school,' suggested Jon. 'The Demetrius School. It must mean something, since that was where Remer went to meet Kortmann's chauffeur.'

'There's something I forgot to tell you,' said Katherina. Everyone turned to look at her. 'When I was sitting alone in the car, while Henning was out surveying the neighbourhood, I tried to pick up if there was something going on inside – if anyone was reading, and if so, what they happened to be reading.' She took another sip of her cognac. 'I was able to pick up several reading classes, words mostly from easy-to-read books, but there was something else – a number of voices that were different, that stood out because the reading was more focused and had a bigger impact.'

'Do you mean . . .' Clara didn't finish her sentence.

'I'm convinced it was a group of transmitters,' said Katherina.

'How many?' asked Iversen.

'Maybe four or five.'

'So is the Demetrius School the Shadow Organization's recruitment centre for Lectors?' said Clara. 'Have any of you heard of the place before?'

Jon shook his head. Katherina and Henning did the same.

'Demetrius?' said Iversen to himself, tilting his head back to look up at the ceiling. 'Isn't that the name of a character in a Shakespeare play? From *A Midsummer Night's Dream*, as far as I recall. Demetrius drinks a love potion and falls in love with the wrong person.' He lowered his eyes. 'That doesn't exactly fit with our situation.'

'Under any circumstances, the school is our best lead,' said Jon. 'I'd like to propose that I go out there and take a closer look at the place. If the school is the centre for the Shadow Organization's activities, there must be something inside the building that will prove it.'

'You mean break in?' asked Iversen.

'If that's what it takes,' replied Jon.

'I'll go with you,' said Katherina.

Jon was about to object but was stopped by her expression. It was obvious she had made up her mind. Iversen, on the other hand, tried to persuade her not to go, supported by Clara, but Katherina firmly believed that a receiver needed to go along, for safety's sake.

When everything had been decided, Pau chimed in. 'If a receiver needs to go along, I want to join the party too.' He got up from his place on the floor. 'You need to have a sceptic present, someone who can keep your feet on the ground so you don't go off on some big conspiracy trip.'

'If that's what it'll take to convince you, it's okay by me.' Jon turned to look at Katherina.

Her resolve seemed to have vanished. Her eyes flickered and she hesitated for a moment before she nodded. 'But we're going to do this our way, Pau,' she insisted.

'Sure, sure,' said Pau cheerfully. 'Don't worry, I'll behave myself.'

They had agreed to meet at three a.m.

Jon and Katherina went together to their respective flats to pick up what they thought they might need. Afterwards they collected Pau at Trianglen before continuing on to the embassy area, which wasn't far away. None of them said anything in the car.

Jon parked the car about a hundred metres from the school and they all got out. The sky was free of clouds, and the multitudes of stars were very bright. Jon's dark jogging suit offered little protection from the night chill and he regretted not dressing more warmly, but it was the only dark clothing he owned aside from a suit.

He'd brought along a sports bag containing various tools from the workshop in the basement of Libri di Luca. He had no practical experience of burglary, so he'd brought a large assortment of tools. Pau was also dressed in dark clothing and he carried a crowbar in a plastic bag. Jon had the feeling that the young man was not altogether unfamiliar with this kind of activity. Katherina had put on a pair of jeans, trainers and a dark windbreaker. Her red hair was drawn back into a knot at the nape of her neck, and she had pulled a black cap down over her forehead.

They walked calmly along the pavement towards the school. The buildings in the neighbourhood were all in darkness. They were mostly large, grand villas, many of them now embassies for smaller countries. At this time of night, the area was completely deserted, almost ghostly, and the few parked cars were most likely overflow from nearby streets that were subject to a shortage of parking spaces.

The street lighting was sporadic, and in the shadows they walked all the way up to the front gate of the school.

Without hesitation Jon reached for the handle and pushed the wrought-iron gate open. He was surprised but also relieved to find it wasn't locked. Even though no one was around, it wouldn't have looked good if they had been forced to climb over the three-metre-high gate in the middle of the night. The three of them quickly entered the grounds and slipped into the shadow of the hedge to the left of the gate. As the last person in, Katherina pushed the gate closed. Then they all stood still for a moment to get their bearings.

To the right of the gate was a wall of a similar height that extended past the building and disappeared into the darkness. The hedge next to them continued along the pavement for the full width of the property. At the end they could just make out another wall, also three metres high, screening off the neighbouring building to the left of the school. In front of them lay the schoolyard, a stretch of asphalt painted with ball layouts and hopscotch grids, and behind that the redbrick school. In the middle of the building wide, granite steps led up to a sturdy front door. The door had a few tiny windows, all of which were covered by a solid-looking grating.

There were no lights on inside the building.

'Can you feel it?' whispered Pau. 'Can you feel the energy?'

Jon held his breath for a moment, trying to sense the force that Pau claimed was present.

'No, nothing,' he whispered back after a few seconds, wondering if Pau was making fun of them.

'Me neither,' said Katherina in a low voice.

'Hmm,' muttered Pau, disappointed. 'That way,' he whispered, pointing to the nearest corner of the building, where a passageway was visible running alongside the outer wall to the back.

They crept along the wall over to the passageway, which took them to the other side of the school. A strip of grass formed a small yard with shrubbery, and a few fruit trees lined the outer walls. The back of the building had two doors – one that opened onto an industrial kitchen, and a basement door at the bottom of a staircase four metres deep.

Jon motioned to the others that they should try the basement door, and Pau stepped forward at once to descend the stairs while Jon and Katherina remained standing at the top. They watched as he first peered into the windowpanes on the door and then tried the handle. When the door opened, he gave a start and glanced up in surprise at his companions. Then he broke into a big grin that gleamed an eerie white in the darkness.

Jon and Katherina crept down the stairs to join the triumphant Pau.

'Please come in,' he whispered merrily, holding the door open for them.

They stepped into the darkness, followed by Pau, who closed the door behind them. Jon reached into his sports bag and pulled out a torch, aiming it down at the floor before he switched it on. They found themselves in a whitewashed corridor with three doors in addition to the one they had just entered by. The panes of the entry door behind them were covered on the inside with sheets of plywood, making it impossible to see in or out. The doors to the right and left were both ajar, and each was adorned with a WC symbol, one for boys and one for girls. The door at the end of the corridor was closed.

'Does anyone besides me think it's odd that the door wasn't locked?' whispered Katherina. Jon agreed.

At that moment a light went on, and the harsh glare reflecting off the white walls made them both squint. Jon instantly spun round. Pau stood behind him with a finger pressed to the light switch inside the door.

'Isn't that better?' he asked without lowering his voice so that his words echoed between the bare walls.

Jon turned off his torch and headed for the door at the end of the corridor. It had white panels and a brass handle. This door was also unlocked, and Jon slowly nudged it open until he could poke his head inside. What he found was yet another hallway, which apparently ran the full width of the front of the school. Up near the ceiling, at intervals of a few metres, were windows that allowed the light from the stars to shine in on the pale walls. A wide-mesh grating in front of the windowpanes cast shadows like a huge spider's web over the floor and walls.

Without opening the door any wider than necessary, Jon slipped into the hallway and motioned the others to follow. Pau closed the door behind them. A series of doors lined the wall they were huddled against, while at the end of the corridor they glimpsed a set of stairs, leading up into the building.

'You mean you still don't notice it?' asked Pau, sounding slightly annoyed.

Both Jon and Katherina said that they didn't notice a thing.

'It's strongest over there,' said Pau, pointing away from the stairs leading up.

Jon turned on the torch and aimed it in the direction Pau had indicated. At the end of the hall another stairway led down yet another level. They crept over to the stairs, with Jon going first, keeping the torch pointed at the floor. Right in front of the stairs was a strong, black iron gate, which stood open.

'I don't like this,' murmured Katherina as she grabbed hold of the gate. The bars were twisted wrought iron, at least two centimetres thick. 'It all seems too easy, don't you think?'

'Maybe they have nothing to hide,' Pau suggested. 'What sort of secrets would a school have, anyway?'

'You're the one who keeps noticing something strange,' Katherina pointed out angrily.

Jon shushed his two colleagues and shone the torchlight down the stairs in front of them.

'You're sure this is the way we should go?' he asked, turning to point the torch at Pau's face.

'Yeah, I'm sure,' replied Pau, holding up his hand to block out the beam of light. 'Can't you sense it? This is where the energy is coming from. Trust me.'

'You've certainly become awfully sensitive all of a sudden,' muttered Katherina.

Jon shone the light back on the stairs and began descending. After a couple of metres the stairs turned sharply round a corner. At the turn, Jon noticed a strange tingling of the hairs on the back of his neck, the same sensation he'd felt the first time he entered the library in the basement of Libri di Luca.

'Okay,' he admitted. 'I think we're on the right track. Now I can feel it too.'

Katherina confirmed that she also felt the energy.

'What did I tell you?' muttered Pau.

Cautiously Jon continued down the stairway. With each step he could feel the energy getting stronger, at the same time as the air got damper and stuffier. At the foot of the stairs was a corridor that led forward a couple of metres before it turned yet another corner. As far as Jon could tell, it ran along the back of the school.

The walls were more rustic in this part of the building, with big uneven patches and exposed granite.

They found two more doors when they turned the corner. The metal door on the right had a peephole of the type that might be expected in the door to a prison cell. The other door marked the end of the corridor and was made of heavy oak with black iron hinges and handle.

Jon peered into the hole in the metal door, but it was too dark to see anything. He pressed his ear against the door and listened hard. When he didn't hear anything, he pressed the metal handle down and opened it.

Inside was a small room, no more than two metres wide and about five metres long. The walls were covered with pale wooden panels. In the middle of the room two big leather chairs faced each other. They both had wide armrests, and over the back of each hung a metal helmet connected to a jumble of wires. With the beam of his torch, Jon followed the wires to where they gathered into one thick cable coming out of the wall. That same wall was dominated by a big window, which provided an adjacent room with a view of the chairs.

Jon found a light switch and turned it on. Fluorescent light flooded the room and all three of them stepped inside. As soon as Jon crossed the threshold, he sensed the energy disappear, as if someone had turned off a switch. Judging by the others' reaction, they had noticed the same thing.

'It must be shielded in some way,' Pau concluded.

'What is this place?' asked Katherina.

'The electric chair?' suggested Pau. 'All teachers must have an urge to use this sort of thing on their pupils once in a while.'

Jon leaned towards the glass pane and peered into the room next door. He glimpsed a series of red and green LEDs, and in the light from the cell he could see a table right on the other side of the window and a row of computers and printers along one wall. On the table stood a computer monitor surrounded by papers and half-empty coffee cups.

'Remer said they had the equipment to measure the powers,' said Jon. 'This must be where they do it.'

Katherina picked up a helmet. 'Very likely,' she said, looking with disgust at the helmet in her hands. 'The shield must prevent the measurements from being disturbed by the energy down here, wherever it's coming from.'

'Okay, Mr and Mrs Sherlock, shouldn't we find out where it's coming from?' said Pau, moving towards the door. 'This place is giving me the creeps.'

'Do you still think this is an innocent school building?' asked Katherina, but Pau didn't answer.

Out in the corridor they again felt the familiar tingling, and it got stronger as they headed for the oak door at the end of the hall. That door wasn't locked either, and it gave them free access to the room they had seen through the window in the cell room. In addition to the rows of computers, the printers and the table with the papers, there was another door leading further into the school.

Jon set his sports bag on the floor and went over to the table to have a look at the papers.

They were covered with graphs, sketches of parts of the brain and rows of numbers, some of them underlined or circled in pencil. At the top of each page was the name and age of the person being tested. Judging by these documents, the latest test subjects were aged ten to twelve. For some of the individuals, the numbers were a measurement of their actual strength, while for others the numbers represented an estimate of the person's expected potential.

'It looks like they can predict the strength of those who haven't even been activated yet,' said Jon.

'Could that be the criterion for admission to the school?' suggested Katherina, who had come over to the table and was looking over his shoulder. Pau stayed near the door, casting nervous glances down the corridor.

'Maybe, but it's hard to imagine how they could take the measurements without arousing suspicion from the parents,' said Jon.

Katherina shrugged. 'There's no limit to what parents will subject their beloved offspring to if it means giving Little Peter a head start.'

'God only knows whether the parents even find out the truth,' said Jon, thinking aloud. 'It's not certain they're Lectors themselves. But what about the children? When are they told? Are the parents informed, or are the kids forced to lie to their mother and father?' He shook his head. 'What would that do to a child?'

'It doesn't sound healthy,' Katherina chimed in. 'They must have more tests than this one to find suitable candidates. It's one thing to possess the powers, either activated or latent, but it's another matter whether the kids are mature enough to join the Shadow Organization.'

Katherina peered under the table and found what she was looking for. She bent down and lifted out the wastebasket. From the wastebasket she removed a number of printouts similar to those lying on the table, folded them up and stuck them in the back pocket of her jeans.

'They won't even notice they're gone,' she said, putting the wastebasket back on the floor.

The monitor on the table was blank, but a quick tap on the keyboard brought it to life. Slowly an image emerged, but Jon was disappointed when it turned out to be a command to enter the computer by typing in a name and password.

'We could use Mehmet's help right now,' he said.

Pau was still standing in the doorway, nervously shifting his feet. 'Shouldn't we get going?'

Jon nodded. 'We're not going to get anything out of this, anyway.'

He went over to Pau and picked up his sports bag. At the next door he nodded to his companions before he pressed down the handle. Pau turned off the light in the room behind them before Jon pushed open the door. It was dark, but Jon could feel a soft carpet underfoot when he stepped inside. After fumbling a bit with the torch, he switched it on and then located the light switch inside the door.

He was standing with his back to the room, Pau stood in the doorway with the crowbar in his hand and Katherina had taken a few steps inside on the carpet. Her eyes were fixed on the far end of the room, displaying both surprise and horror.

'Campelli,' they heard. 'How nice of you to drop by.'

Jon recognized the voice at once.

It was Remer.

'Get out!' shouted Jon, and took a step towards the door, but Pau didn't budge from the entrance. Instead, he broke into a big grin, and without hesitation he swung the crowbar at Jon's head.

Jon was so surprised that he didn't manage to fend off the blow, and a fierce stab of pain shot through his skull.

# 29

Katherina threw herself over Jon's unconscious body. He had dropped like a rock with the blow, as if all his muscles had been loosed at once, leaving gravity to do its work. Blood was pouring from his forehead where the crowbar had struck and running down his cheek onto the carpet. He groaned faintly.

Katherina turned an angry face towards Pau. He stood there with a triumphant smile on his lips and his weapon raised, ready to deliver another blow.

'I don't think that's going to be necessary,' said Remer from the other end of the room.

Pau's smile vanished and he lowered the crowbar.

'I'm sure Katherina here realizes the game is up.' Remer came closer as he spoke and Katherina turned to look at him. He was wearing a black suit with a grey shirt but no tie. His gaze rested on her with no sign of emotion.

'Because you *are* Katherina, aren't you?' he said.

She didn't reply, just turned her attention back to Jon. She stroked his forehead without touching the blood.

'I hope you didn't hit him too hard,' said Remer behind her. 'We need him.'

'He'll live,' said Pau. 'Couldn't be more than a slight concussion.'

'That's exactly what we don't need,' said Remer angrily. 'I told you not to hurt him.'

'I didn't have a choice,' Pau protested.

Remer sighed loudly. 'Do you think you can manage to take care of the girl while the rest of us get ready?'

Pau muttered a reply and Katherina felt a hand on her shoulder.

'Come on, Princess. We've reserved a place for you.'

He pulled her to her feet with his left hand while he held the crowbar in his right. Katherina tried to twist out of his grip but couldn't do it. Two men came into the room and knelt down on the floor next to Jon. One of them was Kortmann's chauffeur, but not once did he look at Katherina. They each took hold of Jon's arms and dragged him out through the door they had just entered by.

Pau led Katherina into the office where he shoved her down onto a swivel chair. Jon was hauled further along the hall and the door closed behind them.

'Where are they taking him?' said Katherina, staring at Pau.

'Not far,' replied Pau and smiled.

Without taking his eyes off her, he reached into a cupboard and took out a roll of duct tape. He turned her round, and she heard him place the crowbar on the cement floor.

That was her chance.

She tensed all the muscles in her body but the instant she was about to leap up from the chair, Remer came into the room. He was holding a gun in his hand. It wasn't especially big, just a little black model with a dark wooden grip, but its very presence changed everything. Even though Katherina knew the Shadow Organization wouldn't stop at murder, up until now the killing had been done by less direct means, as far as she knew. It had been achieved by using the powers – a weapon appropriate to the context – and not with a cold revolver, which seemed strangely out of place in the world of the Lectors.

Pau grabbed Katherina's arms and taped them together, binding them to the back of the chair. Remer sat down at the desk in front of the window and placed the gun on a stack of papers, as naturally as if it were a paperweight. He leaned across the table towards a microphone and pressed a button to turn it on.

'You'd better tie him up properly,' he said, casting a swift glance at Pau. 'We wouldn't want him to get hurt.'

Pau turned Katherina around and taped her legs to the frame of the chair. She glared at him, but he avoided looking at her.

'So you were part of it all along?'

He laughed. 'Don't think I enjoyed it,' he said, sneering at her. 'All your naive piss about reading experiences, literature and "the Good Story". It drove me crazy.' He gave Remer a sidelong glance. 'But now it's over. I've done my job.'

'What about the bookshop?' asked Katherina. 'What about Iversen? And Luca?'

Pau stood up and leaned forward with his hands on the armrests of her chair. He put his face very near to hers. There was loathing in his eyes. He was so close Katherina could hear him grinding his teeth.

'As far as I'm concerned, you can all go to hell.'

Katherina spat in his face and then lurched forward in her chair, but Pau managed to jump back just in time. He straightened up with a grin, wiping his face on his sleeve. Then he took a piece of tape and pressed it hard over her mouth. He stepped back, crossed his arms and regarded his handiwork with a smile. Then he laughed and disappeared into the corridor.

Katherina twisted and turned her arms, trying to loosen the tape, but to no avail. It just bit into her skin, and she would have screamed in pain if Pau hadn't taped her mouth shut. In despair she slumped, noticing that tears were welling up in her eyes. How could they have been so naive? Pau's return should have aroused suspicion, at least enough to keep him out of their plans. But they'd been too concerned about Kortmann's death. She shook her head, as if to shake off the tears. She had to stop it; now was the time to focus all her energy on getting out of this situation. She let her eyes sweep over the room, looking for something she could use.

Remer was studying the computer monitor on the desk and not paying any attention to what was happening at the other end of the room. Katherina was able to pick up only scattered fragments of what he was reading, but it sounded like sheer nonsense. Technical terms, numbers and phrases she'd never heard before, all blended together. Every once in a while Remer peered through the window and signalled to someone in the adjacent room.

From her position Katherina couldn't see directly through the pane, but she sensed that a light had been turned on and that someone was moving around in the room behind the glass. She had no doubt about who had been tied up in there.

By bracing her feet against the base of the chair, she tried to stretch out the tape around her ankles. It gave ever so slightly, just enough to revive her courage.

'Okay,' said Remer into the microphone. 'You'd better leave the room. Now we just need to wait for him to regain consciousness.'

Pau and someone else came back into the office, going over to sit down on either side of Remer. Kortmann's chauffeur hadn't returned.

During the next fifteen minutes Remer apparently ran through a number of preparatory steps and tests on the computer. Pau followed along, occasionally casting a glance at Katherina. The other man looked through a stack of papers, giving brief, routine-sounding replies as Remer asked about 'RL values', tension levels, and 'IR-blockades' – concepts Katherina was unable to decode. In the meantime, she concentrated on working at the tape wrapped round her feet.

'He's back,' said Pau suddenly, and the three men turned their attention to the room behind the glass.

'Good morning, Campelli,' said Remer into the microphone. From a speaker they could hear Jon mutter something incomprehensible. 'I regret the rather hard-handed welcome, but it looked as if you were about to leave us before we had a chance to talk.'

'Pau,' they heard from the loudspeaker, spoken as if it were the answer to a puzzle.

Remer laughed. 'Pau, as you call him, has been in my service the whole time. A product of this place, you might say. He once

301

attended this school and sat in the very chair where you're sitting now, wearing the same helmet.'

'Where's Katherina? What have you done to her?'

'Relax, Campelli,' said Remer. 'The young lady is right here.' He nodded to Pau, who went over to Katherina and rolled her chair over to the window.

On the other side of the glass Jon was sitting in one of the two chairs, tied up with plastic handcuff strips round his arms and ankles. The blood on his forehead had dried and a dark bruise had appeared where the crowbar had struck. When he saw Katherina, an expression of relief washed over his face.

'As you can see, she's unharmed,' Remer went on. 'So far.'

'What is it you want, Remer?' Jon asked, without taking his eyes off Katherina.

'Cooperation. That's really all,' replied Remer. 'A small demonstration to show us what you're capable of, and then an open-minded attitude with regard to my organization. There's a great deal we can offer a man of your talents.'

'What makes you think I want to be your guinea pig? Do you really expect me to participate voluntarily in your experiments?'

'As a matter of fact, I do,' said Remer confidently. 'Anything else would be unwise.' He patted Katherina on the shoulder, and she flinched at his touch. 'As I said, we have a use for her.'

Jon clenched his teeth. 'And if I agree to your experiments, will you let her go?'

'Naturally,' replied Remer. 'That's the deal.'

'It's no good,' said Jon, squeezing his eyes shut and obviously in pain. 'I'm incapable of reading anything right now. You can thank your lapdog for that.'

Remer leaned forward to give Jon an intent look.

'He's bluffing,' exclaimed Pau. 'I didn't hit him that hard.'

Remer shot Pau an annoyed glance and leaned back in his chair.

Jon opened his eyes and stared straight at Remer. 'If you let Katherina go, I promise to stay here until I'm able to do your test,' he offered.

'I'm sure you'll do your best,' said Remer, picking up the gun from the table and showing it to Jon.

Katherina shook her head vigorously but she could see the dismay in Jon's face. The sight of that shabby little object underscored that this was a filthy hostage situation and not a negotiation.

'Okay,' said Jon. 'What do you want me to do?'

'What you're so good at doing,' replied Remer. 'Reading stories.' He nodded to Pau, who left the room.

'First let her go,' Jon demanded.

Remer laughed. 'Now you're being naive, Campelli. The girl stays until we get what we need.'

The door to the cell was pushed open, and Pau stepped inside with a book in one hand and a knife in the other.

'Bastard,' snarled Jon.

Pau laughed as he stepped closer, making sure that Jon saw the knife by holding it up with two fingers.

'Watch out, Jon,' he warned. 'You wouldn't want to get hurt again.' He fixed his gaze on a spot above Jon's left eyebrow. 'Ouch, that looks ugly. Does it hurt?' Pau smiled broadly.

Jon yanked at his arms but they were firmly strapped to the armrests of his chair. He sank back, fixing hostile eyes on Pau.

'So are you going to turn the pages for me?'

'Oh, no,' said Pau. 'I'll be out of here long before that.' He stuck the book in Jon's right hand.

Jon looked down at the cover.

'*Frankenstein?*' he exclaimed with surprise.

From her position near the table, Katherina could see that the book was a paperback edition, as worn as a copy someone had taken on summer holiday. She also noticed that she couldn't pick up anything from Jon's reading of the cover. As they had earlier discussed, the cell room must be shielded in some way.

With one hand Pau gripped Jon's left forearm, pressing it down against the armrest. He used his other hand to cut off the plastic strips holding Jon's arm. After cutting through the bands he swiftly stepped away, out of Jon's reach.

Jon shook his free arm. He grabbed the plastic strips on his other arm but couldn't pull them off.

Pau laughed. 'Forget it, Jon. You can't do it.' He turned round and went out of the cell, followed by Jon's scowling gaze.

'Go ahead and start,' said Remer.

Jon shifted his glance to the window and Katherina gave him a brief nod. Pau came back into the office and stood behind the others at the table.

'Do you have any favourite passages?' asked Jon scornfully.

Remer shook his head. 'It doesn't matter where you begin.' He pressed a couple of keys on the keyboard, and the image on the screen changed to show a number of oscillating curves that slowly rolled from right to left. There was no appreciable fluctuation.

Jon shifted his hold on the book so that he was gripping the spine with his bound right hand and was able to turn the pages with his left. He opened the book to the middle and began to read.

For Katherina it was a strange feeling to hear Jon reading aloud. Up until now she had always been with him when he read so that she could simultaneously receive, but now it was only his own voice she heard, while the book itself remained silent. It was like listening to audio books, which were also devoid of any of the energy with which a reader or a book itself might charge the text. Yet Jon was an excellent reader, and if the circumstances had been different, she would have enjoyed the story. Katherina tried with all her might to stretch the tape round her ankles even more. She felt a little jerk as the tape gave way, and she cast a frightened glance at the others. But they were all staring intently at the monitor on the table and hadn't noticed a thing.

The oscillations on the screen had begun to move. A green line at the very top of the monitor displayed sine-wave oscillations, an image of what Katherina surmised was the fluctuating pulse made by a transmitter's powers. Underneath was a red trace that rose steeply as Jon worked his way through the text.

'Five point one within three minutes,' said Remer, impressed.

Pau sniggered.

The red trace flattened out and stabilized at a level above the halfway mark on the screen.

'Seven,' declared Remer. 'Is he holding back?'

'Well, there aren't any fireworks yet,' said Pau.

Remer leaned towards the microphone, but just as he was about to say something the green sine wave changed shape. The fluctuations increased in tempo, like a metronome shifting gear. At the same time the red line made an almost vertical leap and was now close to the top of the scale.

'Ten,' exclaimed Remer in astonishment.

Behind the glass, Jon seemed apparently unaffected. Only the beads of sweat that were slowly trickling down his forehead revealed the effort he was making.

The fluorescent lights on the ceiling above him flickered erratically a couple of times until one of them suddenly went out, while the two others shone even brighter. Even though the cell room was bathed in light, the glare seemed to be diminishing around Jon. Gradually a sphere formed around him, creating a darker space than in the rest of the room, and sparks and tiny flashes seemed to be racing over the surface of the sphere. Soon they could no longer see him because of the darkness and the increasing energy discharges.

'Shit,' cried Pau. 'He's gone off the scale.'

Katherina cast a glance at the computer screen. The sine wave was still fluctuating regularly but at a faster frequency than before. The red line had disappeared. She twisted her feet free from the tape and set them on the floor.

The now pitch-black sphere seemed to be drawing in the light behind the windowpane, as if it were a black hole. Lightning and sparks slid over the surface in fiery patterns and several leaped from the sphere into the room, where they landed on the objects and wiring surrounding Jon. The sparks danced in the air until all the light seemed to have been sucked inside the sphere with one great inhalation.

Katherina kicked at the floor, sending herself and the chair flying towards the other end of the room, away from the window. As she moved, she made sure to turn her back and lean forwards. Behind her she heard shouting and a great commotion.

Then came the explosion.

The force flung her sideways against the wall and the breath was knocked right out of her. A fierce heat followed and her lungs burned as she gasped for air. After the roar of the explosion came the sound of glass shattering and falling to the floor, and a hissing sound from sparks flying. She heard a whimpering from the other end of the room but all the lights had gone out, and the only remaining light was from the flames that had ignited the papers on the table and floor.

Katherina felt a pain in her arms, on the skin that was unprotected from the heat. The tape round her wrists had started to melt and she could easily slip out of it. She ripped the tape off her mouth and fumbled her way to the door, which she tore open. Before leaving the room, she took one last look at the desk where Remer and Pau had been. She glimpsed people lying on the floor, but she wasn't able to see whether they were still alive.

Out in the corridor a single fluorescent light was flickering, and the strobe effect turned the hall into a nightmarish scene. The metal door to the cell room was bowed outward; the peephole had been blown away and smoke was pouring out of it, as if from a chimney. On the floor in front of the door lay Kortmann's chauffeur. One of his eyes was a deep, gaping crater, and blood was gushing from the wound and down his face into a growing pool on the floor.

Katherina had to push his body aside before she could pull the cell door open. Smoke billowed out towards her. Coughing, she plunged into the room, holding out her hands in front of her. The first of the two chairs was crumpled up like some sort of abstract sculpture; half the upholstery was gone, half was in flames. In the other chair sat Jon.

He was sitting with his head bowed, but otherwise he was completely untouched by the forces that had ravaged the room. He was still holding the book in his hand. Slowly Katherina approached the chair and placed her hand on Jon's shoulder. He raised his head and gave her a strained smile.

'How'd it go?'

Katherina pressed her body close to his and began to sob.

'I'm so tired,' Jon said. He was having difficulty holding his head up.

Katherina released him from the helmet and stroked his forehead.

'We have to get out of here,' she said. 'Think you can manage it?'

'So tired,' Jon repeated.

Katherina tried to haul him to his feet but he was still bound to the right armrest. The explosion had spared the chair he was sitting in, including the plastic strips that held him captive.

'Campelli,' Remer's voice suddenly thundered. Through the hole where the windowpane had been, they could see a figure in tattered clothes, his face covered with blood. 'Welcome. You're mine now.'

'Run,' whispered Jon to Katherina.

She tugged at his bonds, but they refused to give.

With a great effort Jon heaved himself upright in the chair.

'You've got to go,' he croaked, groggy with exhaustion. 'You can't let them take you.'

His words were practically drowned out by a loud explosion. Katherina flinched. She'd never heard gunshot in real life before, but she had no doubt what it was, and the stance that Remer had taken also made it clear enough.

He was holding the gun in his hand, and it was aimed at her.

# 30

With difficulty Jon turned his head towards Remer. He could see the gun in his hand, and Remer's lips were parted in a smile of white teeth and red blood. Jon turned his attention to Katherina and saw the fear in her eyes.

He was still holding the book in his hand, and with one last effort he focused his gaze on the words on the page and read as loudly as he could. Even though he didn't have the strength to charge what he was reading, the reaction from Remer was instantaneous. He took a step back and put up one arm to shield himself.

'Now!' shouted Jon to Katherina, and she leaped away from him, heading for the open doorway where Remer couldn't see her. There she hesitated for a second and turned to look at Jon, but he nodded urgently. She didn't move.

'Run!' he yelled with as much anger as he could muster.

Katherina looked terrified, but she pulled herself together and ran, vanishing from his field of vision.

With relief Jon let go of the book, which fell to the floor with a thud. He sank back with a smile on his lips and closed his eyes. He heard a great deal of noise all around him. People were running and speaking excitedly. Someone was whimpering; it sounded like Pau. Jon hoped that it was Pau.

The smell in the room reminded him of his activation at Libri di

Luca. There was the same stench of burnt wood and plastic, the same feeling of electricity in the air, and he had a metallic taste in his mouth. The exhaustion he felt was also like before, a penetrating fatigue that made it impossible for him to move unless he gave it his full attention.

One thing that was not the same, however, was the way the reading had progressed. He had been completely out of it during the activation. It was like a blackout, and he had been unaware of anything happening around him.

The test of his powers in the cell room was totally different.

At first he hadn't noticed anything unusual. Since he'd been holding the book at arm's length, his distance from the text was further than he would have liked, and he had to squint a bit to be able to read it. The headache from the blow to his head hadn't helped matters, and he had stammered his way through the first pages. Gradually it got easier, and his reading became more flowing and coherent until he noticed the now familiar sense of control.

Jon had read four or five pages of *Frankenstein* without making any major deviations. He just worked his way into the rhythm, which allowed him to orient himself in the space, the text and the energy. He held back a bit, like a runner before the decisive final sprint, tensing his powers like muscles preparing to take off.

When the section began about the revolt of the villagers and the monster's desperation, Jon whirled himself into the story and the images rose up to meet him with clear, sharp colours and distinct outlines. Instead of his surroundings suddenly disappearing, as if someone had pressed a button, there was a much softer transition, like in the fadeout of a film. Objects in his vicinity became part of the stage-set in the story – in this way the chair in front of him became the plank bed on which Dr Frankenstein constructed his monster, and the figures observing him through the glass turned into swaying trees outside the castle windows.

After that Jon turned up the effects. The images acquired a sharp, insistent light, as if they were overexposed. The emotions in the story were so strong that they seemed solid and present, like minor characters in their own right. He enhanced the horror in the scenes, as well as the hopelessness of the monster and the inhuman bloodthirstiness of the masses. The images were almost lifted out of their setting; only the pure feelings on the faces cut kaleido-scopically through the light in an increasing fluctuation of images. He sped things up even more, so the images now appeared as a whirlwind in which faces and scenes became deformed, drawn further into the spiralling movement. The colours flipped polarity, so that the figures appeared like a negative. The characters' teeth, now showing black in their garish grimaces, burned holes right through the images. The white pupils of their eyes gleamed brightly enough to leave after-images on the retina as they swirled around in the maelstrom. Jon made one last effort and threw himself into the cyclone of images.

To his surprise it was utterly dark and very quiet.

'Congratulations, Campelli.'

Remer's voice brought Jon back to the reality of the cell room. Slowly he opened his eyes and peered at Remer, who stood a few metres away. Blood was trickling out of small cuts on his face and one cheek was black with soot.

'You're the new record holder,' he went on, looking around the room. 'At a price, you might say, but very convincing.'

'Katherina?' Jon asked hoarsely.

'Don't worry, she won't get far,' said Remer.

Jon smiled. That must mean she'd at least made it out of the building. Suddenly his own situation was no longer important, and he had a sense of being invincible.

'So, what's my score?'

Remer laughed. 'We don't know the actual number. You went way off the scale. No one has ever done that before.'

'I'm glad I was able to contribute to the entertainment,' said Jon. 'Can I go now?'

Remer laughed again. 'But you've only just arrived,' he said. His smile disappeared, and his grey eyes stared at Jon with a mixture of watchfulness and anticipation.

'We've been looking for someone like you, Campelli. You're the one who's going to take us to the next level.'

Jon shook his head. 'You're crazy. I'm never going to help you.'

'Don't be so sure about that,' said Remer. 'I'm convinced that you'll see things differently once you get a chance to hear what we have to offer.'

Jon snorted.

'And there are always other methods,' Remer went on. 'Methods that don't necessarily involve your girlfriend, should she manage to elude us after all.' He sighed. 'But don't force us to resort to that. The best solution would be for you to join us of your own free will.'

There was something disturbing about the way Remer presented his threats. He wasn't physically menacing or aggressive; instead, he gave the impression of being slightly aggrieved.

'I'm going to have to disappoint you,' said Jon. 'That's never going to happen.' Whatever Remer had up his sleeve, Jon would not give in to the man who was behind the murders of his parents.

Remer turned to yell something out of the door. Then he took a step closer to Jon.

'You're tired, Campelli,' he said indulgently. 'After you get some sleep, you'll see things in a different light. Just wait and see.'

A tall man with dark hair and an enormous jaw came through the door. He handed an object to Remer, who nodded towards Jon's free arm. The man went over to the chair and grabbed Jon's arm before he could move it, pressing it against the armrest with an iron grip. The object in Remer's hand was a syringe, and slowly he approached Jon to inject it into the arm that was still bound.

'You just need to get some rest,' Remer repeated with a smile.

Jon tried to fight it, but he could no longer stay awake.

He hadn't dreamed about his mother, Marianne, since he was a child. Back then the dreams were always about loss. She would be on board a train he just missed, or she would fall into a deep ravine before he could do anything to prevent it. Jon was always alone with her in his dreams, which always ended with her leaving him in some way, most often for good. He'd had some of these dreams before she died, rather like a premonition, and for a long time he'd believed that his dreams had caused her death. Even though he usually awoke in deep despair, Jon later had a sense that the dreams were actually helping him come to grips with his loss, as if they had worn off the edges of his grief. Finally the nightmares disappeared completely, and he hadn't dreamed about his mother since.

All of a sudden she was there, together with Luca. It looked like a birthday scene – Jon's birthday. The table was set for a proper children's party with a paper tablecloth, flags and balloons, but there were so many candles on the cake, more than he could either count or blow out. After he tried and tried to put them out, his happy parents took pity on him and handed him a big present. It was wrapped in blue paper with silver ribbon, but he didn't hesitate to tear off the wrapping. Underneath was a layer of red paper, and under that a yellow layer. It went on like this for a long time, and Jon got more and more frustrated, ripping the paper with ever increasing ferocity while the enthusiasm of Marianne and Luca never waned, as if he were just about to reach the goal. At the very moment when he was about to give up, he reached the innermost layer. He was surrounded by heaps of torn wrappings, and his parents had disappeared in the masses of paper. He could still hear their cries of encouragement if he listened hard, but it sounded as if an eiderdown quilt were covering them. By this time the present had shrunk considerably, and when he removed the last layer of wrapping paper, he was holding a book in his hands.

It was *Don Quixote*.

He had other dreams, but they were disjointed and vague. Several times he saw himself lying in a hospital bed, tended to by a shifting gallery of people. Sometimes it was Katherina, other times Iversen, Remer or people he didn't know at all. In one dream he was diving without any equipment and the water pressure threatened to crush his skull the further down he went, until he lost consciousness in his dream and sank like a rock.

When Jon finally awoke, he knew at once he wasn't dreaming. Even though he found himself in a hospital bed, just like in his dreams, the pain in his throat convinced him he was wide awake. He was terribly thirsty, and his tongue felt rough and much bigger than normal. When he turned his head, he caught sight of a small bedside table with a glass of water on top. But when he tried to reach for it, his movement was stopped by a strap; his body was in restraints. Both his wrists were fastened with leather straps to the metal frame of the bed.

Jon studied his shackles with dismay, as if he might be able to loosen them by sheer force of will, but they were properly secured and refused to yield, no matter how much he tugged at them. He let his gaze slide further up his arm, stopping at the inside of his elbow. On his right arm he saw five puncture marks from syringes. When he examined his left arm, he found seven more.

How long had he been out?

He felt both tired and rested, and when he lowered his head to touch his chin to his chest, he noticed that he was newly shaven.

The room he was in didn't provide many clues either. Aside from the bed and table, there were no other furnishings. There was plenty of space, for at least three more beds, but the room was almost bare, which was further emphasized by the white walls and reddish marble floor. Fluttering in front of a window furthest away from his bed was a white curtain that reached from floor to ceiling; and bright sunlight was trying to force its way through the fabric. Even though the window was open and he was covered only by a thin white sheet, Jon felt surprisingly warm.

The only door in the room was in the wall across from the foot of his bed. A peephole cast an accusatory eye at him from the door, which had no handle on the inside. Judging by the rivets, the door was made of metal.

For a moment it occurred to Jon that he'd been committed to an insane asylum and that the events of the past weeks were all hallucinations. That seemed in many ways a better explanation than what he'd been through, but the illusion was abruptly shattered when the door opened and Remer came in.

'Campelli,' cried Remer with a smile. 'Good to see you awake for a change.'

Jon tried to answer but couldn't get a word to cross his dry lips. Remer noticed his difficulty and went over to the bedside table to

MIKKEL BIRKEGAARD

pick up the glass and offer Jon a drink. Even though the water was lukewarm, Jon accepted it gratefully and emptied the whole glass. Then he let his head drop back on the pillow and set about studying Remer. Something was different. The wounds on his face had healed, and his complexion had a completely different hue from the last time they'd met. The suit he was wearing was light-coloured, loose-fitting summer attire.

'How long have I been out?' Jon finally asked.

Remer shrugged.

'Three or four days,' he replied.

Jon shook his head. That didn't seem right to him. The sunlight, the heat, Remer's clothes. The twelve needle marks on his arms told him nothing. He had no idea what they had given him or how long an effect each injection might have had.

Remer smiled at his confusion and went over to the open door, calling something into the next room in a language that sounded to Jon like Turkish or Arabic.

'How are you feeling?' asked Remer when he returned to the bed. 'Are you in any pain? Do you have a headache?'

Jon shook his head. His back ached, and he was still slightly drowsy, but after several days in bed that was probably to be expected. And he had no intention of showing any sign of weakness to Remer.

'Were the injections really necessary?' he asked, nodding at the marks on his left arm.

'I'm afraid so,' said Remer. 'We thought it would be the safest way to move you.'

He was interrupted by a woman with a dark complexion wearing a white lab coat. Without hesitation she came through the door carrying another glass of water. She didn't look at Jon as she set the glass on the bedside table, turned and left the room. As she passed, Remer said something to her, but the words were incomprehensible to Jon.

'As I was saying,' Remer went on, throwing out his hands. 'It was better for you to be unconscious during the trip. We couldn't have you creating a scene along the way, now could we?' He laughed.

'Look on the positive side. You avoided all the queues, the waiting time and the luggage problems.'

Jon studied him carefully. Even though Remer was blatantly enjoying himself, there was nothing to indicate that he was lying.

'Where exactly am I?' asked Jon.

# 31

Katherina was not entirely sure how she had managed to get out of the school building. It was dark and her vision was clouded with tears, but somehow she had found her way up from the basement and out into the cool night air. There she had paused for a moment to get her bearings. When she heard voices and people come running from the school, she raced to the front of the building, through the schoolyard and out of the gate. Since she didn't have the car keys, that means of escape wasn't an option, so she kept on running, turning the corner at the first side street. There she stopped and pressed her back against some shrubbery as she gasped for air and tried to listen.

Only a second later she heard the front gate of the school open, followed by shouts and footsteps. Judging by the voices, there were at least three people. When she heard steps approaching, she took off running again. Behind her someone started yelling, and she ran even faster. The streets in the neighbourhood were dimly lit, and she turned down one narrow side street after another, making it possible for her to stay out of view. After a few minutes she slowed down and looked back. She stopped in the darkness between two street lights and watched as a figure appeared at the end of the street. The person paused to peer in each of the three directions offered by the intersection.

All of a sudden a dog started barking right behind Katherina and she screamed in fright. The dark shape of a big dog threw itself in a frenzy at the hedge separating them, snarling as if it were a matter of life and death. The figure at the end of the street immediately turned in Katherina's direction, and she forced herself to start running again. Her heart was pounding in her chest and it took all the self-discipline she could muster not to slow down. The footsteps behind her were getting closer, and she could clearly hear the panting of her pursuer. She turned at the next corner and ran fifteen or twenty metres to the middle of the street before slipping through a bicycle blockade. The person chasing her swore loudly. It was a man, and by the sound of it he had taken a fall, but she wasted no time in looking back.

After the bicycle blockade the street got wider, and the buildings changed from mansions to blocks of flats. Katherina was incapable of running any further; her legs could hardly hold her up, and she was more or less stumbling her way forward.

Suddenly someone stepped out of an entrance and blocked her way with arms thrown wide. There was no room to stop, and she ran right into the person, who was almost knocked over. For a moment she got tangled up in the stranger's clothes, and a smell of smoke, beer and sweat filled her nostrils.

'This way, come in here,' said a man's voice and she was pulled through a doorway.

Katherina allowed herself to be hauled along, not voluntarily but because she didn't have the strength to do anything else. She heard the door closing behind them.

'Damn it, Ole,' cried a hoarse woman's voice. 'Didn't I just tell you to go on home? We're closed.'

The man holding Katherina's arm guided her over to a chair and made her sit down.

'Gerly, you can see for yourself that she needs help,' he said in a voice that sounded as if he'd been on a drinking binge for days. 'Besides . . . besides, I happen to know this young lady.'

Katherina was so out of breath she couldn't focus properly and she was in no condition to confirm the man's claim.

Instead, she leaned over the table and buried her head in her arms.

'Okay, Ole,' said the woman. 'But you're not getting anything else to drink.'

A door opened and Katherina gave a start.

'Out!' shouted the woman behind her. 'We're closed.'

Another man's voice, panting for air, started to protest from the doorway, but he was instantly cut off.

'We're closed, I said. Come back around noon.'

The door slammed shut and was noisily bolted.

Katherina could no longer hold back her tears; she started to sob so hard that her whole body shook. She had never seriously believed that the situation would be so dangerous. The fact that she'd been forced to abandon Jon and flee seemed utterly unreal and inconceivable, when she thought about how invincible she had felt when they were together. Katherina felt Ole's hand on her shoulder. He patted her gently, but that just made everything worse.

'Well, a cup of coffee probably wouldn't hurt,' said the woman behind them. The sound of clattering cups and the hiss of the coffeemaker felt as consoling as if someone had hugged her. Her sobs soon subsided to a faint sniffling. Slowly she lifted her head from the table and looked around.

She was sitting in a well-worn pub with heavy wooden tables and chairs upholstered in red leather. A massive bar lined one whole wall and behind it stood the woman called Gerly – a short, stout woman with a ruddy face and eyes that could undoubtedly tame even the most drunken of customers. She came over with two cups of black coffee, which she carefully set on the table.

Next to Katherina sat her rescuer, a skinny, hollow-cheeked man wearing a crumpled suit over a shirt that had once been white but was now a nicotine-stained yellow.

She realized that she knew him.

This man, Ole, was a receiver. The same receiver that Jon had mentioned meeting in the Clean Glass pub after Luca's funeral. She hadn't seen him often. He preferred to take his problems to places like this, but she was positive it was him.

He must have seen the glimmer of recognition in her eyes because he gave her a knowing wink and smiled broadly, revealing two rows of yellow teeth.

'Not bad coffee, Gerly,' said Ole loudly, taking another gulp from his cup.

'Huh. You should try it more often. Then you might even be decent company.' Gerly turned her attention to Katherina. 'Feeling better, luv?'

Katherina nodded and picked up her cup in both hands. The heat felt soothing against her fingers, and she closed her eyes as she took a cautious sip.

'Men are a bunch of bastards,' Gerly went on. 'Nothing but rapists, the whole lot of them. They should all be castrated, in my opinion.'

'Then you wouldn't even have been conceived,' declared Ole, laughing loudly.

'Now don't get started, wise guy. You should see about taking the girl over to the police station instead of trying to be funny.'

Katherina shook her head. 'That's not necessary,' she said quickly. 'I'm fine.'

Gerly studied her intently. 'Are you sure? They shouldn't get off so easy, those fucking bastards.'

'I'm okay,' said Katherina, sniffling. 'Nothing happened.'

Gerly grunted something incomprehensible and went back behind the bar, where she started cleaning up.

'I'll be happy to take you over there,' said Ole, even though his eyes were bleary, and it probably wasn't where he really wanted to be going just then.

'I can't go to the police,' whispered Katherina. 'But I have to get in touch with Clara as soon as possible.'

Ole nodded firmly and sat up straight. 'I'll get a cab.'

He stood up and tottered over to the bar, where he launched into a discussion with Gerly.

Katherina didn't know what she should do. Maybe the police were the only resort right now, but she couldn't face trying to explain the whole situation while Jon was so near and in need of her help. Clara would know how to get him back.

The discussion at the bar had ended with Gerly giving in and ringing the cab company herself. Ole came back to Katherina and downed the last of his coffee.

'We have to go out the back way,' he said, casting a glance at the windows. 'Come on.'

'Take care of yourself, luv,' said Gerly, giving Katherina a nod.

She stood up and followed Ole to a door at the very back of the pub. A faded sign indicated that this was the way to the toilets, and when he pushed open the door she had no doubt the sign was right. The rank smell made her hold her breath. Ole led her over to a narrow back door, which he wrestled with for a moment before it opened with a loud creak.

The back courtyard was quite large – that much Katherina could see even in the dark. As she followed Ole she eyed the few windows that had lights on in the surrounding flats. She wondered how people could get up and go off to work as if nothing had happened. Didn't they realize what was going on in their own neighbourhood? Didn't they know what was at stake?

Ole staggered onward until they reached a dark doorway that opened onto the street. Katherina's rescuer cursed when he couldn't find the door handle. He was moving much too slowly for Katherina, so she gently pushed him aside and opened the door herself.

Unlike the courtyard, the street was brightly lit, and she pressed her back against the wall as soon as she stepped out. Ole practically fell over her, and for a moment he stood in the middle of the pavement, swaying ominously.

'So where's the cab?' whispered Katherina as loudly as she dared.

'It's supposed to be right here,' replied Ole, staggering around until he had to stop so as not to fall. 'Nordre Frihavnsgade. Right here.'

A black car sped past them and Katherina instinctively pressed her body closer to the wall.

'Over here!' shouted Ole, taking a step towards the kerb as he waved his arms overhead. 'We're over here!' A cab pulled up and stopped in front of them.

Katherina quickly stepped away from the doorway and grabbed Ole before he fell. The cab driver opened the window and stuck out his head.

'You are needing help?' he asked in broken Danish.

'Could you just open the door?' said Katherina as she manoeuvred her rescuer towards the back of the vehicle.

The driver got out and opened the door in one fluid motion. Katherina shoved Ole inside, and he collapsed onto the back seat, muttering gratefully. Then she dashed around to the other side and got in next to the driver.

'That is lucky, you are with him,' said the man as he started driving. 'We do not take his kind at this time.'

Katherina didn't have the strength to protest. She merely told him the address of Clara's terraced house in Valby.

The sun had come up by the time Katherina awoke. Thin strips of sunlight were coming through the white slats of the blinds. Still wearing her jeans and T-shirt, she was lying underneath a cream-coloured blanket on a sofa with big, soft cushions with a floral pattern.

The sunroom was where Clara spent most of her time five months of the year, using the rest of the house mostly for sleeping and for storing food. She did her cooking outdoors on a grill or over a small campfire. The walls of the sunroom were covered with white-painted panelling, and flowerpots hung from every beam on the ceiling. All the windowsills were filled with plants too.

Katherina had been here many times before, but she'd never spent the night. She couldn't even remember falling asleep.

When she'd climbed out of the taxi, it was still night, and Clara's house was in darkness. In the meantime, Ole had come to and insisted on continuing on to his own place. Katherina didn't have the energy either to object or to thank him, and the cab drove off, leaving her alone on the pavement.

As she walked up the garden path, she repeated her wish that Clara would be there. She didn't know what she would do if nobody was home. After ringing the bell several times, Clara finally opened the door, and Katherina threw herself sobbing into the arms of the astonished woman.

For several minutes all Katherina could do was cry. She was led over to the sofa in the sunroom, still clinging to Clara. After recovering enough to be able to speak, Katherina asked for a glass of water, which Clara brought at once. She drank most of the water and then began describing the night's events.

Clara listened attentively. All sign of fatigue was gone from her face and she patted Katherina on the shoulder to keep her telling the story. When Pau's betrayal was revealed to her, Clara swore loudly. She had to get up to pace back and forth in order to contain her fury.

'That little . . .' she snarled. 'There's always been something fishy about him.' She brought her temper under control when she noticed from Katherina's face that there was more bad news. She sat down on the sofa again. 'Sorry. Go on.'

It was difficult for Katherina to describe what had happened during the test, and she broke down again when she got to the part about leaving Jon behind in the basement.

Clara brought Katherina some more water and tried to reassure her.

'There was nothing you could do,' she said, putting her arm round Katherina. 'If you had stayed, they would have been able to use you against him. Now they don't have anything to use as a bargaining chip.'

Katherina sniffled. 'But what if they kill him?'

'They won't,' said Clara firmly. 'They need him for something; I have a strong feeling about that. Something that only he can help them with.'

Whether it was Clara's soothing words or the exhaustion after the events of the night that made Katherina fall asleep, she had no idea. But she didn't remember anything else.

She could hear voices coming from inside the house. One of them belonged to Clara.

'Was it really necessary to sedate her?' said the other

voice, which Katherina immediately recognized as Iversen's.

'She was really at her wits' end,' replied Clara. 'You should have seen her. She needed to get some rest, but she was too upset to fall asleep on her own. Sometimes the body needs to rest before the mind can calm down.'

'If you say so,' Iversen said, not sounding convinced.

Katherina heard footsteps approaching.

'How long will she be out?' asked Iversen.

'I'm awake,' said Katherina, turning towards the door.

Clara pushed past Iversen and hurried over to the sofa. 'Are you feeling all right?'

Katherina nodded. 'What time is it?'

Iversen sat down in an armchair across from her. The chair was covered with a multi-coloured crocheted blanket.

'It's ten in the morning,' he said, casting a glance at Clara. 'You've been asleep for nearly thirty hours.'

'Thirty hours!' cried Katherina, jumping up from the sofa. 'How could you . . .' She stopped as everything went black before her eyes and she had to sink back down on the sofa.

'It was for your own good,' Clara assured Katherina, taking her hands. 'You needed to rest.'

Katherina pulled her hands away.

'But what about Jon?' she said. 'We have to find Jon.'

'We're working on that,' Iversen reassured her. 'All of Remer's residences are under surveillance. As soon as he shows up—'

'Has he disappeared?' said Katherina.

Iversen nodded and looked down at his hands, which he had clasped in front of him.

'But what about the school?' said Katherina. 'We have to go back to the school.'

'The school burned down, Katherina,' said Clara and then hurried to add, 'But there weren't any victims. The building burned to the ground only a few hours after you escaped.'

'The fire department thinks it was due to faulty electrical wiring,' Iversen interjected. 'They realized quickly that it was a lost cause, so they concentrated on keeping the fire contained to the school.'

'They're in the process of erasing their tracks,' said Katherina. She looked at Iversen and Clara. They both nodded.

'There's been another fire,' said Iversen. 'Kortmann's villa went up in flames the same night. Kortmann's body was found in the ashes of the library. They think the cause of the fire was a smouldering cigarette.'

Katherina thought back to her last visit to the villa in Hellerup. Henning had carried Kortmann's body into the library, where he had now been cremated, as if on a funeral pyre.

'But he was hanged,' she protested. 'Surely they must be able to see that. The marks on his neck, no smoke in his lungs.'

'Nothing has come out about the circumstances surrounding his death,' said Clara. 'I wouldn't be at all surprised if Remer has contacts inside the police force and is able to influence the investigation.'

'And Remer hasn't been seen since?'

'No,' replied Iversen. 'It's as if he's dropped off the face of the earth. We've rung all the phone numbers listed in the documents about him, but we keep getting the same answer: "Remer is unavailable." ' He threw out his hands. 'As I said, we're keeping his residences under surveillance. In fact, I'm due to relieve Henning in a bit. Don't worry, he's bound to turn up sooner or later.'

Katherina wrung her hands. Sooner or later wasn't good enough. Jon was being held prisoner somewhere out there because she'd left him in the lurch. Unless he agreed to cooperate, it was just a matter of time before Remer would give up and need to get rid of Jon for good. She felt anger welling up inside her. Why had they let her sleep so long? Why hadn't they done more to find Jon?

'We've done what we could,' said Iversen, as if he'd read her thoughts. 'You have to believe us. We even considered going to the police to tell them the whole story.'

'But we gave up that idea pretty quickly,' said Clara. 'It wouldn't help Jon, and Remer's contacts would probably be able to prevent anything from being done about the case.'

Katherina realized they were right. With the information they had at their disposal, they couldn't have done anything more than they had. Her anger was replaced by frustration. What could she do? She had to do something. It was too painful to sit here waiting for Remer to turn up, if he ever did decide to reappear.

'What about Pau?' she asked, sounding agitated.

Iversen shook his head. 'The bedsit where he lived is empty. No one has seen him for the past three days.' He sighed. 'And of course Pau wasn't his real name, so that lead ends in a blind alley like all the others.'

Katherina slowly stood up. She didn't know what she was going to do, but she just couldn't sit here any longer. If she had to search all of Copenhagen to find Jon, she would do it. Anything but remaining passive.

'I'm going home,' she said.

Clara was about to object, but Katherina cut her off.

'It's okay. I'm fine.'

'I'll drive you,' said Iversen, getting to his feet.

'That'd be great. Thanks,' said Katherina as she gave Clara a hug. 'Thanks for everything, Clara.'

'If there's anything I can do, just let me know.'

Katherina nodded. Accompanied by Iversen, she walked through the house and out of the front door. The grass in the little front garden had been recently mown, and it reminded her of summer even though it was mid-autumn. On the pavement at the end of the path lay a bin bag that someone had tipped over, spilling rubbish all over the flagstones. Envelopes, coffee grounds and milk cartons were all jumbled together, soiling the pavement in that impeccable residential neighbourhood.

It was possible to tell a great deal about a person from the contents of his dustbin.

Now Katherina knew who would be able to help her.

Mehmet opened his eyes wide in astonishment when he saw Katherina standing outside his garden door. She had allowed Iversen to drive her home but then went straight to the bicycle shed in the basement to get out her mountain bike and head over to Nørrebro. Something had kept her from telling Iversen about her plans, maybe because she needed to carry them out on her own.

'Well, if it isn't the Lawman's girlfriend,' declared Mehmet as he pushed open the door. He scanned the yard. 'Have you given Jon the slip?'

'You might say that,' replied Katherina, trying to smile. 'I need your help.'

Mehmet gave her a friendly smile as he studied her face inquisitively.

'Sure. Come on in.'

The living room still resembled a warehouse, with boxes against all the walls and cluttering the floor in teetering piles. Just inside the door stood a complete golf set, including bag, clubs and even a tweed sixpence cap hanging from the handle of one of the clubs. Katherina pulled out a club, weighing it in her hands.

'Do you play golf?' asked Mehmet with hope in his voice. 'I can let you have the set cheap.'

'No, I'm afraid not,' replied Katherina.

'I didn't think so,' said Mehmet. 'But that's not why you're here, is it?'

Katherina put the golf club back and shook her head. 'I need you to track down a couple of people for me.'

'No problem.' Mehmet sat down in front of his computer and interlocked his fingers at the same time as he stretched out his arms. His fingers produced an audible crack, and he smiled.

'I need to know where they are right now. You don't have to waste any time on their histories.'

Mehmet nodded.

'First of all, Otto Remer,' said Katherina, pausing as Mehmet typed the name into his computer. 'Next, a man in his mid-thirties who works as a chauffeur for William Kortmann.'

Mehmet's fingers flew over the keyboard as he repeated what she had said. Then he nodded.

'Anyone else?' he asked, looking at her.

'The last one is Jon Campelli,' said Katherina, fixing her eyes on him.

'Jon Campelli?' Mehmet repeated after several seconds. 'You want me to find Jon Campelli?'

Katherina nodded. She could feel her throat closing up at the sound of his name.

'I realize that I said I didn't want to know what you two are mixed up in,' said Mehmet sombrely. 'But what's going on? Did he run off? If he doesn't want to be found, I can't help you.'

Katherina cleared her throat. 'Jon is being held against his will,' she said. 'By the two men I just mentioned.'

Mehmet frowned but otherwise didn't move.

'Otto Remer is the head of a criminal organization that will stop at nothing,' Katherina went on. 'It's extremely important that we find Jon as quickly as possible, or else . . .' She felt the tears welling up. 'Or else they're going to hurt him.'

Mehmet gave a big sigh. 'What the hell have you got yourselves into?' he said. 'I heard that Jon was fired, and now this.' He shook his head. 'Why don't you go to the police?'

'It's a long story,' said Katherina. 'And we're wasting time.'

Mehmet nodded and turned to look at the monitor in front of him.

'Okay then,' he said. 'Let's find our friend.'


The waiting was awful. Katherina had nothing to contribute other than to answer the questions that Mehmet occasionally asked. Otherwise the only sound in the room was the clacking of the keyboard. Mehmet had switched off his mobile phone after the first time it rang, and Katherina didn't want to disturb his concentration. He was her only chance.

While Mehmet worked, Katherina walked around the room, unable to sit still. She examined the assorted wares in the boxes, again amazed that anyone could make enough to live on by entering contests. Jon had told her about a Japanese TV show in which the participants were locked inside a flat and had to live off whatever they were able to win in contests, either over the Internet or from coupons. Most people had to give up from lack of food.

Now and then she slipped behind Mehmet to peek at the

computer screens, but even if she'd been able to read, she was convinced that she still wouldn't have understood a thing. Numbers and symbols scrolled up the three screens at a speed that made it impossible to catch the meaning, and Mehmet's fingers danced over the keyboard.

'Okay,' he announced after searching for nearly an hour and a half. 'I know where he is, but you're not going to like it.'

Katherina went over to the table to look at the monitors. One of them showed a world map covered with lines.

'I checked the airports,' Mehmet began. 'No trace of Otto Remer, but Jon flew . . .' He set the tip of his finger on Denmark. From there numerous lines reached out to destinations all over the world. 'From Kastrup airport to . . .' He moved his finger south along one of the lines.

Katherina opened her eyes wide.

'That can't be right,' she said.

# 32

'Egypt?' exclaimed Jon sceptically.

Remer smiled and threw out his arms. 'The realm of the Pharaohs, the cradle of civilization.'

Jon shifted his gaze from the man in the lightweight suit to the window behind him, where flowing white curtains fluttered gently in the breeze. Even though he felt as if he'd left his geographic sense behind in Denmark, he had to admit that all the pieces did seem to fit. The heat, Remer's attire, the strange aromas. He wasn't keen on trusting Remer about anything, but all indications were that he was telling the truth.

'We left the morning after our . . . meeting,' Remer explained. 'It wasn't exactly easy to arrange a medical transport on such short notice, but we managed to get space on a charter flight.' He uttered a grunt of displeasure. 'Yet another experience you should be glad you were spared.'

'But why?' Jon asked.

Remer smiled again, raising his hand in a reassuring gesture. 'I'm getting to that. Just relax.'

Since he was lying in a hospital bed with restraints after being abducted against his will, Jon had a very hard time relaxing. For him it was no more than minutes ago that he was in the basement of the Demetrius School, watching Katherina run away as he had ordered her to do. Even though at that moment Jon didn't care what might happen to himself, the whole situation was still an outrage that made him boil with fury inside. Several days had passed, he'd been flown to a foreign country and he had no idea where Katherina was, or even whether she'd managed to elude Remer's men.

'You realize I'm never going to help you, don't you?'

'As a businessman I've learned not to use the word "never",' said Remer casually. 'Even though "never" signifies something infinite, it tends to limit the imagination and any potential we may have. As a businessman I need to keep all doors open until the last possible moment, and even then I need to have a cat-flap to come back through.' He clasped his hands behind his back, unintentionally taking on the look of a professor. 'People who say "never" end up regretting it. Did you ever think that you'd give up your job to become a bookseller? Or that your father was the leader of a bunch of gullible, intellectual hippies with magical powers? No, you didn't. Right? "Never," you would have said.'

'That's a grotesque comparison.'

'Is it?' said Remer. 'You have to admit that's what has happened, all the same, and you've actually derived some benefits from it. You've become the owner of your father's fortune, and you've acquired powers that you had no idea existed. You've even found love.'

This reference to Katherina took Jon aback. He looked at Remer. Had the man made a slight nod towards the door, or was that just his imagination? His heart began to pound. If she was here, all would be lost.

Remer must have noticed Jon's reaction because he broke out in a devilish grin.

'See, you *know* you've benefited from it. So much so that you're afraid of losing what you've gained. Just imagine what the future holds for you.'

Jon glanced down at his own body. 'At the moment I'm strapped to a bed,' he stated.

'I know, I know. But that's only for your own protection.'

'Protection from what?'

'From "never".'

Remer turned and strode resolutely out of the room, pulling the door shut behind him with a metallic clank.

Jon stared at the closed door, but it revealed no new information. He let his eyes pass over the empty room, but even though he now knew where he was in the world, it did him no good.

Egypt. What was he doing in Egypt?

Whether it was a side effect from the sedation or whether the light really did disappear as quickly as it seemed, Jon wasn't sure. For him it felt like he'd merely blinked his eyes and it was dark outside. The only lamp was on the bedside table, but the light wasn't strong enough to reach the far corners of the room. The temperature had become more tolerable, but it was still high enough that he felt hot, though he wasn't sweating.

The door opened and the woman in the lab coat came in carrying a tray. Behind her came Remer, and following him were three men who appeared to be of Mediterranean origin.

'Looks like it's about time for you to have some solid food, Campelli,' said Remer, stopping at the foot of the bed. He nodded to the men, two of whom took up position on either side of Jon, while the third remained at the door. At yet another signal from Remer, the straps on Jon's arms were unfastened and the woman placed the tray on his lap.

Jon discovered that he was hungry, but he hesitated to eat the food. He glanced at the guards, who were standing a foot away from the bed and staring straight ahead.

'They don't speak Danish,' said Remer. 'And even if they did, they're loyal to the Order.' He nodded at the bowl of rice and meat on the tray. 'Eat up, and I'll tell you a bedtime story.'

There was no cutlery, so Jon used his hands as he started to eat. He began cautiously, aware of every mouthful, but the spicy lamb and rice tasted so unexpectedly good that before long he was shovelling the food into his mouth as fast as he could.

'The powers you possess know no national boundaries,' Remer

began, nodding at the woman, who immediately left the room. 'That's something you may have surmised. Of course there are others besides you and me in the world, but a text still has a certain limitation because of language. There's no doubt that you could do quite a good job with a text in English, and maybe even Italian, but the effect will always be stronger in your native tongue. In order to charge the text, we need to know the language, and the better we know it, the better the instrument to achieve our goal.'

The woman came back with a tall stool that she placed behind Remer before leaving again. Remer sat down and straightened his jacket before he went on. 'It's a bit different for receivers. They're more able to use their abilities even if they don't understand the text being read. The emotions and images the text evokes are universal, independent of language, but the finer details of influencing still demands knowledge of the language.'

'So you've brought me here to Egypt to neutralize me?' asked Jon between mouthfuls of food.

Remer laughed. 'Certainly not,' he replied. 'First of all, those physical energy discharges of yours are not restricted by whether the listener understands the text or not.' He paused. 'Which is very interesting and without precedent. In fact, we think the phenomenon is simply connected to the reading because it provides a necessary catalyst.' He shook his head. 'But that's something we're going to find out over the course of the next few days.'

Jon snorted.

'Secondly,' Remer went on, ignoring Jon's reaction. 'Alexandria has always been a central location for our organization.'

'Alexandria?' Jon interjected. He tried to associate the name with something familiar, but the only thing he recalled was that it was a city on the north coast of Africa.

Remer nodded. 'It was here in Alexandria that our organization originated,' he explained. 'According to tradition, it was here that the powers that you and I possess were discovered for the very first time.'

Jon finished eating and pushed his plate aside. It was immediately removed by one of the guards, who then offered him a glass of water. Jon took it and drank.

Remer waited patiently for him to finish and then nodded to the guards. They fastened Jon's arms to the bed frame again and left the room without saying a word. When they were gone, Remer clapped his hands and rubbed them together with a look of anticipation on his face.

'Well, Campelli,' he said. 'Are you ready for your history lesson?'

Jon didn't feel the need to answer. He had no choice, after all.

'Alexandria was founded by Alexander the Great around 330 BC,' Remer began. 'The city was intended to be no less than the world centre of learning and scholarship. For that reason, the world's most famous library was built here – Bibliotheca Alexandrina. In addition to being a library, it was a mecca for scholarly studies and intellectual endeavours. Many of the individuals whom we today credit with founding various fields of study worked there, including Euclid, Heron and Archimedes.' Remer cleared his throat. 'The collection of parchments and codices grew, since arriving ships were required by law to leave behind a copy of all the written materials they had on board, as a sort of toll payment. It's thought that there were as many as 750,000 volumes, until a series of wars, plundering raids and fires destroyed this great treasure trove of books. But for more than seven hundred years Bibliotheca Alexandrina was the centre of the world for literature and learning.'

'But it burned down?' said Jon.

'Yes, several times,' replied Remer, lowering his eyes. 'The demise of the library extended over several hundred years, starting with the Battle of Alexandria in the year 48 BC, in which Caesar himself was involved. It had something to do with Cleopatra. The fire ravaged large sections of the library, and countless codices and scrolls were lost. Later the Roman Empire fell, and during the following centuries plundering raids completely emptied the library.'

'And it was in the library that the powers originated?'

Remer raised his index finger. 'Were discovered, not originated. The powers have most likely always existed, but it was only with Demetrius that they were investigated.'

Jon frowned. He'd heard that name recently.

'The school you broke into was named after him,' said Remer, as if he'd noticed Jon's puzzled look. 'He was also the idea man behind the original Bibliotheca Alexandrina, and in addition to being a philosopher, statesman and advisor, he was probably the first head librarian.'

Jon thought back to the meeting with the transmitters at Østerbro Library when the librarian, with a certain amount of envy, had described the influence that librarians once had enjoyed during antiquity.

'Fortunately Demetrius was also a cautious man,' Remer continued. 'He quickly realized what he was on to, and he kept his knowledge of the powers a deep secret. That was how he founded our organization. Back then it was a secret society for those who had been specially initiated, which meant those who possessed the powers and held influential positions. At that time, and for centuries afterwards, there was a virtual thicket of religious and philosophical sects in Alexandria that were more or less secret. Most learned men were members of one or more societies – it must have been the fashionable thing to do back then – and it was probably easy for Demetrius to recruit the right people.'

'Is this what you call recruiting?' asked Jon, tugging at the straps that held him captive.

'It was necessary in order to get your undivided attention,' he said. 'Most likely Demetrius didn't have to resort to such drastic measures. He was a respected man, and I'm sure that everyone he invited to join would have felt honoured, and above all loyal.' Remer's face took on a disappointed expression. 'You should feel that way too, Campelli. Not many are found worthy to join our organization.'

Jon was about to protest when Remer raised his voice to cut him off.

'But I'm convinced you'll come to see things our way. Just wait.'

There was no doubt in Jon's mind that this was meant to be a threat, not a promise, and his thoughts turned again to Katherina. Was she too in Alexandria? Why was Remer so confident of Jon's cooperation?

'With the final destruction of the library, Alexandria also lost its status as a centre of scholarship, and since it was necessary for the organization to be in the place where advances were being made, the group was split up. The members went out into the world to start up local chapters.' Remer raised one eyebrow and gave Jon a curt nod. 'Some of them went to Italy.'

Jon had been counting on hearing at some point what the connection was with himself. There was something that Remer was planning to use to win Jon over to his side.

'Are you saying that my ancestors belonged to Demetrius's sect?'

'There's a good chance they did,' Remer confirmed. 'There are no complete family trees or any surviving lists of members, but all indications are that the pockets of organized Lectors that are found around the world all stem from the original order, established here in Alexandria almost two thousand four hundred years ago.'

'What went wrong?' asked Jon. 'Why haven't you conquered the world?'

Remer grimaced. 'There are lots of reasons,' he replied. 'The decentralization that occurred weakened the organization. Factions arose that had a different agenda, and the various splinter groups wasted a lot of energy waging war on each other. There was also a long period when it was downright dangerous to be a learned person. Scholars were summarily denounced as witches or sorcerers and burned at the stake. That's why it was important to keep a low profile, which didn't make it any easier to find or recruit new members.' He got up to stretch his legs. 'It wasn't until the Renaissance that the organization began gaining ground once again, but it took years before the lost knowledge was reclaimed.'

Even though he was in the presence of his enemy, Jon felt himself drawn into the story he was hearing, but it made him even more surprised that the Bibliophile Society back home hadn't told him about his roots. Maybe they didn't know about the origin of the group; maybe they were keeping it secret until he was ready to hear the truth.

'The Renaissance was a long time ago,' said Jon. 'But again, why haven't you taken over the world by now?'

'Who says we haven't?' asked Remer with a mischievous smile.

'No, you're right. It's only in the last few decades that we've acquired the essential instrument.' He paused.

Jon raised his eyebrows. 'Are you waiting for me to guess what you mean by that?'

Remer laughed. 'Democracy. That's what we've been waiting for.'

'Democracy?' repeated Jon, surprised.

'Democracy is the best thing that's ever happened to the Order. Of course, the monarchy provided a number of opportunities too, but it was much too vulnerable. For one thing, it was difficult to get individuals placed close to the seat of power. And for another, it became dangerous for them every time the power shifted. Most often their heads rolled along with the king's. No, democracy is perfect.' Remer held up his index finger. 'It's relatively easy to get close to those in power, and it's much more effective when everyone thinks they can personally influence the decisions. In reality, they believe whatever we allow them to believe. On top of that, most of our people are able to keep their positions when governments change.'

'They're civil servants?' Jon asked.

Remer nodded. 'Among other things. Remember that we only need to be in the vicinity when those we want to influence are reading. They surround themselves with secretaries, assistants and legal consultants. Even messengers, cafeteria staff and cleaning personnel can be used.'

'So that explains why we can't tell the difference between the various governments,' Jon remarked dryly.

'We're not interested in politics,' said Remer. 'Make no mistake about that. We're just trying to create the optimal conditions for our organization in as many places in the world as possible.'

'You still haven't told me why we're in Alexandria,' Jon pointed out. 'If the organization has spread all over the globe and there's no longer just one centre, then why here?'

'It's true that the original Bibliotheca Alexandrina no longer exists,' said Remer. 'But we've built a new one.'

'We?' asked Jon in surprise.

Remer smiled secretively. 'The Egyptian government, in co-operation with UNESCO, has built a sumptuous new library on the very same site – or at least close to the site – where the original Bibliotheca Alexandrina once stood. It opened in 2002 after twelve or thirteen years of effort, and at a cost of nearly 400 million dollars. An enormous project that has put Alexandria back on the map for information science. The stated goal behind the re-establishment of the library is to restore the region to its previous glory days as the focal point for knowledge and scholarship.'

'And what's your role in the creation of the new library?'

'Let's just say that we've nudged the process a bit,' replied Remer with a smile. 'Ensured that the necessary permits went through, inspired the right people and made sure that our people are among the employees. The sort of minor details that allow us access to the library whenever we like.'

Jon pondered how many other similar projects the Shadow Organization might be behind. The Black Diamond library in Copenhagen? The central library in New York? He pictured monuments going up all over the world like radio towers to disseminate the message of the organization. Even worse was the fact he knew that the goal of the Shadow Organization was not to construct buildings around the world. That was only an administrative manoeuvre along the lines of establishing local offices.

'The Egyptian government, you said? And UNESCO?'

'Trivial matters.'

'So what do you need me for?' asked Jon, raising his arms as high as the straps allowed.

'As you know, you have extraordinary powers,' Remer began. 'Even aside from the physical phenomena, you're much stronger than any Lector we've ever measured. We think that the combination of your powers and this place should be able to take us to the next level.'

'What's the next level?'

'Initially up to your level,' replied Remer. 'After that . . . who knows?'

Jon didn't want to betray his ignorance, but he couldn't quite follow Remer's train of thought. Iversen had told him that all Lectors had their limitations, a certain potential that couldn't be exceeded no matter how intensive the training. Remer was apparently of a different opinion.

'The time is right,' Remer went on. 'More and more countries are choosing the democratic model, and we've never been in a better position. UNESCO and the Egyptian government are small fry. Do the EU, NATO, G8 and the UN say anything to you? Not to mention the FBI, CIA, NSA and most of the other intelligence agencies around the world? Within the next year there are going to be five parliamentary elections in Europe, countless numbers of votes and an endless series of EU meetings, governmental conferences and top symposia.'

'And your people will be sitting at the table?'

'Either at the table or behind those seated there.' Remer pointed at Jon. 'You should feel honoured. They're all here in Alexandria to meet you. You're the one who's going to give them the last push upwards so they can carry out their missions with the greatest possible effect.'

Jon had grown dizzy from what Remer was saying. He felt sick and closed his eyes.

'So what do you say, Campelli?' said Remer, raising his voice. 'Will you join us and have your wildest ambitions fulfilled, or do you want to be a slave for the rest of your life, and know it?'

Jon looked down at the straps holding his arms. He didn't know what was in store for him if he said no, but he couldn't possibly join forces with Remer. He had no intention of helping this man, who had probably murdered his parents and might be holding Katherina captive. He clenched his fists and shifted his gaze to Remer.

'I'll never help you,' he said, putting extra emphasis on the word 'never'.

Remer looked at the floor in disappointment.

'I'm genuinely sorry to hear that, Campelli,' he said. 'But I suppose I didn't really expect any other answer from you.' He got up and went over to open the door. 'Come on in,' he called.

Jon's heart began pounding hard. He'd give anything to see Katherina again, just not right now. If she came through the door, everything would have been in vain. He knew that Remer could make him do anything if they used Katherina as blackmail.

Jon heard footsteps outside the door. He held his breath.

In came a short, thin man wearing sandals, a light-coloured jogging suit and a pair of classic round steel-rimmed spectacles. He was bald and sunburnt, which made him look like a sporty version of Gandhi. He was carrying a small aluminium suitcase.

'Jon Campelli,' the man exclaimed in a voice that was surprisingly deep for his body type. 'I'm pleased to meet you at last, sir.' From behind his spectacles a pair of blue eyes fixed a piercing gaze on Jon.

'Forgive me for not shaking hands,' said Jon. There was something disquieting about the short man, but Jon was so relieved Katherina wasn't there that he regained some of his self-confidence.

'That's all right,' replied the man, placing the suitcase on the foot of the bed. He opened it and took out an object that he handed to Remer. 'I think we might as well start with this.'

Remer went over to the head of the bed and showed Jon a roll of grey duct tape. He tore off a piece and pressed it over Jon's mouth. Jon gave him a hostile glare, but Remer didn't react.

'You'd better leave us now,' the man said to Remer, who obeyed, closing the door behind him.

From his position in the bed, Jon couldn't see what was in the suitcase, but he was prepared for the worst type of torture instruments he could imagine. In a strange way he felt relieved. The pain of seeing Katherina subjected to something similar seemed to him far worse than having to experience it himself.

But when he saw what was taken out of the case, he was seized with panic.

The short man with the steel-rimmed spectacles slowly reached both hands into the suitcase and pulled out an object with the greatest of care.

It was a book.

# 33

When Katherina first heard about where Jon had gone, she was relieved. It meant he was still alive. But the next moment she felt terribly despondent. The distance between her and Jon was pictured on Mehmet's screen as a long, curving arc from Denmark to Egypt, and it seemed insurmountable. She had no idea how she was going to get there or how she would be able to find him in a country of that size. In despair, she simply fell apart standing there next to Mehmet.

He took it well. He led her gently over to the sofa and then sat down beside her, putting his arm around her shoulders. At no time did he ask about the reason for Jon's trip or why she had reacted the way she did. He just let her cry.

When Katherina finally regained her composure, she thanked him over and over, promising to tell him the whole story some day. Mehmet responded by offering his help, no matter what she might need. Katherina was sure that before long she would have to take him up on his offer.

There were probably plenty of questions that she should have asked Mehmet, but she could no longer remain idle. She had already slept away almost two whole days, and all she wanted to do now was drive straight to the airport and catch the first flight to Egypt. But when she said goodbye to Mehmet and climbed onto her bicycle, she thought better of it, and rode instead over to Libri di Luca as fast as she could.

Henning was standing behind the counter. That surprised her until she remembered that Iversen had said he was supposed to relieve Henning and take over the surveillance at Remer's place of residence.

'Everybody can stop looking for him,' said Katherina as she entered the bookshop. 'I know where he is.'

Henning looked at her in astonishment.

'Katherina . . . Aren't you supposed to be . . .' He pointed to the windows. 'Are you okay?'

'I'm fine,' Katherina lied. She didn't have the patience for questions about either her health or her state of mind. 'You can call the others back. Jon isn't in Denmark at all. He's in Egypt.'

Henning's expression was now both annoyed and concerned. He was about to open his mouth, but Katherina was way ahead of him.

'I don't know why. The only thing I know is that they flew him there twenty-four hours ago.'

Henning nodded and wisely didn't say a word until he'd gathered his wits enough to pick up the phone to ring Iversen. Several phone calls later, the message to withdraw had reached everyone involved.

In the meantime, Katherina had found a big atlas, which she placed on the counter, leafing through the pages until she came to North Africa. Her eyes flitted over the map, over the rivers, cities and the wide open areas of desert. As a child she had often paged through atlases, occasionally imagining herself to be a god looking down on her handiwork. If she squinted hard, she could even see the people moving around down there. Right now she wished she could reach down into the sands of Egypt and pick Jon up with her fingertips to bring him home.

Iversen was among the first to arrive, and Katherina told him how she'd found out the information about where Jon had gone. He nodded pensively as he studied the map lying on the counter. The names of countries and cities washed over Katherina as he read, and she tried to cling to the flow of names to find just one that she could link to something meaningful. She focused on Iversen's reading so that he'd be able to scan the map faster, but in her eagerness she pushed him too hard. He calmly placed his hand on hers, asking her to back off. She nodded, apologized and immediately stopped trying to influence him.

'What do they want?' asked Iversen rhetorically, sticking his fingers under his glasses to massage his eyelids. 'Why Egypt?'

'It could be a diversionary manoeuvre,' Henning suggested without sounding convinced. 'If they wanted to keep Jon's whereabouts secret, they wouldn't have used his real passport, would they?'

'Maybe there wasn't time for anything else,' said Iversen.

Katherina stood with her arms crossed. She was having trouble remaining calm.

'Why can't we just go there?' she asked impatiently. 'They're already a day ahead of us.'

'Egypt is a big country,' said Iversen. 'We need to have a better idea where he is. They may have gone somewhere else from there.'

'Not on the same passport,' said Katherina. 'Mehmet checked.'

Iversen nodded.

More of the other Lectors turned up, including Clara, who shamefacedly avoided looking at Katherina, who reciprocated in kind. Katherina still couldn't forgive Clara for letting her sleep so long. Iversen filled in everyone on the situation as Katherina retreated to the background. Before long a lively discussion had started up around the counter, with one theory replacing another, each more outlandish than the last. She didn't understand why they had to waste time on speculation. Of course Iversen was right. Egypt was a big country if you were looking for just one person, but she would feel much better if she was actually there instead of talking about what they should do once they'd arrived.

Katherina went over to the window and looked out. She touched her hand to her chin. It was late afternoon, and dark clouds had gathered over the city, threatening rain at any moment. The wind had picked up, and people were leaning into the gale as they tried to hold onto their overcoats. A figure approached the bookshop and came to a halt at the window, right in front of Katherina. It was a man with a big beard and dishevelled hair sticking out in every direction in the wind. Instead of studying the books on display, he fixed his clear blue eyes on Katherina.

She practically shouted with surprise when she recognized Tom Nørreskov. He hadn't bothered to change his clothes since they'd met at his farm in Vordingborg. He broke into a wide grin.

Katherina ran over to the door and tore it open, making the bells leap on their cords. The other people in the shop turned round to stare, their mouths agape, as Katherina pulled the visitor inside.

Clara took a step closer.

'Tom?' she asked, with doubt in her voice.

Nørreskov nodded and with some embarrassment looked about at the group.

'This is Tom Nørreskov,' said Katherina.

Iversen came forward to take Tom's hand in both of his.

'Welcome, Tom. It's good to see you.'

Nørreskov merely nodded and continued glancing around, as if this were the first time he'd set foot in Libri di Luca. His gaze moved along the shelves up to the balcony and then slid over all the volumes and stacks of books on the main floor. A wide smile slowly spread over his face.

'It's been a long time, Iversen,' he said. 'But the place looks just the same, thank God.'

Everyone present forgot all about the map of North Africa and began saying hello to Nørreskov as if he were an old schoolmate. His eyes flitted from one Lector to the next; there were many he'd never met before, but he studied each of them attentively, as if he were searching for someone.

'Where's Campelli's boy?' he asked at last, reaching into his inside pocket. 'I have a postcard from his father.'

No one said a word, and a strained mood settled over the group.

'It's taken a long time to get here,' he went on. 'More than a month, but it's a long way from Egypt.'

Katherina gave a start and then grabbed the postcard out of Tom's hand.

'Egypt?' she cried, staring at the card.

The picture on the front was dominated by a large, circular building made of sandstone. The sloping roof consisted of glass sections that gleamed like metal in the strong sunlight. It looked most like a flying saucer that had made an emergency landing in the desert sand. With shaking hands Katherina turned the card over.

Never in her life had she felt so frustrated at not being able to read as when she looked at the meaningless symbols on the back of that postcard. Reluctantly she passed it on to Iversen. He grabbed the card and read what it said aloud.

'They are here – Luca.'

For the second time that day Katherina felt a great sense of relief. The card pointed out the city and maybe even the building where Jon was being held. The printed text indicated that the building on the front was the Bibliotheca Alexandrina in the port city of Alexandria.

Iversen's reaction was to put his hands to his head and declare, 'Of course!' He broke out in relieved laughter. 'How could I have missed it?'

Tom Nørreskov looked perplexed as he stared at the others, surprised by the effect of the postcard.

'So where's Jon?' he asked again.

No one spoke.

'Here,' said Iversen at last, holding up the postcard in front of Tom. 'You brought us the answer.'

While Iversen talked to the astonished Tom, filling him in on the events of the past weeks, the postcard was passed around among the others present. Each person studied it intently, as if it were a puzzle picture that concealed more secrets.

When Katherina had the chance to examine the card again, she stared at the picture, imprinting in her mind every detail of the round building and its surroundings. In front of the library was a half-moon-shaped basin, a natural counterpart to the gigantic glass surfaces that made up the slanting roof of the building. The metallic-looking light boxes under the glass served to let only indirect light into the reading rooms below; at the same time they gave the glass surface a futuristic appearance, so that the whole disc resembled a silicon electronic circuit. A notch had been cut into the right side of the circle, creating a rectangular courtyard into which a spherical building was partially sunk. In the notch of the main building was the entrance.

That was where she had to go.

'Bibliotheca Alexandrina,' said Iversen behind her. 'Probably the world's most famous library in antiquity, now rebuilt in the spirit of the original – for the purposes of collecting knowledge and making it available to all.' He sighed. 'We have to hope that it won't suffer the same fate as the original library. Invaluable texts were lost during all the wars, plundering raids and fires. It's said that the building plans for the Cheops pyramid were stored in the library. Just imagine. Who knows how many other important works we've lost because of the voracity of the fires and the stupidity of people. Works that would change our conception of history, culture and science.' He fell silent, out of respect for the cremated books.

'But why have they gone there?' asked Katherina.

'We can only make a guess,' replied Iversen. 'Maybe it's some sort of ritual. The library may be a gathering place for the Shadow Organization.'

'I think it's because of the charge,' said Nørreskov.

Everyone in the bookshop turned towards him, which made him look down at his hands.

'Luca had a theory,' he began in a low voice. Everybody moved closer, crowding around him and listening attentively. 'In his opinion, it wasn't just the force of the book used during activation that was decisive. He thought that the charge that existed in the books surrounding the participants could also prompt the activation, by their very presence. So an activation conducted in the company of the Campelli collection, which we all know is strongly charged, would be much more effective than an activation carried out in a farmer's field, for example.'

Iversen nodded. 'That's common knowledge,' he said, though he didn't sound convinced.

'So the collection in the Alexandria library would enhance the activation?' asked Clara.

'There's one problem with that,' said Iversen. 'From what I've heard, the library is still in the acquisition phase. And since the original conception of the project, the development of electronic media has progressed so rapidly that many works are now on CD-ROM or DVD instead of in printed editions.' He threw out his hands. 'And we know that these types of media can't be charged like real books.'

'Correct,' Tom admitted. 'But we both suspected that a kind of spillover effect could take place in the surrounding area, an accumulation of energy from the charged books, and maybe even from utilizing the powers.'

'That's never been proven,' said Iversen.

'But just imagine what that might mean for the Bibliotheca Alexandrina,' Tom insisted. 'I've been thinking about it ever since the postcard arrived. For more than seven hundred years, at that same location, hundreds of thousands of volumes of the highest quality were stored. We can only assume there were Lectors during antiquity, and with Alexandria being the stronghold of knowledge, there must have been Lectors there – Lectors who could take care of and strengthen the collection.'

No one said a word. Everybody seemed to be digesting the theory Tom had presented.

'I'm positive that an enormous energy source exists there,' he went on. 'And that the new library has been perfectly designed to focus that energy, like a lighthouse.'

'And the Shadow Organization wants to use the energy to activate new Lectors?' asked Katherina.

Nørreskov nodded.

'But why do they need Jon?' she asked, sounding defeated.

He looked down. 'I can't answer that question.'

'I still think it's some sort of ritual,' said Iversen. 'But under any circumstance, everything indicates that a gathering is going to take place at that site. Whether it's to drink tea or to conduct activations, that's not really important. Jon is going to be there, and we have to be there too.'

Katherina nodded eagerly. Nothing was going to keep her away.

'What we need to do is find out what exactly we're up against, or how many people are involved,' Iversen went on. 'We have to assume there will be more than just Remer and Jon present, and it's safe to bet that some people from the school here in Copenhagen will be participating too.' He turned to Katherina. 'Do you think your computer friend could find out whether any pupils from the Demetrius School are taking a trip to Alexandria?'

'I'm sure he could,' replied Katherina.

Mehmet had given her his phone number on a scrap of paper, telling her that she could ring him night or day. He probably hadn't expected to hear from her just a few hours later, but he seemed very amenable when she did ring.

'The Demetrius School, you say,' she heard on the other end of the line. Katherina could already hear the keys clacking in the background. 'Uh-oh, the place burned down,' he exclaimed a second later.

'We know that,' said Katherina. 'Can you find out whether any of the pupils have travelled to Egypt recently?'

'Hmm, provided their Internet server hasn't gone up in smoke too,' Mehmet replied, humming to himself as the keys clacked. 'Nope, here it is,' he exclaimed. 'Alive and kicking.' He started humming again, interrupting himself with little, dissatisfied exclamations and grunts. 'Hey, listen here, Katherina. It's probably going to take me a while. Can I ring you back?'

Katherina said yes and put down the phone.

'Well?' asked Iversen, anxiously.

'He'll ring later,' she replied, disappointed. She would have preferred to be sitting next to Mehmet, or to keep him on the line so she could sense when something happened. She clapped her hands together. 'What now? How many plane tickets are we going to need?'

Iversen gave her a worried look, but he didn't offer any objections. He knew her well enough to realize that nothing he could do would prevent her from going. 'Not for me,' he said, looking down at the floor. 'I'm too old, and the heat . . . I'd just be in the way.'

'That's okay, Iversen,' said Katherina. 'We need you here.'

Iversen nodded without raising his eyes from the floor.

'You're going to need a transmitter,' declared Henning, raising his hand as if taking an oath. 'I'll go.'

The others all exchanged glances.

Tom shook his head. 'I'm already too far away from my farm,' he said with a dejected expression. 'I'm sorry.'

'Maybe it's best with a small group,' suggested Clara.

Everyone agreed, some people showing obvious relief. Katherina didn't care. As long as she could go, it wasn't important whether one or a hundred went with her. Once she found Jon, she'd find a way to free him.

After an hour Mehmet still hadn't called back and almost everyone had left the shop. Iversen had stayed and was pottering about with some books but keeping his distance from Katherina, who was spending the waiting time alternately sitting down and pacing back and forth in front of the windows. She sensed that Iversen was still a bit embarrassed that he couldn't go along. He avoided her eyes and moved quietly among the shelves, as if not wanting to disturb her.

After yet another hour had passed, Iversen went home too when Katherina insisted he needed to get some sleep. She rang Mehmet a couple of times, but he didn't answer. Gradually her pacing around the shop got more and more restless. She walked in order to keep her thoughts at bay. But after more than two hours of pacing, she sat down on the floor with her back against a bookcase. Her legs ached, which provided a welcome distraction from her speculations. She wrapped her arms round her legs and rested her forehead against her knees. When she pressed her eyelids closed, spots danced before her eyes like flies in the afternoon sun. She even felt the heat of the sun baking on her back. The sun of Egypt.

The phone rang.

Katherina awoke with a violent start and looked around in fright. She was lying on the floor in a foetal position. It was daylight outside.

With some difficulty she stood up. Her legs were stiff, and she tottered the first few paces over to the counter.

'Libri di Luca,' she said when she finally picked up the phone.

'It's me,' she heard on the other end of the line.

Katherina recognized Mehmet's voice and was instantly wide awake.

'Meet me at the main library in half an hour.'

'What?' Katherina stammered, but by then Mehmet had rung off.

Katherina broke all the traffic rules as she biked over to the main library. She rode on the pavement, headed the wrong way down one-way streets and used the bus lanes without regard for traffic lights or the honking cars. Her leg muscles, which already ached, began to burn so badly that she almost fell off her bike before she finally reached the main library on Krystalgade. She parked her bicycle without bothering to lock it and dashed through the revolving door into the library.

The white vestibule stretched up through the entire building to the roof, where frosted panes let in the sun to light up the big open space below. Katherina paused in the middle of the hall to look around. The library had opened only an hour earlier, so there weren't many people. She was picking up words from far fewer people reading than she had feared, and she was able to concentrate on those who were present.

At the counter on her right stood a lone librarian who was idle at the moment, while others were pushing carts crowded with books, which they methodically put back on the shelves. A solitary woman was sitting in front of a monitor among a cluster of computers on the ground floor.

Mehmet was nowhere in sight.

Katherina went over to the escalator that led from the entrance up to the floor above. She got off at the fiction section on the second floor and went to stand at the railing so she had a view of the vestibule below. Her heart was still pounding from the mad dash on her bike and she noticed that she was sweating. She fixed her attention on a group that had just come in, but they turned out to be a bunch of students headed for the comic book section.

'This way,' said Mehmet's voice behind her.

She turned to see Mehmet moving towards the escalator that would take him up to the next floor. He was wearing a grey hoodie. She noticed that he was limping, and when he turned his head to make sure she was following, she saw he was wearing sunglasses that didn't quite cover the bruise over one eye.

On the third floor he went over to a terminal that was suitably tucked away between the bookcases.

'What happened?' Katherina asked when she came up to him.

Mehmet sat down with a grimace. 'It'll be easier if you see for yourself,' he said and started tapping away on the keyboard.

A picture of a room showed up on the screen. The image was fuzzy and not particularly well lit, but there was no doubt that it was Mehmet's flat. Even though his living room had never been especially neat, it was clear that something was very wrong. The furniture and boxes were all jumbled together, with the contents strewn across the floor. The desk had been turned over and the monitors that used to sit on top were nowhere to be seen.

'That's what it looks like right now,' muttered Mehmet. 'We have to go back to last night to see why.'

Underneath the picture was a row of buttons with symbols, like on a videotape player. Mehmet clicked on the button to rewind. A time indicator in the upper right corner began counting down. The image was the same, but Katherina could see that the light coming from outside was changing. The counter went faster and faster, and suddenly there was a lot of movement in the picture.

'There,' said Mehmet and clicked on the play button.

On the screen they could see that Mehmet's living room had been restored to its normal appearance and Mehmet himself was sitting in front of his monitors.

'This is right before it happened,' he said.

The pictures showed Mehmet working at the keyboard. He was bobbing his head rhythmically to some tune they couldn't hear. All of a sudden he stood up and stretched his arms in the air as he did a little victory dance.

Mehmet cleared his throat. 'Well, okay. That's when I cracked the school's security system. Good thing there's no sound.'

He clicked on the fast-forward for a few seconds and then on the play button again.

On the screen Mehmet was back in front of his computers, but he stood up abruptly and looked towards the corridor. Through the open doorway they could see boxes cluttering up the floor of the hall. Mehmet went over to the door, but at the same instant a figure appeared behind him and hit him on the back with some sort of club. Mehmet staggered a few steps forward but managed to turn round before the next blow came. He fended it off with his arm and then threw himself at the person, who flew backwards and crashed into a pile of boxes. That gave Mehmet enough time to grab one of the golf clubs from his collection of prizes and he delivered a blow to the chest of his assailant. In the meantime, two more figures entered the living room from the hallway. They too were armed with clubs, and Mehmet had to defend himself from all sides. He was struck numerous times, once on the shin and several times in the face, but he fended them off as he backed out through the garden door.

In the library Mehmet shifted uneasily in his chair and turned to glance around.

On the screen one of the intruders tossed aside his club but pulled out a pistol and aimed it at Mehmet, who raised his hands. But as he stepped backwards he was lucky enough to topple over a stack of crates piled up close to the door. Two quick flashes issued from the barrel of the gun, but by then Mehmet had already got up and out by the garden door. Two of the assailants struggled with the boxes blocking their way while the man with the gun fired yet another shot through the windowpane towards the garden.

'That's about all,' said Mehmet sadly.

On the screen the burglars gave up the pursuit and vented

their frustration on the contents of Mehmet's flat before leaving.

'Are you okay?' asked Katherina, putting her hand on his shoulder.

'I'll be fine,' Mehmet replied. 'Just a few scratches.' He pointed at the image of his ravaged flat. 'Those bastards.'

'Did you manage to find out anything about the school?'

'Of course,' said Mehmet and smiled for the first time. 'I'm about to download the last bit right now.' He glanced around. 'Let's switch to a different terminal.'

They got up and went towards the escalator.

'These terminals aren't good for much,' he said. 'But from here I can go through the library's server and access . . . well, just about anything.'

'If you say so,' said Katherina.

They took the escalator up to the fourth floor.

'It wasn't easy to get into the school's server. Not exactly what you'd expect from a school,' Mehmet whispered along the way. 'But I guess it's not what you'd call a normal school, is it? At least I don't know any other school that has that kind of security monitoring and can react so quickly. In fact, I don't know of *anyone* who can trace a hacker in such a short time and even send out a bunch of thugs while he's working.'

On the fourth floor they found an available terminal and Mehmet sat down and started typing. The screen went blank and then slowly filled up with symbols.

'What did you find out?' asked Katherina.

'I finally got into their security system and found the class lists,' he began. 'As I said, a strange school. It looks like they have their own grading system. All the kids have an RL value, whatever that means. Anyway, I ran the list of student names against the airline passenger lists and got two hits on the same flight as Jon.'

'Only two?' said Katherina in surprise. 'Are you sure?'

'A hundred per cent,' replied Mehmet. 'But then I tried the private charter companies. Even though they don't operate regular flights, they still have to enter passenger lists.'

'And?'

'There have been two departures during the past week. Each flight carried twenty-five passengers who either attend or have attended the Demetrius School. Of all ages.'

Katherina sighed. 'Fifty,' she said, sounding dejected.

'Plus a few more,' Mehmet added. 'There were a few passengers who aren't on the lists of students. Approximately ten others.'

'Can you print out the lists?'

'Of course,' replied Mehmet. 'You can have names, addresses, even photos if you want. At least of the students.' He got up. 'We're going to have to change terminals again.'

They found another monitor at the opposite side of the floor. A moment later photos and lists began scrolling down the screen.

'But now I think it's time for you to give *me* something,' said Mehmet. 'You can start by telling me what the hell is really going on.'

He took off his dark glasses and looked Katherina in the eye.

'It's one thing when the two of you get mixed up in something, but when it starts affecting my business and my health, I think I'm entitled to an explanation.'

Katherina nodded. 'And I'll give you one,' she said, 'but not here.'

Mehmet gave her a dubious look.

She shifted her gaze back to the class lists.

'Stop,' she said, pointing.

With the press of a button, Mehmet stopped the scrolling on the monitor.

'Back up a little,' Katherina told him.

A photo appeared on the screen, showing a dark-haired boy. It was an old picture, but his crooked, arrogant smile was unmistakable.

It was Pau.

# 34

Jon woke with a thundering headache.

Still bleary with sleep, he reached for the glass of water on the bedside table and drank it down in one gulp. There were still red marks around his wrists, and he turned them back and forth as he studied them. Then he broke out into a big smile.

He was part of something amazing.

All his life he'd been held back and robbed of his destiny, but now it was time to regain what he'd lost. It would do no good to cry over time wasted and all the lies that he'd been told. The goal made everything worth it.

Jon got out of bed and went over to the window. It was light outside, and he surmised that it must be early morning. He opened the curtains and looked out at the landscape. Less than a hundred metres away flowed a wide river, its restless surface glinting with sunlight. Between the water and the house were carefully sectioned plots of land with dark green plants in red soil. On the other side of the river the picture was the same: fields with scattered houses in between. On a few of the plots of land he could see people hoeing the ground or carrying away crops.

On the previous evening he hadn't been able to examine his surroundings. Then only single lights were visible in the houses that he now saw before him. He'd also been too tired and filled with his newly acquired knowledge to notice the details of the landscape, even if it had been broad daylight.

Poul Holt, the man whom Jon now regarded as his guide, had read for three hours, sitting next to his hospital bed. Jon felt ashamed as he thought back on it. He had behaved in an ignorant and foolish manner, too proud to see the truth and too weak to reject his past and acknowledge his destiny. But that had changed over the course of those three hours. During that time he had come to a realization, and he had Remer and Holt to thank for the fact that he could now, at last, fulfil his potential.

At first he had fought against it. The book was his enemy, and when Holt started to read, Jon had done all he could to distract himself and focus on anything other than what he was hearing. The reading continued, and gradually he couldn't help listening. It was the story about the founding of the Order and the achievements the group had made through the centuries. The leather-bound book was a chronicle of what he had previously called the Shadow Organization, but now knew as the Order of Enlightenment. The contrast in meaning made him smile at his own naiveté. This Order cast no shadows.

There was no doubt that Holt was a skilled transmitter and that he had made good use of his powers from the very first word he read. Jon could now see that it was necessary. He'd been so frozen in his own world view that he needed help, even though it meant that Holt had to exert a small amount of influence.

During the reading Holt had stopped three times. He removed the tape from Jon's mouth and gave him some water to drink. Each time he asked with concern about how Jon was feeling. Whether he had a headache, pains at the back of his head, or whether he was seeing spots before his eyes. The last time Jon had refused the offer of water. He would rather have the reading continue so he could learn more about the amazing development of the Order. After that it was no longer necessary to put tape over his mouth. And when Poul Holt decided it was time to stop, the leather straps were removed and Jon was allowed to move freely about the room.

Remer had come in a short time later, and from what Jon could remember, he hadn't left until Jon fell asleep. He felt at peace here. More at peace than he'd felt in a long time, maybe even since that time when . . . Jon pushed the thought aside with a grimace of annoyance. He'd been deceived by those he had loved and trusted, that much was clear to him now. He had to put all that behind him and focus on his future.

At that moment someone knocked on the door and Jon turned round.

'Come on in,' he called cheerfully.

Poul Holt came in carrying a tray on which a breakfast of toast and tea had been arranged. There was also a book bound in black leather.

'*Bon appétit*,' said Holt with a smile as he put down the tray.

Jon sat down on the bed, set the tray on his lap and started eating.

'What are we going to read today?' he asked with his mouth full of toast, nodding at the book.

'Today you're going to do the reading,' replied Holt, giving him a look filled with anticipation.

Jon stopped chewing and studied his guide's face. 'Are you sure?' he asked as he swallowed the last piece of toast. 'Last time . . .'

Remer had told him that Kortmann's chauffeur had died during the reading at the school. The chauffeur was one of the Order's true heroes. He'd kept Kortmann under observation for eight years, and in that way he had prevented their secret from getting out. With the permissive way Kortmann and Clara ran the Society, it was only a question of time before their powers became publicly known. They were weak. Even worse, they took pride in using their real powers widely, which resulted in diminished effectiveness and was of no use to anyone. The Order took controlled aim at a few selected individuals, using the full force of their powers and with full effect.

'This time don't try to force things,' said Holt calmly. 'And besides, one of our receivers will be ready to intervene.'

Jon nodded as he drank his tea. During the experiment in the school basement, the cell room had been insulated against the energy discharges so they hadn't had the chance to bring in a receiver to stop him, even if they'd been able to react in time.

'The objective is to find the proper level,' Holt explained. 'It has to be strong enough so that the physical discharges start to manifest themselves but not violent enough to do any harm. We're going to put electrodes on you so we can follow your progress.'

As if on cue, the woman in the white lab coat came in, rolling a trolley in front of her. On it was a helmet like the one in the school, with cords leading from the helmet to a PC.

Jon finished eating and settled himself comfortably. He smiled at the woman as she placed the helmet on his head and made sure it was firmly secured. Determined to do his best, Jon closed his eyes and concentrated. He mustn't disappoint them again. Now was the time to prove he belonged in the Order.

'Start whenever you feel ready,' said Holt, who had sat down in front of the computer screen.

Jon opened his eyes and picked up the book. It vibrated almost imperceptibly in his hands. He opened the book and began to read. Eager to demonstrate his powers, he started accentuating the images after only a few sentences.

Just like during the reading at the school, he felt his surroundings slowly change until they matched the scene he was reading. The white walls expanded into the snowy landscape he was describing, and the bed he was lying on became a sleigh pulled by horses. Trees towered up on both sides of the track they were moving along, and snowflakes whirled around the sleigh, getting thicker and thicker. Time seemed to slow to a lingering panning shot, and he sensed that for each sentence he read, he could create images as detailed as he liked. Every single snowflake was under his control.

Jon turned the sleigh ride into a dark and dreary journey, with the cold pressing over the landscape like a lead weight. Disquieting shadows could be glimpsed in the dense forest, but the speed of the sleigh made it impossible to judge whether they were animals or people or mere phantoms.

The whole time he was aware of the receiver's presence, not trying to disturb or control, but merely offering support, as if a hand were resting on his shoulder.

After a journey that seemed endless, the main character in the book came to a small inn. A shabby wooden door opened onto a pub, and the scene shifted abruptly from greyish-white nuances to golden tones in the glow coming from the fire in the hearth and the oil lamps on the wooden tables. The guests in the pub regarded the new arrival with tremendous suspicion. Their faces were either in shadow or reddish-yellow from the light, radiating an inhospitable arrogance. Jon enhanced the mood into a claustro-phobic nightmarish vision in which the characters' faces pressed closer, their yellow teeth bared, their scars and wrinkles delineated by shadows.

The hand on his shoulder seemed to give him a squeeze and a brief flash of light lit up the computer screen. The images lurched, like a film that stutters.

Jon stopped reading and lowered the book.

'Excellent,' said Poul Holt, nodding to him. His eyes were filled with affirmation and admiration. 'We had to stop you at the end. It was starting to get too strong.'

Jon nodded. He could feel the effect of his exertions, but his joy at having done a good job outweighed the depletion of his energy. His whole body was filled with a pleasant buzzing sensation, not unlike what he had felt from the book, and he noticed that he had goosebumps on his arms. He laid the book aside and rubbed his arms.

'Who stopped me?' he asked, since they were the only two in the room.

'A receiver in the room next door,' replied Holt. 'You need to learn to recognize the signals from the receiver so you'll know whether you can increase the force or have to stop. This time you interpreted the signal perfectly.'

He stood up and helped Jon take off the helmet.

'How did the measuring go?' asked Jon, nodding at the computer.

'Excellent,' replied Holt with satisfaction. 'You held it just below twenty.'

'Is that good?'

Holt laughed. 'You might say that. I measure just under eight, and I'm one of the strongest in the Order.' He carefully placed the helmet on the table. 'It's impossible to know how high you could go. Maybe double that, maybe even more. In that case, we'd need to get different equipment.'

'Does that mean we're done?' asked Jon, slightly disappointed.

'Not at all,' replied Holt. 'But it's important we don't go too fast. You need to rest after each test.'

'I feel okay,' said Jon.

'That's good, but there are other preparations you need to make.'

At that moment Remer came in with a book under his arm. To his great joy, Jon recognized the book of chronicles he'd listened to the previous evening.

'Campelli,' declared Remer heartily. 'I hear the first test went well, is that right?'

'Apparently,' replied Jon, trying to tone down his pride.

'And you're feeling all right? Are we taking good care of you?'

'I feel great,' replied Jon. 'I could keep going right now, no problem. The sooner I get trained, the faster I can be of service to the Order.'

Remer smiled. 'It's important for you to rest after every session. You'll have opportunities to work with us soon enough.' He held up the book. 'In the meantime, there's more about our background you should know.'

Jon reached eagerly for the book, but Remer laughed.

'When I say rest, I mean total rest. Lie down and close your eyes, then Poul will continue from where you left off yesterday.'

Jon did as Remer requested, and he smiled with pleasure when, a few minutes later, he heard Holt's calm voice reading aloud.

The next twenty-four hours were filled with training, sleeping and listening to stories. Never before in his life had Jon experienced a more satisfying feeling. He received approval for his powers, he got better and better with every session, and he kept on discovering new sides to the Order that showed he had found his proper place. For a long time his ambitions had been allowed to hibernate; not since law school had he felt so filled with purpose. Now he knew that with the Order behind him, there were no limits to how far he could go. They could and would support him to achieve whatever goal he set for himself. His success was the Order's success.

Jon hadn't yet sorted out what he might want to do, but Remer had suggested he could establish and run a law firm with offices all over the world. The firm would chiefly have the other companies in the organization as its clients. Most of the employees would be Lectors and, according to Remer, with Jon's powers and background they wouldn't lose a single case. But Remer had pointed out that this was merely a suggestion. Jon could decide his future for himself.

'Time for a day off,' declared Remer when he turned up again. 'We're going sightseeing.'

Jon would have preferred to stay in, but it occurred to him that he hadn't yet been out of the house, even though he was in a foreign country.

The woman in the white coat came in, bringing a suit for him, and he put it on at once. It fitted perfectly. Remer escorted him out to the driveway, where Poul Holt was waiting along with a red-haired man of about thirty. He was introduced as Patrick Vedel, the receiver who had participated in the training sessions. Jon thought it was strange that he sat in another room during the sessions, but Holt had explained that it was at Vedel's own request.

The red-haired man now shook hands with Jon as he stared at him with an oddly expectant expression. He seemed to be waiting for Jon to recognize him. Jon dismissed the idea, and they all got into the Land Rover that Remer had hired and drove into Alexandria.

They drove along the beach promenade, Al-Corniche, which ran the entire length of Alexandria, twenty kilometres in all. Within that area of the east harbour hundreds of stalls stood along the coastal boulevard. Crowds of tourists and local residents were strolling along the wide pavement by the sea. A low stone wall functioned as both a bench and a bulwark facing the water. On the other side of the wall were giant boulders, acting as a defence against the waves of the Mediterranean.

The first stop was the Qaitbey Fortress on the western arm that surrounded the harbour basin. The fort looked a lot like a model made with Lego of various sizes and colours, but it stood on the site where one of the seven wonders of the world once stood, the Pharos lighthouse of Alexandria. It was said that the big reddish blocks of granite came from the ancient lighthouse, which was estimated by some to have been over 150 metres tall. It had made Alexandria into a centre of light, quite literally, just as the library had done the same from a scholarly perspective.

The next stop was a huge square where stalls had been set up to form a marketplace. Some of the stalls were simply cars that the owners had draped with their goods for sale, such as clothing. Other stalls consisted of carpets spread out on the ground and covered with a selection of jewellery, shoes and electronics. The more professional merchants had set up proper stalls made of wooden boards covered with fabric on which their wares were displayed.

In addition to clothes, electronics and antiques, great quantities of foodstuffs were also on sale. All sorts of spices were sold right out of the sacks, and fruit was piled up on tables that looked as if they might collapse under the weight. Meat and fish were on display in the sunshine, and when purchased were wrapped up in newspaper and tossed into a plastic bag. The smells from all the different foods became more and more intense. With each step new aromas joined the mix, forming a stew that became more and more exotic.

Jon walked on ahead, studying everything. He kept having to say no and make dismissive gestures when the stallholders tried to engage him in a transaction. He had moved a good distance away from the others and was beginning to enjoy this excursion. It had been a good idea to take a break from the training sessions.

Suddenly he froze.

Katherina was standing not more than five metres ahead of him.

She was busy looking at antiques and hadn't yet noticed him, but just as Jon was about to move, she raised her head and looked him straight in the eye.

Apparently she was just as surprised as Jon, because her eyes widened and she opened her mouth, but not a sound came out. Then she broke into a big, warm smile and stretched out her arms towards him, as if she expected a hug.

Jon took a step back. The smile vanished from Katherina's face and he could see that she was puzzled. She took a tentative step closer, now with an expression that was both dejected and enquiring. Slowly Jon backed away without taking his eyes off her. He had seen through her. The Order had opened his eyes to her deceit.

'Are you okay?' he heard Remer's voice behind him.

Jon raised his hand and pointed at the woman.

'She's here,' he said. 'Katherina.'

# 35

Katherina couldn't understand it.

For three days she'd been searching for Jon in this Egyptian port city, and suddenly there he stood, less than five metres away from her. But instead of running to meet her, as she'd pictured him doing so many times, he'd pointed her out to his kidnappers.

Shocked, she stood there staring at him, unable to move. His eyes were filled with hatred. Hatred directed at her. Only after Jon was jostled aside and their eye contact was broken did she come to her senses and realize that two men were making their way towards her. Their faces looked anything but friendly. She spun round and pushed her way through the crowd, away from them, away from Jon.

People turned to stare at Katherina as she forced her way past, moving as quickly as she could. The number of shoppers seemed to swell, and they seemed less and less willing to move aside for her. She cast a look back and confirmed that the two men were still after her. A tall, red-haired man and a short, bald guy wearing steel-rimmed spectacles. Her heart was pounding in her chest. What was the matter with Jon?

In one of the narrow market streets there were so many people that no one could move either backwards or forwards. She desperately tried to push through, but it was impossible to make any headway. The stall she was standing next to was selling fish, and the owner of the makeshift shop was yelling at the shoppers as he tried to keep his table from being toppled by the throng.

The face of the red-haired man loomed high above all the others, and when he saw Katherina get stuck in one place, an alarming smile spread across his face. Feverishly she looked around for a way out. The fishmonger was now shouting at her, making a series of sweeping gestures to force her to back up.

Taking a last look at her pursuers, Katherina ducked down and crawled under the table displaying the fish. On the other side the fishmonger greeted her by swatting at her with newspapers and shouting oaths in Arabic. She stood up, only to feel the fishmonger grab hold of her and start shaking her vigorously. The table gave an ominous lurch, distracting his attention for a second. Katherina used the opportunity to give him a hard shove so she could pull free. Quickly she ducked under the next table and crawled into the next market street. There she was able to stand up and begin to jog, zigzagging between tourists and shoppers, the distant crash of the fishmonger's table barely heard behind her.

At the edge of the marketplace, Katherina paused to look back. The two men were nowhere in sight.

She wished the others were with her.

But Henning was back at the hotel in bed with stomach trouble, while Mehmet was wandering around town on his own just as she was doing. After they'd filled him in on the Society's secrets, Mehmet had offered to come along. At the moment he couldn't go back to his flat anyway, and he felt he had a score to settle. Katherina had gratefully accepted his offer. She thought that Mehmet was the one person she could count on. So far he had never disappointed her.

It had also turned out that he had no intention of hanging around idly, just as Katherina couldn't make herself sit still at the hotel. She'd come into town to search for Jon at all hours of the day. Only when she needed to get some sleep or if they'd agreed to meet back at the hotel did she return to the Acropole, where they were staying.

A shout further down the street drew her attention. A short-haired man wearing a light suit was pointing in her direction. It was Remer, and right behind him stood Jon. He wasn't doing anything, just staring at her, as if none of this had anything to do with him. Remer waved one hand towards the marketplace while he continued to point his other hand at her. Katherina followed his gaze and caught sight of the red-haired man in the crowd. At the same instant he saw her.

She took off at a run, turning down the first side street she came to. An old Lada almost ran her over in the narrow lane, and she had to jump aside and press her body up against the wall to avoid the car. Little shops were tucked into niches on either side, mostly electronics shops stacked from floor to ceiling with watches and cameras, phones and computers. A constant flow of motorbikes rushed past at breakneck speed, and Katherina alternated between running along the street and racing along the pavement in order to keep going. At the next corner she stopped and looked back. Just as she thought that she'd manage to escape, she heard a shout.

'She headed to the right,' someone yelled in unmistakable Danish.

Katherina forced herself to keep running as she looked for an exit. This street was slightly wider and considerably longer than the one she'd come from, so they'd be able to see her as soon as they turned the corner.

After ten metres she couldn't manage to run any further, and she dashed inside a shop. It was a bridal boutique. There were almost as many bridal boutiques as electronics stores in Alexandria. One whole wall was covered with bridal gowns, hanging in two rows. Katherina grabbed the first dress she saw.

Aside from her, there was no one in the shop except for the owner, a stout middle-aged woman who got up from her chair behind the counter and came towards Katherina with a smile. Before the woman could even say hello, Katherina had pulled the gown over her head and reached behind to pull up the zipper.

'You want dress?' asked the shop-owner in English with a mixture of friendliness and astonishment.

Katherina turned to face the mirror which was set up at the far end of the store. From there she could keep an eye on the street behind her.

'Too big,' said the woman, laughing. 'Too big.'

The shop-owner began tugging at the zipper, but Katherina stopped her.

'Baby,' she said, pointing to her stomach.

At that moment she caught sight of the bald man from the marketplace. He was staring through the shop window.

'Ahh,' exclaimed the owner, giving Katherina a knowing wink. 'Baby.' She began merrily chattering to herself in Arabic as she continued to nod and smile eagerly.

The man outside paused for a moment. For a split second Katherina met his eyes in the mirror, but he didn't recognize her and moved on up the street.

'But too long,' said the shop-owner and laughed even louder.

Katherina looked down at the dress. It was indeed much too long. She threw out her arms.

'Too long,' she admitted.

The shop-owner helped her out of the dress and began hauling down other gowns for her customer to try on. Katherina kept shaking her head and pointing towards the door.

'Must go,' she said repeatedly. 'Do not feel well.' She pointed at her stomach.

'Ahh,' cried the shop-owner again, this time with disappointment. 'You feel better. You come back.' She patted Katherina's cheek. 'You get good price. Baby price.'

Katherina thanked the woman and slipped out, turning to go in the same direction she had come without looking back. Only after ten metres did she stop at a window to study the display. A number of fake weapons were on view: knives, pistols and larger guns. She glanced back along the street, but the two men were nowhere in sight, so she continued as quickly as she dared without actually running.

After turning several corners and dashing through small, narrow alleyways that she'd come to know from her wanderings, she finally felt sure that she'd given them the slip. She sat down on a doorstep and buried her face in her hands. Tears welled up in her eyes.

She had found Jon and then lost him again. She'd been standing not five metres from him, but then she'd run in the opposite direction. She swore at her own cowardice. If only she'd been able to reach him. It was clear that he had changed, or at least that he didn't remember what they'd shared together. What had those people done to him?

'Have you found anything?' asked a voice.

Katherina raised her head. A man dressed in white robes stood in front of her. He wore a traditional Arabic head-dress that covered much of his face. Only the man's words revealed that he was a European.

'Mehmet,' she cried with relief as she stood up to give him a hug.

Mehmet cautiously placed his arms around her and gently patted her back.

'It looks like you've found something, huh?'

He didn't wait for a reply, nor did he ask her any more questions as he led her back to the hotel through the narrow streets.

'I hope I can figure out how to put it on again,' said Mehmet as he unwound the fabric that formed his head-dress and placed it on the armchair in Katherina's room.

It was a very sparsely furnished room with only a bed, a chair and an armchair with floral upholstery. The shutters were closed, and the room was in semi-darkness.

Katherina was sitting on the edge of the bed with her legs pressed together and her elbows propped on her knees.

Mehmet pounded on the wall to the adjoining room.

'Could you come in here, Henning?' he said loudly. The walls were so thin they could hear what was going on in nearly every room on the floor. As far as they could tell, they were the only Scandinavians in the hotel, so they didn't have to watch what they said.

A moment later Henning turned up, his face pale and with sweat trickling from his scalp.

'What's going on?' he asked as he sat down in the armchair, moving like an old man.

'I saw Jon,' said Katherina.

Mehmet sat down next to her and waited for her to go on.

'At the marketplace,' she explained. 'All of a sudden he was just standing there, giving me a really strange look as if I were a total stranger.' She took in a deep breath. 'Then he sent his bodyguards after me.'

'Bodyguards?' said Henning. 'Are you sure they weren't his prison guards?'

Katherina nodded. 'He pointed me out to them.'

Mehmet looked down at his hands. 'He must have had a good reason for doing that,' he said. 'Maybe he wanted to scare you off, so they wouldn't capture you too.'

'But you should have seen his eyes,' said Katherina. 'The look in his eyes was so different. As if he hated me with all his heart.'

'Maybe he was trying to push you away for your own protection,' Henning suggested.

Katherina shook her head vigorously. 'No, he really *meant* it,' she told them.

'That can only mean one thing,' said Henning solemnly. 'They've been reading to him.'

The idea of brainwashing had crossed Katherina's mind as she searched for an explanation, but it hadn't occurred to her that it might have been done through reading. Even though she'd participated in a reading, she didn't connect it with brainwashing or torture.

'But is that possible?' she asked. 'We were . . . are . . . in love. How could that be turned into hatred in such a short time?'

'It would require an extraordinarily talented transmitter,' Henning admitted. 'And an even better excuse.'

'Excuse?' said Mehmet. 'I don't get it.'

'A reading can't totally replace one attitude with another. It can't turn white to black. If you try to do that, you'll fail. On the other hand, if you try to present an alternative explanation, the subject in question, with the proper sort of influence, will *choose* to change his attitude. The subject will be able to recall everything – the attitude he had previously held, and even the reading itself, but he'll think he made the choice on his own.'

'Man, that's sneaky,' exclaimed Mehmet, leaning back on the bed.

'So Jon made the choice to hate me?' asked Katherina.

Henning shifted uneasily in his chair.

'In any case he was presented with a lie that convinced him he *had* to hate you.'

Katherina got up and went over to the window. Through the slats in the blinds she could look down at the street in front of the hotel. There wasn't as much traffic in this part of the city, only an occasional motorbike racing past.

Had she come all this way to Alexandria in vain?

'Is there anything we can do?' she asked without turning round from the window. She noticed that tears had begun to spill down her cheeks.

Henning sighed deeply. 'That's hard to say. If the conflict between the two choices is big enough, at some point he'll suffer a relapse. I'd think the shock alone of seeing you today would make him reconsider what has happened.'

'Unless more lies are presented to him?'

'Correct,' replied Henning. 'The more arguments they give him for keeping his distance from you, the better.'

'For them, you mean.'

Mehmet stood up and went over to her, patting her shoulder. 'If he loves you, he'll come to his senses.'

Katherina nodded, fighting to hold back the sobs.

'At least we know he's here,' said Mehmet. 'And I think I located some of the others today.'

'Where?' asked Katherina.

Until now they'd been unable to find any of the individuals the Shadow Organization had sent to Alexandria. For days they had roamed around, studying the tourists in the city, the whole time trying to determine whether those sightseers were Lectors as they read their guidebooks or scanned the menus in restaurants.

They had memorized the faces from the black-and-white school photos Mehmet had found, but most of them were taken some time ago, so they didn't expect to be able to recognize the students by appearance alone.

'There's a big group staying at the Hotel Seaview, closer to the harbour,' Mehmet explained. 'One of them might be our mole.'

'Pau?'

'Or Brian Hansen, as he's really called.'

The papers from the school had revealed Pau's real name as well as his RL value. It was listed as 0.7, a very low number compared to most of the other members, who on average had a value ten times higher. It didn't make them feel any better that someone with such a low ranking had been able to fool them for months.

'Couldn't we use him?' asked Katherina, turning to face Henning.

'As a hostage?' Henning shook his head. 'I don't think so. His job is done. After the neutralizing of Luca and Jon, he's no longer of any importance to them.'

'Maybe he could tell us what's going to happen,' Katherina suggested.

'You want to force him to do that?' said Mehmet with a crooked smile.

'We'd just be playing by their rules,' Katherina pointed out. 'Henning could read to him.'

She had no idea how strong of a Lector Henning might be. So far he hadn't been much help. On the very first day he'd taken to his bed feeling sick, and he hadn't been able to take part in the search. Maybe he wouldn't even be capable of reading.

'I'm sure I could get Nessim to find out Pau's room number,' said Mehmet.

'Nessim?'

'The desk clerk downstairs,' replied Mehmet. 'I have a feeling he has a good network here in the city. When he heard that we knew Luca, there were no limits to what he wanted to do for us.'

Before leaving Denmark, Mehmet had dug up as much information as possible on Luca's trip to Egypt just before he died, and one of things he found out was that Luca had stayed at this hotel where they had now taken rooms. Otherwise Luca had left behind very few clues. He'd used his credit card at a few places in town, including at the Bibliotheca Alexandrina, but that was all.

'Was Nessim able to tell you anything about Luca?' asked Katherina.

'No. Nothing except that they talked about the weather, the library and various trivial matters. He described Luca as a friendly man who gave generous tips.' Mehmet went over to the door. 'I'm going to get him on the case right away.'

After he left the room, Katherina sank down onto the bed. She hadn't allowed herself to get much sleep since the night she spent at Clara's. It was only when she was about to collapse with exhaustion that she'd been forced to give in and take a nap for an hour or two. Even then she slept uneasily and usually awoke drenched in sweat without feeling rested, yet unable to go back to sleep. Her encounter with Jon hadn't made things any better. She sensed that if they didn't get to him soon, it would be too late.

She gave a start when the phone rang.

'It'll take a couple of hours before Nessim can get Pau's room number,' said Mehmet on the other end of the line. 'Try to get some sleep in the meantime. Henning too.'

Katherina reluctantly accepted Mehmet's suggestion and put down the receiver. Henning seemed relieved to return to his own room.

Katherina was extremely glad Mehmet had come with them. He had turned out to be the perfect guide; with lightning speed he'd made friends with the locals and developed a thorough knowledge of the city. It probably had to do with the colour of his skin, because she and Henning could hardly walk around unnoticed.

Henning and Katherina had gone out to have a look at the library on the first day, before Henning got sick, but Katherina had been much too worried to enjoy exploring the impressive building. Henning, on the other hand, had been overwhelmed at the sight of the enormous monument – even more so when they entered the huge reading room under the glass roof. They had exchanged

glances at that moment. The energy presence was so massive that
the hairs stood on end on the back of Katherina's neck. It was the
same tingling feeling she'd had in the basement of Libri di Luca
but ten times, even a hundred times stronger. Henning's eyes
shone like a man who was newly in love.

Katherina stretched out on her bed and closed her eyes. Pau was
their last chance, and there was nothing to do now but wait.

She must have fallen asleep after all, because when the hotel
phone woke her, the sun had gone down.

'Mehmet here. We're waiting for you in the lobby.'

Still slightly groggy, Katherina got out of bed and went into the
small bathroom. She washed her face and pulled her red hair into a
knot at the nape of her neck. Then she left the room and went
downstairs.

Henning was still as pale as a corpse, but even so he mustered a
smile when he caught sight of Katherina. Mehmet, who was once
again wearing the head-dress, led them through streets that were
now almost deserted. Only when they were further down in the
city, closer to the harbour, did they find tourist shops that were still
open and much more life on the streets.

The buildings surrounding Hotel Seaview were all taller, so the
hotel looked like it was shrivelling up in their shadow. The facade
was in disrepair with the paint peeling off in big patches and the
shutters faded. It might once have been possible to see the ocean
from Hotel Seaview, but that was long ago. Only the lights on the
hotel sign gave any indication that the building was still in use,
along with a couple of double doors that were open, welcoming
them inside.

The lobby floor was marble, while the walls had coverings ranging from wallpaper to wooden panelling to a heavy velvet tapestry
that hung from the ceiling. The front desk was made of dark wood
as shiny as a mirror; on top stood a highly polished brass bell. On
the wall behind were mirrors in gold frames as well as pigeon holes
containing keys to every room.

There was no one behind the counter, so all three of them

walked silently through the lobby and up a red-carpeted staircase. Every inch of the walls was covered with paintings in ostentatious gold frames.

Not until they reached the third floor did they dare speak.

'Three-oh-five,' said Mehmet, pointing down the corridor, which on this floor had white walls and a pink marble floor.

'Are you sure he's there?' whispered Katherina.

'Nessim said Pau would be in his room now, for about an hour,' replied Mehmet in a low voice.

'How can he be so sure about that?'

'He knows the front-desk clerk here. Apparently they all know each other. At any rate, he was told that ten of the guests are due to be picked up by a minibus in an hour.'

Katherina didn't care for this plan of theirs. She thought it seemed overly optimistic to just stroll right into a hotel filled with Lectors and expect to interrogate someone without anyone else noticing. 'How do you plan to stop him from slipping through our fingers?'

Mehmet stuck his hand under his robes and pulled out a gun. 'It's a toy,' he assured her. 'I'm just going to scare him a bit.' Mehmet smiled. 'But it looks like the real McCoy, doesn't it?'

Katherina and Henning positioned themselves on either side of the door marked 305, while Mehmet knocked. He was holding the gun in his hand, but behind his back.

'What is it?' they heard from inside the room. It was definitely Pau's voice.

'Are you ready?' called Mehmet, disguising his voice.

They heard footsteps approaching the door.

'Ready? What are you talking about?'

The key was turned in the lock and the door opened.

In the doorway stood Pau. He was wearing a long, cream-coloured robe with a snake-patterned black border around the sleeves and hem. The first thing Pau saw was Mehmet in full Arab regalia. He looked the man up and down in astonishment.

'Who the hell are you?' he asked angrily, but at that instant

Mehmet whipped out the gun and aimed it at Pau's forehead. Terrified, he backed away, followed closely by Mehmet. Katherina and Henning entered the room.

'You!' cried Pau when he saw them. 'Shit.'

# 36

Something about Katherina's expression was worrying Jon. Her green eyes had been filled with a mixture of relief and astonishing warmth. How could she believe that such a ploy would still work? Was it a ploy? If he didn't know better, he would say her gaze had been filled with love. Love for him. He shook his head as if to shake off the uncertainty that had seeped into his mind.

'Are you okay?' asked Remer from the driver's seat.

After sending Poul Holt and the red-haired man after Katherina, Remer had hurried Jon back to the car. On the way they once again saw Katherina, this time running away from the marketplace. She saw them too. Jon was struck by her hesitation when she noticed them. For a moment she seemed frozen to the spot in the noonday heat. Then she looked straight at Jon for one last time before she disappeared down a side street.

'I'm fine,' he said moodily.

He noticed Remer glancing at him in the rear-view mirror. Jon was sitting on the back seat, looking out at the city as it passed. There were so many people on the streets. How was it possible that he had run into Katherina, of all people? Was she tailing them? Planning to catch him off guard by turning up at the marketplace? It seemed unlikely. Her surprised reaction looked genuine.

Remer hadn't waited for the two other men to come back. He

started up the car at once and drove off without Poul Holt and the red-haired man, as if Jon were in grave danger. Jon thought he was overreacting. What could Katherina do? On the other hand, he was glad that the Order stood behind him and offered protection. It made him feel important but also a little helpless, as if he wasn't capable of taking care of himself.

He couldn't get Katherina's expression out of his mind. There was something inside him that had been awakened by that moment when their eyes met. As if a fist had struck him square on the chest, knocking all the air out of him and making it impossible for him to breathe. Maybe she really was dangerous after all.

'How do you think she managed to find us?' he asked without taking his eyes off the side window.

'Luck,' said Remer. 'Maybe they have spies in Egypt. Who knows?'

Jon frowned. Something didn't match up. The whole time Remer had claimed that the group in Libri di Luca was a collection of unorganized fanatics who had put all Lectors in danger through the lax use of their powers. Now he was saying they might have a network extending across continents.

'Don't worry,' said Remer. 'We'll be home soon.'

Why should Jon be worried? He studied Remer's face in the rear-view mirror. It looked as if he was the one who was worried. He kept casting concerned glances at Jon, and his driving was bordering on reckless.

They had left the city behind now, and Jon knew it wasn't far to the country house where they were staying.

'Are we in a hurry?' he asked, studying Remer's reaction in the mirror.

'Well, no, not really,' said Remer, casting yet another uncertain glance at Jon. 'But it's probably best if you get some rest before this evening.' He broke out in a big smile. 'We're going to the library tonight,' he said proudly. 'It's important for you to be prepared.'

Jon nodded. He had sensed that there was something special about this day. Partly because of the excursion to Alexandria, but also because a mood of anticipation had infused the whole day.

Right up until Katherina turned up and spoiled everything, that is. He'd been looking forward to this day when he would finally make his contribution to the Order, but now he no longer felt as eager. It was obvious he was going to take part in some form of initiation, but he was no longer so sure what the purpose behind it might be.

They had reached the country house, and several people came out of the building as the car turned into the driveway. Remer got out and spoke to them in Arabic while Jon stretched his limbs after the drive.

'Come on, let's go in,' Remer said, motioning Jon into the house ahead of him.

They immediately went upstairs to Jon's room. He sat down on the bed. He had still not finished working through his thoughts about Katherina, and he would have liked to do it in solitude.

One of the guards came into the room and handed the chronicle book to Remer.

'So, shall we continue?' said Remer, settling himself into the chair next to the bed.

The guard had not yet left the room, but stood just inside the door. Remer looked at Jon with an expectant expression on his face, as if he was the one who was about to listen to a bedtime story.

'I think I'd prefer to wait a while,' said Jon. 'I'd really like to be alone.'

Remer's smile froze. 'It's important for you to be prepared for this evening, Campelli,' he insisted. 'And not just for your own sake.'

Jon was taken aback. There was a threatening undertone to Remer's voice, and he didn't like the sound of it.

'All I'm asking for is half an hour to gather my thoughts,' said Jon.

'I'm sorry,' Remer quickly responded, 'but there's a lot we still have to do.' He turned towards the man standing at the door and gave a curt nod.

Jon got up from the bed. 'I don't think you heard what I said,' he began, but the guard reached him in two strides. He took Jon by the arm and forced him back down onto the bed. With a look of indignation, Jon looked down at the guard's hand gripping his arm.

'This is really not necessary,' he said. 'I just need—'

'It *is* necessary,' said Remer. 'As you'll see.'

Another guard came into the room and went over to the opposite side of the bed. Calmly but firmly the two men moved Jon into a sitting position. He tried to resist but they were too strong, and soon he was held down by the leather straps with no chance of escape.

'What's going on? There's no reason for this. Now tell me why!'

'Don't worry, I will,' said Remer and again nodded to one of the guards.

'No!' Jon managed to shout before the guard pressed a piece of tape over his mouth.

It really had been necessary after all.

That much Jon could now see. He should have trusted Remer's judgement and not underestimated Katherina's power. They were skilful, those Lectors from Libri di Luca, experts in creating discord and distrust between members of the Order if they didn't remain vigilant. If it hadn't been for Remer's quick-witted intervention, they might have succeeded in upsetting Jon so much that he might have denied himself the future he now had with the Order. He might even have turned against them.

After about an hour of reading, they removed the tape from Jon's mouth and the restraints from his limbs. He had been utterly calm, almost exhausted, and was allowed to sleep until Remer woke him again. It had grown dark outside, and Poul Holt had returned. He examined Jon with the routine movements of a doctor, shining light in his eyes, peering down his throat, checking his reflexes.

'You're in top form,' he said at last, giving Jon a smile.

Remer, who had retreated to the background, now came over to the bed.

'You'll have to forgive us for strapping you down,' he said, sounding truly remorseful. 'Unfortunately, it was necessary. I hope you understand.'

Jon nodded.

'It was necessary,' he said. 'I was about to cave in under their influence. It won't happen again.'

'I'm sure it won't,' said Remer, with a nod of satisfaction. 'And don't worry. Tonight you're among friends. Nothing is going to stop us.'

Jon felt reassured. The cloud of confusion he'd felt a few hours earlier had been swept away with such force he couldn't really remember what the whole thing had been about.

'About tonight,' said Remer, pointing at a black robe lying at the foot of the bed. 'Would you mind making sure it fits?'

Jon got up from the bed and held the robe in front of him. It was pitch black with white snakes in a border around the sleeves and hem.

'Are we going to a toga party?' asked Jon.

Remer laughed. 'Something like that.'

Jon put on the robe. It was made of silk, with a thick belt also of silk. Even with his normal clothes underneath, the robe was amply big, and when he pulled up the hood his face was in shadow. It gave him a wonderfully secure feeling. He felt like a monk; he smiled at the thought.

'Perfect,' declared Remer, and nodded with satisfaction.

'What about the rest of you?' asked Jon.

'Don't worry,' said Remer. 'We're all going to wear the same type of robe, but ours will be white.'

'Am I the only one in black?'

'Of course,' said Holt. 'You're the guest of honour.'

# 37

'You bastards,' exclaimed Pau from where he sat on the chair. 'You're never going to get away with this.'

Henning and Mehmet had tied him up with a rope they'd brought along while Katherina had taken over the toy pistol, which she kept aimed at Pau. Now he was spitting venom at them with hatred in his eyes.

'Are you going to a fancy-dress party?' asked Mehmet, holding up Pau's white robe.

'Look who's talking.'

'And what's this?' Mehmet held up the copper amulet they'd found round Pau's neck. 'Is this your VIP ticket?'

Pau didn't answer.

'Let's assume it is.' Mehmet handed the amulet to Katherina. 'So the question is, a ticket to what?' He looked expectantly at Pau, who deliberately turned his head away.

Katherina examined the copper amulet. It was round, about the size of a 5-krone coin, and it had a hole in the centre through which a leather cord was attached so it could be worn as a necklace. All around the edge, tiny characters had been neatly etched.

'What are you going to get out of all this?' asked Henning. 'You're already activated.'

Pau smiled.

'And what an activation it was,' Henning added. 'What was it you have for an RL score? Nought point seven? That's not even enough juice to run a bicycle light.'

Pau's smile vanished. Katherina could see he was gritting his teeth in anger.

'So I suppose it's a good thing you've got the protection of the organization,' Henning went on. 'Weak Lectors like you need all the help they can get. Do they have any use for you at all?'

Fury glittered in Pau's eyes, and his cheeks were flushed.

'Oh, that's right, you infiltrated Libri di Luca, but that was only because Luca took pity on you. He could see from a mile away how weak you are.'

'Shut up!' Pau threw his body as far forward in his chair as the ropes would allow.

Henning leaned towards him, just enough to stay out of his reach.

'So, what now? Your job is done. What possible use can the Shadow Organization have for a weakling like you now?'

'Come back after the reactivation, and I'll show you.'

Henning and Katherina exchanged glances.

'Reactivation?' Henning repeated. 'Is that what's going to happen tonight?'

Pau didn't reply.

'Have you found a way to repeat the activation?' Henning asked. 'A way to enhance it?'

A little smile formed on Pau's lips.

Katherina could see that was exactly what was going to happen. According to the documents from the school, almost all the people who had flown in were already activated. The whole staging of this gathering in this place seemed to point to something larger than a ritual ceremony of no practical significance. She held her breath. If a reactivation could enhance a Lector's powers, then what would happen to Jon? He was already off the scale and deadly dangerous when he was out of control. She could see that the others were thinking along the same lines.

'How much stronger can all of you get?' asked Henning at last.

'Enough to power a bicycle light,' said Pau, then smiled secretively.

'Then it's too bad you're not going to experience it,' said Katherina. She nodded towards the ropes. 'It's going to be hard to go to the reactivation when you're tied up like this.'

Pau looked at her. A hint of uncertainty had stolen across his face. 'They're coming to pick me up,' he said. 'They'll be here any minute.'

Mehmet looked at his watch.

'In half an hour, at the earliest,' he said. 'Plenty of time to get you out of here.'

Pau laughed nervously.

'We have friends in town,' Mehmet went on. 'How else do you think we found you? People who are good at finding things and also good at making things disappear.'

Pau shifted his gaze from one to the other, without finding even an ounce of support. Finally he gave Katherina a pleading look.

'You have to let me go, Kat,' he said desperately. 'I need this. It's my reward.'

'For what?' she asked.

'For Libri di Luca,' he replied, sounding annoyed.

'Did *you* murder Luca?'

'No, no,' said Pau, shaking his head. 'It's my reward for infiltrating you.' His eyes took on a suffering expression. 'Come on, Kat. I promise not to say anything about you being here. Just let me go, so I can get my boost.'

'When is it going to happen?' asked Katherina.

Pau turned his head so he could avoid looking them in the eyes. He was silent for a long time before he answered.

'Tonight, like I said.'

'How?'

'Like an ordinary activation,' said Pau. 'But Jon is going to act as some sort of medium. I don't know exactly how it works. It has something to do with the library's energy and Jon's powers. When they're put together . . . ka-boom! Then we'll all get a boost up the scale.'

'And Jon?'

Pau shook his head. 'Nobody knows. Maybe nothing will happen, maybe he'll get a kick too, or maybe he'll croak.'

Katherina fought back a desire to grab Pau and shake the indifference out of him. They were wasting time while the Shadow Organization was getting ready to sacrifice Jon.

'How do all of you get in?' asked Mehmet.

Pau nodded at the robe.

'We have to wear that, and the necklace.'

'How many are going to be there?'

'Lots. They're coming from all over the world.'

'What about the language?' asked Henning. 'Jon can't very well reactivate people in all the different languages, can he?'

'I don't know! I think it has something to do with the electrical discharges. They'll strike everyone, regardless.'

'And what about afterwards?'

'Afterwards nobody'll be able to stop us.' Pau smiled.

Mehmet nodded to Henning and Katherina and then drew them away from Pau so he wouldn't hear what they said.

'What do you think?' asked Mehmet in a low voice.

'I believe him,' replied Henning with a sigh.

Katherina cast a glance over at Pau, who was sitting there with a satisfied smile on his face.

'I do too,' she whispered. 'Unfortunately. It doesn't look good. This is worse than I had imagined. We're going to have to stop it.'

'But how? There are three of us, and we don't know how many hundreds of them.'

'But there's only one Jon,' Mehmet pointed out.

'What do you mean?' asked Katherina.

'We have to stop him from taking part in the celebration,' said Mehmet bluntly. 'No Jon. No party.'

Katherina didn't really want to know what lengths they would have to go to in order to stop Jon, but she knew Mehmet was right. Jon was the key to the whole thing, and as long as he was on the side of the Shadow Organization – as he seemed now to be – he was dangerous.

'And how are we going to stop him?' asked Henning.

'We have to go to the party,' said Mehmet. He nodded towards Pau. 'One of us will have a free ticket to get in.'

'That will be me,' said Katherina quickly.

The other two looked at her.

'I know him best,' she stubbornly pointed out. 'We've trained together, so I know what he's capable of doing.'

Mehmet nodded. 'Okay. You take the amulet. Henning and I will find another way in.'

Henning agreed with a nod.

'Hey,' shouted Pau behind them. 'I think it's about time for you to set me free.'

The three exchanged knowing smiles before they turned to face their captive.

# 38

In a few hours it would be done.

Jon could hardly comprehend it. For most of his life he had been held back from following his destiny, and until only moments ago people had been trying to lead him astray, but now he would finally have the opportunity to take his rightful place. There had been countless obstacles along the way, and they had caused extraordinary delays. He wished that he'd had more time to prepare. After all, it was only a couple of days ago that he'd been initiated into the true nature of the Order. It annoyed him not to feel entirely ready, even though Remer had said he was. Of course he could see it was important for the Order to launch the activation. The longer they waited, the more chance of losing their influence, but he still felt uncertain. His encounter with Katherina just a few hours ago had shaken him, and if it hadn't been for Remer's intervention, things could have gone terribly wrong.

That couldn't be allowed to happen again.

So it was a focused and silent Jon who sat on the back seat of the Land Rover, together with Patrick Vedel, on their way to the Bibliotheca Alexandrina. In his hands he held the book from which he was supposed to read. It bore neither a title nor the name of the author, and the black leather had no visible markings to reveal the contents. This was the book used for all activations in the Order, specially written for the occasion and charged with so much energy that Jon almost dropped it the first time he held it in his hands. The pulsing from the book made his fingers tingle, but in a pleasant, reassuring way, which helped him to concentrate instead of distracting him. The contents were equally surprising. When Jon had had the opportunity to read some of the pages, he discovered that the descriptions and the images they evoked were strangely compelling. There was no question of any sort of coherent storyline. The book had been written for the purpose of supporting the powers in the best possible way, and it was full of scenes that could be interpreted and charged by the transmitter to great effect. Remer had explained that Jon's copy was only one of a large set of identical books that would be used at the re-activation. All of them had become charged during countless rituals.

Outside the car the weather changed as they travelled from the country house to the city. The wind picked up, and dark clouds drifted in across the evening sky. When they reached Al-Corniche, the beach promenade, they could see the water pounding against the bulwark, the beaten foam tossed over the roadway in great white clumps.

Even though they had driven past the library earlier in the day, it made a different and much more spectacular impression against the backdrop of the sombre sky. The disc of the library roof was illuminated by spotlights, the entire glass surface gleaming an unnatural white. The spherical building on the plaza in front, which housed the planetarium, was girdled by glittering blue bands. Beyond the library was the pyramid-shaped library school; in the darkness it shone green in the glow from powerful search-lights. The illuminated buildings were an incredible sight, and from the sea they must have seemed a worthy replacement for the lighthouse of antiquity.

There were two other people in the car besides Jon and Patrick Vedel. Poul Holt was driving, and Remer sat in the front passenger seat. All four wore the same type of robe; only Jon's was black, the others were white. At first Jon had thought it slightly ridiculous to be dressed in this way, but now he agreed they needed to show the proper respect for the ritual, and this opinion was reinforced the moment he saw the historic setting before him. At the same time, the robe had a reassuring effect, and gave him a strong sense of solidarity with the others. He still felt slightly nervous, but otherwise great, and was looking forward to delivering the best performance he could muster. He recognized this feeling from all the occasions when he had delivered his closing remarks in court, but this time there was much more at stake than the fate of his client or his own pride.

Holt stopped the car right in front of the library and the three other men got out. The wind instantly grabbed at their robes and the trio hurried towards the entrance while Holt drove off. The entry area was made of glass; just inside, a red carpet led the way to the interior of the library. Behind glass doors stood two Arab-looking men wearing the same type of white robes and welcoming the arriving guests. When they caught sight of Jon's black robe, they bowed low and chanted several phrases in Arabic. After that they checked everyone's amulets before the party was allowed to pass through yet another set of glass doors.

The hall they entered stretched ten metres upwards and massive pillars of light-coloured sandstone soared like tree trunks, ending at the metal rafters of the roof. Jon sensed the energy that pervaded the entire hall. It was different from Libri di Luca, not nearly as insistent; instead, it was present in a natural way, like a background radiation that permeated everything.

More than two hundred people had gathered in the foyer, all wearing white robes, some with their hoods up, others bareheaded. There was a buzz of voices as lively discussions were carried on in the small groups that had formed. Jon caught words from a number of different languages spoken by the participants, but as Remer and Jon made their way through, the conversations stopped until they had passed. Then a great whispering followed at their heels.

Remer led the way to a group of about ten people, who greeted the three men in Danish as they approached.

Remer introduced Jon to the group, which he explained was the inner circle of the Danish division of the Order.

All the members of the group carried a book identical to Jon's. Each person stepped forward in turn to introduce himself and utter a few appropriate words of welcome. Jon politely returned the greetings, but he didn't recognize any of them. Judging by their expressions and friendly attitude, however, they all seemed to know who he was.

'The ceremony will be conducted in the reading room,' said Remer, turning to Jon.

'It's an amazing place,' said one of the people in the group, and the others chimed in with eager nods and approving remarks.

'But how are you keeping this whole thing secret?' asked Jon, gesturing towards the assembly. 'It's not exactly a discreet gathering.'

Remer laughed. 'You might well say that,' he acknowledged. 'But often the best way to hide something is to put it right out in the open.' He gave Jon a wink. 'Of course we're not exactly advertising what's really going on here. Officially it's a charity event, and we're also making quite a handsome donation to the library operating fund. Not that it's pure altruism. The staff are our people, of course, even those who work here in the daytime.'

In the meantime groups of Lectors continued to arrive, and Jon estimated the number had now reached well over three hundred. More and more people had begun to pull up their hoods, as a signal that they were ready, and many cast glances filled with anticipation in his direction. He looked up at the ceiling, ten metres above, and suddenly had a feeling that he was the one holding it up and not the massive pillars.

Katherina was shaking with nerves. She stood a short distance from the entrance to the library, observing the other participants as they arrived. To her relief, some of them had already pulled up their hoods, so she did the same. That helped.

Henning and Mehmet had separated from her at a safe distance from the library. They had neither robes nor amulets and would have to try to find another way in. At any rate, the main entrance was closed to them. That became clear to Katherina the moment she saw the two guards at the door. They wore robes just like everyone else but she could clearly see the muscles underneath, and the bulges at their hips indicated they were also armed – with real guns, not toys like the one Mehmet had used to scare Pau.

They had left Pau gagged and bound in the bathroom of his hotel room. Aside from the fact that Katherina considered it an appropriate fate, they had decided it was too risky to try to remove him from the place. And there was little likelihood he would be found before Katherina was safely inside the library. He had put up a fierce struggle when it finally dawned on him he wasn't going to be freed in time for the reactivation. Desperation had shone in his eyes and he tried to break loose in frantic fits of rage. It made Katherina realize that the evening's event was much more than some cosy gathering for bibliophiles. A great deal was at stake, maybe even people's lives. Including Jon's.

Katherina took a deep breath and pushed open one of the glass doors. She was met by a smiling guard who welcomed her in English. He looked at her expectantly. Her heart started pounding even harder. Had he already seen through her? Was she supposed to mention some sort of password? Had he noticed her robe was slightly too long?

The guard patted his chest and then pointed towards her throat. The amulet.

Katherina glanced down and saw that the amulet had slipped inside her robe. Relieved, she pulled it out and murmured an apology. The guard merely gave her an even bigger smile and then gestured towards the next set of doors.

She quickly moved on, pushing open the glass doors to the foyer. The last time she had been here, tourists wearing gaudy clothes and carrying cameras had filled the space with colours, noise and flashes of light. Now several hundred identically clad people stood around chatting to each other as if they were at some perfectly ordinary social function. How was she going to find Jon in this crowd?

Two rows of square-shaped candles in wrought-iron holders lined the corridor leading to the reading room. Katherina started moving in that direction, positioning herself close enough to a group of participants that it looked as if she was one of them, but far enough away so as not to attract their attention. From the words she caught, she thought they were French.

More than half of the participants had now pulled up their hoods, but looking at those who had not, she could see there were people from many different ethnic groups. When she noticed the black book some were carrying she had a moment of panic, thinking the book was yet another item required for admission. But she quickly calmed down when she noticed that most of the people didn't actually have a book. Besides, receivers were not supposed to use books at an activation.

A short distance away Katherina noticed a large group that was getting a good deal of attention from everyone else, and after observing them for a moment she understood why. The robe of one of the group members was black instead of white. The person was surrounded by the others, and she couldn't see much more than a shoulder, an arm and a back when the individual moved to one side. Her hood didn't make it any easier for her to get a good view, so she discreetly moved a little closer.

It had to be the leader. Maybe even Remer.

Katherina held her breath and took another step closer. She knew it was risky because she ended up standing conspicuously separate from the groups around her.

The person in black turned his head, and it felt as if he were looking straight at her.

It was Jon.

His eyes seemed to fix on hers, right there among all the others, but then he let his gaze continue to slide over the assembled crowd, and soon he turned his attention back to the group standing around him. Someone must have said something amusing, because he smiled and nodded to one of the others.

Katherina couldn't tear her eyes off him. She stood there practically paralysed, watching him converse and listen attentively, as if he were among good friends. It was hard to keep her emotions under control. What she wanted to do most was to rush over there, throw her arms round him and hold him tight until the real Jon materialized. It was just too strange to see him enjoying himself in the company of people who had abducted him against his will and even murdered his family.

Jon couldn't quite get used to being the centre of so much attention. He felt as if people were watching his every move, and was aware of a need to ingratiate himself with those standing around him so as not to seem too affected by the situation. One of the participants in particular had been blatantly staring at him. He had tried to ignore it, but even though he had his back turned, he could still sense the person studying him intently. He glanced over his shoulder and saw he was right. The person was standing about twenty metres behind him, a woman judging by the shape of her body. She stood there all alone, observing him from under the shadow of her hood.

He nodded to her in greeting. She gave a start and immediately stepped out of his field of vision. Jon frowned. Was that a lock of red hair he saw as she turned away? No, that was impossible. It couldn't be her. Katherina would never be allowed admittance. And why should she? Besides, there must be other Lectors who had red hair. And it was perfectly natural people would stare at him; the mere fact that he was wearing a black robe made it hard for him to hide.

'Are you okay?' asked Remer at his side.

Jon turned his attention to Remer.

'Yes, sure,' he replied with a smile. 'I'm just feeling a bit tense.'

'We all are,' said one of the others in the group with a laugh. 'And it doesn't help matters that our guide is nervous.'

'Don't worry,' Remer assured them. 'Campelli is totally prepared. Nothing can stop us now.'

Jon nodded. 'When do we get started?'

'Very soon,' said Remer. 'Let me just check with the guards.'

Remer withdrew from the group and headed towards the

entrance. Jon kept his gaze on Remer as he had a brief discussion with the guards, who consulted their watches and nodded affirmatively.

'Is it true you destroyed the test chamber in the basement of the Demetrius School?' asked an elderly man on Jon's right.

'Yes, there wasn't much left of it,' replied Jon, which prompted a worried look in the man's eyes. 'But it was an uncontrolled session. We've been practising since then, and now I can hit the right level with great precision.'

'But we're all at different levels,' said the man nervously. 'How can you be sure the level you choose isn't going to be too strong for some people?'

'We'll start off very gently,' replied Jon soothingly. 'To begin with, the level will probably be too low for everyone to get something out of it, but if things proceed as planned, those who are weakest will be elevated first, and then we can increase the strength and raise up the rest.'

The man nodded and seemed satisfied with the answer. Jon was less convinced about how it was going to work in reality. The re-activation was Remer's theory, and there was no guarantee that it would work, or that it could be kept under control.

'Besides, there are lots of receivers present, and they can modulate the effect if there should be any problem,' Jon added, putting on what he hoped was a convincing expression.

'There aren't going to be any problems,' said Remer, who had rejoined the group. 'And it won't be long now. We're just waiting for a few more people and then we can start.' He pulled up his hood and pointed towards the reading room. 'Shall we go in?'

The others in the group pulled up their hoods and set off after Remer, who slowly walked down the corridor between the rows of candles. Jon followed suit, and everyone else started moving too. Soon the entire assembly had pulled up their hoods to cover their heads and the scattered conversations died out. The only sounds were footsteps on the stone floor and the rubbing of fabric against fabric.

From the foyer the procession moved along the corridor and into the heart of the library to the reading room. The experience of going from the relatively narrow corridor into the vast space of the reading room almost took Jon's breath away. A couple of participants near him uttered little gasps as they entered the enormous room that reached up seven storeys. They entered on the fourth-floor level, and from here they could peer down on the levels below, which looked like terraced fields on a steep mountainside. Mighty pillars held up the floors and stretched even higher to support the disc-shaped roof, which until now Jon had seen only from the outside.

The reading areas had been cleared on this level, but they could see, on the terraces below, that rows of desks and chairs made from light-coloured wood formed the work areas for those who used the library on a daily basis.

The impressive space was one thing, but quite another was the concentration of energy Jon could feel as they moved through the huge room. It was as if they found themselves under a magnifying glass where forces were being concentrated to such a degree that the air seemed saturated with electrical charges, making the hair rise on everyone's arms. Jon felt such a strong tickling sensation that he couldn't help smiling.

Instead of tables and chairs, a circle of candles stood in the centre of this level of the reading room. In the middle of the circle was a dark-wood podium. Jon had a strong feeling he knew for whom that podium was intended.

Slowly and without a sound the people flowed into the room and spread out around the podium. Remer drew Jon over to the centre of the circle of candles. They stood on either side of the podium and silently regarded the crowds pouring in. It was impossible to see the faces under the hoods. Jon felt exposed in his black robe. He was the only person who couldn't hide.

The participants moved in closer and closer as the crowd filled the reading room. Several times Jon thought he saw the woman from the foyer, the one he'd thought was Katherina, but each time there was something about the person's gait or posture that convinced him it wasn't her.

Despite the fact there were so many people, no one said a word. The silence made it possible for them to hear when the doors to the room were closed by one of the two guards, who took up position just inside the doors with his hands behind his back.

As if on cue, Remer stepped up to the podium. It stood on a metre-high platform, and everyone's eyes were directed towards him at once.

He cleared his throat a couple of times and then began to speak. The words were in Latin. Jon recognized them from a section of the Order's chronicles that Poul Holt had read to him. Holt had explained that it was the Order's original mission statement, which exhorted the members always to improve their powers and keep them secret from the uninitiated. The passage also contained an encomium to the powers and the role of the members in the world. Like shepherds, they were to herd the ignorant sheep – which meant anyone without the same abilities.

Jon didn't understand the words Remer read, so he used the time instead to study the people standing around him. They were apparently intimately familiar with the text. They had turned their faces up towards Remer, which made it possible for Jon to see their mouths, which for the most part were shaping the words as Remer spoke them. Only one person was not looking up at Remer but instead was staring straight at Jon. That person was standing a couple of rows away, but he couldn't see the face because of the hood's shadow. Yet there was no doubt the eyes were directed at him.

Jon's heart began beating faster. It couldn't be her. Slowly the person's head lifted to look up at Remer, just like everyone else's. The lower part of the face emerged from shadow. A pair of lips were shaped in a smile.

Jon caught a glimpse of a little scar on the chin. Katherina's scar.

# 39

Katherina was sure Jon had seen her. The first time was in the foyer, where he had nodded at her. What did that mean? That he was ready? That he was waiting for her? Or was it merely a greeting to a presumed colleague? With her heart pounding, she had followed the others into the reading room. If he had recognized her in the foyer, she might be unmasked at any moment. Her nervousness receded as she entered the reading room. The energy seemed more focused than when she was here last. Maybe it was the candles, the robes and the crowds of people, which all combined to draw her attention to the almost tangible excitement in the air.

The second time Jon saw her was right after Remer took up position at the podium and began reading the Latin text. Katherina didn't understand anything that was read; instead she kept her eyes fixed on Jon. He was standing to one side of the podium, letting his gaze pass over the audience, as if he were searching for someone. The hood of his robe was not pulled all the way forward, so most of his face was visible, and she noticed when his eyes fell on her and then stopped. She felt her pulse rise. These same eyes had looked at her with so much love only a short time ago. Now they shone with doubt and confusion.

Maybe there was still hope. Doubt was definitely better than the hatred she had sensed when she saw him at the marketplace earlier in the day. She couldn't help smiling as she turned her attention towards Remer standing at the podium.

There was no doubt that Remer was charging the text he was reading, but since she didn't understand the words, it didn't affect her. But it was different for the person standing next to her, a rather portly gentleman whose robe barely closed around the bulk of his body. After a moment he began to sway lightly from side to side. His hooded head started nodding eagerly at various passages of the text. She looked around and saw more people behaving in the same way. Yet most of the crowd stood motionless, like Katherina, and listened to what was read.

Katherina focused on the way Remer was using his powers. He was a skilled transmitter, perhaps even better than Luca had been. The effect seemed steady and effortless, as if he were producing a strong wind just by blowing gently. When she concentrated even harder, she discovered one of the reasons for this. The majority of the receivers who were present had focused their powers and were supporting his reading in a unified effort. With so many involved, this was a very difficult exercise that demanded a consensus as to what was supposed to be communicated. The slightest hesitation or miscalculation could break the illusion. Katherina knew from her training with the receiver group how difficult this was, but here everyone was totally focused and there was no uncertainty in their performance.

The last sentence Remer read was repeated by everyone present. He raised his head to look out over the gathering, nodded briefly, then stepped down from the dais. Katherina saw him exchange a few words with Jon, who then took Remer's place on the podium. The people around her began shifting their feet uneasily. It was impossible to know what they had been told, but everyone seemed filled with anticipation; they were also nervous.

Katherina used the opportunity to move back a few rows. If Jon had pointed her out to Remer, she needed to be careful. But Remer stayed where he was, standing next to Jon, and he didn't look particularly alert or concerned.

From the ranks closest to the dais, a group of about ten people moved forward. They all held black books which they opened and then raised their eyes to look at Jon. Katherina saw that others in the crowd who had also been supplied with a similar book now did the same.

After clearing his throat, Jon began to read.

The instant Jon started his reading, he noticed a warm, trembling sensation, as if he'd been lowered into a tub of warm water. He was received and enveloped by forces that everyone was using to help him, to support him and carry him, wherever he wanted to go. The restless energy of the book seemed to merge with the massive discharge from the library itself, and the whole thing was further enhanced by the receivers who were present. He recognized the support of Patrick Vedel like a heavy hand on his shoulder, a little more insistent than during the practice sessions, but that was probably just his nerves.

Jon started off at a slow, even pace to make it easier for the Lectors to fall into step, and when the transmitters surrounding the dais joined in with the reading, he sensed another spike of energy. With Remer and Holt he had discussed how the seance should proceed and what phases they should pass through in order to ensure the greatest benefit. It was important not to press too hard in the beginning, to take his time to get into the rhythm of the text and focus his thoughts. That was easier said than done. Catching sight of someone whom he thought was Katherina in the teeming audience had upset his concentration. Was it really her, or was his imagination running away with him? He didn't say anything to Remer as they exchanged places.

When Jon first stood behind the podium, he couldn't locate Katherina again. She was no longer in the same place. He couldn't decide whether that was reassuring or more worrisome.

The scene Jon read took place in a cemetery. The text was wonderfully composed, which made it easy to read the section aloud, and he had many opportunities to colour the situation as he pleased. Having read through the section before, he was familiar with the setting and knew what sort of mood he wanted to evoke.

It was a sunny day and the main character was visiting the grave of his wife and daughter who had been killed in a car accident.

Jon concentrated on the scene, and before his eyes the reading room in Alexandria slowly faded away to become the peaceful setting of the cemetery. The pillars were transformed into beech trees standing along the cemetery walls, and members of the Order turned into the countless gravestones all around him. A warm breeze wafted past, with a scent of spring. The rays of the sun were splintered by the many carved stones and the branches of the trees, and they cast angular shadows across the ground. Jon noticed that he had reached the point where time suddenly seemed to have slowed to a crawl, and that gave him the opportunity to influence the scene as he saw fit, enhancing it to whatever degree he liked.

The main character placed a bouquet of flowers on the grave of his beloved wife and knelt down before the headstone. The grass was damp and soaked his trousers, but he didn't pay any attention. The wind seemed to pick up, and the leaves in the crowns of the trees rustled as the branches swayed.

The widower reached out and placed his hand on the headstone.

The scene shifted as abruptly as a flash of lightning, and Jon accentuated the clarity and speed as much as he dared. They were riding in a car – the main character, his wife and daughter – on their way home in the darkness of night. The couple were quarrelling. The child was crying. Without warning a pair of blinding headlamps appeared before the windscreen; the sound of metal buckling and glass shattering did not drown out the screams coming from the back seat. Lights and images shifted in quick succession as the car spun round and the passengers and everything else inside were jumbled together.

Back to the cemetery.

Jon wondered if he might have pressed too hard. Even though he was keeping to the prescribed level, the shift might have been too violent for some. The cemetery was peaceful and very, very quiet in comparison to the flashback scene inside the car. The enclosed, claustrophobic feeling was replaced by the cemetery's wide-open space. Jon started letting dark clouds appear on the horizon. The wind grew even stronger, and the leaves swirled up and were blown across the ground.

He noticed a little jolt in the scene, as if a single image had been clipped out of a strip of film. He took it to be a signal from a receiver, but not just any receiver. It could only be coming from Katherina – he could tell.

The moment Jon read the flashback scene, a brilliant blue spark leaped out and crept up his black robe like a snake, only to leap to the nearest light fixture many metres overhead. Those who were standing closest took a step back in alarm, and a worried murmur arose. Remer raised his arms to make a reassuring gesture.

'It's okay,' he said loudly. 'This is what we've been waiting for.'

The uneasiness died down and the transmitters who had stopped reading resumed, though with a certain hesitation. Katherina could see that many people were looking anxiously around, and for safety's sake some moved further away from the dais.

Jon continued to read, undaunted, without taking any notice of what was happening around him. His voice was calm, composed and enticing as he presented the story. This seemed to soothe the audience, even as small sparks flickered over his robe.

Katherina looked around feverishly. What had happened to the others? If Mehmet and Henning didn't turn up soon and stop the ritual, the reactivation would become a reality. She could feel it. The whole atmosphere around her was smouldering with energy, the flames of the candles had begun to flicker even though there was no wind inside the reading room and she thought that it suddenly felt colder. Katherina had no doubt that something was about to happen. The question was: what?

The people in the audience who weren't reading stared as if mesmerized by the phenomenon before them. With so many receivers present, and all of them pulling in the same direction, there was nothing Katherina could do. She sensed that Jon's performance was being carried forward on a wave, partly by the library's ancient forces, partly by the support of both transmitters and receivers. To go against the flow here would be like trying to stop a tsunami with a paper bag.

Katherina closed her eyes. The only thing she could do was let herself be carried along, so she focused on Jon's presentation. There was a feeling she recalled from their training sessions, which now seemed an eternity ago. He had a special way of accentuating what he presented, a very special pulse of energy that she would recognize no matter where it occurred. She noticed how most of the receivers had already tuned in to precisely that pulse and were supporting its every beat.

Maybe she shouldn't try to stop him?

She opened her eyes and looked up at the podium. Jon's body stood as motionless as a statue, and only the sound of his voice and the movement of his lips revealed he was even conscious. His robe was like a canvas on which the sparks briefly formed complicated patterns, and Katherina began to see a connection between the frequency of the patterns and the pulse of Jon's energy. By focusing on both what she saw and on the powers, Katherina picked up a sense of the rhythm and could quickly predict where the next discharge would occur. She took a deep breath and waited.

With great mental exertion she shoved Jon's next pulse one notch higher. She noticed an enormous leap in the energy and a violent electrical discharge instantly shot out from Jon's body to one of the lamps hanging overhead. Sparks flew at the impact and drifted down over the audience like glowing snowflakes.

People standing around Katherina instinctively moved back. A few ran away, but most remained there, transfixed by the phenomenon occurring before them and by the irresistible force of the story. They couldn't have left the room if they tried, and they paid no attention to what was happening around them.

In the torrent of images coming from Jon, Katherina suddenly received a glimpse of herself.

It was like a picture from a slide show that was tossed into the scene, almost too brief to catch, but she was positive it was her. Jon had sensed that she was present, and it had broken his concentration. She instantly focused all her powers on loading those same images, and more of them began to appear. Images of them in Libri di Luca, in Kortmann's garden, together in bed, and a glimpse of her in profile against the window of a car. Katherina didn't hesitate to enhance the emotions of longing, love and security in the fragments that turned up.

It didn't take long before she sensed a response. Slowly the images appeared again, filled with a warmth and ardour that was coming from Jon, not her. She could feel tears running down her cheeks. Had she managed to reach him?

Maybe it was wishful thinking, but she seemed to see a change in Jon's posture. It looked as if he was trying to turn his head but was being held back.

Katherina took a step forward, but stopped abruptly.

Remer had changed position. His body was more erect than before, almost frozen solid, and he was staring down at the text without blinking even once. It was as if he no longer had any sense of where he was or what was happening around him. But what frightened Katherina most were the dark little sparks flickering over his white robe.

# 40

The moment Jon realized Katherina was present in the room and was trying to communicate with him, he was overwhelmed by memories. Images of them together kept turning up in his thoughts and were impossible for him to ignore. He remembered that they had been happy, that he had felt happier than ever before, and slowly a desire began to emerge to find his way back to that joyful state. The reading continued, but he was using less time on charging the text so he had the reserves to think back. What was it that had separated them?

In his mind he pictured the test at the school when he had sent her away so that she wouldn't be harmed. The helplessness he had felt then resurfaced; with a jolt, he remembered Poul Holt reading to him for the first time, and how he had at last surrendered.

It was as if he were awaking from a nightmare.

What was it he was in the process of doing here?

Jon tried to stop the reading, but he couldn't. Someone was holding him in place, just as Katherina had done when she demonstrated her powers as a receiver for the first time in Libri di Luca. One of the people was Patrick Vedel, he could feel that, but he wasn't the only one. All Jon could do was keep reading, but he became more aware of how he was accentuating the text.

The main character was still in the cemetery. He had begun his soliloquy to the black headstone in front of him. Jon let greyish black clouds drift in over the valley where the cemetery lay, and the stones around him assumed a raw and filthy appearance. He could feel the weight of the earth beneath the main character, dark and damp, filled with worms ploughing their way through the mould under the grass.

Jon's attention was caught by a patch of greyish fog off to his right. He stared at the phenomenon. So far he'd had total control over the scene; he knew the shape of every single headstone, knew how each blade of grass lay and how it moved. But this grey fog he was unable to steer. It changed, growing denser in some areas, dissolving in others, and soon he could distinguish the outline of a person. He tried to make the wind blow the figure away, but it stood firm and became more and more solid. A ghost? The setting fit, but there were no ghosts in the text, and this was not something that he himself was adding.

It started out as a hazy human shape, but the molecules suddenly rearranged themselves and with one stroke the figure became as solid as a statue. The details of the face were the last to fall into place, and then there was no longer any doubt in his mind.

Jon had never considered the possibility that he, as the Lector, might be part of the scene he controlled. He had regarded his role as that of an outsider who influenced the presentation in the same way a film editor does at the editing table. When he saw this manifestation of Remer, Jon realized that he himself had to be somewhere in the world framed by the text. He was unable to glance down at himself to confirm this personally, but it seemed clear to him that the moment when the energy discharges began was the moment he had crossed the threshold and entered the space of the story. That explained the feeling he had had of being liberated from his physical body.

Remer's appearance meant the reactivation had worked, and that he had now acquired some of the same powers Jon possessed.

The Remer figure seemed to be looking about. His eyes didn't move but his face kept turning to take in the world in which he found himself. When his gaze fell on Jon, or rather on the place where the image of Jon stood, the Remer figure stopped moving. His lips, which were still colourless, formed into a smile.

A mixture of fear and anger welled up inside Jon. He had to stop Remer from getting any stronger, no matter what it took. Mentally he clenched his hands into fists and put all the force he could muster into the effects. The colours became so saturated that the scene looked like a computer-generated reconstruction, with razor-sharp edges and a clarity even the best monitor couldn't reproduce. By aiming all his focus on the area surrounding Remer's figure, Jon tried to erase him by enhancing the intensity of everything else.

Remer's facial features became distorted and the details of the figure slowly began to blur, as if he were a statue made of sand in a strong wind. The surface seemed to dissolve into atoms that were stretched out like the tail of a comet, pulling away from the figure; the smile dangled from the back of the head until it was one long streak, and the connection between the body and its limbs faded more and more. An eerie lament issued from the haze, a sound that seemed to come from a throat that didn't belong to the animal kingdom.

Jon exerted himself even more, but he could feel he wouldn't be able to maintain the intensity much longer. The figure had been reduced to half-size, with its molecules pulled into a long streamer behind it, but Jon couldn't penetrate to its core to erase it permanently.

Slowly Jon felt his concentration weaken. The colours and sharp outlines around him disappeared. The sound emitted by the figure changed, becoming an angry snarl, and Remer's figure began building itself anew, as if it were on rewind. Soon the figure was back to human form, with its features even sharper than before.

'Campelli,' panted Remer's voice after his body was re-constructed. 'Impressive trick, but not a very nice way to welcome a friend.'

In shock, Katherina took a couple of steps back.

A violent spark had leaped from Jon to Remer, hovering between them and growing in thickness and intensity. Remer's body shook for a moment and seemed to shrink in on itself, but at no point did he lift his eyes from the book he was reading.

Panic had broken out among the participants. Some were trying to escape by running for the door, but in the confusion a number of people fell, tripping up those who were behind them. That caused others to flee by jumping over the railing to the terrace below. Still others crawled along the floor or tried to seek protection along the walls or next to the pillars.

Remer's expression was contorted with pain, but he still kept reading, practically doubled up over the book, as if he wanted to protect it with his body.

There were still about a hundred people standing around the dais and taking part in the ritual, either by reading or by supporting the readers. Most of them kept casting anxious glances at Remer and Jon before they once again returned to the text.

It smelled as if something was burning, and the air was charged with electricity, which made the hairs stand up on Katherina's arms.

The spark between Jon and Remer seemed pale. It started very slowly to move at a calmer and calmer tempo, diminishing in size and luminosity. At the same time Remer began to straighten up, and the expression of pain vanished from his face.

Completely new sparks surrounded two other Lectors. Those who were standing too close leaped away, screaming with pain, while some people fainted on the spot. Others in the vicinity moved aside or ran off. A great noise erupted from those who were reading and from others who were talking or screaming and trying to get away. Accompanying everything was an angry hissing from the sparks.

Katherina cautiously backed further away from the podium as she tried to maintain her support for Jon and also take a look around. The others had to turn up soon. It was too late to stop the reactivation, but they needed to do everything they could to limit it. She reached a pillar and pressed her back against it. More Lectors ran past her, headed for the exit. Terror shone in their eyes. She tried to shut everything else out and focus on supporting Jon.

One of the Lectors, the latest to be reactivated, collapsed with a shriek. It happened without warning. He'd shown no signs of weakness or pain before he passed out, and Katherina had the feeling the same thing could have happened to anyone in the crowd.

On either side of Remer two new clouds had appeared. They had human shape, but were not yet fully formed.

Remer smiled.

Jon noticed another jolt in the images, a signal from Katherina which he took to be a warning. He sensed her support grow and he gathered all his forces. The cloud cover became pitch-black and the wind raged through the cemetery. Headstones toppled, pulling up the earth, which was whirled through the air in little tornadoes.

Maybe he couldn't fool Remer again, but the two new arrivals were in for a surprise. Before they were fully formed, Jon ratcheted up all the effects surrounding the figures. He wanted to make them disappear, remove them from the story, erase them like the misprints they were. They started to dissolve. One of them vanished almost instantly, whirled away in one of the tornadoes like smoke into an exhaust vent. The other stood its ground.

Remer was no longer smiling. He looked first at his companion and then at Jon.

Suddenly the headstone next to Jon changed shape, and in fright he lost his concentration. Before his eyes the granite liquefied and the stone changed from a rectangular shape into a cross.

Jon looked about in confusion. More changes were occurring all around him. Railings appeared, the vegetation shot up in some places and vanished in others. The sky grew lighter and the wind subsided.

'This is amazing!' shouted Remer with delight, stretching his arms up in the air.

The figure next to him was now fully formed, and Jon recognized him as one of the Lectors he had greeted in the foyer. The new arrival looked around in astonishment. Behind him three more hazy figures appeared.

Remer laughed. 'You don't have a chance, Campelli,' he shouted. 'Give up.'

'Why?' replied Jon. 'You've already got what you need.'

'True enough. But we still have room for a man like you in the Order.' He threw out his arms. 'Just look what we can accomplish together.'

'You duped me,' snarled Jon. 'Forced me to betray my own people.'

'You had it in you already, Campelli. I just brought it into the light.'

The three figures behind him were gradually becoming more solid.

'And pushed everything else into the dark,' said Jon. 'Katherina, the bookshop, my family. You made me forget my own family, Remer.'

'It won't do you any good to dwell on the past,' said Remer with annoyance. 'Even your father would have realized that. He would have loved being able to step into the story and change things the way we now can.'

'But you never gave him a chance,' Jon pointed out. 'You killed him.'

Remer shrugged. 'It was necessary,' he said. 'We would never have been able to turn him.'

Jon felt anger welling up inside him. With a flash of light the clouds overhead once again turned pitch-black, and lightning shot across the sky with an angry crash.

Remer cast an uneasy glance at the clouds.

'Who did it?' asked Jon through clenched teeth.

'What difference does it make?'

'Who killed my father?' shouted Jon, accompanied by yet another crash of thunder overhead.

'Patrick Vedel, the receiver,' replied Remer indifferently. 'It was necessary.'

'Patrick Vedel,' repeated Jon. It wasn't more than an hour ago that they were sitting side by side in the car on their way to the library. His anger grew stronger, and he knew that Vedel could feel it, because the hand he felt on his shoulder seemed to lose its hold for a moment, but then gripped even harder. Vedel was still keeping Jon inside the story, and he was wise to do so.

'Luca found out about our activities down here,' Remer went on. 'I think he realized he was out of his depth.'

'My father was here?' asked Jon. The idea that Luca would put so much distance between himself and the bookshop seemed unlikely.

'He could have been a good detective,' Remer acknowledged. 'Just like you, but even so I think he was shocked.' Remer shook his head. 'A man struck by panic could do anything. He had to be stopped.'

'So you killed him.'

'He might have gone to the authorities. That would have been equally bad for your little girlfriend and her reading buddies. It wouldn't have benefited any Lectors, any of us.'

The three figures behind Remer had assumed their final form and stood there looking about in amazement. One of them was Poul Holt.

Remer smiled. 'So, Campelli, what's it going to be?'

Katherina gasped for breath. The air in the reading room seemed to be getting heavier by the minute and the smoke was tearing at her lungs. Big sparks kept reaching out and making contact with the overhead beams, the pillars and other random objects. Some struck fleeing Lectors who were flung to the ground and either lay where they fell or tried to crawl away.

The energy in the room was stronger now than when they had arrived. At first it had seemed like an eiderdown settling over the space, but now it had changed character and felt like a rushing river, violent, roaring and overpowering.

Katherina had positioned herself next to a pillar so she could see both Jon and Remer. In the flow of images coming from Jon, she had caught a glimpse of a red-haired man. She recognized him as one of the men who had chased her through the marketplace, and judging by the emotions Jon attributed to the images, the red-haired man wasn't exactly a friend of his either. The accompanying anger was enormous, and when brief picture sequences of Luca got mixed in, she understood why.

The red-haired man was the receiver who had killed Luca.

Jon's concentration weakened due to his anger, and Katherina had to set aside her own fury to help him. Even though it pained her to do so, she muted the emotions in the pictures of Luca and instead supported the story as best she could. Slowly Jon regained his focus and began working his way through the text. She couldn't tell exactly what was happening in the place where he found himself, but something was certainly going on that went far beyond the words and sentences of the text, as if each letter of the alphabet was a landscape in and of itself.

Katherina moved closer to the podium and Jon. She didn't cover much ground, but she felt better being slightly nearer to him. Nothing was visible on his face – no emotions or expressions she could interpret.

She felt the hood of her robe being tugged from her head. A hand landed on her shoulder and slowly she turned around. In front of her stood the red-haired man, the man Jon had just pointed out as Luca's murderer.

'You shouldn't be here. You must have taken a wrong turn somewhere,' he said with a triumphant smile.

Katherina's heart pounded and she couldn't breathe. Without the protection of her hood she felt helpless. It was a hundred against one, and there was no place for her to flee. She had failed.

'You'd better come with me,' said the red-haired man.

The pictures of him she'd received from Jon popped up again, but now they were coloured by her own rage.

Katherina took a deep breath.

With a violent shove she sent the man toppling backwards. He staggered a few steps before he fell on his back with a yelp. Several people standing close turned towards Katherina with shouts of surprise. She started screaming as loud as she could and pushing at those who were nearest. The first participants moved away in fright, but she kept running into people and yanking at everyone she could reach. She managed to grab some of the books and tore them out of the hands of the astonished owners, hurling them as far away as she could. There was no chance that anyone would come to her aid, but she could at least break the concentration of the crowd, maybe long enough so that Jon could stop the reading.

The people around her began to understand what was going on, and more and more hands reached out for Katherina. She repeatedly tore herself free, but the crowd was getting rougher and rougher, and agitated voices were pelting her with words in many languages. She fought back as best she could, but then someone shoved a book at her face and stopped her shouts.

A voice cut through the noise. It was one of the hooded guards, pushing his way through the excited participants and speaking to them in an authoritative tone. He got Katherina in an armlock and one by one the others retreated. The guard ushered Katherina towards the door. The Lectors moved aside, glaring at her as they did. Almost everyone was watching the commotion while Jon still continued to read, as did a number of other Lectors close to the podium who appeared not to have noticed a thing. Desperation surged inside of Katherina, and she almost didn't have the strength to stay on her feet, but the guard ruthlessly pulled her along. When they had nearly reached the door, she made one last effort to tear herself away, but the guard merely tightened his grip.

'Take it easy, damn it,' he whispered in unmistakable Danish. 'It's me, Mehmet.'

# 41

Jon noticed when Katherina's support vanished.

The colours of the surroundings abruptly lost their strength and the details around him became blurred. He had to work harder to keep the scene intact. The features of the cemetery weakened and the atmosphere was not as palpable as it had been before.

At the same time a violent commotion occurred in the energy field. Instead of being a unified support that reinforced the intensity of the scene, the force now fluctuated for shorter or longer periods. It seemed like the signal from a transistor being run through the whole range of frequencies.

Remer had also noticed it, but instead of faltering, he smiled. 'Don't pay any attention to that,' he said confidently. 'We don't need them.' He held his arms out to the sides and tipped his head back to look up at the clouds in the sky.

The colours changed, starting from above and flowing downwards, as if someone were pouring paint over the landscape. Everything that was pale and pastel became so sharp and bright it hurt his eyes. The headstones moved back into place and acquired detailed decorations including gargoyles and mythical creatures.

Jon couldn't keep up. He'd lost control of the scene. The ball was now in his opponent's court. 'Not bad,' he admitted as he tried to hide his concern. What had happened to Katherina? He didn't have the strength to hold on much longer alone. Maybe she had escaped. He hoped she had. If only he could make sure she was safe. If only he could poke his head outside to determine whether she was okay.

Three more of Remer's people appeared.

It looked like he was defeated. Without Katherina's support, and with more and more of Remer's people being reactivated, he couldn't keep going. He noticed that his energy was fading, but he still couldn't stop reading. Patrick Vedel's influence had vanished, but there were other receivers who were keeping every-one captive in the text.

The main character at the grave stopped speaking, closed his eyes and bowed his head. Slowly he leaned forward until his fore-head touched the stone.

Darkness. They were back inside the car. The sides and roof were pressing so close he couldn't move. He heard screams from behind him, inside the car, muted, as if someone were shouting into a quilt, but insistent and impossible to ignore. A strong smell of petrol made the main character cough. A shudder rippled through his body and a violent pain in his legs made him scream.

Jon was caught off guard by the change of scene, but he quickly recovered. The darkness limited the possibilities for manipulating the surroundings and gave him a chance to relax. He tried to gather his forces, though he knew it wouldn't be long before the scene changed again.

'Are you okay?' asked a voice outside the car door.

The main character could do nothing but scream.

Then other sounds. The sound of metal against metal, faces that bent close and then vanished, the chassis of the car creaking and groaning. Petrol fumes filled his lungs and made him cough again. He felt someone grab hold of him. The pain was unbearable. He screamed. Someone was yanking violently at his body. Suddenly he felt water on his face. Rain. He saw the outline of the car as he was dragged away. He saw the crushed roof and the crumpled bonnet. He saw a blue spark issue from the rear of the car.

Then he felt the heat washing over him.

Mehmet and Katherina came out into the corridor, beyond the crowd's field of vision, and hugged each other.

'What happened to the two of you?' Katherina asked.

'It wasn't all that easy to get in,' replied Mehmet. 'And we also had to convince a couple of guards to loan us their togas, if you know what I mean.'

'Where's Henning?'

'He's there,' said Mehmet, nodding towards the stairs. 'He started reading from another book we found.'

They hurried up the stairs to the next level. Here the tables and chairs had not been removed. They stood in long, even rows – a sharp contrast to the chaos below. Henning was sitting with a book in his hands in the middle of the floor, a couple of metres from the edge of the terrace. As they approached, they could hear him reading in a clear voice.

'Watch out,' said Katherina, holding Mehmet back. A spark raced across the pages of the book Henning was reading. 'He's been reactivated.'

'Is that good?' asked Mehmet.

'I have no idea,' replied Katherina and sighed. She stepped closer to Henning and studied his face. His eyes were staring down at the book but they seemed to be seeing more than just letters and words. A few drops of sweat glistened on his brow and his cheeks were flushed.

'He's completely out of it,' declared Mehmet.

'Leave him be.' Katherina moved over to the railing. They were standing right above the podium with a full view of the floor below. Jon was still standing there, reading, paying no attention to the fact that scattered all around him were bodies lying on the floor along with a jumble of candles and books. Discharges from the electrical fixtures sent constant showers of sparks out into the room, and bolts of lightning leaped between Jon and the eight other Lectors standing around the podium who had been reactivated. It was as if they were feeding each other with energy, sometimes in random bursts, at other times passing the charge from one person to another like a relay baton.

'Shit,' said Mehmet next to her. 'What the hell is going on?'

Before Katherina could reply, they heard a clattering sound behind them. Henning's body had straightened up and was arched like a bow over the chair he had been sitting on. Foam was seeping from the corners of his mouth and a horrible hissing sound had replaced his reading voice. Katherina ran over to him but didn't dare touch his body, which began to shake violently. His eyes were no longer staring at the book but were looking up at the ceiling with an empty, frozen expression. A drop of blood ran from his nose to his lips.

'Henning!' she yelled. 'Can you hear me?' There was no reaction on his face.

Katherina didn't know what to do. She wanted to wrap her arms around him and hold him tight, but didn't dare. Tears began to well up in her eyes. She took a step back, never taking her eyes off Henning's face.

Suddenly his body stopped shaking and his features once again looked human. Then he closed his eyes and collapsed back onto the chair.

Mehmet took a hesitant step towards the Lector and studied his face closely before he pressed two fingers to Henning's throat. After a couple of seconds he removed his hand and sighed.

'He's dead,' he said.

It was raining in the cemetery. After the darkness of the flashback scene, the rain was a much-needed breath of fresh air. The stench of petrol had been replaced by the smell of wet grass and flowers.

'Wow,' exclaimed Remer. 'Nice little intermezzo.'

Another grey cloud appeared and began taking shape.

Remer smiled. 'Give it up, Campelli. It's now eight against one.' Then his smile froze and he frowned.

The new arrival was Henning, who looked around in astonishment.

'Henning!' shouted Jon in relief.

Henning took a moment to get his bearings and then caught sight of Jon.

'Jon!' he cried. 'Is that you?'

Remer uttered an angry shout and held his hands out towards the spot where Henning was standing. A strong wind began blowing around them.

'Ignore it, Henning!' yelled Jon. 'It's not real. Focus.'

Henning stared in bewilderment at his feet. The wind picked up. A whirlwind rose up around him until he was surrounded. It had torn up earth and leaves as it emerged, encircled him at an ever-increasing tempo.

'Katherina,' Henning shouted. 'She's . . .' The wind stole his words. 'Lightning . . . have to go back . . . out . . .' A panicked expression spread across his face.

Jon tried to neutralize the tornado, but Remer's supporters made sure that it got even stronger, rotating faster and faster. Jon tried to change its path but it refused to budge. Henning's figure grew weaker. His shouts could no longer be distinguished from the roaring of the wind and his body grew fainter with every second. Finally his figure was no longer visible in the centre of the storm.

Suddenly the whirlwind vanished, and all the stones, leaves and earth it had contained came raining down. Henning was gone.

Remer seemed to be examining the pile of dirt that remained on the spot where Henning had stood. 'I think you're right, Campelli,' he said. 'It's a matter of faith.' He smiled. 'And I don't think we've seen the best yet.'

Around them the scene changed again. Lightning sliced across the sky and rain began to fall, at first in big, heavy drops, then in columns of water. The grass grew higher as Jon stood there looking at it, and the walls of the cemetery seemed to move further away to make room for new rows of headstones, white crosses beneath grey clouds.

Remer laughed. A maniacal tone had crept into his voice. 'Nothing can stop us now!'

The wealth of details seemed to explode. Jon could see the very structure of the bark on the trees, microscopic fungi on the surfaces of the gravestones, vermin underground, moisture that had collected in the carved surfaces of the headstones. It was almost too much for him to take in; so many impressions forced themselves on him, filling his head until he thought he would faint.

One of Remer's comrades in arms sank to his knees, holding his head. He started screaming, and the outline of his body slowly blurred. The sound of his shouts grew fainter as the Lector's molecules separated from one another, cloaking him in a cloud of particles that vanished in the wind.

'Remer,' said Poul Holt, sounding strained. 'You need to hold back a little.' His face was contorted with pain.

'Hold back?' Remer shouted. 'We haven't come this far to hold back.'

'He's right,' said Jon. 'You've gone too far.'

Angry, Remer turned to face him. 'Too far?' He smiled.

Jon sensed the wind growing stronger around him. Dirt and rain-drops whirled past. He was bombarded by impressions of the shape, speed and path of every single drop, but he had no control over them. Remer was steering and shaping them, down to the individual molecules.

Instead of fighting back and trying to regain the upper hand, Jon tried to concentrate on one thing. One small step. Even though he couldn't feel his physical body, he tried with all his might to move his left foot backwards. He pictured it scraping along the floor of the dais, centimetre by centimetre, further and further back. It filled his thoughts. One small movement.

More and more loose objects were being swept along: leaves, stones, planks, branches and signs all rushed past him at an ever-increasing speed.

One step.

'Is this far enough, Campelli?' shouted Remer jubilantly. His voice was barely audible in the wind.

A pain at the back of his head sliced like a bolt of lightning through Jon's consciousness. He was lying on his back at the foot of the dais. His fall down the steps had made him drop the book that had been holding him captive. He couldn't see where it had landed.

Eight Lectors remained by the podium. Jon stared at them. He now understood why the other Lectors had been so terrified of his powers. The air felt electric; the smell reminded him of the metallic odour of leaky batteries.

Jon tried to stand up but a sharp stab in his left foot made him groan aloud with pain. He looked down. His foot was turned at a strange angle. Even thinking about moving his foot made it hurt.

'What's going on?' said a nervous voice behind him.

Jon turned and caught sight of Patrick Vedel, only two metres away.

'We have to get out of here,' said Mehmet.

Katherina nodded, but she couldn't take her eyes off Henning's lifeless body.

'Did you hear what I said?' Mehmet stepped in front of her so they made eye contact. His gaze was steady and insistent.

'Jon,' said Katherina. 'We have to take Jon with us.'

They went over to the railing and looked down at the floor below. The electrical activity seemed to have increased. They heard the constant, dry crackling of discharges and the sparks were lasting longer than before.

As they watched, yet another one of the Lectors fell away from the circle surrounding the podium. His white robe might just as well have been empty. He fell to the ground without a sound. A dark liquid spread across the floor from the body.

'We have to go down there,' said Katherina firmly.

'Wait.' Mehmet grabbed hold of her.

Beneath them Jon's body began swaying. Katherina gasped and put her hand to her mouth.

At that moment Jon fell backwards, toppled off the dais, and landed on his back with a horrible thud. The book he was holding disappeared into the shadows. He lay still for a moment – much too long, it seemed to Katherina – but then he started moving again. He lifted his head and managed to prop himself up on one elbow and look around.

Katherina sobbed with relief. Her emotions had been on a roller-coaster for the past couple of days, and she knew that soon she wouldn't be able to stand any more. Even though she wanted to run down to Jon at once, her body refused to obey her. She was shaking so hard she could hardly stay on her feet.

'He's okay,' said Mehmet with a grin. He put his hands on her shoulders and gave them a squeeze. 'He's okay,' he repeated.

Down below Jon had turned towards the shadows behind him and a figure had stepped into the light. Katherina recognized the man with the red hair. They couldn't hear the exchange of words that followed, but Jon was clearly upset, though evidently unable to stand up. The man with the red hair squatted down next to him, but Jon pulled away and began looking about.

'A book,' Katherina decided. 'He needs a book.'

'What sort of book?' asked Mehmet.

'It doesn't matter,' she replied. 'Just find a book and I'll try to get his attention.'

Mehmet disappeared.

'Jon!' shouted Katherina as loudly as she could. 'Up here!'

Jon looked about in confusion. The man with the red hair stood up and let his gaze sweep over the terrace.

'Up here!' she called, waving her arms over her head.

Jon raised his eyes and finally caught sight of her. Even though he was some distance away and the light was bad, she could see that he recognized her. A big smile spread across his face. The man with the red hair straightened up and put his hands on his hips. Jon used this momentary distraction to seize the man by the ankles and yank on them so his body fell backwards. Jon then scuttled away on his hands and knees. Katherina couldn't understand why he didn't stand up.

Mehmet was back with a book.

'Here,' he said. 'It was the first one I could find.'

Katherina took it from him and again called Jon's name.

He turned around in time to see her waving the book. He nodded eagerly and she tossed it down to him. It landed a few metres away and he struggled to reach it. In the meantime the man with the red hair had hauled himself to his feet.

It was the anger that kept Jon conscious. His body was drained of energy. It required the greatest effort for him to make the slightest movement. The pain in his foot didn't make things any easier, but at least it helped to keep him alert.

At the sight of Patrick Vedel, Luca's murderer, Jon had to restrain himself from assaulting him on the spot. But his position, lying on the floor and presumably with a broken ankle, didn't give Jon the best advantage, so he made himself stay calm.

'What's going on?' asked Vedel again, squatting down next to Jon.

'Your boss has lost his mind,' replied Jon. He looked around. There was nothing within reach he could use as a weapon.

Vedel's eyes flickered. 'Remer knows what he's doing,' he said. 'He's doing what's best for the Order.'

'He's in the process of *annihilating* the Order,' snarled Jon. 'Can't you see that? He's gone too far.'

Vedel shook his head. 'No, the Order is his life, *our* life.' He stared with admiration at his boss. 'He'll do anything to preserve it.'

'Yes, he'll even kill for it,' said Jon.

Patrick Vedel gave him a searching look.

'What's the life of an old bookseller worth compared to this?' said Jon bitterly, as he maintained eye contact with Vedel. Jon could see that the man was trying to work out whether he knew the truth or not.

Vedel lowered his eyes. 'It was necessary,' he said.

'You went too far,' said Jon. 'Just like now. Who do you believe that Remer is thinking of right now, himself or the Order? I've been where he is. I know the answer.'

Vedel clenched his teeth. 'He would never—'

'Jon!'

Jon recognized Katherina's voice and looked around. Vedel stood up and did the same.

She called his name again. This time it sounded as if her voice were coming from overhead, and Jon caught sight of her on the terrace above. A huge feeling of relief washed over his body.

'That bitch!' yelled Vedel in annoyance.

Jon's anger flared up again, giving him renewed strength. He reached out for Vedel and grabbed him round the ankles. With a violent yank, he pulled the Lector's legs out from under him, making him fall heavily on his back.

Jon pushed and dragged himself away from Vedel as fast as he could. He hadn't gone more than five or six metres when he heard Katherina calling him again. She was waving a book. Out of the corner of his eye Jon saw that Vedel had stood up and was coming towards him.

The book landed a couple of metres away from Jon and he struggled to reach it as Vedel came closer. It was a small, slim, leather-bound book. Jon opened it with shaking hands. He might still be able to get out of this situation.

Vedel stopped when he saw the book Jon was holding.

'Now, just take it easy,' he said, holding up the palms of his hands. 'There's no reason to . . .'

Jon's courage sank as he read the first words.

The book was in Italian. It wasn't possible. Not here, not now.

The expression on Vedel's face changed from nervousness to relief. 'Not a book to your liking?' he asked and laughed.

Jon turned his attention back to the book. He *did* know Italian, after all. It had been a long time since he'd read the language, and he doubted he knew it well enough to protect himself, but he had to try.

He felt Vedel grab hold of the collar of his robe and start dragging him across the floor.

Jon kept his focus on the book, stammering his way through the first words. He was sweating. His hands shook. The first sentence meant nothing to him. He was having a hard time concentrating, but he forced himself to continue.

Vedel laughed again and kept dragging him towards the railing.

Word by word Jon stuttered his way into the next sentence, and then he realized that he knew this text. He recognized the sentence he had just read, and he knew what would come next.

He had read this book before.

# 42

Jon couldn't recall how many times Luca had read *Pinocchio* to him.

His mother once told him that it started even before he was born. Luca had read aloud to her and their unborn child almost every evening. They liked to compare her growing belly to the whale in the story, and then they would laugh so hard that Luca couldn't go on reading. During Jon's first years, it was the story he wanted to hear most often. He never grew tired of it, and every evening he pestered his parents with his requests for just one more chapter. Usually they gave in. Especially his mother. She too enjoyed the story, and she performed all the roles with such feeling and using so many different voices that Jon never forgot them.

It was a magical book written in a magical language that only he and his parents spoke. That was how it seemed to Jon, at any rate. He had loved the sound of the words and quickly memorized entire passages. Luca would often test him by starting a sentence and then Jon would finish it, regardless of whether they were sitting on a bus, standing in a queue at the butcher's shop or seated at the dinner table. His mother would shake her head at them, but it didn't matter. It was the game he shared with Luca, and Jon loved it.

Even better than the words were the images they created. Jon knew every stone and every blade of grass in the story. He had walked through that landscape countless times and knew precisely what the houses looked like, how the tree branches curved, and what the facial features and gestures were of all the characters. There was no doubt in his mind about how the waves moved, the size of the boat or the colours of the whale.

Jon had pictured these images so many times they practically sprang forth as he began to read. The reading room in Alexandria instantly vanished, to be replaced by the story's gently shaded colours and the soft undulations of the landscape. He hardly had to make any effort at all. This was completely different from the other seances when he'd really had to work to make the images flow. This time they emerged all on their own, leaving him energy to enjoy the experience. Gone was the pain in his foot, and Remer was no longer a concern. He was overcome by a serenity he hadn't felt in years, and the sense that everything was going to work out fine.

It occurred to Jon that the images he was creating were really not his own. Luca had most likely passed them on through his readings. If he had been as skilled a Lector as everyone claimed, it stood to reason that he would have given his child the best possible experience. That it would one day save his son's life was not something Luca could possibly have foreseen, but Jon didn't think it was accidental. Why would he end up with this particular book, in the least imaginable place, under the most improbable circumstances, exactly when he had the most use for it? The odds of that happening had to be astronomical.

Jon took another look at the scene. Everything was in its proper place and the story was proceeding as it should. He found it reassuring to know this was Luca's work. The images were as clear and pure as if Luca had read the story to him yesterday. After Jon had learned to read, he had gone through *Pinocchio* many times, but he still preferred to have Luca read it aloud to him. Even when Jon started getting interested in more action-packed stories, it was always *Pinocchio* he wanted to hear at bedtime. He loved to fall asleep to the sound of Luca's voice.

He could almost hear it now.

*

After tossing the book down to Jon, Katherina prepared herself to support him as soon as he started reading. She was ready the second Jon reached for the book, but when he stopped after the first glance, she got nervous.

'What was that book you gave me?'

Mehmet shrugged. 'I have no idea. It was just the first one I could find.'

The man with the red hair had seized hold of Jon.

'We have to go down there,' said Katherina.

Mehmet set off at a run, but Katherina stopped abruptly.

Jon had started to read.

'I'll be right there,' she called, and then focused on Jon's reading. She concentrated all his remaining energy on moving through the text, trying to keep out other impressions and fixing his attention on the story. Slowly he got into the rhythm.

After only a few sentences the red-haired man began to scream. He had a firm grip on the collar of Jon's robe and didn't let go, even though his body was shaking violently. Suddenly there was a loud bang and the red-haired man was hurled away from Jon with great force. He flew backwards until his body slammed into a stone pillar and he sank to the ground.

He didn't get up again.

Katherina slid down with her back against the railing. She closed her eyes and concentrated on receiving. The images emanating from Jon appeared as gentle, calm pictures – pictures she realized she recognized.

The energy in the room began to change. What had felt like a rushing torrent now little by little diminished in intensity and speed until at last it stopped altogether. Instead of moving in one direction, it began steadily pulsating, like gigantic inhalations and exhalations. The energy encircled them in a completely different way, feeling closer and bringing with it a warmth and peace quite unlike the frenzied and insistent mood that had reigned up until now. All the accumulated energy in the library was directed towards a specific pulse, a pulse determined by Jon.

Katherina sensed it was now safe to stand up. Jon was still lying in the same place, calmly reading *Pinocchio* from his position on the floor.

Over by the podium stood five people who were still reading. The expression on Remer's face was strained, the veins clearly visible at his temples, a glistening film of sweat on his brow. Katherina could tell from what she was receiving that they were working hard to maintain their concentration. They must have noticed the shift in energy and were fighting back with their last strength.

Katherina ran out into the corridor and down the stairs. They had to seize the chance to escape while Remer was preoccupied. On the floor below she practically ran into Mehmet, who stood as if paralysed, regarding the scene before him.

'What the hell should we do?' he said. 'This is going to end up bad.'

Katherina cast a glance at Remer. His facial features had changed. His expression was tormented and his body had started to tremble.

'Jon is the only one who can stop this,' replied Katherina. She ran over to where he was lying. He looked quite unaffected as he almost sprawled on the floor with his eyes on the book. She focused on his reading, homed in on the rhythm and gave him the signal to stop. The pulse of the energy made an extra leap, then a few irregular beats before it finally stopped. Jon's expression changed as he turned towards Katherina. He smiled but then seemed to remember where he was. His smile froze as he looked at the podium.

Remer's body was now shaking harder than before. The energy was no longer under control and had lost its focus so it was striking out in all directions. Katherina sensed that Remer was stubbornly fighting to regain control. It was an impossible battle. There were far too many opposing surges of energy and there were no receivers left to help him, but he refused to give up. A couple of sparks enveloped him for a moment; blood began running out of his ears, down his throat and into the collar of his robe, which slowly turned red. He kept reading through clenched teeth. His face was now drained of all colour, an eerie white in contrast to the blood, and contorted with great pain. Streams of blood started pouring from his nose and running down his white robe.

Even from this distance they could hear that a hissing sound had crept into his reading. There was an enormous bang and Katherina was blinded by a flash of light. Silence descended over the library. The sound of sparks igniting had stopped; no was reading any more. The bodies of the five remaining Lectors stood upright for an instant until gravity won out and they toppled to the floor.

Jon ached all over and he felt unbelievably tired. When he tried to move, he groaned from the stabbing pain in his foot. Katherina was sitting beside him, looking into his eyes. She alternated between laughing and crying. Her face was covered with dust and the dirt on her cheeks was streaked with tears.

'Are you okay?' he asked with an effort.

Katherina nodded and kissed him on the forehead. He raised his hand to wipe away a tear from her cheek. Her green eyes filled with more tears and she buried her face in his neck. He put his arm round her and pulled her close.

Only then did Jon notice Mehmet, who was standing a couple of metres away. He was surveying the room; every now and then he would shake his head and mutter something incomprehensible.

'What the hell are you doing here?' asked Jon. 'Are you on holiday?'

Mehmet laughed and came over to join them.

'Something like that. Thought this might be a good place to borrow a book for a trip to the beach.'

Katherina and Jon couldn't help laughing.

Jon cleared his throat. He felt unable to move. It was only with Katherina's help that he was able to sit up.

'I think I've broken my foot,' he said.

'Yup, that's what it looks like, boss,' said Mehmet. 'We're going to have to carry you.'

Katherina nodded, wiping the tears from her face.

'What about Henning?' asked Jon.

Mehmet shook his head. 'He didn't make it.'

Anger gave Jon the necessary strength to stand up, with help from his companions.

'Let's see about getting out of this place,' he said. 'We're done here.'

Mehmet and Katherina each took Jon by an arm, and together they left the Bibliotheca Alexandrina in silence.

# 43

It was a strange feeling for Jon to be heading home when he had no recollection of ever leaving. He'd been unconscious on the flight to Egypt, and it was as if his sense of place had stayed behind in Denmark without having a chance to catch up with him.

The events in the library hadn't yet sunk in either, and the more days that passed, the more unreal it all seemed. He remembered everything that had happened, but it was as if it had happened to somebody else. Katherina had told him about the events he hadn't witnessed himself, and they were just as incredible. A deep sense of gratitude washed over him every time he thought about what they had gone through to come to his aid. He couldn't help thinking about all the possible scenarios when things could have gone terribly wrong, and how lucky they had been. That didn't apply to Henning, of course, and Jon realized that he owed the man his life. That made it even more painful to have to leave his body behind in the library, but they kept assuring each other that they'd had no choice.

According to the newspapers, a bolt of lightning had struck the library and caused a small fire, but there was no mention of either the injured or the dead. It was obvious that the Shadow Organization still had members in the city who were able to control what the public was told. Not even Nessim, the desk clerk, who otherwise had plenty of contacts, was able to ferret out anything more.

Katherina, Mehmet and Jon had kept a low profile for a couple of days and then jointly decided that enough blood had been shed. The Shadow Organization had been dealt a death blow. Only the strongest had been able to enter the space of the story, and they were the ones who had lost their lives. The only thing they could hope for now was that the whole event had put the brakes on the organization.

There was nothing to be gained from staying any longer in Alexandria, so Jon and Katherina reserved seats on the next plane home. Mehmet was enjoying being in Egypt and had decided to stay for a couple more weeks. He'd established a solid friendship with Nessim, and since his work merely required a computer with access to the Internet, he could do it anywhere. Besides, he wasn't in a hurry to return to the autumn weather of Nørrebro and his ravaged flat.

Jon had had his foot examined by a doctor Nessim had recommended. It turned out that his ankle was only sprained, but he couldn't put any weight on it and he had to use a crutch. That made it a bit difficult to board the plane, but it meant they were given seats with extra leg-room.

Jon studied the other passengers. Aside from a couple of businessmen with laptops they were eager to switch on, most of the people looked like tourists on their way home from holiday. Jon was fairly sure their holiday memories wouldn't measure up to his own.

Other than discussing the factual events, Jon and Katherina hadn't spent much time talking about the meaning of what had taken place in the library. It was still too fresh in their minds, and Jon was having a hard time putting his experiences into words. The feeling that Luca was protecting him had been so strong that he first needed to digest what had happened. But there was one thing he knew for sure: he would never be able to be a lawyer again.

So it wasn't his job that was making him long for home. It was an urge to hear the bells above the door of Libri di Luca again, a yearning to breathe in the smell of parchment and leather, an almost physical need to touch the books on the shelves. At the same time he had the feeling that he was expected, that he would be received with a nod of acknowledgement from Luca, who would be sitting in the leather chair with a book on his lap; that he would be welcomed with a warm smile from his mother who stood leaning on the balcony with her elbows on the railing; that he would be silently accepted by his grandfather Arman, who stood with his back turned as he shelved books in their proper places. They were all there, the Campelli family, present in the dust on the shelves, in the shadows between the bookcases and in the air that only reluctantly circulated whenever the front door opened.

But more than anything else, he wanted to see Katherina in Libri di Luca again. In fact, he could no longer imagine the bookshop without her – in the place where he had met her for the first time, floating among words and letters she could never comprehend but to whose essence she was so obviously devoted.

Jon cast a sidelong glance at Katherina, who was sitting in the seat next to him with her head resting on his shoulder. She had closed her eyes and most of her face was covered by her red hair, which she had pulled loose from the knot at her neck as soon as they sat down. He reached for the in-flight magazine in the pocket in front of him. Katherina didn't react, and to everyone else it looked as if she were sleeping. But Jon could clearly sense her alertness as soon as he began to read.

It was a nice feeling.

He no longer needed to feel alone.

THE END

# The White King
## György Dragomán

---

Winner of the Sandor Marai Prize

'Electric, ominous, urgent . . . a coming of age tale with a difference'
*DAILY MAIL*

Eleven-year-old Djata makes sure he is always home on Sundays. It is the day the State Security came to take his father away, and he believes it will be a Sunday when his father finally comes home.

In the meantime, Djata lives out a life of adventure, playing war games in flaming wheatfields and watching porn in the back room at the cinema. But lurking beneath his rebel boyhood, pulling at his heart-strings, is the continued absence of his father. When he finally uncovers the truth, he risks losing his childhood forever.

An urgent, humorous and melancholy portrait of a childhood behind the Iron Curtain, *The White King* introduces a stunning new voice in contemporary fiction.

'Dragomán is superb at the paraphernalia of boyhood . . . so much intense experience is on offer . . . a poignant and big-hearted book, firing the imagination long after the pages have stopped turning'
*SUNDAY TELEGRAPH*

'It's the *Just William* books teamed up with *Nineteen Eighty-four*, a superb novel about childhood, schooldays and gang fights . . . sums up the lunacy of Ceausescu's regime better than anything else I've read'
TIBOR FISCHER, *GUARDIAN*

'Disturbing, compelling, beautifully translated'
*THE TIMES*

9780552774536

# Cathedral of the Sea
## Ildefonso Falcones

*A spell-binding drama of love, war, greed and revenge
in medieval Barcelona . . .*

A young serf in fourteenth century Spain, Arnau is on the run from his
feudal lord. Through famine, plague and thwarted love he struggles to
earn his freedom in the shadow of the mighty Cathedral of the Sea: a
magnificent church being built by the humblest citizens of the city.

Arnau's fortunes begin to turn when King Pedro makes him a baron in
reward for his courage in battle. But his new-found wealth excites the
jealousy of his friends, who begin to plot against him, with devastating
consequences.

A page-turning historical epic, the tale of Arnau's journey from slave
to nobleman is the story of a struggle between good and evil that will
turn Church against State, and brother against brother . . .

'Falcones' intricately plotted novel . . . binds you into its thrall. A
bold work of imagination, which pays homage to lives gone by as
well as to the great church itself'
*DAILY EXPRESS*

'An exciting, very readable adventure novel, enriched by realistic
descriptions of medieval life, work, finance and politics'
*INDEPENDENT*

9780552773973